Praise for

We Cast a Shadow

"Good questions breathe life into the world. *We Cast a Shadow,* Maurice Carlos Ruffin's debut novel, asks some of the most important questions fiction can ask, and it does so with energetic and acrobatic prose, hilarious wordplay and great heart. . . . Love is at the core of this funny, beautiful novel—a father's love situated firmly in the jaws of a racist society that threatens to swallow everyone in different ways. . . . At any moment, Ruffin can summon the kind of magic that makes you want to slow down, reread and experience the pleasure of him crystallizing an image again. . . . We're never far from an alliterative flourish ("flaky fried fowl fingers") or a stroke of sudden beauty ("I grabbed the knob with both hands, a transparent crystal bulb, a dollop of frozen light") that makes us pause and say, damn. . . . *We Cast a Shadow* churns fresh beauty from old ugliness. What injustices have we as a culture come to accept as normal? What are the pitfalls of our complacency? And how can anyone survive this? . . . Read this book, and ask yourself: Is this the world you want?"
—*The New York Times Book Review*

"Inventive and shocking."
—*Los Angeles Times*

"Stunning and audacious . . . endlessly perceptive . . . Ruffin proves to be a master. . . . A fast-paced and intricately plotted book . . . The real draw of the novel is Ruffin's gift at creating unforgettable characters. . . . He writes with a straight face, never in love with his own cleverness—there are echoes of Ralph Ellison's intelligent, unshowy prose. . . . It's a razor-sharp debut from an urgent new voice in fiction."
—NPR

"Set in a painfully recognizable future wherein whiteness is attainable through expensive surgical alterations, this is the story of a father grappling with his son's multiracial identity in a world which preys upon any semblance of otherness. *We Cast a Shadow* is a gripping speculative tale that investigates traditional notions of family dynamics and redefines the limits of the lengths one will go to protect his beloved."

—PEN America

"This riotous novel details the farcical lengths this father will go to in order to afford the surgery and save his son from the fate of Blackness while simultaneously hiding his mission from his wife. The novel straddles many modes of storytelling—adventure story, family drama, political satire— but it shines because of the jocular voice of the narrator."

—*Los Angeles Review of Books*

"There are some first novels that exude a technical mastery of character, pacing, plot and description. There are others that exude relentless audacity and ambition. But few in the history of American literature do both. *We Cast A Shadow* feels like it was written by an author who wants to create a literary classic that will outlive us all. Maurice Ruffin pulls off, especially at the level of subtext and temporality, something I've never seen from a first-time novelist. The book wants us to be radically better, and to do that it realizes it must force us to ask bruising questions that will outlive its readers. *We Cast A Shadow* is the finely crafted quake the American novel needed."

—KIESE LAYMON, author of *Heavy*

"*We Cast a Shadow* is like a dispatch from the frontlines of the African-American psyche. Written with ruthless intelligence, it's the story of a father's love and how he tries to protect his son in a country that devours black lives through violence, incarceration, and poverty. . . . [Ruffin] can drive his story to the outer limits and beyond, and never lose the threads of bitter reality that make it so haunting. *We Cast a Shadow* soars on Ruffin's unerring vision."

—*The Boston Globe*

"An incisive and necessary work of brilliant satire. Set in the post-post-racial South, *We Cast a Shadow* tells the story of a man—one of the few black men at his law firm—desperate to pay for his biracial son to undergo demelanization, desperate to 'fix' what he sees as his son's fatal flaw. It is this desperation that drives this novel, that haunts this novel, and in this desperation, we see just how pernicious racism is, how irrevocably it can alter how a man sees the world, himself, those he loves. In that, *We Cast a Shadow* is not so much a work of satire. Instead, it is a chilling, unforgettable cautionary tale, and one we should all read and heed."

—ROXANE GAY, author of
Hunger and *Bad Feminist*

"This ingenious debut novel asks some of the most important questions fiction can ask, and it marks the debut of an abundantly talented and stylish satirist."

—*The New York Times*
(Editor's Choice)

"Daring . . . In Ruffin's debut, set in a near-future American city plagued by vicious racism, a couple wrestles with whether to protect their biracial son by subjecting him to a new demelanization procedure."

—*HuffPost*

"A biting satire of anti-blackness in the United States."

—BuzzFeed

"In Ruffin's debut novel a racially divided world, and constraints that come with it, are disturbingly compared to our own. In the book the narrator fears for his biracial son Nigel's life in a near-future of increasing racial segregation and privatized prisons. In order to afford an operation that will save his son's life by turning him white, he must put his relationships, happiness and better judgment on the line. A racial satire with echoes of *Get Out,* Ruffin's world is brilliantly drawn and uncomfortably close."

—*Esquire* (U.K.)

"Rakishly funny . . . [The narrator's] intensely rhythmic and colorful voice lifts you along with him on his frenetic odyssey. Ruffin's surrealist take on racism owes much to *Invisible Man* and George S. Schuyler's similarly themed 1931 satire, *Black No More.* Yet the ominous resurgence of white supremacy during the Trump era enhances this novel's resonance and urgency."

—*Kirkus Reviews*

"[A] brilliant, semisatirical debut . . . Though Ruffin's novel is in the vein of satires like Paul Beatty's *The Sellout* and the film *Get Out,* it is more bracingly realistic in rendering the divisive politics of contemporary America, making for a singular and unforgettable work of political art."

—*Publishers Weekly* (starred and boxed review)

"Heart-wrenching and morally ambiguous . . . a challenging, thought-provoking debut."

—Associated Press

"I've been thinking hard about Maurice Ruffin's new book, *We Cast a Shadow,* this year. Beyond being one of the most audaciously imaginative books I've read in a long time, Maurice is really demanding we think about the debt we leave our children by not reckoning with the mess of race and power in this country. It's a crucial offering to anyone thinking about what's beneath the scabs of America."

—*Nylon*

"A chilling, satirical look at an openly racist culture where the schism between black and white has widened. *We Cast a Shadow* pits an African-American father against a *Get Out*–worthy world of white imperialism."

—*The Atlanta Journal-Constitution*

"Gripping . . . It truly shines. . . . It serves as a reminder that at the heart of politics and turmoil there is family, and that is what motivates us and gives us hope."

—*The Michigan Daily*

"A full-throated novelistic debut of ferocious power and grace . . . a story that refracts the insanity of the world into a shape so unique you wonder how this book wasn't there all along."

—*Literary Hub*

"A powerful novel of just how far one father will go to keep his son safe from the outside world."

—*Parade*

"Brilliant and devastating."

—*Booklist* (starred review)

"An ambitious debut novel, *We Cast a Shadow* is a surrealistic satire about identity, race, and family relations. . . . Ruffin [is] a talented, genre-bending writer to watch."

—*Garden & Gun*

"Vital . . . set in a beleaguered Southern city of a fictional future in which the father of a biracial son seeks desperate means in order to protect his son from violent racism in America."

—*Southern Living*

"Maurice Carlos Ruffin's debut novel is both funny and distressing, often at the same time. Using satire to throw race relations into sharp relief, *We Cast a Shadow* is endowed with a particular blend of foreboding and derangement that encapsulates present-day America."

—*Antigravity*

"It's a wonderful thing when the stars align for a book, when the book is brilliant, the writer is ready, and the readership is eager."

—*The New Orleans Advocate*

"A provocative debut novel along the lines of *The Sellout* by Paul Beatty . . . It's gutsy, it's electrifying, and it's fan-freaking-tastic."

—*Bookriot*

"Razor-sharp and darkly satirical, this novel nudges you to question everything at every turn."

—*Harper's Bazaar Australia*

"*We Cast a Shadow,* a sharp satire and also a tragic story of family, will give you major *Get Out* vibes."

—Popsugar

"Maurice Carlos Ruffin's thrilling debut, *We Cast A Shadow,* is haunted by the ghosts of writers Ralph Ellison and Victor LaValle. But Ruffin, and the terrifying racial landscape he renders, is a world unto himself."

—NAOMI JACKSON, author of
The Star Side of Bird Hill

"Riotously hilarious and resoundingly heartrending . . . Ruffin performs literature's noble alchemy—making the unseen seen."

—T. GERONIMO JOHNSON, author of
Welcome to Braggsville

"When we live in times so absurd and frightening that the only plausible reaction is nervous laughter, we need fiction as strange and revelatory as this landscape. Maurice Carlos Ruffin's *We Cast A Shadow* is an always inventive story of race, longing, and self. Like *Invisible Man* and *The Wig* before it, it takes all the shabby myths of race in America and sews them together into something new, an altogether wondrous fabric, to warm us in this not-so-brave new world."

—KAITLYN GREENIDGE, author of
We Love You, Charlie Freeman

"An urgent, exuberant, and important work of fiction that is also wildly hilarious . . . With *We Cast a Shadow,* the talented Mr. Ruffin has arrived."

—JAMI ATTENBERG, author of
All Grown Up

"A glorious debut, *We Cast A Shadow* is a disturbing, empathetic, and ultimately illuminating story about race and family."

—LAILA LALAMI, author of
The Moor's Account

"Maurice Carlos Ruffin writes with a conviction that turns skeptics into believers. A novel that has nearly every pressing issue of the modern moment in its crosshairs, *We Cast a Shadow* is likely to be mistaken by some as a dystopian satire but recognized by many more as America's unfortunate realism. One of the most original novels I've read in ages, *We Cast a Shadow* immediately renders any discussion of contemporary fiction, especially Southern fiction, incomplete without it. This one will be on nightstands and in classrooms. Don't miss it."

—M. O. WALSH, *New York Times* bestselling
author of *My Sunshine Away*

"Maurice Carlos Ruffin joins the pantheon of great satirists as he trains a distorting lens on America, bringing its corruption into clearer focus. *We Cast a Shadow* is madcap and merciless, tender and terrifying as it explores the lengths a father will go to protect his son in a vicious world."

—C. MORGAN BABST, author of
The Floating World

"I couldn't stop reading *We Cast A Shadow*—and I couldn't stop thinking about it. Blazingly witty, bitingly funny, and both sharp and shrewd in its take on race in America, Maurice Carlos Ruffin's debut is an instant contemporary classic."

—ALEXANDRIA MARZANO-LESNEVICH,
author of *The Fact of a Body*

"In his debut novel, Maurice Carlos Ruffin brings the South out of the past into the here-and-now, and beyond, to the future. *We Cast a Shadow* ranges from Nabokovian humor to "the lower frequencies" invoked by Ellison's *Invisible Man*—incandescent, vexing, not unlike America itself."

—ZACHARY LAZAR, author of *Vengeance*

"This novel terrified me because it's real, real in its imagining of a near-future I can and can't believe at the same time. Much like the present. But Maurice Ruffin's hapless narrator is irresistible, even as you wince at his decisions, and this novel—part satire and all heart—will tug at you long after you've put it down."

—TOM FRANKLIN, author of
Crooked Letter, Crooked Letter

"*We Cast a Shadow* is both hilarious and heartbreaking. A fellow New Orleans native, Ruffin reinterprets old Creole anxieties about 'passing' in a futurist context, and with comic genius skewers the window dressing of 'diversity' in a racist police state. Like all great satire, this riveting novel isn't angry, but you might be after reading it."

—JAMES NOLAN, author of *Flight Risk:
Memoirs of a New Orleans Bad Boy*

WE CAST A SHADOW

WE
CAST
A
SHADOW

A NOVEL

MAURICE CARLOS RUFFIN

ONE WORLD
NEW YORK

2020 One World Trade Paperback Edition

Published in the United States by One World, an imprint of Random House,
a division of Penguin Random House LLC, New York.

ONE WORLD and colophon are registered trademarks of
Penguin Random House LLC.

Originally published in hardcover in the United States by One World,
an imprint of Random House, a division of Penguin Random House LLC, in 2019.

LIBRARY OF CONGRESS CATALOGING-IN-PUBLICATION DATA
Names: Ruffin, Maurice Carlos, author.
Title: We cast a shadow: a novel / Maurice Carlos Ruffin.
Description: First edition. | New York: One World, [2019]
Identifiers: LCCN 2018021024 | ISBN 9780525509073 (paperback) |
ISBN 9780525509080 (ebook)
Subjects: LCSH: African Americans—Fiction. | BISAC: FICTION / Literary. |
FICTION / Satire. | FICTION / African American / General.
Classification: LCC PS3618.U4338 W4 2019 | DDC 813/.6—dc23
LC record available at https://lccn.loc.gov/2018021024
Printed in the United States of America on acid-free paper

oneworldlit.com
randomhousebooks.com

9 8 7 6 5 4 3 2 1

Book design by Diane Hobbing

For Tanzanika, I bet you a fat man

There are few things in the world as dangerous as sleepwalkers.

—RALPH ELLISON

See how elastic our stiff prejudices grow when once love comes to bend them.

—HERMAN MELVILLE

Look at this tangle of thorns.

—VLADIMIR NABOKOV

Part One

1

My name doesn't matter. All you need to know is that I'm a phantom, a figment, a man who was mistaken for waitstaff twice that night—odd, given my outfit. I managed to avoid additional embarrassments by wallflowering in the shadow of the grand staircase. Their cheeks pink from Southern Comfort, the partners—or shareholders, as the firm called them—stood chatting in clusters around the dining room.

I had been invited by my law firm's leaders to attend their annual party at Octavia Whitmore's mansion on the Avenue of Streetcars. It was a highlight of my life, an honor for a lowly associate just to be invited, although I was surprised to be told to show up in a costume.

Rough fabric chafed against my collarbone. I was dressed as a Roman centurion. I had rented the mega-deluxe option, no expense spared: full tunic of lamb's wool, leather sandals, and five—count 'em, five—Hollywood-prop-grade weapons: a sword, a javelin, a bow and arrow, a shield, and a dagger. I never knew that Roman soldiers used daggers. But the costume guy assured me that they did too use daggers, the dagger being the preferred weapon of choice for when shit got real, which apparently it did from time to time.

The first floor of Octavia's mansion was a series of large rooms. Playful notes of sandalwood and jasmine lingered in the foyer. I spotted my fellow black associate Franklin beyond that entryway. Franklin, who got white-girl drunk at every firm function, karaoked "I Feel Pretty" into a microphone. Franklin had come wearing the perfect icebreaker. He wore a white smock and a black bow tie, the uniform of every black busboy and waiter at every old-line restaurant in the City. Café des Réfugiés, Carnation Room, Pierre's—no, not Pierre's; there were no brothers at Pierre's. I wasn't sure what must have been more mortifying for Franklin: that he was singing so poorly or that no one paid him any mind. It couldn't have helped that he was too black to be pretty.

My frenemy, good ol' back-slapping Riley, was bent over a table giving the managing shareholder, Jack Armbruster, a foot massage. Sweat made Riley's bald head glow. He looked like a scoop of chocolate ice cream melting under the parlor lights. Riley was dressed as a parish prison inmate, which rankled my sense of propriety. They saw enough of us dressed that way in news reports. However, I had to admit it was an impressive getup. He wore a Day-Glo orange jumpsuit, and even a fake chest tattoo. He carried clinking leg shackles slung over his shoulder, as if ready to reincarcerate himself on request.

Riley was working the old fart's feet, feet so gnarly they seemed like roots ripped from the field behind the mansion. He dabbed his dome with a handkerchief. Was a promotion and bonus worth the kind of humiliation Franklin and Riley were undergoing? Confetti rained down on the junior shareholders in the adjacent parlor. You betcha.

My son Nigel's procedure would be expensive. After feeding the snarling, three-headed beast of mortgage, utilities, and private school tuition, I only managed to pocket a few copper coins each month. But if I were promoted, I would earn a fat bonus, and Nigel would finally get a normal face, over his mother's objections.

I idled on the sidelines, nursing a rum and Coke, which, in turn, nursed my ever-present migraine (thankfully, almost down for the night). I had lost count of how many drinks I'd had over the last few hours, which meant by now my blood was probably 75 percent alcohol by volume. And that was on top of the dissipating effects of the Plum I took that morning. I told myself on each awakening that I didn't need Plums anymore. I told myself I could quit anytime I chose. But I knew better. Those petite purple pills, which turned my nervous system into a tangle of pleasurably twinkling Christmas lights, had become a constant companion.

Riley ambled over. He exaggeratedly wiped his palms on his jumpsuit pants. Smiling, he jabbed his hand out for a handshake. I shook my head.

"Where is the love?" Riley glanced at his hand and sniffed. "I don't blame you actually. I think Armbruster's been on his feet all day." He grabbed the sleeve of my tunic, tossed his head back, and chuckled. "You don't think you're going to win in this, do you?"

"I like my look," I said, taken aback. "Check out this hand-stitching—wait. Win what?"

"Win this hazing ceremony. Tonight is a competition, after all. There's three of us, but only one promotion. You knew that." Riley raised his eyebrow. "You didn't know that."

"But this is just a party."

"And one of us will have something to celebrate." Riley always seemed to have inside knowledge about the firm's workings. But he was also the kind of person to say things just to get a reaction from me. Still, he wouldn't joke about this. The stakes were too high.

"What happens to the losers?"

He leaned in to whisper. "You know how it works. It's up or

out." Riley adjusted my breastplate. "I didn't mean to mess with your confidence. You're right. This is a great look." He straightened up and nodded. "Really authentic."

Riley patted my shoulder and trotted off, his manacles clattering against the back of his jumpsuit. He shook the hands of a couple of shareholders and laughed.

I suddenly realized I had made a serious miscalculation. Riley's costume was a great way to get attention and spread good cheer. Mine, on the other hand, was the sartorial equivalent of a glower. Centurions were badasses who killed anyone who crossed them. The only way I could have made this group any more nervous was if I showed up as Nat Turner, but I knew better. Or I should have. There were many unknowns in my pursuit of happiness, but one thing I understood: law firms like Seasons, Ustis & Malveaux didn't hire, let alone promote, angry black men. If this was a competition, I needed a new strategy. The shareholders wanted entertainment. They wanted a good time. They also wanted subservience. They did not want to feel threatened. If I was going to win, I would have to demonstrate I was willing to give them exactly what they wanted.

I quickly moved from room to room searching for anything that could help me. In the back den, I spotted Octavia Whitmore in a gingham dress, carrying a terrier in the crook of her elbow and a drink in each of her hands. If anyone could help me find an advantage, she could. After all, she was a senior shareholder, and I her legal footman. I was the associate who did the grunt work that was beneath her valets. She needed me.

"You look just like Judy Garland," I said. Octavia hadn't noticed me, so her face momentarily lit up in surprise as I approached. I kissed her cheek.

"Well, aren't you sweet?" she said.

I liked Octavia. She was one of the good ones, even if, as she once drunkenly admitted to me in a stalled elevator, she sometimes fantasized about wearing blackface and going on a crime spree. After shattering storefront windows and mugging tourists by the Cathedral, she would wash the makeup from her face, content in the knowledge that the authorities would pin her deeds on some thug who actually had it coming.

That was when I realized that the Toto in her arm was a cat—a Ragamuffin cat wearing a wig. I'd never seen a cat wearing a wig. It was a night of wonders.

"Why you off to the side like this, sugar?" Octavia licked her thumb and polished the foot of a gilt bronze cherub.

"Someone has to stand watch over these rabble-rousers." I puffed my chest out and stamped my javelin on the marble floor.

"But who's guarding you? Here, this will freshen you right up." She took the javelin and handed me another glass. I gave my empty rum glass to one of the waiters, an onyx-skinned man who would have otherwise eluded my attention if not for the fact that he'd clearly undergone enthusiastic rhinoplasty, his broad-winged brother's nose replaced by a narrow, upturned pointer. Such procedures had become much more common among black folk lately. I couldn't tell if he'd only had his schnoz done because he was too poor to afford the full procedure or because he was afraid. Half measures were such a waste of effort. If you were going to skydive into whiteness, aim for the town square, not the outskirts.

"What's this?" I said.

"A Sazerac," Octavia said with a wink. Her hair's silver streak glinted.

"But you know I don't drink," I said, drinking.

She chuckled.

"I don't think I'm a fan favorite in this." I gestured to my clothing.

Toto growled at me. That cat took its role seriously.

Handling my javelin as if it were a pool cue, Octavia leveled it at the crowd, but I couldn't tell who she was shooting at. She leaned it against the stairwell banister. I reached for it, but she stopped me.

"Leave it," she said. "I have something for you upstairs."

We climbed the stairs until we reached a side gallery that looked down on the atrium. Powder-blue shapes shimmered from the aquarium and formed waves across the checkerboard floor. Riley passed behind the bars of the staircase, dragging his chain. I was glad to be away from the scrum of shareholders with their plastic smiles, the smiles of sharks before a feeding frenzy. You really shouldn't be able to see a person's molars when they grin. The whole situation made me jumpy, as if a squid were twitching around in my tunic. I should have worn underwear.

Octavia led me into a long room. Every wall was covered with leather-bound books. *Eyes Without a Face*. *The Hip Hop Ontologist's View of Leda and the Swan*. *Blackstone's Law*. I pulled that book from the shelf and opened the cover. Dust motes pirouetted into the air. I sneezed.

"You read all these?" I asked, wiping my nose with the back of my Sazerac hand.

"Shit, no." She ran a French-tipped nail along the rim of my glass. "Neither did my father. They're real, but mainly for effect."

"Oh."

She pointed past me, and I followed her line of sight.

Statues lined the back wall. Just like me to notice books but not creepy wax men lurking in the shadows. One mannequin was Chinese, I guessed. He wore a fulvous robe and had long tufts of hair along his chin. Another looked like a Jack Kirby Thor, square jaw, blond hair, and Mjolnir, the magic hammer. I caught the theme even though there were no placards. Gods of the Human World.

"What do you think of this one?" she said.

It was a black man. He wore a headdress, face paint, and a bone necklace. I had no idea which African deity he was supposed to be, but I'd read enough to know there were more black deities than anyone could possibly keep track of, so many, in fact, that it cheapened the idea of godliness. If everyone was a god, no one was a god.

Whoever made the statue apparently believed the myth that all us black men were hung like Clydesdales, a myth that led to plenty of awkward dating experiences since I was only average in the Joe department. The African god's loincloth did little to obscure his bulge. It was a safety hazard. Someone could poke their eye out.

As for my overall opinion of the statue, whenever a white person asked me any question just because I was the onliest black guy in the room, the possible responses rattled around my brain like dice in a cup: one, answer with anger; two, answer with humor; or three, answer with a question.

The first, I practically never used. Anger, of course, could get you killed.

The second, humor, was fine in most situations, but it was only something I deployed in safe environments. This was not a safe environment. Octavia was up to something. Something dangerous, or brilliant, or both.

"Is this a museum?" I asked.

"My father's private collection." She trailed her index finger down my bare arm. She walked behind the African god. From its perch on Octavia's arm, Toto sniffed the statue's butt. "These were sculpted by the same man who did the original Madame Tussauds. The hair is real human hair. Even the eyelashes. Even the eyeballs, I think." She squatted by a low drawer and rummaged through it. She pulled out a gong. "There are accessories all around the room. You can upgrade your look to something more . . . appropriate."

She struck the gong with her glass, producing a hollow sound.

"Why are you helping me?" I asked.

"I like you. Always have, but also I put a dollar on you winning." Octavia stepped into me, the way she might if we were about to tango, close enough that I could smell her liquor-drenched breath. "If you want to win, gather your balls and get out there, boy."

"Thanks?" The only non-black person with permission to call me "boy" was my wife. Yet I knew I couldn't say anything. Octavia had probably consumed a liter of Sazerac, and who could fault anyone who had probably consumed a liter of Sazerac?

She flourished her hand and strutted toward the door. "Don't worry. I won't watch you change," she said. "This time." And then she left.

I don't know how I missed the giant figure just inside the door back to the gallery. He was easily double the size of the other gods. He wore a toga and had a beard that would have made Jerry Garcia proud. Actually, given Octavia's wealth, it could have been Jerry Garcia's actual beard. The statue held a lightning bolt. Zeus! That was who I wanted to be.

Zeus was a shameless choice in my quest to climb the social step stool. Who could fault me for choosing the ruler of Mount Olympus? Victory was close at hand. Possibility whisked me away. I wondered whether the virtuoso plastic surgeon I had in mind for Nigel's procedure preferred credit cards or cashier's checks. I imagined my boy's wedding day in the distant future, his cheeky face flawless as a seaside sunrise.

No. I couldn't be Zeus. If I went back to the party as the king of gods, the shareholders would think I was conceited, crass, uppity.

I needed something that would give me a fighting chance against Franklin's Stepin Fetchit uniform and Riley's "20 to life." I had to sink to the level of the shareholders' expectations. My fellow melanated associates fit in better than me because everyone was used to seeing black waiters tending to tourists or black convicts being led to work in neck shackles. There was a comfort in these familiar images, as reassuring as steaming apple pie or drones dropping barrel bombs on terrorists. The Zulu chief stared over my head. I only had to fulfill an expectation. I only had to say yes one more time, right? Examining the various fasteners and clips of a remnant barely large enough to cover a child's bottom, I thought: *I can totally do this.*

Once I finished changing, I inhaled, threw my shoulders back, and descended the curving staircase with all the resolve of an over-looked but hopeful debutante. I anticipated a collective pause when people noticed me. There was. Entering a crowded room full of intoxicated lawyers wearing nothing but a loincloth, leg tassels, and feathery headdress is bound to attract attention. What I didn't expect was that Jack Armbruster, who prided himself on never wasting so much as a molecule of bourbon, dropped his highball glass. It shattered with a satisfying crack against the mar-ble. Liquor spread, a pale imitation of lifeblood.

I gazed at the shareholders in their costumes, a zombie pilgrim, a cheerful Madame LaLaurie, and a diminutive Honest Abe, all silent for what felt like an hour at the bottom of the ocean's deep-est trench. Armbruster whipped out a silk handkerchief from his blazer—I think he was the Millionaire from *Gilligan's Island,* but it was hard to tell because that was more or less how he always looked—and wiped his mouth with a flick. Everyone watched him. He chuckled and clapped once. The room burst into ap-plause.

I realized that I'd walked out smack into the middle of the judg-ing session. The other associates had been cleared out, probably into the field behind the mansion. The big plate-glass windows reflected the interior of the room, the shareholders, and myself. But by concentrating, I caught a glimpse of the world beyond the mirror. Sure enough, amid the restless security personnel who guarded Octavia's neighborhood with machine guns, Riley and Franklin stared at me from the grass, their faces featureless in that spectral mansion glow. They clapped, too. My chest tightened as if someone were squeezing my lungs from the inside of my chest.

Then the drumbeat kicked in.

The firm had hired an Afro-Cuban quartet, trumpet, keys, drums, and congas for the party. Possibly sensing a chance to fill their tip bucket, the band stuttered into a dark tribal beat. Not the kind of rhythm that rock and roll was built on, but the kind of rhythm that predated *bluesuederockaroundtheclockpleasepleasefightfor-yourrighttoparty* by at least a thousand years.

I danced. I wasn't a dancer, but I was a decent mimic. I'd watched Mardi Gras Indians buck jump my entire life. I'd seen people around the neighborhood twerk and p-pop. I'd seen crackheads have seizures.

Facing the shareholders, I couldn't see myself. But if I could have sprung from my own body and watched myself from Zeus's perch upstairs, I would have seen a skinny, nearly naked Negro in a sumo squat, flapping his arms and legs as though they were on fire. People laughed and imitated my movements. Flashes popped. The videographer swung in for a close-up. It's a strange thing to feel so alive even as a part of your soul turns to cold green goo and oozes out of your heel. Every time I raised my spear, they cheered louder. The higher I raised it, the louder they roared.

And then suddenly the music shifted—like a runaway tour bus transitioning from cliff to air. Silence. Armbruster covered his mouth with his handkerchief, his eyes locked on me. Octavia fanned herself. Somewhere in the room a camera clicked twice.

It must have been the buzz of the alcohol and pill that delayed the feeling of a licking breeze across my lower body. The loincloth had come undone, and I was naked as a peeled egg.

Do you know how eerie it is for a hundred people to go completely quiet at the sight of your manhood?

Toto ran over, and I backed into the wall, all eyes on me against the world. I snatched him up, using his furry body like a pom-pom. I stumbled out of the mansion's back door and into the field.

2

We lived, at that time, in a part of the City once inhabited by Mosopelea Indians who migrated to the marshlands to avoid the white man, then by immigrants from Continental Europe who, having left behind crowd, famine, and disease, fled the City to escape the black man, then inhabited by blacks who were vigorously reappropriated to the penitentiary at the parish line, and finally by the descendants of those earlier whites who returned when the coast was again clear. Except for me and half of my son, there were no other blacks in our neighborhood.

Our enclave was not without its charms. Sometime before we bought in, our neighbors prosecuted an altogether different kind of war of the roses so that every porch and garden box was an explosion of floral fireworks: elephant ears reared back from mouse flowers, pineapple lilies and calla lilies brushed sisterly hips, a Mexican hen and chicks soundlessly clucked from a terracotta pot left behind on our porch by the previous owners.

Our house was very fine, long and narrow as a folio book, so it seemed quite quaint from the front. But inside, the house, with its long, left-centered hallway, went on for many chapters.

Past the den where our frumpy paisley couch nested, past the dining room where the drop-leaf mahogany table gave port to an armada of Penny's acrylic paint tubes and brushes, past the second bedroom where Nigel's vintage Rev. ManRay McKintosh poster (gifted by his grandmother) hung, was our kitchen, where my wife and son gathered the morning after my failure at Octavia's mansion. From the bedroom door in the back corner of the kitchen, I entered in rumpled, kaleidoscopic pajamas, hyperactive gorillas pounding kettledrums in my head. I wore opaque safety goggles left over from a welding-accident case I'd worked years earlier. I could hardly see a thing, but they served a purpose. They were meant to buy me time.

"You look like you lost a wrestling match." Penny poured orange juice into the leaf-green carafe without looking at me. As usual, she was already ready for work. Whereas I took an eternity to put myself together, Penny wasn't the kind of woman to overdo it with hair or makeup. She was a pragmatist. A little foundation. A little blush. No lipstick. She still wore her red curls long, although not as long as she did in the early days of our marriage. Her light green blouse matched the underside of the leaf she had just filled. "Doesn't he, munchkin?"

"My dad doesn't lose fights." Nigel poured batter onto the well-seasoned iron skillet, a wedding gift from Penny's mother. My nose twitched to cinnamon and a hint of ginger. Eleven years old, and it was an accepted fact that Nigel was the most talented chef in our tribe. We discovered this at age three when he grabbed a shaker of seasoning salts and dumped it into my bowl of bland grits.

"He won, and I bet the other guy looks way worse."

"Crap." Penny righted a quart of chocolate milk that had spilled on the counter. I asked if she needed a hand, but she was already pushing the lake of dairy into the sink with a ream of paper towels.

I returned my gaze to Nigel. "That's my boy." I ran my hand through my son's hair, a velvety tousle of black laurel, and poured a cup of coffee. He didn't have to attack his hair with noxious chemicals, like I did, to make it unkink.

Penny jotted a note on the fridge to-do list. Her chicken-scratch was almost impossible to read, except for the note that had been next to the door handle for years. In block letters, it clearly read, "I love my boys!"

I gestured. She folded the paper she'd just written on and stuffed it into her bra. "I'm calling the City about those surveillance vans," she said.

"They're safety patrols, not surveillance vans," I said. Yes, the City Police van visited our block twice a day. And yes, it had cameras and infrared devices that could look into the deepest reaches of our home. But the vans checked in on any neighborhood where black folks lived to monitor vital signs: low heart rates suggested barbiturate use, elevated heart rates meant conflict, no heart rate was self-explanatory. It was for our—that is, black folks'—own good. When I was growing up, it wasn't uncommon for people to attack us in the streets.

Since Nigel and I didn't live in a black neighborhood, the poor officer assigned to protect us had to ride all the way over from the Tiko. He had to speed to stay on schedule.

"Those goons almost hit Mrs. Kravits this morning." Penny tossed the soiled paper towels into the garbage and pressed down with both hands.

"Okay. I'll call, if it makes you feel better," I said.

"It would." She washed her hands.

"May I?" I gestured toward her chest. She smirked. I removed the reminder note.

"So are you going to explain that?" Nigel pointed at the goggles on my face.

"I have no idea what you're talking about." I parked at the head of the table. Penny pitched a look of disgust over Nigel's shoulder at me. We had fought a few minutes earlier about my behavior. That is to say, my darling dragon fruit did not appreciate my stumbling into the house sometime around three A.M. wrapped in the plaid picnic blanket we kept in the trunk of my car. Nor did she enjoy my bleary recitation of the night's absurdities before falling asleep on the floor at the foot of our bed or my presentation of red-rimmed eyes on awakening that were a sign of—well, she knew what they were a sign of.

I caught Penny's look and stirred it into my bitter coffee. "Oh. You mean these?" I removed the safety goggles. Beneath them I wore a small pair of dark sunglasses.

Nigel screwed his mouth up in mock derision. "Jerk."

On checking myself out in the mirror that morning, my eyes were puffy, pink, a side effect of all I'd ingested the day before, plus a lack of sleep and a bellyful of stress. I didn't want to miss seeing Nigel off to school, I never missed doing so. So I plied my peepers with the prescription eye drops I kept for just that purpose and donned the goggles and glasses to give the drops time to do their thing.

Penny asked Nigel to go grab her phone from the bedroom, and he went. Ah. Coffee. No sugar. No cream. I liked my java so black, the police planted evidence on it. And I was such a lucky man. My beautiful wife. My lovely, intelligent, redheaded wife swung across the room, her hips, about which she was unduly self-conscious, clicked in sympathy with my cuckoo clock heart. Then my amazing soulmate whacked me in the back of the head so hard, coffee squirted from my nostrils.

"Ow," I said. Penny smiled slightly. Plums were sometimes called zombie pills due to their anesthetic effect. My pain proved to her that I was still with her in the land of the living.

"Why aren't you dressed?" she said through clenched teeth so Nigel wouldn't hear.

"I told you I'm not going," I whispered. After the previous night's debacle at Octavia's mansion, I had no doubt that Franklin or Riley had already been promoted. The sun was still scrubbing darkness from the sky outside the high window, but I was sure that Administration had already ripped my nameplate from my office door and deleted my biography from the firm website.

"So that's your solution?" she said. "You won't even find out what actually happened?"

My hand trembled and coffee splashed out of my mug. Without my job, we wouldn't be able to keep the house, the cars would get repoed, and worst of all, I wouldn't be able to pay for Nigel's procedure. But I couldn't change that. I had been held up to the light and found wanting. I could imagine Penny's estranged parents guffawing at the thought of her being forced to move back in with them. Interracial marriage was perfectly legal, of course, but it— along with mixed-race births—had been on the decline for years, especially in the South. Our dissolution would be proof that her folks had been right about the folly of such unions.

Penny wasn't on speaking terms with her family. They hadn't come to our wedding, not that they would have, if invited. Penny had grown up in a highly exclusive planned community upstate. The only people of color she knew were her Filipino nanny, Esmeralda, and Mr. Bowman, the elderly black man who handled the lawn care. When she dated a Muslim boy from an equally successful family, her parents almost disowned her. She broke off that relationship, which she would regret, but moved to the City as soon as she finished high school. She was in college when I met her.

As for my failure to procure Nigel's treatment, Penny didn't want some mad scientist fooling with her baby's face anyway. She thought it best for him to learn to love himself rather than slice and dice his little body in a quest for acceptance. It was the only area of discourse where there was daylight between us.

Nigel reentered and threw his hands up. "Ma," he said, "I didn't see it anywhere."

"Really," she said, rummaging through her burlap purse on the hutch. "Here it is. If my head wasn't stapled to my shoulders . . ."

Penny and Nigel decked the table with pancakes, vegan bacon, and a bowl of raspberries. We ate. The flavors wreathed my stomach in joy.

"Mm," I said, drowning the last of my cake in maple syrup. "So good. Who gets to eat like this on a Friday morning?"

Penny reached out to touch Nigel's face.

"Ma!"

"You've got gunk in your eye." Of course, I didn't see any gunk. I saw the thing on my son's face.

It was very small at first, the spot. After Nigel was born, cleaned, and placed in Penny's arms, I had to count backward from ten three times before I stopped shaking enough to actually see him. He was a gorgeous ball of fat with a miniature version of my family nose and Penny's pinkish coloration, the shade a fingertip turns once released. I finally understood why little old ladies, when pinching chubby toes in sequence, often spoke of wanting to "eat the child right up!" Until that moment, the notion had been a dark one, bringing to mind flashes of Goya's *Saturn Devouring His Son*.

There was a speck, like a fleck of oregano, on Nigel's eyelid. He had been baking in Penny's oven nine full months, so it made sense that there would be bits of gristle in hard-to-clean creases. I gently touched the spot and realized it was part of him, a birthmark.

Nigel pulled the sunglasses from my nose. He gave me a queer glance, then put the frames on his face. The birthmark flashed at me. It had metamorphosed over the years. First, it had grown. By preschool, what had been a dot had spread to the ridge of his eyebrow, and, eventually, down the side of his face. Second, it changed shapes from a rough circle to a wedge to a silhouette the shape of New Zealand or perhaps the Wu-Tang Clan symbol turned on its head. Third, it darkened with him. Nigel's general shade stabilized to an olive tone so that he might be mistaken for a Venetian boy who spent his summers cartwheeling across the Rialto Bridge, but the birthmark colored from wheat to sienna to umber, the hard hue of my own husk, as if a shard of myself were emerging from him. It was the reason I encouraged Nigel's love of baseball caps. Anything to keep the birthmark from blackening.

I asked him where his hat was, the new neon-yellow one that I had gotten him. It was a kind of anticamouflage, really, a target designed to draw the viewer's eye away from his beautiful but distorted face.

"Oh"—Nigel glanced at his book sack by the exit door—"I must have left it in my room."

"So today is the big day, huh?" Penny said.

Nigel nodded and grunted, knowing that talking with his mouth full was verboten.

I wondered what they were talking about. My boy was involved, in varying degrees, in so many school activities that one could easily lose track: the visual arts society, soccer, the *Big Fish* lit mag, the keyboard chamber orchestra, peer tutoring in math, speech and debate, the drama club, and kiddie slam poetry every third Thursday. We kept a calendar on the fridge, but the shorthand that Penny used was as indecipherable to me as Chinese *hanzi*.

What big day was it? How did I get here? Why couldn't I ever follow the plot? I bet even that busybody down the street knew what big day it was. A tiny me, feet propped up in the back-theater row of my mind, spilled his popcorn and let loose a Bronx cheer.

"How do you feel about it?"

"Like I'm going to win, Ma." Ah, Nigel's class at the School Without Walls—an offshoot of the Montessori tradition—was having a creativity show-and-tell. Students were encouraged to "make the impossible possible." Favorites would be selected for display in the auditorium. Nigel's project had something to do with the magic of mirrors, but between Elevation Night and working late all week, I wasn't able to help out. Not that this was any great loss to Nigel. Penny was the hands of the family. My fumbling efforts at arts and crafts usually led to a frantic bandage search, both for my damaged digits and for my ecchymotic ego.

Nigel skipped away from the table. Penny raised her hand to

whack me in the back of the head again but stopped and did that thing she did when she wasn't whacking me in the back of the head; she swept her hand sideways like a blackjack dealer laying cards on a table. The lower edge of her tattoo said hello to me from behind her blouse sleeve. I could only see the bottom tendril of a vine that led up her forearm to a garden above her elbow where a butterfly—a Leopard Lacewing, if that was the artist's intention—hovered over a white-haloed flower on her right shoulder blade. She shoved the bowl of leftover raspberries away and held my chin between thumb and forefinger.

"I know things have been crazy at work, but you worked like crazy to get there. Maybe it's over, but if there's any chance of changing their minds, you're the only one who can do it." She grabbed the scruff of my neck like a lioness taking a cub between its teeth and pulled me closer. "I'm sorry I thumped your noggin, baby." Her breath smelled like citrus. Citrus and embers.

"Who doesn't love a good thumping?" I leaned in for the kill.

"Gross!" Nigel stepped back into the kitchen. He wore the neon-yellow baseball cap. "Again with the kissy face."

Penny and I straightened in our seats. She gave me a look that said, *Could you just try to keep it together for our son?* I gave her an *As you wish.*

"Tooth inspection," I said.

Nigel groaned.

"You'll understand when you're older," I said. "Cavities are the great scourge of adulthood."

Nigel carried a box-shaped arrangement of cardboard and plastic. He set the box on the table and pointed at the plastic window on its side.

"You have to get really close and stare inside," Nigel said. "Go on."

I stared. A light snapped on. A diorama appeared. It was a simple reconstruction of Nigel's bedroom, the bed and dresser made of folded jacks and queens—Nigel and I sometimes played euchre or Forty-fives—and near the wall, to the right, was Nigel, or rather a cutout of a photo of him with his arms thrown up victoriously.

I recalled that photo well. I had taken it on a Gulf Coast beach two summers earlier. The scent of seawater assailed my memory, the murmur of waves. A seagull wing whirled cryptically out of view. Nigel and I raced from the car parked on the coastal highway. I gave him a head start, but soon found that I couldn't catch him. His long-toed feet beat against the clay until he stopped at the water's edge and a cloud of water surged around his calves. He turned back to me with a smile so bright, I was shocked it didn't reduce me to ashes. Penny was just beyond the frame when I took the picture. A moment later her arms were wrapped around him, and I took that picture, too, of them so deliriously happy in the surf, but the shot came out blurry.

I couldn't help but notice how much he had grown in so short a time. He had been shorter and rounder of face then. Plus, the birthmark had been smaller.

Suddenly, mini-Nigel vanished, although the rest of the tiny room remained exactly as it was. Where did it go? Despite myself, I gasped and drew back.

Nigel and Penny watched me with complete satisfaction. Penny smacked the table and guffawed, her somewhat wheezy laugh that jangled the keys to my heart every time. They had gotten the response they wanted. Penny kissed Nigel's forehead.

"Pretty good, right?" Nigel blushed and adjusted my sunglasses on his face.

I sputtered for a moment asking how, shaking my head. Nigel explained about relative levels of light and the expectations of the person watching, but I was distracted as Nigel brought his hand to the birthmark and lightly scratched. Dermatologists assured us long ago that the mark was no danger to him in any way and that it certainly wasn't infectious or spreadable by rough handling, but the cup clanging against the bars of my mind said that scraping it might make it worse. It could inflame; it would spread to other parts of his body. What if the dermatologists were wrong? My medical malpractice cases had taught me that doctors are no better at predicting the future than weathermen.

"Don't do that." I grabbed Nigel's wrist, harder than I intended, and saw framed in the oval lenses my own frantic, bloodshot eyes.

3

Firings at Seasons were low-key affairs, or so I'd heard. I'd never witnessed one, and I certainly didn't plan on witnessing my own. Yes, I had promised Penny to make a run at saving my career, but the escalators changed my mind. They were out again, which I took as an omen. How could I secure my position if the skyscraper itself, all sixty-two stories of it, was against me?

The Sky Tower, where Seasons' offices nested, was a sprawling affair. A rotating, highly illuminated steel sculpture fountain—it blinded you if you looked at it the wrong way—sat in the center of the ground floor. Above, the rippling, curvaceous terraces surrounding the atrium seemed to spawn and respawn into infinity. But the diagonal distance from the concourse to the lobby—where a trio of middle-aged black female security guards chatted like a Greek chorus—was only about three stories via a series of M. C. Escher–like mechanical stairs, all frozen now.

By the time I made it to the main elevator bank, I was clammy and winded. Deflated, I understood that talking my way back into the firm was a fantasy in the same way that I thought my voice sounded great, even angelic, in the shower. Occasionally, I went so far as to record myself. On playback, amid the pinging current of water and our crusty, clanging pipes, I heard my voice. What a whiny, keening instrument fate had saddled me with.

No. I needed to slip into my office, grab my things, and slink out unnoticed. I'd tell Penny I gave it my all. As for Nigel's procedure, there were no better-paying jobs in the City, but I'd simply have to find another way.

Getting in and out of the office unnoticed wouldn't be difficult. In a firm of more than five hundred employees, you could do almost anything without causing a stir. Last year one of the transactions shareholders had died cradling a telephone. No one noticed until Accounting came by to check his invoices. When they touched his shoulder, his body exhaled.

Behind me, an elevator arrived. I climbed into the vertical coffin, careful to avoid making eye contact on the way up. My fellow passengers stared at their devices.

The firm's receptionist didn't give me a second look when I padded into the vestibule.

Something crinkled in my breast pocket. I pulled out a folded receipt. Penny had written on the back of it, *"Nihil taurus crappus."* Penny never cursed in real life, but her cornydog Latin had been drawing a smile from me since the day we met. My best friend.

Etherine passed me in the hall, carrying a tray of utensils and saucers. She wore her everyday uniform, a gray housekeeper's dress. I told her good morning. She harrumphed and kept walking. Nothing unusual there.

I went to the kitchen. Coffee and a few minutes of quiet would calm my nerves. I opened the door and stopped midstep. People were in the room. I leaned backward, hoping to leave without being noticed, but I knew the door would squeal like a pig the second I moved. So I froze in place, with half my body in the kitchen and the other in the hall. My brogue hovered above the threshold.

Dinah Viet Dinh stood by the sink, dumping out her thermos. "God." She removed her horn-rimmed glasses and stuck out her tongue. "It tastes like liquid butt."

"Speaking of which"—Paul Pavor leaned against the refrigerator, running a hand through his blond hair—"I wouldn't be surprised if they cut all three of those boys loose."

"From last night, you mean?" Dinah asked.

"I *would* be surprised," Quentin Callower said. "I gather the major shareholders were rather impressed with those dehumanizing displays." He hunched over his herbal tea, his bald spot showing.

"Look, Riley's prison rags had me rolling on the floor. I mean, I like a little fun as much as the next man," Pavor said, winking at Dinah, who rolled her eyes. "But the last thing we need to do is keep dead weight for the sake of meeting some quota. Someone better missed out on a shot at working here because those clowns were in the way."

Dinah opened her mouth to speak, but shook her head and inhaled.

We had all gone to law school together and were hired as part of the same class, although Callower was older than the rest of us. Pavor was from upstate; tall and blond, he left a failed acting career in his past. Today he looked like someone who might play a lawyer in a twentieth-century soap opera about attorneys and their convoluted love lives. He was biding his time until his parents believed he was responsible enough to take over the family marijuana empire back home.

Callower was the great-grandson of a former mayor of the City, a staunch segregationist who left town during one of the waves of white flight. His family lived in the suburbs, and the rumor was that they had disowned him for living in the city limits.

Dinah and I went back to grade school. We played strings in a youth orchestra together along with Riley, who was the pianist.

Dinah was born in Vietnam, but her mother got an engineering job at a solar company and moved the family over. Dinah used to say her parents never wanted to come to America because white people would expect them to assimilate. She took to the City quickly, even telling everyone to call her Dinah instead of her birth name, a fact she hid from her parents. But she was only doing what the other Vietnamese kids did. The members of the Vietnamese community in the City were known for fitting in and sacrificing for one another. The other Vietnamese kids I went to school with got mad when I asked them to teach me Vietnamese phrases or to tell me about Vietnamese culture. They didn't even live together in clusters like most of the black folk. They were spread out, almost like they were trying to hide in plain sight.

Dinah, Callower, and Pavor had all been promoted months ago. They worked upstairs and only came down to fifty-nine because that's where the best espresso machine was and to cat-and-mouse the rank and file.

It was tradition for new shareholders to give the subordinate lawyers ludicrous assignments that seemed more or less legit. Dinah had gotten me good. She asked me to run a legal analysis of porn shops under the City code. The firm served every vice company you could think of—bars, tobacco distributors, massage parlors—so it wasn't an off-the-wall ask. When I brought the memo to her, she sat me down and held a straight face for all of five seconds before losing it and almost falling off her chair, laughing.

"I think this new executive assistant"—Dinah was still working her mouth as if to roll the taste out—"I think this new executive assistant is really trying to poison me." She said "executive assistant" with air quotes. She wasn't big on political correctness. She had run through four secretaries the prior year.

"It's not like you don't have it coming," Pavor said.

"It's not like you don't have a drone strike coming to your condo," Dinah said.

"It's too early for violence." Callower held his face in his hands. "And talking. Everyone should just be quiet for once, for me."

Pavor and Callower had been at Octavia's last night. They had been trading shots of Jägermeister in a side parlor last I saw them. Was that confetti in Callower's hair?

Pavor pinched Callower's cheek. "Aw, sugar plum's got a sore noggin?" Callower pushed Pavor's hand away.

That was when Dinah noticed me. Pavor turned my way. Callower didn't.

I shrank back, not wanting to give away how vulnerable I felt, but that was a giveaway in and of itself.

Dinah walked toward me, her silver stilettos sparkling.

"Hey, buddy." Pavor saluted me with his cup of vodka.

"What the fuck are you wearing?" Dinah pointed at me.

My stomach turned. I sported a three-piece rose-tinged seersucker with saddle shoes and a favorite fedora. They all had on seersucker suits, too—Dinah's was a skirt ensemble with those extra-high heels she favored. Seersuckers were the firm uniform, of sorts. I never wore them—striped linen doesn't go that well with brown skin—but this morning I had figured, what the hell? I donned it out of protest. A sign that I could have been one of the club if they hadn't pulled the treehouse ladder out of reach.

"That was one hell of a performance you put on last night." Pavor crouched and threw his elbows out. "You were like a dancing ninja." He wiggled in place.

"The funky chicken on LSD," Callower said.

"Today's the day," Dinah said.

"Yeah," I said.

Her eyes widened. "You don't think you made it," she said. "Hey, he thinks he's been pushed out."

"Really?" Pavor said with too much perk in his voice.

"Have you heard different?" I said.

Dinah said nothing. Callower furrowed his face. Pavor sipped vodka.

Etherine entered the kitchen, laid her serving tray on the counter, and wiped her hands on her apron. What kind of black person came to work dressed like Mammy in *Gone with the Wind*? Etherine did, that's who.

One night, years earlier, I was at the firm late. Some clients from out west were in town, and the shareholders were having a big to-do for them in the conference center. Walking by the prep area, I saw Etherine putting away flatware.

She glanced over at me. "Why you shaking your head?" she asked.

I was startled because I hadn't realized I was doing it. "It was nothing."

"You think I don't know you look down on me just like them people?"

"I'm just trying to go home."

"I know you," she said. "You think you so fancy with your degrees and everything."

"I just don't know how you can dress like we're in the antebellum South."

"You think we ain't?" she said. "I got two daughters in college and a house that'll be mine after I pay out the mortgage. That's how I do it." She shook her head. "You wearing that fine suit now, but give it some time. They'll have you in a butler getup before too long. That's when you'll see."

"Did you set up the big room?" Dinah asked Etherine.

"I did, Ms. Dinah," she said.

I was struck by two feelings at that moment. One was that once I left the building, I'd never see any of these people again. The other was, thank goodness that once I left the building, I'd never see any of these people again.

I went to my office. I couldn't believe that I'd put so much of myself into Seasons. Eight years—and for what? So they could

raise Riley and Franklin up and shove me out? I was a better lawyer than either of them or Dinah and the others. I won hearings. I
settled cases. I made Seasons look good. And why should I work at
a place that made Etherine walk around looking like the resurrec-
tion of Hattie McDaniel? I shouldn't. Seasons was just a den of
thieves. It had stolen the best years of my life, my vigor, my self-
esteem. I would leave and never look back. But first I'd leave a
parting gift.

I went to the supply room. I scanned the shelves. I saw what I
needed: a green spray can.

Malveaux was more a trophy case than a conference room. It
was named after one of the long-dead early shareholders. Plaques
covered almost every inch of wall space: plaques for donating legal
services to the homeless, for representing death row inmates, for
sponsoring Little League games, for every good deed imaginable.
I thought the firm protested too much. There was a blank wall at
the far end of the room. My perfect canvas.

Frosted glass separated Malveaux from the rest of the firm. I
turned off the lights and lowered the blinds. My heart hammered.

But what should I write? For some reason, Sir, my dad, came to
mind, sitting in his lonely prison cell, but I pushed him out of the
way. I ran through a raft of possible messages and rejected them
all: *Give me liberty or give me death.* (Too patriotic.) *In the hands of the
Almighty.* (Too religious.) *Freedom suit!* (I wasn't even sure what that
meant.)

I thought about drawing a scene, like when Huckleberry Finn
meets Nigger Jim. (Too unrelated, and I couldn't draw.) A yin-
yang symbol. (Too abstract.)

Maybe a simple word would do. *Love.* (Hell no.) I dropped the
can. *Fuck.* Yes, that old stand-by. *Fuck.* No. Too generic. Anybody
might write that—

Etherine shuffled by on the other side of the frosted glass but
didn't seem to notice me. I could just make out the silhouette of
her dark head floating above the frilly lace collar she wore.

Suddenly, one word screamed to the front of my mind. I raised the spray can.

Someone cleared their throat behind me. "What are you doing?" Dinah asked.

"I—I was just . . ." I lowered my arm.

Dinah sat on the edge of the conference table. "I mean, word travels fast, but you're celebrating already?"

"What?"

"The shareholders were just saying nice things about you." She told me the executive committee had met up on the top floor, sixty-two. "They picked you."

"You mean I'm not fired?"

"No."

A heat rose in my body. I had been so afraid. I wanted to break-dance at the news. Instead, I pumped my fist. "Wait, you're on the EC?"

"As of today." She placed a golden doubloon in my hand.

It had the firm's name on one side and the logo, a crescent that looked like a frown, on the other. "What's this?"

"It's yours," Dinah said. "You're the new diversity chair."

I laughed. "That's impossible. The committee is all white."

You had to be a senior shareholder to be on the committee, but there were no senior minority shareholders in the firm. Ergo, the committee was all white. The exclusion of the firm's minority members from the diversity committee wasn't racist. It was simply a matter of protocol. Franklin used to say the committee was a regular rainbow coalition that anyone could serve on provided they were ivory, eggshell, or pink.

Then it struck me. Not only was I on the committee, but I was the head. That could only mean—

"So I'm a shareholder," I said. The house, the cars, Nigel's face. Everything would be saved.

"Um. Not exactly. You need to talk to Octavia." Dinah walked toward the elevators.

I dodged the mail girl pushing a cart full of folders, one for each attorney, and held Dinah's shoulder. "Why, what's going on?"

"You wouldn't believe me if I told you I didn't know, would you?"

"No," I said.

Dinah was Octavia's right-hand glove. Anything Octavia touched, Dinah did, too.

"I know what you know," Dinah said. "She's supposed to fill me in at the plantation."

The plantation? Since when did the firm have a plantation?

Dinah stepped into the elevator. My device rang. Nigel's school. I couldn't get into the box without losing the signal.

"Wait," I said. "Tell me more."

Dinah pointed at her fingers. She was going to get a manicure. She waved, and the elevator doors closed.

Octavia pinged my device. She wanted to immediately meet in her office to discuss my position in the firm. My heart fluttered. Finally, I would find out what was really going on. I turned down the hallway toward Octavia's.

But my device rang. The connection was fuzzy, although the voice on the phone was familiar. Mrs. Beardsley, a dean at the School Without Walls, said Nigel had had an incident.

"Is my son okay?" I asked.

"More or less," the voice said.

"What kind of answer—is he bleeding? Is he unconscious? Has an ambulance been called?"

My device pinged again—question marks from Octavia.

I returned to the reception area. I couldn't just blow off my boss. Perhaps I could just talk to Octavia for a minute. But Nigel.

"Your son is physically okay, but he's asked for his mother," Mrs. Beardsley said. A pause. "And for you."

I jabbed the elevator button, which lit up and went dark every time I touched it. Such unreliable machines. The stairwell was a few feet away. I took it.

4

I probably shouldn't have left the Bug sputtering smoke in the front yard of Nigel's school, the School Without Walls. Dashing, I left the driver's door ajar, the bumper kissing a fire hydrant, the windshield wipers squeaking against dry glass. The School Without Walls was a compact compound of buildings made of simulated logs in a miniature wood. Largest of the buildings was the Central Hall, situated on the left edge of the property.

It had been the site of the first Negro school in the City and later, during the Jazz Age, home to several speakeasies. Once the old structures were razed, the City planted trees, which over decades sprouted toward heaven, muffling the moans of displaced ghost clarinetists. Even though the area looked like something out of a Harriet Beecher Stowe novel, the City skyscrapers played peekaboo just above the crenulated treetops. The Sky Tower, tallest obelisk in the state, was clearly visible, as it was from nearly anywhere in the City.

I should have centered myself. I should have taken a few deep breaths of evergreen oxygen. Instead, I took Central Hall's stone steps two at a time. I scared some students hanging out there. Or I would have scared them if I hadn't run into the locked main door and bounced off like a pebble. The students' laughter fell around me. My fedora tumbled across the landing.

"The other door open," a girl in a purple fur-collared coat and plaid skirt said. She had innumerable knots of twisted hair—some in red or green ribbons—and was darker-skinned than me, darker even than Franklin, blue-black, the dark of a shadow in a cave. She grabbed my hat and twirled it on her index finger. I reached, but she swiped it out of reach, a pocket-size matador. They didn't exactly teach respect for elders at the School Without Walls. I snorted at the girl.

"What's your hurry, mister?" she said.

"It's kind of an emergency," I said.

"What's with the hat?" She bent the brim back.

"What's with the coat?"

"It's cold," she said.

I didn't have time to jaw with some brat. The call from Mrs. Beardsley (a call while flying across town confirmed that it was her), dean of student growth, had been stymied by bad reception. Sunspots. Then in the car, reception was worse than in the Sky Tower. Our conversation was a jumble of gerunds and inquisitives, a discourse in Cubist style. *Locking what? You're telling me— telling me he's all right, right? Okay, don't go calling his mother—his mother—okay?*

Nigel had been doing well that year. No random shouting. No throwing of history books. No flameouts in the boys' lavatory. His grades were good. He seemed to like his teachers. Why would he have barricaded himself in a utility closet?

A wailing, then a fire truck—the station was only two blocks away—trundled up the narrow clay driveway. No doubt called by the school to deal with my son.

I ran inside and swam through an eddy of children on my way down the interior stairs. It wasn't one of those schools where the kids wore uniforms. This let the kids conform to mass media culture by wearing gaudy, real-fur coats, often dyed an eye-torturing violet, the uniform of that annoying pop princess whose face popped up in every ad on every device I owned. Of course, the School Without Walls was so permissive that no one objected to all the mama rabbits and baby foxes that died to make the coats. Banning any fashion would have been considered fascist by the parents on the board.

I had wanted to send Nigel to a more mainstream school, one that required khaki uniforms and distributed little folders with crests on them, somewhere he could socialize with the children of the shareholders I worked with at Seasons. But the private schools only had so many slots for kids whose parents weren't alumni and megadonors and connected enough to know how to navigate the arcane application process. My top choice for Nigel, the Morrison School, hadn't admitted a child of color in over a decade. Ultimately, Penny's argument won out. If I was so worried about Nigel's face, why not send him to a school where appearances didn't matter? But appearances always mattered. He was one of perhaps six students of color in a body of several hundred, and he reported bullying at the School Without Walls, just like at his previous learning institutions. At least the School Without Walls had an on-call therapist to help him with his anxiety.

I made the first floor. Mr. Gonzales's art class, the same room as at the last open house. Some kids gathered around the classroom door.

Mrs. Beardsley, in dark trim slacks and a button-down shirt, threw her arms out. "Clear this area, children." She shooed the kids, and they fluttered away like pigeons. As soon as she turned her attention to me, a round-faced but otherwise nondescript girl pecked closer again. Beardsley escorted me into the room.

Penny was kneeling at the closet door, her ear pressed to the wood. She stroked hair away from her ear and rose when she saw me. We hugged. She had somehow made it across the entire city, a ten-mile swing from Personal Hill Hospital, where she worked as a social worker, in the time it had taken me to make the relatively short drive from the Sky Tower downtown. Beardsley must have called her first and well before me. Penny's forehead was pink with worry, a condition that yanked my strings out of tune.

Mr. Gonzales stood near the chalkboard, a sweater tied around his neck. He ran fingers over his knuckles and wouldn't look at me.

"He's in there?" I said.

"Nigel won't tell me why he went in," Penny said.

A white smudge trailed from the center of the classroom several yards toward the closet door. The mysterious substance, which had a yogurt-like consistency when I nudged it with my brogue, led under the closet threshold.

"The class was in a free-painting session," Mr. Gonzales said. "There was a commotion, and he ran inside. I simply don't know what started it. The drama helper ran to call the fire department. He's very swift."

The door was decorated with cutouts of a pocket watch, a cuckoo clock, a sundial. Nigel was behind that barrier. He could be bleeding, or unconscious, or eaten by rats. All I wanted was to go to the far side of the room and launch my body against the door. Whether I killed myself in the process wasn't important. I needed him out of there.

"Hey," Penny said. She squeezed my hand. "You with me?"

I glanced back at the door and bit my tongue.

"He'll be all right," Penny said.

We went to the door.

Penny leaned on it. "Baby?" she said. "It's Mommy."

Nigel's voice, a sob from the other side.

"Nigel boy?" I yelled.

He called for me.

I grabbed the knob with both hands, a transparent crystal bulb, a dollop of frozen light. The beveled edges grated my skin. I pulled. The knob twisted free from the door. Now the door couldn't be opened from the outside.

I stared at Penny, horrified. She pressed her hands to the door. "You can come out now," she said. "We're here to bring you home."

"Open the door, kid," I said.

Penny gave me a look. Teachers and children watched us from the doorway to the hall.

"I'm sorry," Nigel said, his voice muffled.

"That's okay," Penny said. "Just let us in." She lightly drummed an offbeat rhythm on the door.

Nigel matched it. The door clicked but didn't open. He couldn't get out. "It's locked," he said.

"In times like these," Mrs. Beardsley said, "it's important to remember the school's philosophy of nonconfrontational optimism. We'll sort this out. The firepersons are just outside."

Yes. The firepersons were outside. All that malarkey about them being heroes—pshaw. Hype! Probably polishing their helmets and checking the certifications on their ax handles. Regulations. Procedures. Whatever they were supposed to be doing, they weren't in the room rescuing my son.

I scanned the area for something to batter the door open with. The chairs and easels were too lightweight. Mr. Gonzales's desk was too heavyweight. Mr. Gonzales himself? Right weight. Battering ram. Could I, in my adrenalized state, toss a 180-pound Latino man through the door? *Yes!* Wait. *No.*

I went to the hallway, shaking my head. Students crowded me, some slurping ice cream cones as they enjoyed the spectacle of me. I barked, but they kept slurping. That was it. *Ice cream. Whipped cream. Foam. Fire extinguisher.* Super genius me, I patted one of the kids, a tall boy with a mop of tawny hair, on the head and found a fire extinguisher in the hallway. It was heavy, solid as an anvil. A twinge buzzed in my lower back, but it was a muted pain, easily ignored.

"Wait," Penny said.

I told Nigel to get away from the door and cover his eyes. I rammed the butt of the canister into the knob apparatus. Nothing. Again, harder this time. The door cracked. Once more with feeling! Fell through the doorway, end over end, onto my face.

Nigel was not there. It should have been dark in that closet, but daylight from the hallway washed in through an open-air grate in the wall. I crawled through it.

Penny was on her knees hugging Nigel. My Nigel. He must have crawled out through the grate before I broke in. A white smear had splattered half his face.

"I'm sorry," he said. "I'm so sorry, I didn't mean to."

"Are you okay?" Penny asked.

"I'm okay," Nigel said.

By this point, I was on my knees, too, the three of us roped together by our arms. Something struck me as odd. I reared back, rubbing my thumb along his cheek. That white obscured most of Nigel's birthmark. So help me, he looked like a normal child.

"Is this paint?" Penny licked her fingers and scrubbed Nigel's cheek.

"No. Skin cream." The girl in the fur coat stood next to Penny. "Nige was putting it on, and someone called him a beauty queen." The girl produced a plastic container of face gunk, gunk that I was very familiar with, and gave it to Penny.

"Who called him a beauty queen?" I asked.

"I did." The girl in the fur coat shrugged.

"Madam C.J.'s Lightening Formula?" Penny asked.

I shook my head, but Nigel didn't notice.

"Dad gave it to me," Nigel said.

"You gave our son skin bleach?" Penny said. "Tell me you didn't give our son this shit." Penny, like most people, had different levels of anger. Cursing in front of our son meant that she was near the max level. The only higher level was the one where she separated my head from my body before driving a stake through my heart with her bare hands. "What's wrong with you?"

Of course, it shouldn't have been that big a deal. Skin toning cream has been around for millennia. It was the secret weapon of Egyptian pharaohs, Indian hijras, and legions of heads of state who had been unfortunately born a few shades too dark. People everywhere used it for their beautification needs, but I knew well enough that Penny wouldn't appreciate me giving it to Nigel to reduce the appearance of his birthmark. That's why it was our little secret. Or had been.

On the outside landing, Penny ran her hands through her hair and tugged hard, a nervous tic.

"What are those firemen doing to Dad's car?" Nigel asked.

"What?" Penny asked. She ran down the steps. "Guys, don't do that."

Smoke streamed from the back of my Bug, that muffler I needed to replace. A fireman unleashed a torrent of water into the interior. Another fireman raised his ax above the back window.

I noticed that Penny's rubbing had removed some of the cream from Nigel's face, revealing a dime-size view of his stain. I opened the container, which Penny had dropped on the landing, and worked a fresh glob of the cream onto the birthmark.

"I love you," I said.

"I know, Dad."

5

I needed to connect with Octavia, who was probably not pleased that I had ignored her request to meet. With the antic activities at Nigel's school, I forgot to at least tell Octavia why I didn't show up. Having ghosted her for nearly eighteen hours, I figured messaging her would be less effective than meeting in person, which meant driving to a restored plantation one hundred miles out of the City. The firm retreat, Seasons's annual orgy, where sex was replaced by talk of market trends, potential clients, and how to best take over the world, would begin in a few hours. There would be much maniacal laughter and twirling of mustaches. And while associates like myself were encouraged to go, the shareholders liked it just as well if we stayed back in the office and churned billable hours for them.

Maybe it would have been better to wait until Monday. After all, I hadn't been canned, and Octavia would be back in the office by then. Yet I also hadn't been promoted or gotten my balloon bonus, pending for 96,342 hours, not that I was counting. No bonus meant no procedure for Nigel's face, a situation I could not abide.

I was loading my overnight bag into the hood trunk when Penny sauntered up—no woman anywhere sauntered like my Penny—carrying a floral-print duffel decorated with *Hibiscus mutabilis*.

"You're coming?" I asked.

"On one condition." She dropped her bag. "Two conditions, actually."

"Shoot."

"Apologize for hiding that cream from me, and promise you'll never have our son use that crap again."

My cheeks flushed. I was more embarrassed, I realized, that I'd been caught than that I'd given Nigel the cream behind her back. But a part of me wanted to make the promise, to give in to the possibility that maybe Penny was right. She always thought I was overcompensating in my attempts to protect Nigel. She seemed to think I saw monsters everywhere I looked, which was correct, of course.

"That's a nice offer," I said, "but I got this. I'll just go, handle my business, and come home."

"Dammit. Don't be an idiot. Can't you see I'm worried about you?"

"I'm all good."

Penny grabbed my face. I tried to look away, but she wouldn't let me. "Are you really? All good? I need you to be better for your son. I need you to love this family and love yourself."

I knew what she meant. We got along pretty well most of the time, the three of us. But most of the emotionally violent arguments Penny and I had pertained to Nigel and how to best help him. Like what had happened at the school the day before. As usual, Penny was reacting to something I said or did that caused Nigel's anxiety to manifest. If I hadn't pushed the cream on him, he wouldn't have wound up cowering in a closet. I needed to say less and do less. My family could be happy. We could be grinning fools.

"I'm going with you," Penny said. "That's all there is to it." She raised an eyebrow, and those eyes, those sea-green peepers, washed away my remaining resolve.

"Fine," I said. "And I'm sorry."

"For what?" She crossed her arms.

"For hiding the gunk from you."

"And?"

"And I won't let him use it again." I sighed and put her duffel in the trunk next to my battered canvas valise.

"Now, give me your palm."

I extended my hand. Penny took out a blue permanent marker and drew a misshapen circle. She often did this when we first met. She had a philosophy about focusing on the basics, the people in our orbit who mattered, the actions that supported instead of harmed. She chose a circle as a symbol of inclusion, but also because it was impossible to hand-draw one perfectly. Perfection was the enemy.

Suddenly, I felt ashamed for hiding anything from her. It felt good to be forgiven. "Shouldn't you be at work?"

"I called in," she said.

"What about kiddo?"

"We can leave him with your mother. They don't spend enough time together."

Leaving Nigel with Mama meant he would spend the weekend in the yard behind her restaurant in the deceptively hyperborean sun, drying up and darkening like a raisin, my warnings that she was setting her grandson up for lethal melanomas notwithstanding. Not to mention all the propaganda she would cram into his head. Black empowerment. Racial righteousness. Resistance. The woman fed filthy protesters for free.

"Let's make a family outing of it," I said. "Bring him along."

Once I covered the Bug's waterlogged seats with plastic, we hit the highway.

"Look at this, Dad," Nigel said. "It's like a sponge."

I glanced over my shoulder. Nigel was pressing his outstretched fingers into the seat cushion. Water bubbled through a hole in the plastic.

"Don't do that, son," I said. "Why don't you sketch for a while?"

"I don't want to sketch now." Viewing him through the rear-view mirror, the shadows of trees flowed over his face. "It smells like dog back here."

"Just occupy yourself, kid."

"And put on your seatbelt," Penny said. "We should've taken the van."

"Wouldn't have made it." We prided ourselves on not having car notes. My car was an unfortunate bit of forced inheritance, given to me as my father had no use for transportation. He was an indentured servant—had actually cut organically grown sugarcane—in the fields not very far from the plantation we were headed to. As for Penny's ride, we'd paid that off years earlier. The minivan was safe for her commutes around town, but it shook with righteous indignation at being forced to travel at highway speeds. My Bug, although an antique, was a solid bet on long trips. I drove it to hearings in small-town courts all over the state without incident. I was sure the car would cruise the highways and byways of my nation long after I, and everyone I loved, went dust to dust.

When we hit the northbound interstate, I put on *Pet Sounds*. Penny turned to me from the passenger seat. I didn't look, but I could tell she was studying my face as if to say, *I can't believe you still listen to that crusty old white boy music. My grandparents didn't even like the Beach Boys. You must be the whitest black man on earth. I thought it would just be a phase.*

"It is," I said, forgetting the nonverbal aspect of our chat. "A very long phase."

"What?" she asked.

"Nothing," I said and wobbled into the second verse of "God Only Knows," but Carl Wilson's tenor was far too high for me to glide with for long, especially with other people's ears at stake. After the bridge, Penny's voice came in as clean and clear as the original. Nigel leaned forward from the rear, gripping Penny's seatback for stability. By the swirling, three-part finale, we were all singing together.

Penny and I both looked back at our son for an extended beat. Nigel smiled at us. He was missing a canine tooth then.

"Put on your seatbelt," we said in unison.

"Okay, okay," he said. "Jeez."

We exited the highway and dashed into molehill country. Somehow Nigel convinced us to take the scenic route for the last leg. Country towns in the South gave me the jimjams. I worried about every police station, every church I saw. I wondered what evils were done in the name of separating the whites and coloreds, as if people were nothing more than dirty laundry. We passed brick-faced homes that sat far back from the road like they were waiting to pounce. Some had little American flags on their rickety mailboxes. Scarecrows. Spinning windmills. It must have been anxiety-inducing to travel those roads many decades earlier, say, in the time of my father's father or even earlier yet—like in the 1950s.

What would the people in those houses think of a well-dressed Negro, a redheaded beauty, and an olive-skinned boy puttering by in a spotless German car? Would a patrolman pull us over? Would Penny have to explain that I was her chauffeur? Would the cop knock out a headlight and write us a ticket? Or would he bring us to an abandoned schoolhouse for reeducation?

Still, there was something about that shadowless afternoon, wheeling the freeway with my family. I wasn't particularly religious, but I noted brief sequences in my life where the invisible medium—air, mist, water, I could never say what the medium most resembled—seemed to drain away. In those moments, there was nothing at all between me and them, the two souls I cared most about in all the unknowable universe. Those were the times when I believed that there was a plan, although I wasn't privy to the details, and that it was a just and good plan designed to benefit Nigel, Penny, and perhaps even me. Those slim fissures in my logic never lasted long enough.

6

I'd never been to Shanksted Plantation. Actually, I'd never been to any plantation. I actively resisted it. Every time someone tried to lure me to Harper's Alley or Carriageway for a day trip, I begged off. I'd lived in the City my whole life and swore that I would drink a cup of bubbling battery acid before I dipped my ladle in the polluted cultural springs of the hinterlands. In my thinking, the entire South beyond my hometown was just one sprawling countryside of ectoplasmic Colonel Sanderses on horseback chasing runaway spirits until the Rapture. Hardly my idea of a refreshing getaway.

Of course, I knew the basics from movies, books, and Joey Watson's fifth-grade *Gone with the Wind* poster board, which I poured chocolate syrup all over before the start of class. (Joey still won best presentation. He hung a Mammy/golliwog/gorgon from the board. How could he not win?) However, none of my vicarious experiences prepped me for being on plantation soil. I'd never done a double-take at a gleaming white chateau with shadowy, Dracula-teeth columns. I'd never ridden up a rustic promenade, across the same twigs and pebbles over which somebody's barefoot mom once hauled kindling. I'd never wondered if it was better for a pregnant woman to die from strangulation or a broken neck.

"What are those?" Nigel asked.

Penny squinted, her mouth agape. At first, I thought the wavering golden-brown shapes dangling from the branches were Spanish moss, but I'd heard that all the moss was eaten by pests years ago. The shapes were fabric, perhaps a tip of the hat to what the plantation had lost. Strange fruit indeed. Good Lord. The Shanksted trees were positively crawling with banshees.

"They look like strung-up people," Nigel said.

"God," Penny said. "I hate this place so much."

I steered us toward a clearing in the distance. The mansion was only a front. Behind it, in the forest, was a complex of hotel buildings all done in an antebellum theme. The Big House, a building with covered galleries on each of its four floors, was where check-in awaited our arrival.

"I don't know how this happened, sir," the lanky brunette at the front desk said. "Your name is here, but somehow we don't have a room for you."

"We'll take whatever you give us," I said.

After a conversation with her supervisor, the lanky clerk returned from the hidden room behind the desk and said, "We've found a solution for you, sir." She gave me a key card and beneficently pointed us to the narrow staircase at the back of the lobby.

Upstairs, we found our accommodations, a megaroom called the Planters Suite. The bellboy, a little guy who could have been an older cousin, brought our bags up. He could have been a cousin except for the work he'd had done to his face. His lips had been deplumped so that he seemed to grimace in pain as he pointed out the myriad gracious features of our quarters, the hot tub, the balconies overlooking the whole property, a basket full of complimentary chocolates—dark, milk, and premium white.

At the door, as I counted off his tip, the bellboy gave Nigel a strange look. In such situations, I had to figure out what the person found unsettling: Nigel's face, my marital relationship, or the offspring of our union. These shadows followed us wherever we went. Sometimes I felt like we all had birthmarks.

The bellboy shook his head. I realized from the way his eyes swept over each of us that it was likely a combination of all three reasons. Penny didn't notice. She was opening the curtains to let some daylight in. Nigel furrowed his brow. I sent him to his room. I was no stranger to such audacity.

Mixed-race couples were rare these days, having reached a climax during Sir's youth, before the authorities overreacted to a protest by a black nationalist organization. As for the porter's distraction by Nigel's birthmark, that was just one more reason Nigel needed the procedure.

I pinned the money to the bellboy's chest with my fingers. "That's enough," I said. He took the money and left.

I went to Nigel's room, one of three bedrooms other than the master suite allotted to Penny and myself. The balcony doors were open, and a brisk wind swooped in. Nigel sat on his bed, flipping through a book of colorful sea creatures. He wasn't looking at the pictures, just turning the pages absentmindedly. Nigel loved real books made of real paper. Bless him, the little weirdo. But occasionally he stroked the page as if trying to switch over to the next screen.

"This place is cool," he said.

"It is, isn't it?" I said.

Nigel glanced at me, then averted his eyes back to the book. I closed it. He lowered his chin.

"That man," Nigel said. "I don't like being looked at that way."

"Some people lack all refinement," I said.

"Would you speak English?" Nigel sat up. "It's like he thought I was an alien or something."

"Hey." I grabbed Nigel's chin and considered what Penny would say if she were in my position. "None of this is your fault,"

I said. "Don't let anyone else's opinion cross you up. You're exactly the way you were meant to be."

"You sound like Mom."

Such a smart boy. "She knows what she's talking about." I wanted to tell Nigel about temporary injustice and how everyone had to persist in difficult situations until things cleared up, but the strings in my chest were too tight. Words were only words after all. "You— Do you want a chocolate?"

He nodded.

I made a wrapped square of milk chocolate appear then disappear, using sleight-of-hand Sir taught me when I was around Nigel's age.

"You're going to show me how to do that," Nigel said.

I reproduced the chocolate between my thumb and forefinger. "Maybe when you're ready." I dropped the chocolate into his palm.

"I'm ready." He unwrapped the package and ate.

"Not quite."

Nigel groaned.

"Do you have your comics?" I asked.

He gave a thumbs-up. I switched on the light because he'd read in the dimness if I didn't.

"Look, Dad." Nigel took a jar of Madame C.J.'s cream from his book sack. "I remembered the cream!"

I glanced over my shoulder to make sure Penny wasn't around and placed a finger over my lips. I'd forgotten that I'd stocked Nigel up with several jars of the stuff weeks earlier. Based on my promise to Penny, I should have taken the jar away and explained that he no longer needed it. But the bellboy's gawking reminded me of reality. The cream was for Nigel's own good. "But remember," I said, "between us." I kissed him on the forehead and went to the door. "Be sure to wear your big hat when we go out. It's getting sunny."

Then I closed his door. In the hallway, between his room and the master suite, I pulled a Plum from my shirt pocket. The pill slipped through my fingers and bounced across the carpet. I picked it up and, without checking it for debris, popped it into my mouth. My esophagus lit up as that little elevator descended into my basement.

Penny lay on our bed, a four-poster canopied special, like something out of Lady Chatterley.

"Everything all right?" she asked.

"*Hakuna matata.*" I locked our double doors and turned on the stereo. There's a point where you've been married long enough that you can pluck hidden meanings from the ether. In the middle of our ongoing fight over Nigel's skin cream and how best to handle his adjustment problems, Penny had chosen to join me on this expedition into the heart of darkness. During meaner times, she would have let me drive off without a word. Her singing in the Bug was another such sign. In a full-on argument, she would have grumpily turned off the stereo. The slight blush on her cheeks as the song ended, and that mischievous glint in the corner of her eye as the last note echoed against the glass. The subtle presence of feminine pheromone only detectable by the ever-so-slight itch at the back of my throat. Unspoken communication. Married-folk semaphore. An invitation to a truce. A man has only two options in circumstances like that: play it cool and risk the train chugging from the station without you, or climb into the engine cab, knock out the engineer, and toot that horn.

I tossed my fedora onto a wine rack by the fireplace and undid the first few buttons of my shirt. The overhead fan shook and the ferns around the room dipped in sympathy to those currents.

"You called for your Mandingo, Miss Penelope?" I asked.

"Oh, hush, boy," she said, and flipped the smoke-gray sheets away from her naked body. I kissed the top of her foot and yanked her closer to the bottom of the bed. Once the sheets settled, we fucked a flame into being.

7

In the late afternoon, I decided we should go down to the Old House, the mansion we had driven by on the way in. Octavia was not responding to my emails, but she had to be somewhere on the property. The resort offered golf, skeet shooting, a spa. Tennis courts, bike rentals, and canoeing. Scavenger hunts. A tour would depart from the Old House soon. Tour title: "Paradise Lost— A Survey of Antebellum Farming Life." The tour was my best chance to locate Octavia, so I signed us up.

The sun came out from behind the clouds. Nigel seemed to have left his own black cloud in the suite. Hauling his book sack of widgets and goodies—magnifying glasses, jars for insect collecting, soy jerky, etc.—he slid down the staircase railing in the Big House, laughing, and we set off for the tour. We immediately got lost. Penny, Nigel, and I wandered out onto the property, using a cartoonish map provided by the concierge. Not only did I find the mascot icon—a dark-skinned man in tatters—offensive, but the map itself was useless. Penny was better with maps than me, but even she was confused. The chart wasn't to scale. The proportions were way off. Those tennis courts weren't right behind the Big House as suggested, but a few hundred yards away, behind hedge-obscured fences. The lying map claimed the swimming pools were slightly east and the amphitheater slightly west, but everything was due south.

Penny and I held hands as Nigel orbited us like a proton. We passed a neatly trimmed garden. Then another set of tennis courts. And another neatly trimmed garden. No. The same neatly trimmed garden. We were trapped in a loop.

"Is this really happening?" Penny laughed nervously.

"Maybe we went forward when we should have gone back," I said. Between Penny's and my linked bodies, Nigel passed, a neutrino. The fishing hat looped around his neck brushed against my side. It should have been on his head, not his back. "Put it on, son."

"Aw, but it's too big."

"Don't back-talk your father." Nigel righted the hat on his head. "And don't you roll your eyes, young man."

"There's got to be a way out of here," I said.

Nigel trotted to a hedgerow a few yards away, his fists clenched to his sides. The fishing hat bobbed in time to his footfalls. He had grown considerably in recent months, but he was still on the smallish side, and the brim of the big floppy hat brushed his shoulders on the downstroke.

"That hat is a little obnoxious," Penny said, grinning. "He looks like Dumbo before he learned to fly." I shrugged. It could be hard to tell where the line was with Penny. Whereas I felt Nigel should only go outside in a mirrored hazmat suit to protect his mark from darkening, she was sanguine about the whole affair. Sure, there were various no-fly zones in the airspace of Nigel's birthmark. Penny was 100 percent opposed to lightening cream, for instance. Yet she more or less agreed that hats were sensible protection from the genetic-mutation-inducing qualities of the jolly old sun. She wore a field hat and sunglasses herself.

Nigel found a knob and pulled a door open, hedge and all.

I glanced at Penny. "My side of the family," I said.

"Might be." She took a protein bar from her purse and tossed it to Nigel, who grinned.

The main hall of the Old House was flanked by two broad staircases. Freshly waxed wood and engine oil scents predominated. About thirty shareholders were gathered, dressed in khaki shorts, maxi dresses, and flip-flops. There was enough wrinkly flesh to challenge a pugs-only dog show. I waved at Paul Pavor, who sipped something from a go-cup, then gave me finger guns. I didn't see Octavia.

Our tour guides, a man and a woman in period clothing, introduced themselves as Nathan and Mary. The woman wore a complicated wig-and-bonnet arrangement.

"Why are they dressed like that?" Nigel asked.

"We should go," I said to Penny.

"No." She pursed her lips. "I want to see this." I didn't want to spend any more time with my superiors than I had to, but my nervous system was too happy to argue much. Penny rarely turned away from incidents of obvious racism or bigotry. She jumped into them like a Viking with a long sword, her neck flushed as she dismantled her opponent's arguments.

The pair led the group through the mansion, pointing out Venetian drapes and fine china, over here the property owner's desk for writing letters to his business partners, over there Old Miss's pouting room.

In the grand ballroom: "Andrew Jackson Smith's troops ransacked this very home." Nathan had a high-country accent. "It took over a decade to restore the property to its original splendor." He jammed his hand into his gray overcoat and sniffed as he walked past us.

The guides brought us to the back porch and offered white parasols from a copper drum. I didn't take one, nor did Penny.

"It can get awfully bright out there," Mary said, fanning herself. She smiled from the cheeks down, but her eyes were dead. She adjusted her wig. "A small price to pay for a nice Southern life." Her crinoline was so wide, I was sure she'd get stuck in the door, but she turned sideways and popped through with no trouble.

She and Nathan led us across the field, the one I'd seen from our room at a distance, and the crowd closed into a dense semicircle around us. A pair of iron doors erupted from the grass several yards away.

"What's that?" Deb, a labor lawyer from one of the Carolina offices, asked.

"Looks like a storm shelter," Pavor said.

"That's a hotbox," Nigel said.

"Very good." Nathan wiped his forehead with a handkerchief.

"How did you know that?" I asked.

"Mom's genes," Nigel said. Penny laughed that wheezy laugh of hers.

"You have to remember," Nathan said, "there was no police force or easily accessible court system. The farmers needed a simple but humane way to maintain order hereabouts. The box was rarely used because it was so effective."

"I bet," Penny said.

"You didn't want to end up in that box." Mary chuckled.

"Good way to kill people, too," Penny said.

Everyone stared at her. The sun was unusually intense, so much so that the grass seemed more yellow than green.

Nigel had taken his hat off again. I told him to put it back on. "Aw." He furrowed his brow.

"Be like your old man." I tipped my straw fedora and nudged him.

We continued into the woods and stopped at a small clearing. Nathan took off his wide-brimmed hat and held it with both hands at his waist. I could tell he had said whatever he was about to say a hundred times before. Someone stepped in a cow pie and cursed.

"The Southern economy," Nathan said, "of the mid-1800s was a powerhouse of the world. A land of unheard-of splendor." His accent got thicker in the woods. *Southern* was "suh-thun." *Power-house* was "pow-ah-haus." Every time he said *splendor,* I thought he was talking about the sweetener I used in my coffee. Mary talked the same way. I couldn't tell if they were laying it on thick as part of the show.

"See these individual pine trees here?" He threw a thumb over his shoulder. "There are hundreds of them. Today they stand where acres upon acres of grade-A-quality cotton, sugarcane, and tobacco once grew for export the world over."

"The Southern economy," Mary said, "was such that Southerners enjoyed a level of opulence not seen since the time of the pharaohs of ancient Egypt."

Penny clenched and unclenched her fist. Her knuckles were white. "Can I yank that animal off her head?" she asked.

"Easy," I whispered. "I have to work with these people."

"You'll recall," Mary said, "that the Northern section of this present nation launched its war of unprovoked aggression on the presupposition that it was sovereign supreme. To wit: the North believed it had the right to impose absolute authority over the economic structure and governing freedom of these Southern states. This was in no way different than the tyranny the founders fought and defeated in the Revolutionary War."

Penny's nose twitched. She raised her hand to her shoulder. I pulled her wrist down. She reraised it.

But Nigel beat her to the punch. "What about slavery?" he asked.

Some of the shareholders grumbled. Pavor snorted. It struck me that this was the first time I'd seen Pavor without Dinah nearby in a while.

"Is that a question?" Nathan asked.

Penny stepped forward. "This place only has nice furniture and tapestries and shit because everyone was forced to work for free. They were denied their human rights."

Sometimes I almost forgot about Penny's activist streak, that I'd

met her at a protest against low wages in the retail sector, that I'd
bailed her out of jail. My little insurgent. She spent her present
days, pen in hand, jotting notes about her clients. But I could still
see her angrily charging across a parking lot with a red placard
because of some real or imagined slight.

"Well, I never," Mary said, still in character, fanning herself.

"She has a point," I said. "The Civil War started because of slavery and the—"

Mary held her hand out to stop me from talking. This shouldn't
have worked, but I found that I couldn't say a word. It was almost
like she had my vocal cords in her grip. She stared at me. Or maybe
through me. She was looking at the Old House behind the group.

That's when I noticed that she was a lot older than I thought. It
must have been the humidity that revealed her. Her makeup was
running at the cheeks. Underneath the melting foundation, her
skin was mottled, the color of raw beef tongue.

"Sugar," she said, "every schoolboy knows the Civil War didn't
start because of slavery. That was just spin Lincoln's cronies put
out to keep the Europeans from joining the Confederacy. Read a
book."

"How much do they pay you to tell these lies?" Penny asked.

"Wait just a minute, little miss," Nathan said.

Penny gestured at Mary. "This kind of stupidity and romanti-
cizing a past that never existed—"

Nathan waved his hands as if trying to put out a fire. "I do not
think—"

"People like you"—Penny stepped toward the guides—"are the
reason everyone is confused about what actually happened."

"That's it!" Mary yanked off her wig and bonnet. "You got
some nerve, sister." Out of character, Mary had a New Jersey accent. "Busting my hump when I'm just trying to make a living."

"Let the composed head prevail," Nathan said, still performing.

"Stuff it, Jake!" Mary threw her wig and bonnet to the ground and stormed back to the Old House, holding her skirts up the whole way. At the top of the stairs, reduced to the size of a poodle by distance, she turned back. "I quit."

"Come on, Merle," Jake said. "Don't be that way." He gave us a nasty look and jogged away. The group walked back to the mansion.

"Where's Nigel?" Penny asked.

Pine branches swayed overhead and a rabbit jumped into a hole in the middle of the field. We called for Nigel, but he didn't answer. I hoped this wasn't another of his disappearing acts. He'd been better recently about not scurrying away like a field mouse when he was stressed. But the incident at the School Without Walls had been a reversion to form. I didn't want him to have to go back on anxiety meds. He was doing so well.

"The hotbox," Penny said.

We went to the box. The iron doors were too heavy for me to open alone, but with Penny's assistance, I managed to crack one open enough to see that our son wasn't inside. I pressed my hands against the side of my head.

Nigel wasn't in the gallery of the Old House, the pouting room, or the kitchen. No one had seen him. I called security. Sometime later a man with a bloodhound showed up. It was the bellboy who had brought up our bags and gawked at Nigel. He said his name was Moses.

"The security man on the other side dealing with some foolishness, so the manager sent me over with Rufus here to help you folk find your young one."

"I guess you won't need a picture," I said. "You got a good enough look at him earlier."

Penny gave me a *Don't be a jerk—he's here to help*. Moses wondered out loud if we had anything of Nigel's that Rufus could sniff. Penny produced Nigel's hairbrush from her purse.

Before long, we were in the woods. Since the end of the tour, the sun had receded a good bit, so the woods were more shadow than light. We couldn't see that well. Moses took a stick from the ground and wrapped it in a greasy cloth. He lit the assembly to make a blazing torch. Rufus, jowls shaking, woofed in delight.

At the entrance to the woods, Moses took Nigel's brush and held it to Rufus's nose. The dog leaped forward, pulling Moses along.

"Y'all try to keep up. No time for lollygagging. I'm missing tips for this."

Penny and I followed.

"Oh. He must got him a good scent," Moses said. And it did seem as if Rufus had read the directions. Unlike our earlier stroll, we didn't double back or wander. We moved more or less in a straight line for a good while until the woods thickened considerably. A little ways off, a pack of coyotes ran away from us, and I realized the sun was completely gone. The orange flicker of the bellboy's torch provided the only light. Then, as unexpectedly as he had started, Rufus stopped.

"Would you look at that?" Moses said. I couldn't tell what he was talking about since Rufus's jowls covered whatever it was he sniffed. The dog gathered the thing in his mouth, but Moses made him give it up. The bellboy deposited the wet ball in my hand. A crumpled dark-chocolate wrapper.

"You don't think Nigel came this deep into the forest, do you?" Penny asked.

I shrugged, not wanting to stoke the hysterical fire building in my gut. My shoulder was still sore from breaking through that door at the School Without Walls. And in the forest, I felt especially helpless without any doors to ram through. What could I do? Knock down a tree? Dig a new route to China? *My son is resourceful. My son is okay.* I repeated these words in my head like an improvisational drum solo. *My SON is resourceful. My son is OKAY.* I yelled his name.

Rufus took off again, pulling Moses and, by extension, us. But a few moments later Penny cried out. She reached down and grabbed a small high-top shoe. Nigel's shoe. The other one was a few feet away. A coyote yowled. Penny and I locked eyes for an extended moment.

Moses motioned for us to come over. I spotted a protein bar wrapper near Rufus, who sniffed the base of a nearly vertical earthen structure. It was almost more of a wall than a hill. Moses said Nigel was up there.

"There's no way," I said. "Not unless he grew a tail."

Penny went to the wall, grabbed some exposed tree roots, and climbed. I leaned on my knees to catch my breath. I wished I had gone along with Penny and Nigel to the indoor rock-climbing facility those few times they had gone. A section of soil broke loose and showered down on me. "It's not safe," I said. But Penny wasn't listening. All this, and I never caught up with Octavia.

Then something happened that I never forgot and could not initially explain except to say it was confusion of my senses, a synesthetic illusion. I heard splashing, laughing, singing, and in leaves above the hill, I saw the twinkling of stars that could not have been so luminous or active.

Penny climbed faster. I called Nigel's name again. No answer, but the singing stopped. I grabbed a root and followed Penny. Without the torch, my eyes adjusted to the night. The far side of the hill was steep, but not as steep as what we had just climbed. It was there, atop the hill, we found Nigel's hat, shirt, and a ribbon, the color of which I couldn't make out in the gloom.

"What's that?" Penny asked. A bulb of light drifted into her hand. A firefly. Beneath us, dense foliage partially obscured a stream.

I lost my footing and dirt-surfed down the slope of the hill. A short way off I saw my son, buck naked in a burbling current. He was waist deep and standing motionless, as though waiting for me to collect him from the sidewalk outside school. A rustling in the brush, as if from a gaze of rabid raccoons, sent a prickle down my ribs.

I asked Nigel what he was doing. He drew his hand across his face in an attempt to dry it. "Just swimming."

"But why didn't you tell us where you were going?"

Nigel had the strangest smile on his face and looked fit to burst into laughter.

Penny appeared. She looked worried, relieved, confused.

"You knocked them over, Dad."

A mason jar lay on its side at my foot. I had knocked the lid off. Fireflies flew out of the jar and lit into the treetops.

8

Although I was an average talent, I always possessed a great love of sport, competition, game. In high school, I was mildly athletic, the kind of boy who could run the expected number of laps without complaint or deploy any number of defenses in a chess club match to keep my king out of serfdom for a reasonable time. But my love of competition outstripped my talent: I couldn't outrun the speedsters, and my deflections rarely led to victory over my young masters.

I played, for a single season, on our basketball team, the Chickenhawks. *Hootie hoo!* I wasn't particularly tall, fast, or agile. I certainly didn't have the hidden ankle wings of my fellow airmen that allowed them to dunk the ball from the concession stand. However, I was blessed with a facility for ball control. I became the team's point guard after the starting senior was arrested on possession charges and died of a rare and undiagnosed heart problem while in custody. A terrible loss, as he'd already got an offer to go pro. I remained Chickenhawk number one until I blew out a knee while blocking the shot that would have knocked us out of the state playoffs. My sacrifice was all for naught. Three nights later I sat on the bench, my leg in a black brace, while Royceland, a crew of upstaters that preferred three-pointers over dunks, bombed my beloved Chickenhawks to smithereens, 114 to 81. What was the Royceland Red Roosters' cheer? Ah. "Death from Above," son.

"If you could have played on crutches, you would have," Nigel said.

"You've heard this story before, eh?" I tugged his baseball cap down.

"Just once." He smirked and pulled the cap back up. "Or a million times."

The Monday after Nigel's plantation bath, he and I were in the bowels of the City's professional b-ball arena, Secret Nine Arena. There were two reasons I had never brought Nigel until that night. First, I almost always had to work late.

Second, Nigel had always shown an innate ability as a young sportsman. At age six, he could cartwheel and leapfrog like any other American boy, but he could also drive a soccer ball like a transplanted Brazilian. Whatever gene existed in me had combined with Penny's fairer ones and amplified Nigel's sportiness, even in informal settings. I was disturbed no end that whenever he visited my office, he'd stand as far away from my wastebasket as possible and plunk crumpled balls of paper into the receptacle like so many pennies into a well. The last time I brought him to my office, I snapped at him to stop, and he did. I felt guilty, of course, but for the love of Meadowlark Lemon, did the world really need another child of the diaspora with highly developed ball skills? The answer was in the question, and I made all indirect efforts to discourage his growing love of sports. America could cheer someone else's brown boy down a field and, after he'd wrecked body and mind, into an early grave.

It was an irresistible magnet that drew us to the cavernous arena that weekday evening. Octavia pinged me with a message: "Meet at the firm suite and bring your kid. Seven-thirty P.M. Gate seven. Suite 342. Do not miss."

We breached the building through a restricted side entrance reserved for kings and their retainers. We were early and wandered the semiprivate corridor, where workmen sped by in motorized carts and vendors offered frozen drinks, pretzels, and gaudy, glossy pamphlets. My son fairly hummed with electricity. He was dumbstruck by the many people milling about, the glowing advertisements floating above, the echo of the arena announcer's voice telling us not to miss our shot at a photo with the team mascot. Nigel's joy flowed into me, and we carried his awe in tandem.

As we rounded the base of the arena, we came to a darkened tunnel. At the far end of that tunnel was a clear view of the bright, marqueted hardwood floor where players in warm-up suits dribbled basketballs in and out of view. Faint holographic shapes—circles, lozenges, clouds—appeared on the floor and vanished to a rhythm I couldn't catch. Nigel paused midstep and watched. It was during this reverie that I bought him an oversize We're Number One foam hand and a veggie hot dog. In retrospect, I probably should have purchased the foam hand after the hot dog because my son refused to put down the one in order to eat the other. I found some amusement in watching him solve this puzzle by using the foam hand as a food tray.

I also noticed that his baseball cap had disappeared.

"Where is your hat?" I asked. Nigel shrugged. He said he must have lost it. "How is it possible that you lose every hat I buy you?"

He shrugged again. "There's not even any sunlight in here," he said. "It's nighttime." I realized he was right.

Across from the tunnel where we stood, an older white woman in chintz smeared balm on her lips with a pinky. "Do you know where the garbage cans are?" she asked.

"No," I said.

"Oh. Well, can you take this?" She offered her plate of picked-over crab claws to me. She thought I worked for the arena, that I was a janitor.

I glanced down at my T-shirt and immediately regretted my choice to dress like a normal person going to a basketball game rather than wear a top hat and tails. Of course, then she would have thought I was the doorman. I shoved my hands into my pockets.

"That's nice team spirit you have," the woman said to Nigel.

"Thank you, ma'am." My polite boy. I placed a hand on his shoulder.

"Where did you get it?" she asked.

"Right over there. I think." It was about then that I noticed she was concentrating quite deliberately on Nigel to the exclusion of me, but this wasn't about his birthmark. The woman wasn't judging the composition of his face so much as his relationship to me. She was a Good Samaritan. I'd participated in this puppet show before, too. It wasn't the first time someone, thrown off by the variance in our physical appearances, thought that I'd kidnapped my own child.

"Did this man buy it for you?" she asked. She had a booger of garlic on her lip.

"Uh-huh," Nigel said, dropping a bit of veggie chili on the smooth concrete below.

I nudged him. "Don't speak with your mouth full, *son*."

"Sorry, *Dad,*" Nigel said.

A giant security guard, possibly a failed player himself, seemed to be trying to decide whether to cross over from his comfortable post on the far side of the corridor.

The woman knelt and grabbed Nigel's wrist. "You can trust me."

"Don't touch my son," I said.

The woman ignored me. "Are you okay, young man?"

Nigel looked at her, his eyes wide. For a blink, I worried he might say that he wasn't. "Miss, can you let go of me?"

The woman shook her head, as if casting off a spell. She rose to her feet and walked away, her Birkenstock sandals slapping her heels. She glanced back once more before dumping her trash into a receptacle and turning in to the arena proper.

Someone tapped my shoulder. It was the security guard, who stared down on me from two and a half heads up.

"Is there a problem?" I asked.

"Are you with the firm up in the Seasons Ustis suite?"

"So what if he is?" Nigel said.

"A lady asked me to escort you."

"How did you know it was me?" I asked.

"She described you to a T."

We followed the guard into a side tunnel, passed a couple of paramedics smoking cigarettes, and rode an elevator to suite level. The firm's spacious suite loomed near center court several stories up. Mixed in with numerous shareholders, including Armbruster, his right-hand man, Scott Forecast, and Callower, were heavy hitters I was more likely to see on television than in person. Armbruster and Forecast spoke to Mayor Chamberlain, with her signature bouffant hair, who was preparing to run for her second term. Dinah was removing lint from Pavor's lapel. Pavor grabbed her other hand, but she brushed his away and glanced around to see if anyone noticed.

A young man who'd starred in an action film about shapeshifting gnomes tucked into a slice of marionberry pie and wrinkled his nose. I had tried a slice on the way in and agreed with his assessment. On a ten-point scale, I wouldn't have given the stale-crusted, gloopy wedge much more than three and some change.

I escorted Nigel to the exterior seats that afforded a view of the game with the unwashed masses just below our feet. Men careened across the court. Whistles blew. Someone did a 720 dunk, and the whole cave rocked with applause. At halftime, the arena lights dimmed, and a squad of cheerleaders with small wings on their backs appeared and flew around under laser beams.

A waiter offered a tray of cocktail wieners. Nigel took some, but I didn't. I was too shaken to eat. In fact, I probably hadn't said much more than yes, no, or maybe for some time. To Nigel's question as to why Herman was the only one with gold-plated kicks, I replied, "Maybe." My wistfulness wasn't the result of a pharmacologically induced state. I hadn't had a Plum since the morning, although it was high time.

Octavia sat next to me, removed her sunglasses from her face, and put them in her hair. "I was starting to think you made other plans."

"Not at all." I gave her a double-cheeked air kiss.

She glanced at the cluster of men talking to Armbruster. "The good old boys have run this place long enough. Do you know Seasons hasn't had a woman managing shareholder in twenty-seven years, three months, and eight days?"

"I had no idea," I said.

"It all comes down to who society chooses to respect. Like when you didn't come to my office on Friday when I messaged you. That was disrespectful."

"I'm sorry about that—"

"I'm talking. Do you know why I called you to my office that day?" Octavia went into her suit jacket pocket and pulled out a lapel pin. One of her sun pendants. "To congratulate you for winning on Elevation Night." She attached the pendant to my T-shirt. "A lot of people had money on that Riley, but I knew you were up to the task."

I exhaled. The pendant meant I was one of Octavia's people, which afforded me a measure of job security. Job security meant I was that much closer to helping my son. "Thank you," I said.

"Don't thank me. You've got your work cut out for you, and people who wear my pendant aren't allowed to slack. But you knew that."

I pointed at the pendant. "So this means I'm promoted to shareholder."

"About that. No. A majority of the executive committee had to sign off on it. None of you got a majority of votes, but you got the most. So you're not a shareholder, but you're not canned either. You're provisional until a revote or I release you." Octavia glanced up toward one of the suites that ringed the arena. "You should have cleared it outright, but I think Armbruster convinced a few of the others to turn their nose up at you to spite me."

"Why?"

"Because they know I've got aspirations. I've got a potential client on the hook, a real whale who'll give me enough juice to make a run at head honcho. That's why I need to know that you're in up to the hilt."

"Of course I am."

"If you come through for me, I'll have enough clout to get you that revote. Of course, if you crap out or I do, we'll both be in the unemployment line. People who make a run for the top of the mountain and miss don't last very long. But you knew that, too. Any questions?"

I swallowed—ludicrous, considering we had worked together for years. But I couldn't shake the feeling that everything I cared about was at stake in how I handled the next few minutes. "The diversity committee. Why did you put me on it?"

She tilted her head in the direction of Armbruster, who was chatting up a leggy young brunette. "What do you see when you look at old Jack? Be honest."

I didn't want to insult Octavia. But I knew she would see through any attempt to be tactful. "I see success. Some deserved. Some not. I heard he was in line to be in charge after only a few months in. Big clients flock to him because he's got the look and profile that people buy. It's a closed loop, a self-fulfilling prophecy."

Octavia pursed her lips and nodded. "That's good. I couldn't agree more. I've spent my whole career paddling in his wake. I made my group number two by force of will, and now it's time to overtake that big rusty cruise ship. Know how we're going to do it?" I shook my head. "We're going after PHH."

Personal Hill Hospital, or PHH, as people called it. I wasn't surprised that her target client was the hospital where Penny worked.

PHH was one of the biggest employers in the City, and if Octavia managed to bring it in, she would become one of the wealthiest shareholders in the history of the firm. PHH had a level-one trauma center and an acclaimed, renowned cancer treatment service, but its plastic surgery clinic was all over the news since that pop singer underwent a transformation there. It was where I planned to bring Nigel when that sunny day came. Rumor had it that Octavia herself had had a good deal of work done. Franklin once told me that Octavia was just another light-skinned black who had her nose sharpened so she could pass. I never believed that story. After all, her family had owned that mansion on the Avenue of Streetcars since before recorded time.

"That's where you come in," Octavia said. "I need to show that the firm cares about the community. It's the price of entry to even be considered for their approved-legal services list."

"By community, you mean black people."

"Don't be crass with the race talk, but that's right. That's how the game is played. They lose their federal funding without the right mix of vendors."

"What can I do?" I asked.

"I need you to put together a campaign that proves the firm is committed to diversity."

A great roar erupted in the arena. Nigel jumped up, pumped his fist.

Octavia tilted her chin up and smiled. "I remember your résumé. You were what? Second in your class?"

"First."

"See that there. You'll think of something. I'm a big believer in putting my people in position to do their best. Callower has a job to do. He'll be running down the permitting and licensing side to see if we can find something that will increase PHH's profits. Companies love when lawyers find money just lying around. Dinah has a job to do. She'll keep track of the competition and ensure that we're one step ahead. And now you have your orders."

Made sense. Dinah and the others all seemed extraordinarily busy with things other than drafting briefs and going to depositions. I had to grab the reins while the grabbing was good.

"I'll need a budget," I said.

"Oh, you're quick," she said. I tossed out a number, not really knowing what I'd do with the money. "You can make do with half that."

"Do you want PHH or not?"

Octavia sniffed. "Fine. If there's one thing I cotton to, it's initiative. Take this puppy, for instance." Pavor stooped next to Octavia and licked barbecue sauce from his thumb. Octavia squeezed Pavor's cheeks like a cheerful aunt. "Look at this face. Wouldn't you vote for this man?"

I had no idea what they were talking about.

"I'm running for mayor," Pavor said. "The firm is backing me."

"You?" I asked. "Since when do you care about politics?"

"Since boss lady needs someone on the inside to move things along," he said. "I qualified this afternoon." Pavor noticed a line of sauce on his blazer and cursed. He wandered away wiping it.

"He and that Dinah make a pretty effective team." Octavia gestured toward Dinah, who was pouring club soda onto a cloth. "What do you want?" Octavia asked. "I mean psychologically, if you catch my drift. What do you need as a human-type person?"

"To do my job well." I studied my hands. It was true, in a sense.

"Nice answer, boy-o, but body language doesn't lie. I saw you look over at your kid again."

Nigel leaned forward at the rail, waving his foam finger.

"You're a good heart," she said. "That's what I like about you."

Armbruster walked down the steps to where Nigel was. He patted Nigel on the back.

"What about Armbruster?" I asked.

"What about him?" she whispered. "Managing shareholder isn't a lifetime position. If he's smart, he and his contingent will back me. I don't think he's that smart, though."

Nigel led Armbruster over. "This is your boy?" he asked.

"Last I checked," I said. A small part of me wanted to feel sorry for Armbruster. He was a grandfather, after all. Chairman of the water utility board. A respectable man. Octavia usually got what she wanted, and with Armbruster in her sights, he was as good as done.

"I had no idea. Such a handsome boy. A good-looking young man. Must have got it from his mother." Armbruster guffawed. I chuckled, too. "I bet you're good at basketball."

"Not really?" Nigel glanced at me, apparently wondering if that was the right answer.

Armbruster plucked a cigar off a server's tray. "Too bad."

Octavia and I both noticed my knee, which was leaping up and down like a thrown engine rod. I put my hands on my knee. The shaking stopped.

"Did you see that, Dad?" Nigel asked.

"What, son?"

"Some stuff happened," he said, twisting on one foot, "but we won."

"Never doubted we would." Octavia extended a hand. "Did you?"

"Not for a second." I clasped both my hands around one of hers, the universal, diplomatic black man's handshake.

Part Two

Part Two

9

"The face of Seasons Ustis law firm, huh?" Mama adjusted her kente cloth chef's hat. "You better hope you don't get punched in the face."

We were in the Chicken Coop, the fried chicken restaurant slash community center slash sometime boardinghouse Mama had taken over and put me to work in when I was a teenager. A place I avoided as much as possible as an adult. It was bad enough to participate in a cliché. How much worse to propagate one? A black family selling fried chicken to black people in the ghetto? Even a racially insensitive hack screenwriter would avoid that setup. Yet to be honest, my difficulty with flaky fried fowl fingers had a more personal dimension.

In high school, in the second half of my sophomore year, I dated a girl for about two weeks. Or rather I should say she, Sharane, dated me. She became an eventual Rhodes scholar and CEO of an entertainment company out west. However, when I knew her she was a cherrywood-skinned goddess—the cheerleading captain!—with all the physical bells and whistles necessary to send the hormones of an apelike teenager such as myself rocketing into the magnetosphere. Any neutral observer could have taken one look at me—the thick glasses I wore over my uncorrected eyes, the hair parted straight down the middle—and seen that I was outclassed. I questioned whether her interest was an elaborate setup to shame me at some upperclassman's upcoming drinking party. But it turned out that she just really liked Mama's chicken. She would show up to the restaurant shortly after I wrapped an apron around my waist and wait for Mama to step into the pantry. Then with the stealthiness of an American spy tiptoeing through the lowest subbasement of the Kremlin, I would smuggle a few extra-crispy thighs over the counter. Not that I fooled Mama.

Our liaison reached its sell-by date pretty fast. As soon as Mama announced that I could no longer just give Sharane half our stock, the girl's presence became scarce. For my part, I lost my taste for eating fried chicken around then. And for years afterward, I suffered nocturnal indigestion every July 6, National Fried Chicken Day.

Mama went behind the counter, slipped on a pair of plastic gloves, and mixed flour and seasonings in a bowl. "My son a figurehead," she said. "You've always been different, but I thought you had better sense."

I glanced at Penny, seated next to me. "I thought we weren't going to bring up my work stuff." When I had told Penny about the situation, her face turned red, and she sliced an eggplant right down the middle. She saw it not as an opportunity but as an exploitation. If the firm really wanted to show their appreciation for me, they should have given me a raise or made me lead on one of our major client cases.

"It just slipped out."

Penny rolled her eyes upward. The restaurant air conditioner clunked to life. "But see? Your mother thinks it's a horrible idea, too." Mama thought the firm wanted to use me as blackface. A way to make the organization more palatable to the clientele. She was right, of course. But it would put me in position to help Nigel. I couldn't tell her that. I knew my mother well enough to understand that she would object to my plans for Nigel even more vehemently than Penny did. Best to avoid the topic and enjoy time with my family.

"Forget that they're not paying you extra for doing it." Mama cracked several eggs into another bowl. "Why can't one of them do it? And what in the world qualifies you to be the face anyway? Lord knows you don't look like most of them."

"It's the chance of a lifetime," I said. "A chance to break new ground."

Mama opened a beer and poured some into the wet ingredients. "Boy, Uncle Tomming existed way before Harriet Beecher Whatsherface wrote that novel. You ain't doing nothing new." She poured more beer, then stopped. Her banana earrings swayed as she gulped the remaining contents of the beer can. "Don't mind me none." Leaning toward Penny for effect. "He always been stubborn."

Penny stepped to the register. "I have a dream that one day he'll come to his senses, and we'll live happily ever after in a little cabin in the woods."

"Don't hold your breath, sister," Mama said. "He's just like Sir."

I grunted.

Mama placed the battered chicken into a basket and lowered the basket into the deep fryer. It was hard to believe that when Mama and Penny first met, they both confided in me their reservations about each other. Penny found Mama overbearing and self-concerned. Mama thought Penny was clueless white trash. The tats and black eye makeup didn't help.

Nigel entered through the double doors that led to the community center's day room. "Where is everyone?" He washed his hands.

"Honey, they at that protest."

"The kids, too?" Nigel dipped his finger into the dry ingredients. He tested it on his tongue and pointed at the pepper mill. Mama smiled and nodded. Nigel ground three heartbeats' worth of pepper into the mix. "Shouldn't we be there, too? I mean, maybe they could use our help." He tasted the mix and gave Mama the thumbs-up.

"Protest?" I said. "No son of mine is going to stand shoulder to shoulder with a clot of troublemakers. You could be arrested or shot. And besides, they probably don't even know what they're protesting for. Is it higher wages? Is it banking reform? They probably think it's for longer kennel hours."

"You don't even know about the protest, do you?" Mama put her hands on her hips. "Look at him."

"Well, I— That's not the point."

"Hello?" Penny said. "We talk about it almost every morning." She reminded me that the protest was at PHH—not the main building where she worked, but at the plastic surgery clinic. For the past few weeks, she had to drive through angry people at the employee entrance. "Not that I'm mad at them. Their hearts are in the right place. Even if they shake the van sometimes. Someone graffiti-bombed the clinic building with these big, weird letters. . . ."

Although it beat discussing my work obligations, I wasn't really interested in talking about protesters. An envelope lay faceup between the register and the condiments caddy.

"Oh!" Mama said. "It's for you. A letter from Sir."

I held my hands up. "I don't want that."

"I'll take it." Nigel grabbed the envelope.

I took it from Nigel and ripped it in half. "We don't associate with criminals."

"Your father is no criminal."

"That's not what the court said."

"Well, if he is one, that criminal put food on our table," she said. "That criminal paid for your frou frou edumacation. That criminal is your father." Yes, Sir was my father. "Sir" was the nickname Mama gave him for what she sometimes described as his "particular bearing." I now found the usage of the nickname creepy and disturbing, like those parents who referred to each other as "Mother" and "Father." Also, it was hard to fathom that my father and I had once been so close that people took to calling us Big Sir and Little Sir, an appellation that I now strictly forbade even Mama to use.

"What did I do to deserve such a siddity son?" Mama turned her nose up. "You need to come around here more and stop acting like you weren't raised right. It's not healthy to spend all your time up in that white tower."

My field of vision went dark. Someone had placed their hands over my eyes.

"What's up, Frank Sinatra?" Only one person ever called me that. It was a reference to my fedora, which lay upside down next to me.

"What you selling today, money?" I asked in light Ebonics. Supercargo released me, mussed my hair, which I hated, and stepped into view. He had taken my fedora and put it on. Supercargo was my cousin. He had lived with me, Mama, and Sir for years. We'd been close as kids—I taught him how to tie his shoes—but I'd kept my distance from him after he dropped out of high school and got himself locked up in City Prison. He said it was all a setup. That white people had more use for him as a felon not in direct competition with their sons and daughters. Supercargo was a little nutty. *Choose your company wisely,* I always told Nigel.

"I see you still conking your fro, brotherman." My fedora sat atop his wild dreadlocks like a bird on a hippo's back.

"I see you're still annoying as ever." I turned to Mama. "I told you about harboring all these agitators in the restaurant. The City will be after you."

Mama raised her pinky. "Shut up, boy," she said, and laughed.

"What's up, girlfriend?" Supercargo kissed Penny's cheek.

Nigel came around the counter and tried to hug him, but Supercargo held his hand out to give Nigel a pound. "I'm too ripe for a hug," Supercargo said. Nigel hugged him anyway.

Supercargo said the riot squad moved the barricades back one hundred more feet from the hospital. Now they were confined to a small patch of grass near a drainage canal.

Mama asked him about the two bundles he dropped by the door. Balled-up banners in one.

"And those tablecloths you asked me to pick up from the Kendrick's cleaners," Supercargo said. Mama thanked him. "There were a couple of guys in robes and hoods."

"That's rich," Penny said. "They must think it's 1968."

Mama placed a hand on her collarbone. "Did they cause trouble like before?"

"Nah. We run them off."

"Now, that's how you handle an issue," Mama said. "Why don't you handle your problem like him?" Sometimes I could swear Mama liked my cousin better than me. He wasn't even my real cousin, just a crumb-stealing stray whom I loved like a brother.

"What problem?" Supercargo asked. I explained. "So, basically, your job want you to be more black so they can look like they care about black people."

"In a nutshell," Penny said.

"Sounds like he's doing what he gotta," Supercargo said.

Penny and Mama looked surprised.

Nigel tapped Supercargo's arm. "I'm going to be main guy in the school musical."

"Main guy?" I asked. "Musical. What foolishness are we speaking of now?"

"Not quite the lead yet." Penny pulled Nigel to her body and curled an arm around him. "He still has to win the role."

"Oh," I said. "That." My jealousy mounted. There was something about Nigel's ability to create words that my presence warped. Around me he sometimes seemed like Charlie Chaplin or Fancy Fox, able to act but not speak for himself. But in my absence, Nigel apparently reached Proustian heights of discourse, detailing the colors and smells of his life with startling clarity. He had known about his audition for the School Without Walls' production of *The Musical Life of Cletus Prufrock Morris,* the blind black organist and, later, blind black vice president, for days before I overheard Penny and him talking about it. Supercargo walks in and Nigel tells all in under sixty seconds. I took my fedora back. I didn't want it sullied.

"You know how to play the keys?" Supercargo asked.

"A little." Nigel hung his head slightly.

"That's nonsense. Nigel is a veritable virtuoso."

"Thanks, Dad," Nigel said.

"The new teacher at school, Mr. Riley, has been showing me. He's really good."

"Riley?" I asked.

"He said he used to work with you," Nigel said. So that was where Riley wound up after the firm dumped him on Elevation Night.

"Mr. Riley said if I stuck with it, I could get really good." We had brought in a tutor and paid him handsomely for weeks before Nigel admitted he didn't like the man. Following those sessions, Nigel could play "Yankee Doodle" and "Twinkle Twinkle Little Star" but little else. He couldn't be a natural at everything, apparently.

"You just need to practice more, baby," Penny said.

Supercargo gestured for Nigel to follow him into the community center, and I received a jig of haptic feedback from my amygdala. My cousin was mostly a good guy. Maybe the countless times he had been stopped by the police and occasionally been taken into custody and sometimes even charged and now and again incarcerated—for vagrancy or carrying a joint—weren't his fault. But fault wasn't the question.

I couldn't help but feel that every time he left my sight, the next thing I would hear about him was that he was profiled, chased, arrested, shot, killed, or any combination of the above. Still, I put a lot of the trouble on his appearance. He often dressed well, if a bit too garishly, during his leisure. But his various work uniforms, frumpy and bland, put him in the same visual class as the brothers begging for change at the soup kitchen. And his hair, his magnificent, unstructured, unprofessional hair—the huge locks branched off in five or six directions, a photo negative of the final fireworks of New Year's Eve—made him a target. I had been trying to convince him to cut the growth or at least tame it for years.

A slightly out-of-tune piano interlude to an R&B song emanated from the other room. The syncopated interlude played a couple of times before stopping midnote. It restarted shakily, like a fawn using its legs for the first time.

"Is that Nigel?" Penny's face lit up.

"Sounds like it," Mama said. Penny went to see. I was going to follow, but Mama said that she bet I had forgotten how to prep an order. I bet her she was wrong. As I mixed wet and dry ingredients into a steel bowl, I realized Mama was watching my every move, studying my face.

"It's just the kind of opportunity I've been waiting for. I slaved for this."

"Don't con me," Mama said. "I won't take it. You still trying to bring that boy in for that procedure. I know you."

It's impossible to outmaneuver the person who taught you how to walk, talk, and lie. "We don't have to talk about this now."

"But we do. You losing yourself. Your heart. Your roots. Like another man I know." She grabbed her own forearm and wrenched her fingers around it as if trying to take herself apart.

I looked away and grabbed the pepper Nigel left behind. "I'm not about to wind up in prison."

"They transferred him to City Prison, you know," Mama said. Sir had been at Buckles Correctional for the length of his term. The idea of him being in the City—barely a mile away—startled me. I struggled to suppress my surprise. "I'm going to visit him during open hours next week."

"Great," I said.

"Don't sass me." Mama raised her pinky. "I know you ain't well.

It'll break me if you let whatever is chewing on you hurt that boy."

"We're fine, Mama. I promise."

"Stop," she said.

"But we really are."

"The mix." She grabbed my hand. Without noticing it, I had emptied the pepper mill. The mix was pitch black.

10

Despite Mama's misgivings, I knew I had to stay proactive, so I went to my friend Jo Jo's place out in Sunny Vale. Sunny Vale was once a gated community, but the fence boards had rotted out before the most recent recession and were never replaced. Now nothing separated its nearly identical rows of fussy American Craftsman–style homes from the service road Nigel and I waited on. We were in the Bug. We were caught in a long line of cars turning into the subdivision. My knee quivered.

Nigel watched my knee. He wore my fedora, which, although pushed back from his face, sloped down to cover his ears. As he leaned forward, with his palms pressed against the dash, I had that hiccup-in-time feeling, as though I were the passenger and Nigel were driving.

"Can you see what the holdup is?" I asked. Nigel slid back the fabric sunroof, gleefully climbed onto the seat, and peeked out. This was all strictly verboten in Penny's presence, of course. But my dove wasn't around, and I needed a distraction, because to answer Nigel's unasked question: Dad was not okay. Dad was not in the same ballpark as okay. Dad was on a cruise missile headed in the opposite direction of okay at hypersonic speeds. My throat was a knot of twigs. Eyes sat on rusty ball bearings. Left heel swarming with bees. I had another more pressing reason for going to Sunny Vale. Imagine my surprise when I found my pill holder, a Daffy Duck Pez dispenser, empty.

My desperate state was my own doing. I should have planned ahead. I should have restocked days ago. I should not have brought Nigel. But with Penny at work, I couldn't explain a midday disappearance, leaving Nigel at home.

"What's the deal?" I asked Nigel.

"It looks like some kid dropped a ball," he said.

I stood up through the sunroof, crushing Nigel to one side of the gap. A ball was wedged under the bumper of a dump truck.

"This calls for evasive maneuvers, petty officer." Thus continuing a role-play we engaged in less and less frequently as the world adulterated Nigel. The narrative was ridiculously complex by that point, but the basics were easy enough to understand. We were in a submarine when we received a garbled command to attack the mainland of that tragic kingdom, our homeland. Meanwhile a distress call came in: innocents trapped on a sinking ocean liner. Nigel: *We should probably save those kids*. The captain: *Hell no*. Me: *Oh well*. Exposing the captain, Captain Swartzman, as a double agent, Nigel confined the cretin to quarters. We usually succeeded in our rescue mission. But in recent times we tended to arrive belatedly due to a confluence of quick-moving icebergs and demonically possessed winds, which hampered operations and, by extension, saved lives.

Nigel saluted. "Aye-aye, XO." He wiggled back down into the car.

I followed suit. "Safety first," I said. "Prepare to surface."

"Preparing to surface, XO." Nigel clipped on his seatbelt.

"Blow the ballast." While I depressed the clutch, Nigel threw the stick shift into drive. "Brace yourself," I said. And we swerved around the kerfuffle. Horns honked. Voices called out angrily. I cut through a backyard, glimpsing an elderly woman on a radioactive green Slip 'n Slide.

Entering the neighborhood proper, I clipped a yard jockey, putting him out of his eternal misery. After I killed the engine in Jo Jo's circular driveway, the Bug's rear engine pinged in well-earned exhaustion. Nigel was pressed against his seat.

"Did we save them?" I asked.

"Some," he said.

Inside, Jo Jo greeted us wearing jodhpurs, riding boots, and a black beret. He was dressed like someone's idea of a film director from the silent era. He even wore a floppy black mustache that didn't match his sandy brown hair or pale skin at all. Same old Jo Jo. My college roommate had a penchant for the oddball, the whimsical, the obscure. I fit all the categories, which I suppose is why we hit it off from the day we met in freshman orientation. Our tastes were generally different—I liked classical pop, he enjoyed contemporary avant-garde; I favored dandyish clothes, he liked whatever didn't stink too bad that day; I tended to date white girls, he never went out with anyone lighter than a paper bag (until he met Casey)—but our energy signatures were the same. We rarely had to explain ourselves to each other. Like we'd been separated during a mix-up in the maternity ward.

In our undergrad days, when it looked as though we might get a black woman president, it seemed as if the country were turning away from the old troubles of systemic racial oppression. Jo Jo used to say that one day we would walk into a room and people would see us as the twins we were, despite the fact that he was white and I wasn't. I bought into the hopes, too. But those hopes died fast. It sometimes felt like we were the only people in the world who experienced the whiplash and loss of those years, because no one else talked about that era. Not that Jo Jo and I did.

"There's my handsome brother," Jo Jo said.

"What's with the Cecil B. DeMille?" I asked.

"Dress for the job you want, killer." Sometimes Jo Jo worked in the local film industry as the guy who stood a mile away from the action to ward off the public. He had wanted to make movies— used to make funny-as-shit shorts starring me and our classmates— before he became a pharmacist and, later, a discredited pharmacist. He got a headless teddy bear each month from the mother of the child he'd inadvertently poisoned.

"Where's Randy, Jerry, Reynaud, and Milford?" Nigel asked.

"You didn't tell him?" Jo Jo asked.

I hadn't brought Nigel to Jo Jo Baker's in a long time. His wife and kids had moved out the previous year. Casey and the boys were replaced by a rotating cast of scruffy subculturalists who loved the irony of Jo Jo's suburban compound: a local experience so authentic that it was more or less exactly like where they came from, only with endless Plums and other exotic nipple twisters like ziziphus berries.

Jo Jo, the poor bastard, seemed to think Casey would step out of the kitchen at any moment and declare that all was forgiven.

A woman stumbled from the kitchen on one platform heel. Her hair was piled into a crooked beehive, and she wore little more than an unsashed kimono that revealed one light brown breast. Mild, hard-to-pin-down accent when she spoke.

"*Tozz fiik,* Jo Jo. You could have warned me that you had a kid in here, no?" The woman cinched the kimono together with a looped metal belt.

Jo Jo introduced her as Polaire from Egypt. A friend. He told her who I was.

"I've heard much about you, Jo Jo's friend. You have such a fantastic complexion. Like the chocolate they melt onto strawberries."

"Um. Thanks?" I said, my cheeks warmed.

"Oh no. Did I embarrass you?" she asked.

"Honestly? A bit."

"Good," she said.

Nigel and I stepped into the kitchen and opened Jo Jo's fridge. I saw an empty egg carton, some Camembert, and a cornucopia of beers, but there was a container of freshly squeezed lemonade. Nigel removed the container.

"Whoa, *kemo sabe*." Jo Jo took the container from Nigel and turned to me. Jo Jo took off his mustache. "Not for the little one. Not unless you want him seeing orange stars and green clovers. Would you?" He nodded at Polaire, who grabbed Nigel's hand.

"Want to see something spectacular?" She gestured toward the staircase. I gave Nigel the okay signal. "Come, my little chimpanzee," she said, and led him out of the kitchen.

"Is she safe?" I asked.

"Her? Safest person in this flying circus. Daughter of a sultan or something, but don't bring it up. Speaks like a dozen languages. Brilliant photojournalist, too, although she's too busy trying to get back to that war zone. Those animals shot her. She barely made it out."

I asked him how he was doing lately. He said his life sucked, but at least he kept busy. "You didn't come here to check on me, brother." He placed hands on both sides of my neck, squinted, and sniffed. He snapped his fingers. "A little out of focus."

"It's not just the Plums. Work trouble." I told him about the diversity campaign. I sipped juice from another cup and immediately spat the liquid out. "Castor oil?"

Jo Jo handed me a napkin from his sleeve. "Probably."

"So I need a director to make a commercial. Someone with style. I'll need some stills, too."

"I can help you with that."

With Octavia's budget and leeway, I could build any team I needed to get the job done. Jo Jo was flaky, but he knew his shit. He'd gone to school to become a pharmacist, after his parents' wishes, but he blew that off and eventually found success as an independent video producer. He started out doing weddings, then training films for midsize companies. Now his artistic video installations were the talk of the City and quite lucrative. It turned out my pal was a creative genius after all.

And while a normal person couldn't pay him enough to do commercial work, he could help me make an Afrocentric Seasons ad campaign to impress Octavia and PHH. Octavia would be one step closer to her big deal. When she closed the deal, I'd get my cut, and Nigel would be healed.

I grabbed Jo Jo's shoulder. "I'm thinking something light and quick. Lots of smiling black faces. Upbeat music—"

"Like one of those Caribbean tourism commercials," Jo Jo said.

"Precisely—"

"But with local flavor."

"Correct."

"We'll need some good locations," Jo Jo said. "Location is everything."

"I know just the place."

The doorbell rang. I opened the door and a man in fatigues stood there, a shotgun slung from his hip. I raised my hands. He shoved me into the wall, choking my windpipe with his forearm.

"Hey, hey, hey," Jo Jo said. "Easy, officer. The good brother is with me."

"Oh. I didn't know." The officer released me. I grabbed my throat.

"Why'd you do that, man?" Jo Jo said. I gasped and coughed.

"I did it for his safety."

"My safety?" I asked. "How is that possible?"

"I had to make sure you weren't a danger to me or yourself," the officer said. His neck was bigger than his head. "I'm not used to seeing black guys around here. You can't be too careful these days. There was a robbery—"

I was still coughing. Jo Jo patted my back. "Just take your goods," he said. He threw a stuffed brown paper bag to the officer. The officer tossed a stuffed envelope to Jo Jo and left.

"Sorry about that," Jo Jo said. He explained that the cop wasn't a real cop. Not anymore. He and his buddies had a camp out in the swamps where they ran tactical maneuvers 24/7. They needed stimulants to stay alert.

"You mean they're a group of crazies," I said.

"By definition, any gathering of humans is a group of crazies." Jo Jo waved at the man as he drove off in his gigantic black pickup. "You look like you could use a backrub."

"No, thanks. Maybe a medic."

"Not that kind of backrub. A Blue Geisha Backrub. One of the kids camped out back said I should call it a Blue Geisha Blowjob, but that's just crass, y'know?"

Jo Jo explained that the Blue Geisha Backrub was a Plum, so it did what all Plums did: pumped the air back into your soul. "Two differences though," he said. "It's a little slower on the uptake, but more powerful. And you know that stuff I add to the Plums that warms your insides? It's got a lot more of that."

"That's three things."

"I guess so." Jo Jo gave me a packet of regular Plums. Then he counted out three Blue Geishas into his palm. "You don't want to take more than one of these a week. Trust me on this."

I swallowed one. Jo Jo sipped lemonade. He clicked on the television. A commercial for Paul Pavor for Mayor came on. Jo Jo sipped lemonade, which had somehow taken on the appearance of Malbec, and made finger frames with his hands. *Terrible composition.* I had the sensation of time stretching like a wad of currently-being-chewed gum. He sipped lemonade. *Actually, it's Zinfandel.* Although I didn't recall asking Jo Jo aloud. *You can't escape. The wall is real, and it goes on in both directions forever.* Eventually, Polaire and Nigel appeared at the bottom of the stairs.

Nigel was in blackface. My words came out in the strangest

way, like cannonballs down a children's slide: "Why. Does. My. Boy. Look. That. Way?"

"He said he's playing a famous musician in a play but he's too light."

I tried to stand but collapsed onto my knees. Soon I was crawling. Spit drooled from my lower lip.

He can't look like that.

11

The massive Tikoloshe Housing Development aka Da Tiko aka Cargoland aka Mondayville aka The Big Oil Slick/The Oil Slick/The Slick was one of the last projects in the City and the perfect place for my guerrilla marketing squad to capture video of black locals. The Tiko was important enough to have made the National Register of Historic Places, although there was a debate as to whether it dated to the silver age of high-density housing or whether it had always been there in one form or another. It was also where I had lived for a sizable portion of my childhood, where I watched the world from the bubble-glassed bedroom of our third-floor walk-up.

The complex was surrounded by a tall barbed-wire-rimmed fence, and we had to show our IDs to get inside. If we lost our IDs, they wouldn't let us out.

I was still a bit bouncy-castle-brained, so Jo Jo drove while I reclined in the back of the Bug next to Polaire. Nigel had called shotgun.

"How about over there?" Nigel asked. I sat up, struggling, as my arms still felt like noodles. We were riding by the central field, a round patch of brown grass called Wright Park. The red-brick buildings were arranged in a multiringed circle, broken up by alleys that communicated to the gates. I once saw the complex from above while flying out of town on business. The arrangement seemed like a stylized impression of a gun muzzle, seen dead-on.

I began to question the wisdom of coming back here, a neighborhood I assiduously avoided, especially with Nigel. The unit where I grew up was on the back side of the Tiko. And although I couldn't see it, I smelled it as if it were landfill just upriver. And too, the Chicken Coop was just outside the fence. If anything really wacky happened, Mama would hop the fence to tell me what an idiot I was being.

Jo Jo hopped a curb, rattling us around. We stopped. Everyone got out except me—I fell out. Jo Jo helped me. Then he squirted something up my nose, and my vision cleared.

"What was that?" I asked.

"Placebo," he said.

Our plan was brilliant. Create an attractive nuisance. We would set up a giveaway table and place props to get the attention of Tiko residents. Once they came around, Jo Jo would take pictures and video of me with my fellow disadvantaged people. Then he'd convert the pics and vids to pamphlets and commercials that showed how much the firm cared about "the community." The props? Little old me and a teepee. At Jo Jo's place, Polaire had found a double-breasted khaki tux—Jo Jo's wedding getup—which I now wore. We'd borrowed the teepee from the smelly kids in Jo Jo's yard, fastened it to the Bug's roof.

We erected the teepee, surrounding it with a few cardboard boxes of T-shirts that Polaire insisted had fallen off a truck. She draped the boxes with their contents: purple Crooked Crown T-shirts. The finishing touch was a prominent, hand-painted sign that said FREE. We were like a purple blossom in the middle of the field. The bees would swarm shortly.

An older man walked up. "What is all this?" He stood with one hand on the front of his hip, his other hand shoved into the pocket of his football-logo jacket.

"Take a picture with my celebrity friend and get a free shirt," Jo Jo said from behind his video camera.

"Celebrity? I ain't never seen none of him."

"Well, you do see him now, no?" Polaire said. I shook the man's hand. Polaire leveled her still camera and quickly took a few pictures of us.

"I guess." The man rubbed his chin. "What kind of shirt we talking?"

Nigel held up a shirt. "Exclusive Crooked Crown shirts, sir."

The man's face lit up. I never understood what people saw in Crooked Crown, the purple-clad pop star who seemed to be everywhere lately, on shirts, on TV, in jail. I only knew her name because Penny had been a fan of hers back when she was the lead singer in that R&B group, the one where the members each wore distinctive black face paint. But that was before Crooked Crown visited PHH for lip thinning, a nose job, skin bleaching, and the Devil knows what else, a process called demelanization or a demel or a scrub. She had been a black girl from Baltimore. Now she looked more or less like a Greek woman.

Surprisingly, Penny seemed to like her music more since the changes. When I ribbed her about this, she said that you can't judge a person's artistic creations in relation to the choices they make in their personal life.

Nigel thought Crooked Crown made good music. "We're the only place in town that has them. And now it's yours." He handed over the shirt.

The man held the shirt up and drew his hand along the fabric as if it were the finest Egyptian cotton. "She the one beat that cop up on that reality show?"

"She was defending herself," Polaire said.

"My granddaughters love them some Crown."

"If you take one, mister, it would help my dad get a promotion at work." Nigel smiled.

The man grunted. "I'll pass the word," he said.

And that's how it went. Dozens of people passed by. Polaire took a bunch of photos. The boxes were soon nearly empty.

"Maybe I give the next people a little makeup?" Polaire tapped Nigel's head. "A darkener to bring more of an authentic atmosphere?"

"What is it with you trying to make everyone look blacker?" I asked.

"Not blacker. Browner. Don't you think rich brown skin is beautiful?" She pinched my cheek. "No blue veins. No irritated reds. Just smooth, gorgeous brown."

I couldn't tell if she was shitting me.

The sun was setting when we realized that our otherwise successful plan had a flaw: no bathroom facilities. Nigel announced he had to go. I concurred that I was in the same leaky boat.

"Me three," Polaire said.

There were several shelters, as they were called, positioned around the Tiko. I had been taught to avoid the shelters growing up, as most residents referred to them as flytraps. But it seemed like some effort had been made to upgrade them to a reasonable level of safety and security. The one nearest to our setup, a flytrap with an orange-and-white-polka-dot roof, was clean swept and guarded by potted plants around the perimeter.

But as we approached the shelter, I realized how shabby the Tiko actually looked. Yes, the high-density, brick living units were still intact. But gutters dangled from brackets. Paint flaked from doorsills. And basketball-size chunks of earth were missing as if someone had gone at the grounds with a giant ice cream scoop.

Near the shelter, a streetlight had been knocked over, the light's globe shattered, the globe crystals scattered like salt across a marble counter.

"That y'all?" someone said. A man crossed the grass, avoiding the strange potholes in long strides. His dreads frolicking with his motion, I didn't recognize him as Supercargo until he was nearly upon us. "What y'all doing up in here?"

Nigel hugged Supercargo. "Mr. Jo Jo and Ms. Polaire took pictures of Dad with some people to make some advertisements to post on the Net so Dad can impress his boss and get a fat raise," he said. "This is Mr. Jo Jo and Ms. Polaire."

Supercargo gave Jo Jo a pound and Polaire a cheek kiss.

"Didn't I meet y'all at this one's wedding?" Supercargo asked.

I wanted to correct the flap, since he was clearly confusing Polaire for Jo Jo's ex, but Jo Jo intervened. "You met me, bro."

"Well, either way," Supercargo said, "you can't be using these." He glanced around. "Even if the popos are playing hide and seek. Come use my place."

I never visited Supercargo in his nest because of my fear of the Tiko, its inhabitants, and the goings-on. I was aware of the oddness of these feelings. After all, this had been my home first. My culinary-school-trained mother and professor father picked this place as the launching pad for our family. Rougher elements of the City's black community didn't become the key demographic of the Tiko until their developments and neighborhoods were razed to build that NASCAR track, that apple orchard, that megamall, all following a series of unfortunate calamities, some manmade, others heaven-sent.

We climbed the narrow stairs of building number seven. My building had been number fourteen, but the hallway smelled the same, the same sharp stink from the chipping green paint I always imagined was full of lead specifically placed to sap the intelligence of any kid unlucky enough to eat it.

"This reminds me of my grandmother's flat in Tunisia," Polaire said.

"Did your gramma like to toke up?" Supercargo asked.

"All the time," Polaire said.

Nigel giggled. Some boys sat on the third-story landing, smoking weed. They tightened up when they saw us but immediately decided we weren't a threat and went back to smoking and talking.

This was an L-shaped building. Some were square blocks. Others, like the one I grew up in, were long rectangles. We traveled down a hall and hung a sharp left past the elevators. The elevators were a great idea, but they hadn't worked even when I was a kid, and none of the adults I encountered back then recalled them working. If you wanted to get anywhere in the Tiko, you had to do it under your own power.

We passed an open unit where tidy-looking white people in business casual clothing sat upright on a couch. One man, his hair neatly parted, loosely lolled his head. The women on either side of him were zonked out also. One of the boys from the hallway checked his device clock and stepped into the unit. The trio's time was up. The Tiko was a good place to find your jollies for those with free right-of-access. Fly in from out of town. Stop at the Tiko for a tune-up and make your noon meeting with time to spare.

Supercargo opened the door to his apartment, and a musky but not entirely unpleasant smell, like that of a recently burned forest, filled the hallway.

"Welcome to Supercargo's abode," Supercargo said. "Supercargo'll be your guide to all things Supercargo. Please leave all negativity outside. If you can't, please leave yourself outside." He took Polaire's hand high and guided her into the unit. The rest of us followed.

"I'll give y'all the tour." He gestured around the room, explaining that we were standing in the den, dining room, computer center, and kitchen, all of which happened to double or quintuple, you see, as his bedroom.

"Who sleeps back there?" Polaire pointed at a door in back.

"Uncle Tyrod." Supercargo chuckled. "He's probably knocked out. Ladies first."

Polaire excused herself to the restroom. Nigel had gone right to a large TV and activated a video game.

"Nice place you got here," Jo Jo said. "Reminds me of my college pad."

"This is so cool." Nigel hopped onto his haunches.

"That boy act like he don't get out."

"Dad doesn't allow video games."

Polaire reentered carrying a small djembe drum. She sat next to Jo Jo on the sofa. They patted the membrane arrhythmically, making animal noises with their mouths.

"This reminds me of my visit to Mauritania when I was a child. Those savages would . . ."

In the restroom, I took my time collecting myself. I cupped cold water in my hand and popped a Plum. I smoothed my eyebrows with wet thumbs. I spun on my heel and did finger guns. I squatted in place and rubbed my knuckles along the bristly fibers of the rug. I was just ascending when I heard a scream from the main room.

A giant stood in the room.

"What kind of party y'all having up in here?" It was Uncle Tyrod. He stank of gingerroot. His black hedge of an Afro probably hadn't been trimmed in months, if not years. The hair seemed to reach in all directions like an animated shadow. How long since last I saw him? Five years? Twenty-five?

"How's your daddy?" he said, looking down on me. I'd forgotten how tall he was. His fingernails were brown, at least two inches long, and curled like pork rinds.

"He's fine." I was struggling not to look disgusted.

"I guess I look different," he said.

"Little bit," I said.

"He one of yorn?" Uncle Ty knuckle-pointed. I told him Nigel was indeed mine. When he asked about the white people, I told him that they didn't belong to anyone.

Lean and muscular from his job delivering furniture, Uncle Ty had been the one all the Tiko women loved, everyone loved. He was charming, a man's man who could cook a pot of gumbo, then go out and beat anyone in a footrace. Not anymore.

Now Uncle Ty was shapeless and hairy and generally seemed like something that had crawled from a swamp. Something inside me twisted and fell over. My father and Uncle Ty had never exactly seen eye to eye. Sir thought of Uncle Ty as common and not living up to his potential. Uncle Ty saw Sir as confused and siddity. But they were both strong men in their own right, the patriarchs of strong houses. The last time I saw them just kicking it together was in our old unit. Sir wore an argyle sweater vest. Uncle Ty in his oversize jersey called Sir "Carlton." But Sir was hardly a paragon of fatherhood these days. And Uncle Ty—he was hardly even a person now.

Of course, Uncle Ty wasn't my real uncle any more than Supercargo was my real cousin. The authorities often threw people together with no regard for their connections or lack thereof. If you needed a place to call home, you had no right to be choosy. That's how two grown men of different generations came to live together.

"Sorry," Jo Jo said, gulping. "So sorry. I must have caught a bad one earlier."

"You had me so worried." Polaire stroked his hair and kissed his forehead.

"It's okay, Mr. Jo Jo," Supercargo said. "I feel kinda the same way when I drink lactose."

Uncle Ty sat on a stool. He seemed dreamy-eyed. "Y'all like my place."

"It ain't your place no more, Unc," Supercargo said. "I'm on the rent-control papers."

"Whoa," Jo Jo said. He stood. Polaire tried to stop him, but he shrugged her off and went to the mantel above the bricked-over fireplace. "It's you."

"How does it compare to your crib?" Uncle Ty asked.

"My house is okay," Jo Jo said. "It's empty of the people I want to see and hear though." He glanced at Polaire. "Except for this one." He asked if he could pick up the framed paper on the mantel.

"I was possessed." Uncle Ty forced his way into the spot between Polaire and Supercargo. It was a big sofa, but the middle of the thing sagged so that the three of them fell in together. Even Supercargo looked uncomfortable.

"You don't need to talk about problems, Unc," Supercargo said, "not tonight."

"That minister who used to check on me said I'm supposed to talk," Uncle Ty said, "and ask for forgiveness. I spent five years in Woodville before they transferred me to City Pen Special with the other crazies."

Supercargo stood up and grabbed Uncle Ty's arm to pull him to his feet, but it didn't work. Supercargo wasn't strong enough.

"What's this about?" Polaire said.

"I ate my boy," Uncle Ty pointed his knuckle at me, "your cousin Jacques."

"Ho ho ho." Polaire placed her fingertips against her neck. "You're him? *Le Cannibale Noir*?" She snapped a shot.

"I had a nightmare where I was buried under the ground. I had dirt in my eyes and mouth, but I could hear footsteps over my head." Uncle Ty shook his head. "I was scared, and it felt real. I knocked myself out inside the dream. Then a mob with broomsticks was chasing me across a hot place, and sand turned to waves of water that washed me away. Next I knew, I was in a valley where the Devil was waiting with a pack of hellhounds. The Devil looked like a normal dude in a tracksuit, but I knew it was the Devil all the same—don't ask me how I knew, I just did. The hellhounds weren't even pit bulls, just Snoopy dogs—you know, beagles—but I knew they were hellhounds all the same. I run as fast as I could, but they was after me. Seemed like no matter how fast I run, they was on top of me. I climbed a mountain of dirt, and I was happy because I knew I was free. The Devil and hellhounds were ghost, and I was by myself. But my stomach was sunk in like I was wasting away. So I got on my knees and dug out all the seeds and ate them. But when I woke up for real, I was in the kitchen." Ty pointed at the stove. "Little Jacques was in the stew pot—what was left of him—and my stomach was swole full."

Polaire had been darting around the whole time, taking pictures of everything from different angles. She must have gotten a few shots of me with my mouth hanging open.

"Stop telling stories," I said. I didn't know what kind of scam Uncle Ty had going, but I wasn't going to take his lies. All that stuff about hellhounds and Devils was straight out of old blues songs, and I'd had enough embarrassment for one night.

Supercargo grabbed my arm and whispered in my ear.

"Don't contradict him," Supercargo said.

I drew back to see his face.

"He can't take it, cousin." Supercargo gestured to his own mouth. "The blood. You know he ain't been right since the shooting."

The memory came rushing back. Uncle Ty and Jacques. Stopped by an officer as they walked home from work. Jacques with an outstanding warrant for not paying court fees on an expired driver's license conviction. Jacques shot in the lung for resisting arrest. Uncle Ty attempting mouth-to-mouth but finding only his son's lifeblood.

I glanced at Uncle Ty, who hadn't stopped talking to the others. He knew the truth but couldn't face it. The murder of his son had deranged him.

"It wasn't your fault, Uncle Ty," I said.

He pointed at me. "I ain't lying, boy," he said. "I was in the mental hospital till last year. A woman came around talking about paying me for Hollywood rights. She wasn't the first one. I never had so many people offering me money before all this started. Then they was coming out of the woodworks. Sneaking in and shit to see me like I was some kind of griot."

Uncle Ty said they let him out of the hospital because of overcrowding. He wasn't a danger anymore.

"I wanted to stay though," he said.

"I cannot believe you are real," Polaire said.

"I got something." Uncle Ty dug in his pocket.

Supercargo quickly got up. "Don't be showing that."

"Did you take any of the money people offered you?" Jo Jo said.

"Nah," Uncle Ty said. "It didn't seem right."

"I can pay you for your trouble," Polaire said.

"He don't need your money," Supercargo said.

"Ah, here." Polaire took a triangle from her purse. "Take this."

"What's this?" Uncle Ty flipped the triangle. It was her calling card.

"Call me," Polaire said, "and we'll do a proper shoot one day."

Uncle Ty said he'd never been the modeling type and he didn't want to start now.

"Well, at least give me another good shot."

"Okay." Uncle Ty took a bone out of his pocket. It was a sliver of a long bone, a fragment broken from a whole. He put the fragment in his mouth.

"Oh yes!" Polaire said. "Perfect."

Supercargo grabbed Polaire's camera by the lens. "It's time to go."

"Careful with that," Jo Jo said. "It's her art."

"You don't leave now, I'll put her art up your ass." Supercargo turned to me. "You too. Nigel can stay. But y'all got to go."

12

However, before we leave the Tiko, I feel I would be remiss if I didn't share, in these notes, an early experience from when I called the development home.

Picture, if you will, the swarm of flies that used to gather around the garbage can at my childhood home. What if I told you that the flies were one City patrolman and the can my old neighborhood? One man orbited the Tiko incessantly, maniacally.

Officer Dred Douglas was a hero, a myth, a legend. Judge, jury, and occasionally, hangman. A national news anchor once called him America's top cop. He seemed to work 24-hour shifts 7 days a week, 365 days a year. And perhaps he did. It was not unusual to find him napping in his squad car, wearing highly reflective sunglasses so as to make us residents think he was watching, always watching.

Douglas's omnipresence was the way of Douglas. Sometimes during the ride from school in the Bug—back when it was still Sir's—we'd see Douglas sitting in his patrol car near the entrance of the Tiko.

"There's that windbag cop," Sir would say, glancing in the rearview. I wouldn't look back for fear that Douglas was monitoring me through the side mirror reflection. Yet by the time we arrived at our building, which was about a two-minute drift into the center of the development, Douglas would be waiting at the corner, pretending to check the channels on his walkie-talkie—*click click clicking* from one line to the next. Douglas, in this way, could come up at the start of a sentence and also be the last word in it.

"That guy gives me the jeebies," Sir might say. Or "You would think they would have promoted him out of here by now." He would then rub his forehead beneath his fedora.

So Douglas was everywhere, and he saw everything. Like a football referee who ejected players for improper shoe lacing, no infraction—no matter how apparently insignificant—escaped his Argus-eyed view. Douglas would have made an excellent poster child for the community policing/broken windows war, if the City produced such posters. Douglas was a paragon, his light blue shirt and dark blue pants starched and creased to military specifications. In the summer, he wore a wide Stetson, and in the winter, he grew a beard that he didn't cut until after the New Year, so that by Christmas he looked like Black Santa. But he delivered abrasions, contusions, and shattered bones all year round.

Although he had the look of the kind of officer who might appear in a public service campaign, directing pregnant mothers to avoid live power lines, he hated children. He hated adults, too. He even hated pets—I once saw him punt a cat. Neither Sir nor Mama spoke to him. No one did because talking to him meant you'd have to make eye contact. And eye contact was highly suspicious to Douglas. As was the conspicuous avoidance of eye contact. The best policy was to maintain a distance of about five hundred yards from him at all times, which basically meant you had to stay out of the Tiko to avoid him. (This was before the City began expanding the Tiko's fencing to accommodate new settlements for people who lost their homes in other parts of the City.) He seemed to think he was stationed in a war zone. And that if he only held out, his reinforcements would be along at any moment to shock and awe us with Daisy Cutter bombs dropped from helicarriers disguised as cirrus clouds. We were all the same to him: nurses, bus drivers, drug dealers, preachers, car thieves, and professors alike. He'd show us good when the time came, his baton seemed to say, as he paced the Tiko slapping the stick against his thigh.

I suppose under one analysis, Douglas was a good man doing the job he was hired to do. No one could deny that he was a diligent officer of the law. He was like an overeager linebacker who blitzed on every down. It didn't matter if he got the sack as long as he disrupted the play. And he disrupted both work and play. During the years we lived in the Tiko, I personally observed him bodily searching nearly every man, woman, and child at least once. It didn't matter if he had a reason to suspect that some crime was being committed. No body was left unturned. Yes, all the swaggering Jeromes with their baggy pants and fitted T-shirts, but also the mothers and daughters. And if he could find them, that is to say, if they existed outside jail or the cemetery, the fathers, too. I saw it all. Elderly men with their pockets turned out. Girls dressed for parties in platform heels with the contents of their purses scattered across broken concrete. Splattered ice cream cones. Overturned red wheelbarrows. So much depends upon a man with a hatred of his own.

13

I stood between my open office door and the wall, where hung a three-quarter-length mirror. I had come in a few days before to find Melvin Marvin, the frumpy facilities guy, supervising some other frumpy facilities guys as they transported my belongings from my cramped space on fifty-nine to a new office only two doors down from Octavia's on the sixty-second floor. Sixty-two was unofficially the senior shareholders' floor. Octavia had pulled a string, inviting a mere mortal to frolic among the masters of the mountaintop.

Sixty-two was the main floor of the firm. The firm library, which still contained honest-to-goodness physical books, was here, as was the demonstrative trial exhibits room. A sky lobby looked out over the river and a winding staircase, whose elegance suggested a river flowing backward up a hill. Even the pile of the carpet was more luxurious on sixty-two. I didn't belong here. But I could.

Leaning toward my office mirror, I tried to tame my tie, but it refused to cooperate. The tie's divot was crooked, and the whole thing kept bunching up under my neck like a sharp-knuckled fist.

My office door swung into me from behind, pushing my face into the mirror.

"Mfft," I said.

"Showtime, sweetheart," Octavia said. I wiped the mirror made greasy by my face, but that only made it harder to see. Octavia pushed her sunglasses to her forehead. Her silver streak darkened behind the lenses. She gave me elevator eyes and chuckled. "Oh ho ho. Somebody's ready for the prom. And maybe a little action behind the bleachers. Are those spats?"

"Fortune favors the well-dressed."

I adjusted one of my yin-yang cuff links. I felt ready. Every strip of fabric, every accessory, every button and aglet projected an image and reflection. The suit as armor, talisman, lure.

My links were from Penny. Mama had given me the tie for graduation. Crammed into the inside coat pocket was a folded sheet of paper Nigel had made when he was only five. The outer leaves said "World's" and "Best." It could unfold to the size of a large placemat. Although I had expected the inside to say "Dad," the interior featured a giant stick-figure head with charcoal-shaded skin, clawlike hands, and furrowed eyebrows that lent it a pensive look. I patted my heart. The paper crinkled.

"The executive committee is happy, sugar, so you know what that means."

"You're happy?" I said.

"You damn skippy I am. My office." Octavia's corner office was a crowded one, full of objects from her exploits. A dusty trophy from the year she was the fastest teenager in the state sat on a low table by the window. Exotic hand-woven rugs covered the hardwood, hardwood she installed when she became a capital shareholder. There was a painting of a woman who could have been an ancestor tilling a field in World War II England. Photos of Octavia and two different presidents, one Republican, one New Whig, hung behind her desk, near a small picture of her adopted daugh-

ter, whom I'd never met because she was a relief worker in Finland
and refused to reenter America on moral grounds. Then a pic of
Octavia, in fatigues and brandishing a spear, next to a wild boar
she had brought low.

Octavia unclipped the portfolio—prepared by Jo Jo and Polaire—
that I'd given to her the day before. She removed a stack of glossy
eight-by-tens and flipped through them, showing me each as she
went. A shot of me posing with two button-nosed children. Me
laughing with an elderly woman with cornrows. Me and Uncle
Ty, that thigh bone in his mouth. I thought Jo Jo had destroyed
that one. The copy read: "Together for a Better Tomorrow."

"I'm glad you like it," I said.

"Like?" Octavia asked. "This is better than I imagined. The firm
will fund a full campaign around these. So I don't have to pay out
of my own pocketbook." Octavia's candy dish was a Punu mask
turned on its face. I felt a pang of envy at the fact that she had been
to the African continent a half-dozen times whereas I had never.
Would never. But it was a mild pang. Even though some African
Americans bought into the Garveyan notion of going back to the
Motherland and others thought of it as a war-, famine-, and
disease-infested land, I knew the truth: It didn't matter whether
Africa was great or awful, nor did it matter how much dark blood
coursed through my veins. Africa wasn't home. For better or
worse, this vicious hamlet—where I dreamed perchance of a
bright future for my son—was home.

Octavia tossed a hard caramel from the bowl and chewed. "Pop-
up ads. Billboards. Inserts for firm client brochures." The single
silver streak in her hair reminded me of our polluted river. When
sunlight hit the diluted particulates just right, it was quite beautiful.

"When?"

"Already in motion. I'll show you." She explained that we
couldn't play around. Armbruster's group was making a play for
that international media conglomerate, the Darkblum Group,

which recently placed a major office in the City. Octavia went to the window and pointed at the McNamara Building. It was only a third as tall as the Sky Tower, so it was perfect for a rooftop billboard. An advertisement for Blanco's Chocolate Milk with a screen capture of that actor in elderly woman drag struggling with a cute black-skinned kid over a comically large jug. Tagline: "You bet not steal my good milks!" The ad shimmered like falling stars and shifted, winkingly, to reveal the next ad in stages: the firm logo, a forehead, the edge of Uncle Ty's bone. I turned away.

"What?" Octavia asked. "You don't like it."

"Um. No. Yes. It's great."

"Good," Octavia said. "You're really on your way, you know that?"

"Really?"

She gestured to the abacus on her credenza. The executive committee kept track of our efficiency with the Racing Form. Although any shareholder could pull the Racing Form up on their computers, it was hidden from the view of peons like me, but I knew what categories it contained: billable hours worked, billable hours written off, billable hours paid by the client, and bonus points for special work that added value to the firm. Octavia's abacus was a physical manifestation of the Racing Form.

Instead of beads, her abacus had rows of colored semitransparent stones, a different-colored row for each person in her group. I didn't know who each row stood for, but Dinah was clearly the top rung, where half of the amethyst stones had already been shoved to the complete side weeks ago. As Dinah worked harder than anyone I knew, she racked up stones faster than anyone I knew. My sardonyx stones were second from the bottom. A quarter were on the complete side.

"I'm not even close," I said.

"We close this PHH deal, you're all set. Even if I have to kick in some of my goodwill on loan. Let's go."

We left her office. We passed various staff people in the halls.

We must have looked impressive or, at least, determined, because they nodded or smiled at us with a peculiar intensity, as if they all knew we were going hunting. I tripped on the rug in the lobby, but didn't fall.

By the time we exited the Sky Tower garage in Octavia's sports car, which sat so close to the ground I could feel the pebbles in the macadam and hear the pleas of ants, storm clouds hovered above. As we reached the Personal Hill complex, the heavens let loose.

Personal Hill Hospital occupied fifty-five acres of prime City real estate just north of the business district. It was once two hospitals. Adelaide Hill Medical Center dated back to the Civil War, when a wealthy Northern heiress moved to the City and established a hospital for injured Confederates. The Personal Clinic Corporation bought out the old AHMC. The new buildings surrounded the old AHMC building, which was punctuated by turret-like projections. The new buildings were outsize and prone to taking off at odd angles. The old building looked like a Gothic castle surrounded by a Rem Koolhaas–designed castle.

Driving up the private boulevard that bisected the campus, we saw steel barricades that held the protesters back on either side— get back, you dogs—their placards melting in the rain. I searched for Supercargo but didn't see him.

The general counsel's secretary set Octavia and me up in a waiting room, where we sat until a group of people, three men and two women, came in.

Octavia had met with some of them in preliminary meetings before. The group was mostly white. All I knew was that the CEO was a man named Eckstein. A square-jawed, graying-at-the-temples man in nautical blazer approached with hand extended.

"Mr. Eckstein," I said.

Octavia shook her head and gestured at the only black person in the group. An elderly black man in an ascot with big active eyes and conked hair not unlike my own. "He's Mr. Eckstein." I apologized, but Eckstein shot me a fearful look. We took our seats around the conference table.

We exchanged social lubricants. Eckstein's son went to the same school in London as Octavia's daughter. A red-nosed man quipped about the protesters drowning outside. We passed our materials around the table. One of the underlings gave Eckstein a brass-handled magnifying glass that he used to examine Jo Jo and Polaire's photos. He didn't look pleased. Then he scanned some of the text I'd ginned up to give the portfolio the semblance of substance. One section boasted statistics about cases and projects Seasons had done for the City's poor; another explained Seasons's efforts to recruit local minorities from a shrinking pool of applicants.

Eckstein pushed the documents over to his assistant, who carefully rearranged them.

Eckstein crossed his hands. "Have you ever done prison time?" He was staring at me.

I pointed at my chest. "Me?"

Octavia squirmed in her seat. I had never seen her uncomfortable before.

"I'm a direct person. I don't mind telling you the truth. I know you've noticed me staring at you. You remind me of a young man who mugged me after a parade on the avenue years ago. Took a family heirloom. A stopwatch that belonged to my mother."

My mouth swung open at the accusation. I wasn't sure whether to laugh or yell.

"This one?" Octavia said. "He's safe as they come."

"That's right." I patted my chest. "I'm firm catastrophe warden for the fifty-ninth floor."

"Three years running," Octavia said.

Eckstein raised his hand. "That's not the reason I'm not going with Seasons. It's your firm profile. I'm sure you know by now how important a strong respect for diversity and community involvement is to us here at PHH. That comes from the board, not me."

"What did you think of our materials?" Octavia asked.

"The numbers don't convince me that Seasons has been dedicated to it for long enough. Offer your services again next year, and we can reevaluate."

Eckstein got up. His upper lip curled. "For what it's worth, the marketing campaign disgusts me, but it's also exquisite—it's just the kind of thing people in this town respond to." I thought he might spit on us, but instead, he left.

Octavia and I walked down the hall. I moped. Octavia fumed.

I was the first to speak. "What do you think we should—"

Octavia shot a look of disgust. "Those bastards. Armbruster and his frat boys are going to have a field day when they hear about this. You think the firm wants me to succeed? They would just as soon have me sit quietly in the corner during shareholder meetings, batting my eyelashes and laughing at all their jokes. I'm the one who made them bring in you and Dinah and the rest of them. They would love if the firm were lily-white forever. Now this Eckstein thinks I'm some kind of poser, and you're asking me what to do. How about you bring some ideas for a change?"

"I'm sorry," I said.

"No. It's not your fault." Octavia stopped and placed her palms against the wall. She wasn't breathing. I was about to ask if she was okay when she kicked the metal panel that covered a fire extinguisher. She kicked the panel repeatedly until her shoe flew off. The panel was dented.

I grabbed her arm. "Stop. You'll hurt yourself."

She kicked the panel with her other foot and swiped hair out of her eyes. "I'm not going down quietly. It's always men standing in my way. Well, not this time. I've only just started." She told me to meet her in the garage and entered a restroom.

In the lobby atrium, a woman in a skimpy purple getup and matching fur coat stood on a temporary stage. She was thin, pale, and being questioned by a swarm of reporters.

In the garage, I was almost to Octavia's Aston Martin when someone called to me. "Excuse me, but Ms. Breedlove would like to speak with you." A man walked toward me from the stairwell. He wore a plastic purple kilt and a helmet with built-in sunglasses.

"Who?" I asked.

An entourage stepped out of the garage stairwell. There was something Picasso-esque about the group of young people with their architectural hairstyles and violet-color-schemed clothing. They arranged themselves on either side of the door. A musical cue, like digitally altered flutes, played from one of their devices. A musical herald.

Crooked Crown, her platform heels clicking on the cement, entered. Beneath her purple coat, which I now realized was more of a shawl, she wore a form-fitting outfit composed entirely of sizable purple patches, some of which seemed made of taffeta, others wool, and still others lace. Yet the patches exposed portions of skin in her R- and X-rated areas. This was to say nothing at all of the monitoring collar she wore around her neck.

Last year she had attacked a police officer while taping a locally shot live TV special for NBCBS. Most people would have gotten years in prison or been put down in the case of repeat offenders. But her record label lawyers had worked a deal that required she (1) dump a few hundred thousand dollars into the City coffers, and (2) not leave the City until the judge decided she'd suffered enough.

"Who are you?" she asked, her hips swinging like church bells as she approached. There was something otherworldly about her. "I saw your face on a billboard whilst being driven." That was another thing I joshed Penny about: her phony British accent. But she had the involuntary effect that all celebrities had on me. Each time my cheeks flushed, and my IQ seemed to drop by a third. She must have seen the firm billboard that Octavia had put up.

I said I was a lawyer. I gave her my card.

"How do you live in this place?" she gestured as if to suggest my bed was stashed behind a pickup. "This town is like a vulture burning the flesh from my soul."

"I get by," I said.

"Do you know who she is?" the one in the kilt asked.

I told them I did.

"Only Crown, dahling," another of the entourage, a girl wrapped in a purple cylinder, said. "She dropped the Crooked part when she went solo."

"I fancy your style," Crown said. "It's rare that a body captures my attention. I wager you're wondering why I'm here. Can I sign anything for you?"

"Sign?"

"My autograph. People seem to like when I do that."

"Well, I don't have—"

Crown raised a hand to her shoulder. One of her people placed a marker in her hand. She uncapped the marker, grabbed my shoulder with her free hand, then drew on my jacket what appeared to be a backward C.

14

I was a killer in court, a master of oratory, an unstoppable disciple of Cicero, Nelson Mandela, and Sukarma Kamenetz. But I hated going to court. Why? If you watched enough award-winning films or read a bunch of crime thrillers, as I did as a boy, you would get the distinct impression that courts of law, indeed, the entire system of codified expectations, was fueled by the search for truth. This was not so. Our courts were powered by two things and two things alone: fear and fear itself.

In court, I was afraid of everyone: the client who relied on my competence and zeal; the armed bailiff, whose job it was to subdue zealots like me when we overstepped our bounds; my opposing counsel, whose raison d'être was to cut my limbs from my body until I was nothing but head and torso; and the judge, whose duty was to pound me into the floorboards like a railroad spike. My opponent feared their own client, the bailiff, and the judge as I did. And even the judge feared the appellate courts that could overturn any decision with impunity. And the appellates feared, presumably, God. But who did God fear?

Dinah Viet Dinh sat to my left, fondling rosary beads, our elbows rubbing. We were on a pew in one of the lower chambers of

City District Court surrounded by dozens of other attorneys. We were the only two non-whites in the hall. Not that I was counting.

It was Rule Day, a time for prayers and complaints to be heard. Every lawyer in the room had filed a pleading during the prior month, motions to stop things, motions to start things, injunctions against up, exceptions in favor of down. All throughout the hallowed courthouse, on each of the five floors, counselors perched on the edges of their seats, ready to grumble and carp on behalf of their patrons.

"Jesus Christ." Dinah Viet Dinh folded a sheet of blue paper and slid it into her little metallic purse. "Does he ever show up on time?" The woman in the row in front of us, a blonde in a yarmulke, glanced back at Dinah. When the woman turned away, Dinah snarled her lips. Dinah was right, of course. Judge Lordes was notorious not only for showing up long after scheduled hearings but also for faulting lawyers who did the same. His disciples— for example, the court reporter who never pronounced my name right—ratted out the tardy. If the judge learned that you'd arrived, say, ten minutes late, he might kick your case to the back of the docket, make you wait until the end of the day to be heard. One poor sap complained about this treatment and was sent to the north tower brig on contempt charges. He was supposedly still chained to his cell like some anchorite. More than likely court legend. But maybe true. I hadn't seen the guy in at least five years.

Dinah and I were there on separate cases. If it were anyone other than Dinah, I would have been pissed. Callower, for example, tended to bring his intemperance to court. Last time, he slipped a silver flask into my trial bag to avoid a snooping bailiff. And Pavor was just as likely to duck out at the last moment and ask me to cover for him. Not Dinah. She was a pro. She took the calling as seriously as I did. Still, today there was also something a little off about my friend. I couldn't pinpoint what it was. New eye shadow?

Dinah was involved in a settlement involving some local musician. "So what's your problem?" she asked.

"No problem," I said. "I'm ducky."

"You're nervous."

"Am not!"

"Are too!" Dinah nodded toward my lap. I was unwittingly doing that thing I did when I had pregame jitters: crafting origami out of court papers. It was something I'd learned from Penny back when we were dating. I tucked the last edge of paper underneath, creating a powder-blue butterfly. I unfolded the paper until it was again a show-cause pleading.

"What are you here for?" Dinah asked.

"Hitch," I said.

"Jesus Christ." *Karol v. Hitchens Corporation* was an all-purpose punchline. Had a bad case? Least it wasn't *Hitch*. Ran up astronomical expenses on a file? What did you think this was—*Hitch*? Long wait for a ruling from the Supreme Court? Poor sucker. *Hitch* will come down before you get word.

Over the last fifty years, nearly every attorney who worked at the firm touched the file at one point or another.

The plaintiffs in my case had sued after their house was atomized by space junk. My client's entire defense of the claim was based on the argument that a falling satellite was an Act of the Big Fella Upstairs. Sometimes while puttering around His workbench, He dropped things: screws, satellites, asteroids. No mortal creature could be liable for an accident set in motion by a celestial butterfingers. Just ask the dinosaurs.

I glanced at the roll call screen on the wall. Dinah's name scrolled past, followed by the real name of Crooked Crown.

"How could you not tell me you're representing that singer?" I asked. "I mean. She's on TV every day."

"It's no biggie. The firm is representing her. So technically you're her lawyer, too. She's kind of not as much of a douche as I thought she would be. She came to my apartment the other night when Pa—when this guy I've been seeing was there. We lit a few up and played with tarot cards. You mumbled something about needing my advice. Well?"

I explained how Octavia and my visit at PHH had imploded. "Octavia is pissed at the situation, pissed at me, too," I said. "And that Eckstein treated us like we were telemarketers."

"You're toast," Dinah said. "She's going to fire you. You should start looking for a new gig, maybe like a teaching job or something at a bank. I have a hookup— What?"

"Thanks a bunch."

"Your problem is that Eckstein wants you to be different, so be different. Go volunteer at a school for delinquents or raise money for a Little League team like car dealers and moving companies do."

An idea hit me. "Supercargo!" I said. Dinah stared at me in confusion. "My cousin's been asking me to get involved with his civil rights group for years."

Dinah laughed. "I wouldn't buy you as an activist."

"Have some faith. I'll be the most activistic person you've ever met."

"Thine eyes of mercy toward us," Dinah said, playing with the last bead of her rosary. "And after this our exile—"

"All rise." The court crier, a man wielding a ceremonial truncheon staff, opened the rear chamber door. We all stood.

A black-robed figure stepped into the room and quickly ascended the steps to the bench. This detail caught my attention more than any other: the judge had very bony hands.

"That's not Lordes," I said.

"Nice going, Dr. Watson," Dinah said. "Has your investigation revealed anything el—"

"*In re Tyresha Breedlove-Eckstein,*" the judge said.

"Jesus Christ," Dinah said, gathering her purse and briefcase. She passed the bar and took her place behind one of two counselors' tables. "Dinah Viet Dinh on behalf of the petitioner, Your Honor."

As she launched into her argument, a surprisingly poetic, roaring soliloquy on the dangers of avarice, I realized that I was only slightly prepared. Of course, I had read the plaintiff family's latest brief in my case—they alleged *res ipsa loquitur,* the idea that some offenses are so obvious and indefensible, there is only one side to the story. And you, defendant, must pay all the monies. But it struck me just then the precariousness of my position. If I lost the hearing, the firm would finally realize how clueless I was. They would recall Franklin or Riley or find some other fresh-faced indentured servant. I'd be out on the street. Nigel and that spotted face of his would never be corrected, perfected.

He sat on the head of a stone lion in City Park. He seemed younger than he should. More innocent. "Come on, Dad," Nigel said. "You can see me!"

"Am not?" I asked.

"Wake up." Dinah shook my arm. I glanced around the room, which had taken on a sickly green hue. Most of the other lawyers were staring at us. The plaintiff family's lawyer was already in position at counsel table one. Why wasn't Dinah at the podium? I was in the front row? I'd seen Dinah at the podium just now? But she was at my side? I had the same emerging-from-the-depths feeling I had every morning when I awoke. Like I was piloting a submarine from the bed of the Dead Sea. Dinah jabbed her elbow into my ribcage. This was happening more and more frequently. Time jumps. Spatial hiccups. Distorted sensory processing. Brought on by Plums and Japanese women? No. Jo Jo's Geishas. But I couldn't remember if I'd had one that morning. Or maybe I'd had three?

I wiped my forehead on my suit sleeve and walked to the free counsel table. If there was only one really important rule in running onto the playing field, it was, *Don't let them see you stumble, don't falter, get to the huddle in a calm, orderly fashion—women and children first.*

This ship is unsinkable. I smelled delicious maple bacon.

The opposing lawyer stood up and took her place at the podium microphone. It was the woman in the yarmulke. She smiled, introduced herself, and pointed in my direction a couple of times. I wiggled my fingers at her.

"—a clear-cut instance of fault occasioned by wantonly negligent actions," she said.

A fly buzzed my ear. For a moment, I saw the whole insect, the antennae, the wings, and the hind legs quivering with life. It was tired, hungry, nervous. I caught the fly, in the palm of my hand—in one quick snap—and squeezed. A burst of energy faded in my palm, which prickled as it cooled.

The plaintiff's lawyer went back to her seat. I stood up and wiped my hand on my coat. Two pulsing stalks of light on her back at the shoulder blades. The plaintiff's lawyer seemed to have blue butterfly wings sprouting from her back. But some Muppet inside me yelled that this did not compute and that I'd gotten a bad Plum before, so I'd better find my center and dunk that ball!

"Your response, counselor?" The judge was an undifferentiated blob of robe and shadow by then.

"I thought—" I grabbed the podium and clutched it. I felt like I had grabbed the vibrating world by the neck. The room stabilized. "I thought you'd never ask." Cotton mouth. I spritzed Binaca. Shit. It tasted like bacon.

15

I read somewhere once, perhaps in *Family Health* magazine (or was it *Hearth and Home*?), while waiting in some foyer for a Plum to kick in, that museums are proof of humanity's narcissism. A museum with its glass display cases and terse, descriptive cards is a way of declaring how important we are. We rock. We *matter*. On approach from the Oort cloud, aliens probably wouldn't be sure whether we were an intelligent species. They would scream across the sky, in their aluminum saucepans, atomizing entire shopping districts—bye-bye Dolce, *poof* goes Gabbana—until they came across a museum, at which time one of the horrified Plutonians would exclaim, "Stop the culling, Xerblatz. We have made a horrible miscalculation. These creatures *feel*." A museum is proof positive of a community's heart and values, its history, manner of speaking, culture, its soul.

Of course, a museum is also a boneyard.

The Musée du Nubia du Africq, also known as the Musée or the MdNA (the second *d* was omitted), was founded before most of the City's blacks were swept out of the main body of the City and into the Tiko or the hinterlands. The museum founders must have somehow sensed what was coming, the way a bird intuits the coming of a particularly harsh winter.

In their panicked foresight, the founders of the Musée collected core samples of blackness from various eras and areas of the City's history: a sepia-toned color wheel used by a protester during the Brown Bag Riot of '24; a set of turntables owned by DJ Oya; an ankle monitor worn by the City's last African American mayor before her unfortunate demise; a chisel purportedly used by the Invisible Artist, who engraved the Sky Tower's calcified walls with gargantuan abstract faces that peered vacantly into the hinterland swamps until the faces were sandblasted off by management. In this way, the MdNA was something like Noah's Ark. Only the Musée saved Nubian gewgaws, not stone tablets. Also, the waters were not liquid but purely metaphorical. The reversal of white flight, a white scourge.

I had heard others complain about this passage of our village's history, but I was of the belief that history is neither good nor bad. History is landscape. History is backdrop. It is context. Anyone who peers into a canyon and finds something hateful in it is seeing their own reflection.

"You're a good man, Jo Jo Baker," I said, glancing at him in the passenger seat.

"Why am I doing this again?" Jo Jo motioned at the camera around his neck.

"Because I need a wingman." Dinah was right. I felt better now that I was back on offense. All I needed to get into the good graces of the organization that ran the museum was a positive attitude and a few handshakes. Once I insinuated myself, I would present proof to Octavia that I was hard at work making Seasons look good. She would be able to parlay my efforts into something useful.

"I thought I was promoted out of that spot when you got married." He snapped a shot of me.

"Once a wingman, always a wingman." Pulling into the parking lot, I remembered the bombed-out storefronts and drugged-out bums who populated the neighborhood during my childhood. The Musée was now flanked by a lovely patisserie and a classical mime college.

The organization that owned the museum, the Blind Equality Group, nearly lost the franchise due to a tax debt. The BEG, as it was sometimes called, believed in creating a completely color-blind world. Their ongoing fight was against those who would divide the citizenry by race, even if that meant ignoring history, statistics, policy, and rhetoric. They just wanted us all to get along. But hopes and dreams don't pay the bills. To raise funds, they converted the property into a tourist attraction. As I recalled from school trips to the establishment when I was a boy, it was more of a gift shop than anything, trading in the iconography of blackness throughout the decades, from baggy jeans and head wraps to big red wax lips and combs shaped like clouds. (Someone—maybe Sir—had told me that the combs were originally fist-shaped but the fists were outlawed by City ordinance. The idea of a comb shaped like a folded hand sounded like one of my father's typically dubious ideas. He had been a frequent purveyor of the big fish tale, a veritable fishmonger.)

The Musée was one of about a half-dozen places where Supercargo worked part time. Most of my cousin's jobs were like that. Fifteen hours here. Eight hours there. A graveyard shift when he could swing it.

Supercargo greeted us with a flurry of daps and hugs as soon as we entered. "Cuzzie," he said. "I never thought I'd see you up in here, but I'm glad you came. And you brought my man Jo Jo. Give me a second, y'all." He went behind the checkout counter and righted a discount sign. A group of tourists in hockey jerseys clustered around a turning rack. A brunette woman clutched a familiar-looking plush doll to her chest. I purchased a vanilla-crème-filled chocolate eclair from the patisserie. A dollop of that delicious, wholesome goop dropped onto my shoe. As I reached into my blazer for a handkerchief, I was suddenly taken over by nostalgia.

I picked up a doll that was identical to the one the brunette had held.

"What is that thing?" Jo Jo finished his baklava and wiped his hands on his pants. I gave him the doll. It was a representation of the civil rights leader—that former mayor I mentioned—Jacquelle Suhla, herself. It was clad in a gray pantsuit and brown bow tie. Of course, the doll's humanity was substituted for something more salable. An adorable monkey.

Some people thought the Suhla Monkeys were racist. But others believed they were a preemptive strike against bigoted minds. If we could transform our best leader into a marmoset, then what did it matter if certain people wondered if we blacks had tails that we tucked into our underwear? As for me, I found the monkeys cute. I'd had one when I was in grade school. It occupied a prime position in my childhood bedroom: hanging from a strap over my dresser mirror. Whatever happened to my monkey?

"How much?" the woman asked me. "This is the cutest thing. My niece will just love her."

"Well, I—"

"He doesn't work here," Jo Jo said.

"Everything is twenty percent off today, miss," Supercargo interrupted, pointing to a sign hanging from the rafters.

"You work here?" the woman asked. Supercargo said yes. "You have amazing hair." The woman's eyes widened. "May I?"

Supercargo offered a length of his dreads, which she stroked as a child in a petting zoo might.

"Such an earthy, soulful texture," the woman said, and wandered off to gather more swag.

Supercargo smiled at me. "It's better to meet her type in here than in a darkened alley. I'd never make it out alive." He flipped up the counter and stepped from behind it. "Come check out the hall. I'm glad you came, cuz. You too, Jo Jo." I palmed a tube of skin toning cream from a stack on the counter with the intent to purchase it later. Supercargo parted a beaded curtain.

"What, no secret handshake?" I asked.

"Would you know it if I asked, brother?" Supercargo asked.

"He's got a point." Jo Jo took a picture of Supercargo and me.

"So he does."

The hall was a simple, wood-paneled affair with metal folding chairs arranged in rows. At the front of the room, a microphone jutted from a podium. Affixed to the front of the podium, a placard said, BLIND! EQUALITY! NOW! A few people were already seated. I was no stranger to such rooms. When I was a boy, Sir had brought me to this lecture or that sermon. To protests and strategy sessions. To the inner sanctums of community, resistance, and struggle. Such events fit Sir like a well-worn pair of slippers. Regardless of the audience or location, he was always ready with a word of support for the cause, even when it wasn't clear what the cause was. After all, what was equality other than a typographical error in the Constitution?

Yes, the Founders had meant that all men were created equal, but they failed to include an index of defined terms. Ever since they drafted that screed, no one wanted to admit that Washington, Jefferson, and the rest of those guys meant only to protect the rights of white, landowning men. Through sloppy copyediting, our illustrious forefathers set off the human rights skirmishes that would beset the nation all the way to the present. If any of the seventy-plus delegates at the Constitutional Convention could have bothered to bring along a gray-wigged man of letters or even a lowly print shop owner, the document would have been clearer, so generations of people wouldn't have spent their lives dreaming of rights they were never meant to have, wrongheadedly attending protests, getting beaten or killed.

Had Sir tried to make me more like him, in visiting so many of these struggle spaces? He must have realized somewhere along the way that he'd failed. And how would he have felt about me bringing Jo Jo? Sir wasn't a racist. *The oppressed can't oppress, boy. That's like blaming the lobster for the temperature of the pot.* But he never met a white person he didn't have a problem with. Bringing Jo Jo into a historic inner sanctum such as the back room of the MdNA would have been like inviting the Sons of the Confederacy into a planning session of the original Million Man March all those decades ago. Every time I wondered what he would have made of Penny, I short-circuited the thought by trying to recall the name of Jacqueline Kennedy Onassis's black great-grandfather.

"Tyson?" I mumbled. "Jenson? Or was it great-great-grandfather?"

"What?" Jo Jo asked.

"Nothing," I said.

"I'm thinking of taking a trip up to Brooklyn—"

"To see Casey? That's not a great idea."

"She can't keep my kids away from me." I reminded Jo Jo that his ex-wife could indeed keep the boys away from him until his attorney, another law school classmate, managed to garner visitation rights for him. Against my advice, Jo Jo hadn't had representation during the divorce or custody hearings. Now it was up to his new lawyer to wrench him out of the hole he'd dug for himself. I sometimes questioned the plausibility of two people so deeply in love ending up as mortal enemies. Maybe love was just the larval stage of hate, the comely caterpillar in advance of the hideous butterfly.

I had come to the Musée with a simple plan: Join up with BEG. Maybe get Seasons to sponsor the organization's Christmas party. Then use Seasons's support of the race community's activities as one more arrow in the quiver next time Octavia and I made a run at the hospital.

I was surprised to see that at least a third of the room was white. After all, Supercargo, like Sir, was not above throwing up an occasional black power fist. I expected a room full of sixth-wave Black Panthers, but the gathering was a mix of people from various races and classes. Supercargo introduced us to a few people. A brother with surgically recolored blue eyes—it was easy to tell, the blue was too blue, the perfect, beautiful blue of a Midwestern sky—who drove streetcars. A woman who worked on the janitorial staff of the School Without Walls; she seemed perhaps Afro-Latina by her accent and medium-light brown skin, but her nose had a papery aspect to it, a telltale sign of early-process demelanistic reconstruction. A youngish white couple in dashikis. The Galton–van Riebeecks, Jan and Marie, I would later learn. Supercargo and Jo Jo fell into conversation with some of the others.

Near the back of the room, a man in a seersucker suit bent over a cardboard box and fiddled with the contents. That bald head. That almond skin tone. My mind served up an image of the same man bent over at Octavia's mansion, rubbing Armbruster's gnarly, waxen feet. He recognized me as soon I recognized him.

"Riley," I said.

He placed one fist on a hip, a standard Riley pose. "Well, if it isn't the boy who lived," he said, his weight shifting from foot to foot. He was a beast in doubles. "Give me some!" He threw both arms around me and gave me a lingering, almost tender hug. "How are things on the Great White Way?" He covered his mouth and glanced around with exaggerated sheepishness like someone from one of those historical *Wayans Bros.* clips. "I shouldn't say things like that, especially around here, but I've had it rough since they fired me, and I'm dying to know if the place has burned to the ground yet. Least they deserve." Riley told me he had gotten his pink slip as soon as he came in the morning after Elevation Night. He'd made a few calls and snatched a teaching job at Nigel's school. "School pay is godawful, but there's a little less intrigue, as you can imagine."

A clot of schadenfreude rose up the back of my throat. Riley had always been a social climber with an air of superiority about himself. It was funny to see him humbled to a profession that society deemed hardly as important as street sweeper, given the pay scale. But I felt a twinge of shame. I couldn't deny that I missed him at the firm. He usually knew what was going to happen before the rest of us associates did, and he shared information freely. Beyond that, he could be a good guy, even selfless. Like the time he took me to lunch and explained all of Octavia's expectations and pet peeves.

"You always did land on your feet," I said.

"That's me," he said, "part pussy cat."

"How's my kid doing?"

"Oh. We get along eminently, but he's on a different schedule, so I don't see him much." Riley cupped my elbow. "Listen. You really shouldn't be here."

"That's no way to welcome an old buddy."

Riley's face suddenly darkened, and he punched my shoulder hard. "I'm serious." His face went back to normal as a couple walked over. "Have you met Marie and Jan? They're two of BEG's biggest benefactors."

"No." I rubbed my shoulder.

"That was before our diamond stocks plummeted," Marie said. She grabbed my forearm. "I thought he'd be blacker."

"Yeah," Jan held out a pale hand next to my dark one. "We're more African than you."

How much shock registered on my face? Did my eyes bug? Did my tongue loll in my open mouth? Supercargo pointed at me. Jo Jo chuckled. So did the Galton–van Riebeecks.

"They're from Namibia," Riley said.

A short sister in a pantsuit entered. I'd seen her on television. She was the granddaughter of Suhla, the former mayor.

"Oh, baby," Riley said. "Zora doesn't look happy." I shrugged my shoulders interrogatively.

"Funding issues," Marie said. "The City keeps futzing around with the grant allocations. They keep the organization on a tight leash so we don't escape from the yard."

"Don't look at me," Riley said. "My contacts in the City Finance Department don't return my calls now that I don't have that Seasons Ustis Malveaux shine."

Supercargo gave Riley a nasty look, then showed me to a seat near the front of the room. The Galton–van Riebeecks sat behind me. Supercargo played MC and called Zora to the podium. She said a prayer, her wide, open face turned up to the fluorescent lights. I found a meeting agenda on the seat next to me. I scanned it. There were slots for old business. Marie oversaw BEG's fundraising. Intake was up. Supercargo was the recruiting coordinator. New member enrollment was down, but hopefully my presence was a sign of change. Then the testimonials started. The streetcar driver spoke in stilted terms about the value of everyone coming together and "rolling along the same track." The janitorial woman said we shouldn't fear "sweeping changes" because sometimes you have to "clean the mess out and start from fresh." It was Supercargo's turn up.

"Y'all know we been working a long time for the dream. We trying to bring our community together in a new way, a permanent way." Some people nodded. "It's been a long time coming, but I can feel that we turning a corner. Our protests at the hospital have been making a difference. People are paying attention and hear our message."

A few in the room clapped. But not everyone. For instance, the janitor wrung her hands, while the streetcar driver stared straight ahead. The Galton–van Riebeecks, though, clapped vigorously. "And now ain't the time to back down or let up. I don't know about y'all, but I ain't about to back down. I don't even know how." Another smattering of appreciation. "But I ain't going to run on because I want y'all to hear a word from my best cousin. He a good dude. He really is." Light applause.

I didn't move. They couldn't make me move. If I just sat, eventually they would move on to other business. It was a familiar fear, always present the moment just before I spoke in court. In that moment, I considered the possibility of failure, of humiliation. Jan tapped my shoulder, and I popped up like a piece of burned toast.

Supercargo took the seat I had vacated. More light applause. Jo

Jo snapped shots of me in rapid succession. I tried to clear my throat, but there seemed to be a gigantic ball of wet, warm cat hair lodged in my esophagus. Somehow the audience took this as cause to clap harder. I didn't want to argue in favor of the protests at PHH. I liked the work PHH did. After all, I would be sending Nigel there soon enough. And how could the BEG be anti-demelanization when at least three people other than the streetcar driver and janitor had obviously undergone procedures?

But then I remembered why I was there. I needed to build a foundation that Octavia could relaunch her PHH campaign from. If I could convince the group to accept me as one of their own, I would quickly move up the ranks. They would vouch for me when the time came. Along the way, I would make sure there were plenty of photos documenting my place—Seasons's place—in the movement. Eckstein wouldn't be able to say we had no commitment to the black community. We would *be* the community.

I employed a technique I learned back in law school. I placed my hands on either side of the podium, firmly gripping the edges. I spaced my feet shoulder-width apart. I took three deep breaths. This trick was given to me by my mentor at the University of Alabama Law School, a beautiful sister called Mimi LaVon of Chicago, who was two years ahead of me. Mimi's technique grounded me in times when it seemed like the whole planet was vibrating on an untenable frequency.

"Brothers and sisters," I said, "there is a black cloud over our city. A wave of darkness that threatens to wipe away our identity. We've all seen the nefarious work being carried out at the shadowy clinic. The thinning of lips. The whittling down of noses. The whitening of skin."

"You tell it," Marie said. Several people leaned forward in their seats. Jo Jo clapped a little too loud—I didn't know he cared. I wasn't quite sure what to say next, so I used Penny—that is, a word salad of things she had said at one time or another—to make the point.

"And for what purpose? To divide us. Now is the time for us to prove to our fellow citizens the value of self-love. The value of accepting one another as we are." I pulled my monogrammed handkerchief from the inside of my jacket and wiped my forehead, then my cheek, as I had seen my pastor do in the church my parents brought me to before it was condemned. An eclair crumb lodged in the corner of my lip. I ate it. Chocolate. "My dear brothers and sisters. Countless people have climbed this mountain before us. Countless have suffered indignity and even death to open this path. But today we have reached the other side and find a valley filled to the brim with the briars of iniquity. It's up to us to chop down those briars, to clean out the vestiges of a caste system based on the color of our skin!"

At the last line, I pounded the podium. The room rose to its feet in response, as if I'd just brought down the hammer at a state fair, and they were the puck. Everyone clapped, even Mr. Streetcar and Janitoria. Except for Riley, who remained seated with his arms folded. But never mind him. There was an electric vibration inside me as they chanted my name. Supercargo led me from behind the podium. People grabbed my hands, hugged me, kissed my cheeks.

"I guess this means you in," Supercargo said.

"You reckon?" I asked.

16

Nigel had too many birthmarks to count. If this fact surprises you, it's because I've done a poor job of describing the true wingspan of the albatross hanging around my dear boy's neck.

I knew the blot on his face greeted him in the display cases of the School Without Walls. I knew he saw his defect in the black mirrors of electronic devices. I knew his stain was apparent in the barely disguised reactions of strangers who had been smiling the moment before they recognized his defect.

I won't take you through all the myriad incidents that we—that's him as a boy, me as a boy, and us in our patrilineal relationship—experienced in the course of events. It would be impossible to do so. But I could randomly flip through my journal, a Big Chief Bigboote tablet where I kept a written record of all the indignities my son and I experienced.

Memories could be questioned, distorted, forgotten. But a transcript could not. The physical act of remembering is a bulwark against insanity. Against the possibility that the insidious big white machine exists only in my head and in the heads of similarly delusional persons. That the big white machine's carcinogenic pheromones and countless rows of razor-sharp teeth are the result of indigestion, a bad Plum, an inferior mind. In any event, my written journal was far more secure for posting these thoughts than some digital cloud where Uncle Sam, Anonymous, or God could get their talons on them.

I'm seated now under an Adansonia looking at a page that I opened to by chance. Here are notes from a long-past outing: It's the summer before Elevation Night. An ideal Saturday afternoon. A well-maintained, semipublic pool. Only a five-minute stroll from our house. To get in, I showed the desk clerk my neighborhood association card. Then he asked for my federal ID, which he held up to the light. We wetted ourselves in the exterior shower. Matching swim trunks purchased by Penny. Blue field with Captain America shields in an orderly pattern. Deck chairs mostly occupied. Pool active, but not crowded. Nigel and me not the only ones like us. A black family already splashing around in the shallow end. Joyous and common like any family at any pool on any hot day anywhere. But even I wonder where they came from. Lifeguard hunches on his perch. Stares at them. They ain't done nothing. The lifeguard ain't done nothing. But I staple my eyes to the scene. And that's something. The act of observing rewrites reality.

Nigel swims back from the deep end. A strong swimmer. Water streams over his small back like encouragement.

He climbs out. "I think somebody spilled soda in the pool." He sticks out his tongue, flicks water from his face. "What?" he says.

I grab his shoulder and spin him around. That dark medallion of skin on his tummy is bigger. Nigel's other blemishes cover his body. The greatest concentration of marks: belly and back. A dark asterism. Some flaws approach the size and complexity of the stigma on his face. Some discolorations have undergone transmutations similar to the facial mark. Some even seem to have moved over time from one hemisphere of his body to another. My fear is that these islands will merge to form a continent. The lesser smudges, they're just ordinary freckles. But what image would emerge if I traced those dots? His mother's face? Our home? A playground viewed from a hilltop? But there I go again being melodramatic with a capital dramatic.

"Maybe I should go home with them." Nigel nodded toward the black family. "I bet they're really nice people." My boy's mark humor, his scar-chasm.

"No," I say. "You're all mine."

After my speech at the Musée, and after I dropped off Jo Jo, I drove home, mentally mulling over Nigel's blemishes as I pulled in to our driveway. I brought the Bug so close to Penny's minivan's rear bumper that my vehicle seemed to be puckering for a kiss. Inside our house, Penny was swabbing her decks and battening down her hatches, so she could shove off for her shift at the hospital. I'm being too coy. Have I mentioned the giddiness I inevitably felt watching my wife prepare for her day? She stood, leaning slightly over the bathroom sink, on tiptoes. My girl. I'll spare the reader my X-rated thoughts. But I'll confess that they involved a lightning-quick reimaging of the Rapunzel myth, which, of course, is nothing more than a prudish allegory about sexual desire and climbing with one's lover to orgasmic heights.

Actually, whenever I think back to that time and Penny's pre-work prep, I'm drawn to an entirely different fantasy. One where animated nightingales float down through the skylight to land on her shoulder. A white rabbit scurries up from a hole in the hardwood to say, "You're late. Hurry up. Get your sun shades. Because it's bright and you're late!"

"Ground Control to husband." Penny pinched my cheek.

"What?" I asked.

"You were off planet again." Penny crossed into the closet and grabbed a jacket. "Nigel does the same thing. How was the museum thingy?"

"Weird," I said, "but that's to be expected with anything Supercargo is into."

"Well, I'm glad you went, even if it was work-related," Penny said tersely. That tone had been entering her voice more and more since I told her about my assignment as the Face of Seasons.

"You should spend more time with your cousin anyway. He adores you."

"I guess. How's the kid?"

"In his room. There's something different about him lately. He didn't want to help in the kitchen just now."

"It's a hard age." I leaned in for a kiss.

"Just talk to him." Penny bopped my nose. "There's Tater Tot casserole in the oven."

Nigel's room was situated in such a way that the sunlight poured in during the morning. But by late afternoon, as our snow globe city spun away from the sun, his chamber grew dark. It was his habit to spend entire weekend afternoons on his bed reading classics or doodling in his sketch pad or playing with his device if he was very bored. The world shadowed around him. He never bothered with the lights.

Nigel's position was usually such that, standing in the long hallway, I could silently watch him without being noticed. An invasion of privacy? Yes. A little creepy? Prolly. But doesn't every parent do this in some fashion or other? Don't we all feel that some substantial portion of our essence has made its way into the child? In this sense, the voyeuristic parent is really watching herself and hoping for some revelation. Or at least a tip.

I had seen all the seasons of our child's life: the winter he stacked a set of alphabet blocks to spell *safe* even though he was surely too young to know what that word meant; the spring he ran a remote-control school bus into a crowd of action figures and, seeing the horror of his actions, gathered the figures in his arms and laid them under bedsheets to recuperate; the fall he pulled one of my hats over his eyes and shadowboxed an invisible gang.

Now Nigel lay on his bed, a sketch pad open before him. In small, cramped strokes, he created something I couldn't make out.

Nigel glanced at me. "Dad," he said in a way that was both cheerful and wary. He swept the pad closed.

"What you got there?" I asked.

"Nothing. Just drawings."

"Can I see?"

Nigel pulled the pad away from me. "That's okay."

The truth is I knew precisely what was inside. It was the latest iteration of a comic Nigel had ginned up years before during a particularly difficult time in our household. Our caped hero was a stand-in for my boy, of course. A kind of Nig-El. The baddie was a weasel-faced villain he called the Fascist Fedora, who went around forcing the citizens of Sun City to wear super fancy hats: top hats and bonnets, derbies and Gainsboroughs, etc. This didn't bother me. The family organizational chart listed me as "father, breadwinner, protector, role model." The part about me as a best bud was somewhere in the addendum.

"I brought you something. Take off your shirt." I said. Nigel sat on his haunches in bed but didn't take off his shirt. I showed him the tube I'd gotten from the Musée.

"Super extra strength," I said. It was bad enough that skin toning cream was relatively hard to find within the City excluding the Tiko, which I avoided for reasons already described. Even within the Tiko, so much of what I found was watered down. Lower percentages of active ingredient. The jar of Madame C.J.'s that Penny chucked off the steps of Nigel's school was an example of the lower-quality product. But not J.B.'s Whitener. It was the skin-toning equivalent of acetone.

"I don't want to," Nigel said.

"Don't be that way," I said. "We'll go out for ice cream after. Won't that be great? Maybe head over to the bowling alley."

"I just don't want to."

"Why not?"

"It stinks, and it stings." I knew that Nigel was right on both counts. I had, many moons earlier, smeared some J.B.'s on the right side of my torso over the ribs. It smelled faintly of sulfur and burned worse than an analgesic. The next morning there was a faint patch of reddened skin that seemed somewhat lighter if viewed under the powerful light of the vanity from a certain angle. I never used the cream again because I recognized how silly I was to try it. I would have had to dive into a pool of the ointment to fix my skin. I was too dark all over. A full body stain.

But even with my personal experience, I knew Nigel wanted the cream. How did I know? Because he held the hem of his shirt between his thumb and index. I knew my son.

Of course, we had discussed this before. We didn't have to during those times when he relented without comment. But during other times, I had to remind him of where I was coming from. Of whose side I was on in the war we were fighting.

"Why do we do this?" I asked.

"So that I can get better," he mumbled, sounding for all the world like his five-year-old self, that being the first time we did this.

"And what happens when you're better?"

"We won't have to do it anymore."

"There are dark things and light ones, and you're the very best thing in the world." I threw my arm over his shoulder. "You know I love you, right? One day this will all be in the rearview."

Nigel nodded. The edges of his eyes were wet. Such a sensitive boy. But my eyes were wet, too. Empathetic me. Nigel removed his shirt and his shorts. My son in intermezzo. The interplay of his light skin and dark spots brought to mind the *stracciatella* in the freezer. I stretched a latex glove onto my hand and let go with a *snap*.

Now, I'm perfectly aware of the judgmental thoughts running through your head as you read these words. I suspect your pupils have dilated, your lips are agape, your heart filled with venom toward me. But let me make an attempt to clarify my position as this is neither the time nor the place for the mincing of words or slightest prevarication of any kind.

I am a unicorn. I can read and write. I have all my teeth. I've read Plato, Woolf, Nikki Giovanni, and Friend. I've never been to jail. I've voted in every election since I was eighteen. I finished high school. I finished college. I finished law school. I pay taxes. I don't have diabetes, high blood pressure, or the *itis*. If you randomly abduct a hundred black men from the streets of the City and deposit us into a gas chamber, I will be the only one who fits this profile. I will be the only one who survives. Is it because I'm better than the other ninety-nine? No. It's because I'm lucky, and I know it. Somehow the grinding effects of a world built to hurt me have not yet eliminated my every opportunity for a happy life, as is the case for so many of my brethren. The world is a centrifuge that patiently waits to separate my Nigel from his basic human dignity. I don't have to tell you that this is an unjust planet.

A dark-skinned child can expect a life of diminished light. This is truth anywhere in the world and throughout most of history. But let's stick to the Home of the Free. Place young Jamal on an all-white basketball team, and guess who will get ejected from the game more often for normal rambunctious behavior? Give a hiring manager a stack of applications. Let him choose between an equally qualified Jamal, Jane, or Jonathan. See Jamal waiting at the unemployment office. Again. (Admittedly, none of these examples are particularly shocking, and I fear that I risk insulting your intelligence, dear reader, but ride with me awhile longer.)

See Jamal evicted from his apartment. See Jamal arrested for vagrancy. See Jamal mysteriously die in a transport van on the way to the City jail. A brief interlude of cursing the heavens. Resurrect Jamal with lightning. Smoke. Sparks. The smell of burning cocoa butter. Put a toy gun in Jamal's hand in an open-carry state. Wait for Jane or Jonathan to call the police due to a "suspicious-looking black guy." See the cavalry show up and scalp Jamal. No questions asked. Jane is heartbroken for the tragic misapprehension of the situation, she says over a pumpkin spice latte, as Jonathan bites the tip off a double chocolate biscotti.

I have a natural aversion to numbers and statistics, as they can be manipulated by any reactionary with an agenda. But that doesn't change the objective fact that prospects for African Americans have devolved even since my grandparents' time. Black women make thirty cents for every dollar a white man does, and 90 percent of black moms are single mothers. Unemployment among black males is the norm, not the exception, and nine out of ten brothers have done time. And virtually none of us black guys and dolls can vote since felons and the children of felons need a voucher from an upstanding citizen to earn a voting pass. (Jo Jo was mine.)

None of that even takes into account the fact that every black person is a de facto enemy of the state. They used to call bringing every able-bodied black male to jail for questioning racial profiling. Now it's called excellent police work. Did I mention that blacks in most major cities live in fenced-in ghettos just like the Tiko? There may be beauty in my blackness and dignity in the struggle of my people, but I won't allow my son to live a life of diminished possibility. I see a constellation of opportunity that those of my ilk rarely travel to. I see my Nigel at the center of those stars.

This reraises the question I've occasionally concerned myself with during Nigel's life: What if I can ensure that my boy is not perceived as a black man? What if he is simply a man?

"Ah." Nigel winced. Did I enjoy using the noxious stuff on my son? Of course not. What parent likes to see their baby cry at the barber or squirm beneath the dentist's drill? But weaker creams weren't effective.

As for Penny, she loved our son as much as a person could. She gave more hugs. She provided more words of encouragement. She was the practical one, the reason Nigel got all his shots on schedule and never missed a day of school. But what did my amazing, considerate wife know of the unseen slights our son experienced, the monstrous episodes so internally disturbing that our doomed boy would never tell anyone—not Penny, not even me—about? Still,

I didn't have to hear words to understand. Wasn't I also among the marked?

He stood in front of his bed in skivvies while the cream dried into his skin. I couldn't have him rolling around and spreading it on his bedsheets. Even the milder version stained.

"Last spot," I said. "Close 'em tight." He shut his eyes. This was the most important part of the care. But also the trickiest. The tarnished skin around his eye was naturally quite tender. And then there were the delicate membranes nearby. I had to use finesse. I squeezed a teardrop's worth onto my purple-gloved pinky and gingerly applied the unction. I was nearly done when Nigel flinched.

"Keep still," I said.

"Ah!" he said. "It burns."

"Hold on."

"Dammit. Stop!" He grabbed my hand, roughly.

"Ow," I said.

For a moment, Nigel glared at me with one eye clamped shut. He let go. He went for the open door. All along his back, blotches of white cream gleamed like gems.

I had talked with the parents of older kids about the transition to teenagedom. Nigel was on the cusp of that ever-expanding dark interior world. Even in moments of small rebellion, there had always been an agreement that he was not the final arbiter of his own life. But I could tell that my job of preparing him for the best of all possible worlds had just gotten harder.

In the second bathroom, Nigel ran the sink. In the kitchen, I tied off a garbage bag containing the soiled latex gloves. I opened the door and ran the overhead fan. I couldn't leave any evidence in the house for Penny to find. As I walked outside to the garbage can, the white sack dangling from my fingers, I heard something like Nigel's laughter from back inside my home.

17

Those were the times when I thought about Sir locked away in his rusty prison cage. Sir, whom I had only spoken to once since his arrest, when Mama had, after some considerable prodding, convinced me to see him in his new native captivity, a visit the three of us would come to regret.

But it wasn't that encounter that came to mind now. What I recalled was a family reunion we attended when I was a precocious preteen, just before Sir's arrest. Ours was a large family, although the great body of us lived in the state next door or the state next to that one. I'm excluding the overhanging branch, our distant light-skinned cousins; those yellowish leaves had grown in California valleys for generations. They never showed up for anything.

The reunion was an especially auspicious gathering as it marked my grandfather's ninety-ninth birthday, which would turn out to be his last, as he would die suddenly a few days later. I didn't know him very well, in part because he sired Sir late in life, shortly before abandoning my sainted, deceased grandmother and moving to the country. He and Sir didn't get along.

He was a scary guy to young me. In retrospect, I had no good reason to fear the man, who worked multiple jobs until his eighties. But also, in retrospect, I realized that my fear had something to do with my father's attitude toward him ("He's just another wog") and with the clothes he wore when not working: stiff-billed snap-back caps, baggy white T-shirts, baggy blue or black jeans that slouched low on his waist and occasionally below his butt. In other words, he dressed like an old-timey thug. In still other words, I was scared because I was supposed to feel scared, in the same way that one is jokingly terrified of a faux-blood-covered man in a haunted house. As I grew older, I recognized the ridiculousness of my position and, that day, consciously tried to correct my attitude and treat him as if we'd gone crabbing every summer of my young life.

"Do you feel ninety-nine, old man?" I knelt next to him, in the respectful way that I had seen some of the grown men—my cousins and half-uncles—do, with my forearm resting against the side of his wheelchair. The metal frame felt like ice against my skin.

"Every bit of it, caterpillar. Every one of those years was a different problem. And now those problems done piled up on top of me. Hurts to move. Hurts to breathe. They shove a hose up my Johnson so's I can pee. I'm just about done with all this. This world been too many for me. I had dreams when I was an up-and-comer—"

He stared out at the reunion. We were on a park knoll in the state next door, where he lived. From the knoll, it was easy to watch the family, the many dozens of us, on the field below gathered around grill pits, playing bid whist at picnic tables, boys tackling each other with a contraband football, old ladies praying hand in hand. My parents had walked to the small promontory by the lake and were making their way back, two shadows beneath the evergreens.

On the opposite end of the green, a trio of state troopers, in their black armbands and Stetson hats, observed our gathering. The white lights on their interceptors blinked slowly and out of sequence.

"I'll tell you something, lil shorty." He put his hand on my forearm. His skin was wrinkled, but not as much as I would have expected. And his fingernails were as large and clear as if each were a window into his body. "I tell you this because you special even iffen you too young to feel me." He leaned toward me. "You listening?" I nodded. "Peep this. I spent my whole existence working for white folk, and I did good for myself and all of you. I was a chef for forty-five years at the Wallace National Golf Club. I worked odd jobs to make ends meet. I been an under-the-table butcher 'cause I ain't have no certification papers. I worked nights at Loafer's making French bread for fancy restaurants all over the South. I been a chandler, too. I tell you to watch out for them though." He squeezed my wrist. His eyes popped. "White people ain't no more evil than the next man, and don't let nobody tell you they are. But white folk radioactive, too. Because they got the top card and always will. 'Cause they glow in the dark, they can't help but hurt you like what make cancer. You get me?"

I didn't nod, but I didn't shake my head either. I froze. Clearly, my grandfather's brain was infected by devils.

He turned me to face him and gestured with his hands. "We like snails at a parade, and they tossing salt from the floats. Onliest thing you can do to shut it off is to use guilt for your umbrella. Guilt them into respecting you. When I die, tell 'em a Klan man killed your old grandpa. Tell 'em whatever you want to keep them off your back. Make them feel like they owe you something. Shame 'em to death. It's the only way you'll make it with them in this world, believe me, I tried. Self-respect will be your end."

"Time to go," Sir said.

My grandfather seemed to suddenly deflate, as though Sir's presence sapped his strength. Grandpa stuttered when he spoke, and his hand shook. "Y'all raising this boy right," he said. "He going to be a real gentleman."

I stood and went to Sir's side.

"You would know." Sir rubbed his elbow patch. We had driven

straight over from the college where he taught, so he was still in his sweater vest and blazer. Not that he would have changed clothes. That was his standard look.

Mama rubbed Sir's shoulder. Her flowy orange and brown top fluttered in the breeze. "Thank you, Mr. Ben. You look hip with your Kings hat."

"You so sweet, honey," Grandpa said. "I wish y'all would bring this boy around more."

Mama said something affirmative. But Sir muttered, "Not a chance."

"What was Mr. Ben talking about?" Mama asked when we were a distance away.

"Nothing," I said.

"I didn't have to overhear to know," Sir said. "He was trying to turn his head into a landfill. But the facility was closed, right, son?" I nodded absentmindedly.

As we walked, Sir placed a hand on the back of my neck. "You understand the importance of personal pride, and you certainly understand that life's rewards come from knowing you're as good as anyone else, as important."

My grandfather was still seated in his chair on the knoll. Some family girls brought him a second helping of sweet potato cake, his favorite.

"You listening, son?" Mama asked.

"Yes, Sir," I said. "I mean, yes."

18

It turned out that Jan Galton–van Riebeeck, the white guy in the dashiki, was BEG's director of strategic initiatives, one of the few paid positions in the organization. This meant he was linked into all things BEG. If I could impress him with my dedication to the group, then he would explain things that a peon like Supercargo wouldn't know. Organizational structure, current methods, future plans. He would roll out the carpet so I'd know exactly where to walk.

Several days following my induction, I left the office early and met up with Jan and Riley at the organization's downtown satellite office, an old book depository. The office was tiny—only two small rooms and a closet full of crabbing buckets—but it was to be used at my leisure once Jan cleaned the cobwebs out of the space— and my mind. We were going over BEG's core tenets, which had been developed and deployed by our forebears, most of whom were lost to history.

On the table before me lay a half-dozen pastel pamphlets with cartoony figures of many skin tones—including jaundice yellow and fabulous magenta—holding hands, hugging, or ululating. One sloppily drawn figure probably should have been pointing his finger at his heart. However, the errant digit angled toward his head. "We're All the Same Where It Counts," the thought bubble read.

Jan chewed a plastic straw and paced. Riley stood over me with his arms folded over his olive suit vest.

"Okay," Jan said. "Now, what does it mean?"

"It means that regardless of a person's skin—"

"No, wait." Jan stopped walking. He took off his round glasses and pinched the bridge of his nose.

"We just went over this." Riley turned from me to Jan. "I don't think you even understand what we're all about."

"Give him a chance," Jan said. He sat on the edge of the desk across from me.

"It's simple. You've got to stop thinking of America in racialized terms." Jan wiggled his fingers. "Race is nothing more than an idea, like city-states or heaven. Whenever you call me white and yourself black, you're falling into a trap laid by bigots. We've got to ignore race to transcend it!"

"He won't get it," Riley said.

"Hey, take it easy," I said. Ever since that day at the Musée, Riley had been brusque with me. I couldn't tell whether it was because of envy that I'd outlasted him at the firm or anger that I'd moved in on his territory within BEG.

"Let's take a break." Jan grabbed his page boy cap and took a smoke break. Riley took a phone call—"I'll have that shocker good to go in a couple days, hun," he said. I took a spot at the window. HI! HOW ARE YOU? a billboard said. These New Truth advertisers and their gimmicks. This whole situation took me by surprise. A drizzle fell, silver sheening the streets of the business district. A green and white banner flapped.

Of course, I knew the theory that race was a figment. Who didn't? Sir himself had explained it to me when I was about nine, while mocking his department head at the university.

We were in our living room–den–kitchen in the Tiko. Sir paced back and forth by the open window. Mama sat at the table with me, eating lemon petits fours while I gorged on a slice of home-made chocolate cake and milk.

". . . and she had the nerve to get upset with me." Sir gestured at his chest. "Called me a Cro-Magnon. I may be an iconoclast scofflaw, but I'm a thoroughly modern iconoclast scofflaw." Sir sipped his to-go coffee, which had been sitting on the open win-dowsill. "And another thing—"

Mama stopped him by raising her pinky. "You ever stop to think she might have a point?" She bit another petit four, her dan-gly earring swaying as she chewed. Her right ear was bare. Her earrings were perpetually escaping and turning up in unexpected places.

"Not you too, Sadie."

I laughed.

"Oh, you think I'm funny, young man?" Sir held his coffee cup toward me. "Thy tongue outvenoms all the worms of Nile."

"Thou art a villain," I said. I wasn't as versed in Shakespearean insults as he was. I hadn't taught a class on it. I was only nine.

Mama waved him off. "I'm saying some people think too much about it. It gets like weeds choking off the good growth."

He rubbed his hand across the side of his prematurely graying hair. "Listen, Magee won't have a point when I hammer a stake into her heartless heart."

I snorted milk out of my nose.

"You like that one, huh?" Sir wiggled his eyebrows.

"See that?" Mama slapped the table. "Knew I was right."

"What?" Sir asked.

"You only think about violence when you losing the argu-ment."

"I do n—" Sir shook his head and smiled, his signature grin, sheepish and glowing at the same time. Sir and Mama had been high school sweethearts. They knew each other's ticks and tells. "Yeah. Well. Just because I'm losing doesn't mean I'm wrong. I could lose all day and still win." Sir folded his arms. Just when his hands came to rest under his armpits, a muted thud came from across the common outside the window. "Get down!"

Mama grabbed my arm and pulled me under the table. We lay on the spotless floor, which Sir mopped every night before he bedded down. Sir was on his belly ten feet away, his eyes locked on us, commanding that we not move until the coast was clear. The wake of Mama's breath hit my ear, and out of the silence came the sound of distant firecrackers—gunshots, a flurry of them so fast that had the police been aiming at a paper target, the target would have instantly vaporized.

"Not yet," Sir said. *Pock pock*. The sound of a small gun at close range. His shoulders loosened.

Mama got up.

"Wait," Sir said. "We don't know if—"

But Mama was already on her feet and headed to the window. Her socks whiffed across the tile. Sir wasn't about to let her look on without him. I went over. At windows all over the Tiko, people, their faces terrifyingly angelic from the amber ground lights, glanced down on the entrance to Building Seven where a group of Anti-Violence Task Force police—heavily armed and armored— streamed out of the doorway like a long muscular centipede.

I was used to hearing the voices of women screaming after these incidents. But there was no screaming. Whoever had been in that apartment, whatever their gender or age or employment, was dead now.

"That ain't right," a woman's voice said. It was Ms. Wendy Woods, in her hotel maid's uniform, bulling her way through a collapsible barricade. "That ain't even much right!" A man, Bowman, the street sweeper driver who had been courting Ms. Wendy Woods for decades, followed and begged her to come back. One of the police officers' helmet lights swept across the cement and landed on her face, which I couldn't see from my angle at the window.

"Wendy!" Mama said, and Ms. Wendy Woods looked back. The helmet light turned red. Something pierced my bare foot, Mama's missing earring, a golden scythe.

I jumped in place when Riley grabbed my shoulder. A fire truck passed below the window. The truck cast light—red-white-red—against the rain-soaked nearby offices. No siren.

"Maybe you can get it," Riley said. "Who knows? But you think I don't know what you're up to? I know all the plays, baby. You feel like being here is good résumé padding, but you need to step off that right away. BEG is all about the UNITY. You're part of the problem we're trying to fix." He spoke under his breath while gesturing toward the world beneath the window. The marble plaza steps of the Sky Tower, like the terraced pages of an open book, were just in view.

"I didn't hear you complaining when you thought you were about to be promoted," I said.

Riley sneered. "And since when do you care about human rights anyway? This whole thing seems like a put-on." He crossed his arms. "I changed, okay? Some things are more important than a bigger paycheck."

"Would you feel better if he did his trial by ordeal today?" Jan asked.

"My what?"

"In this slop?" A slow smile spread across Riley's snout. "That's the best idea you've had all year, Janbo."

Apparently, trial by ordeal was a requirement of membership in BEG instituted after Suhla's failed reign as mayor and BEG leader, after the Teleprompter Massacre where a school full of black children and teachers were gunned down by a half-dozen white nationalist crazies, two of whom were black. The City went nuts about then. Suhla was jailed for the protests she had led in the past, which were characterized as riots, riots that led to the police leveling several city blocks where activists had holed up. I'd seen the photos. It astounded me how much damage a barrel bomb from a drone could do.

The organization was nearly disbanded by decree, but instead a placeholder leader was installed. One of the jobs of the caretaker was to lower the temperature of discourse among the City's people. One way to do that was to encourage members to get out into a community that was increasingly dismissive and fearful. If a potential member could go out into the City streets and spread BEG's message without getting beaten, arrested, or shot, then they were BEG material. Trial by ordeal.

Riley had stuck a BEG sticker—block-printed white letters on a black background—to my chest. My job was easy enough, on its face: hand out one hundred pamphlets in one hour. I stood at the corner of Avenue and Planter Street, an umbrella vibrating in one hand, a sheaf of pamphlets tucked under my other arm. Drizzle swirled.

"Excuse me," I said to a group of well-dressed white women walking toward the river where that Myrtles mall was. If I could convince the seven women to take a pamphlet, I'd be almost 10 percent to goal. BEG had a handful of approved introductory statements. One for every occasion, including women who looked like they were returning to the salon after only twenty-four hours away. "Ladies, have you considered that your children and my children were created equal under the Constitution?"

I was greeted by dismissive hand waves. A man in a business suit—similar to my own—didn't respond to my line that equality was good for the bottom line. A group of tourists in cowboy hats crossed to the other side of the street. One of the men kept his hand near his six-shooter.

And that was how it went for the better part of an hour. Meanwhile BEG's office windows were in view a hundred yards away. Blond Jan stood in one, dark Riley in the other. Like a pair of mismatched irises.

I noted a red smudge on the ground that I would come to learn was all that remained of a homeless black who had illegally camped at the corner of the Sky Tower for some time. A black eventually identified as a former employee of a local firm. It was unknown whether he worked in facilities management or cleaning services.

"What are you doing?" a man asked. He was blond and skinny, like he could have been one of Jan or Jo Jo's cousins. He wore City maintenance overalls.

"Sir," I said. "What is your name?"

"No, thanks."

"Have you considered that the best way to fix our future is to come together as one American people?"

He glanced at my sticker. "Oh. You're one of those guys." He turned away.

"Don't let me scare you off."

"I'm not scared. I'm just not interested." He walked. I fell into step next to him.

"Please take one of these." I flapped a pamphlet at him.

"I don't want one."

"What's your name?" As it turned out, we shared the same surname. I jogged around in front of him. "Please please please please please take one."

"What's it to you?"

"Do I have to get down on one knee?" I asked.

The man raised an eyebrow.

He was halfway down the street to the shuttle that ferried workers to the suburbs. A pamphlet jutted out of his back pocket. My pant leg was wet, and my knee somewhat bruised, but I had found an effective technique. After ten minutes of groveling, I was empty-handed.

19

Another day. I cut out of the firm early to visit the Nzinga Clinic because Jan and even Riley were pleased with my results from the trial by ordeal. After I'd given out all the brochures, one insistent couple even followed me back to the BEG satellite office to get their own. Jan said I could consider the satellite office my domain. I'd receive further instructions soon. That's why I was at Nzinga's. I'd just jumped from the backroads to the highway. It was time to map the final route to Nigel's future.

The clinic was in the medical annex adjacent to Personal Hill Hospital. Sitting in Dr. Nzinga's waiting room, the short medical tower where Penny worked was clearly visible. Fourth floor, northeast corner. I could feel her in there. Her heartbeat. Her breath. I was sure the hairs on the back of her neck stood up just then.

In the foyer was a maquette of a proposed massive new clinic large enough to service the City for generations to come. I imagined Dr. Nzinga, that tall, noble dark-skinned—but not too dark-skinned—man, somehow still practicing at the age of 101, holding the hand of my future granddaughter and telling her that life would eventually improve.

I see you have your grandfather's nose. Do not worry. It is easily resected.

Life did eventually improve. But hope wasn't enough. You had to work at it.

In the distance, the Sky Tower roof floated beneath milky clouds.

I had visited the clinic once before on my original fact-finding mission. That time the waiting room was populated by all kinds of people: a girl with a partially corrected cleft palate, a large-bellied man, a redhead in cycling clothes. I had quickly downloaded the demelanization brochure (only available if you stopped into the clinic) but accepted a couple of brochures about varicose vein correction to cover myself and giddily ran out. This time everyone was black (and half of the room wore purple faux-fur coats). This time I checked in at the counter and took my seat in a far corner with my back to the wall like a mafioso. I needed to meet Dr. Nzinga. I needed to tell him about my intentions for Nigel.

"Hey, brother," the man next to me said. It was the streetcar driver from the Musée. The one with the stained blue eyes. "You here for a scrub, too, huh? What you looking to have done? Nose? Lips? You got some real repugnant back-to-Africa lips, for sure. Need to trim them shits down."

"I'm just here for work," I said.

"Makes sense." The man sipped a can of P. Cola, the can's pulsing blue a color I always found happy and hygienic. "I saw this thing on TV about folk who get some of this done. They get paid more. That's why I'm going to get this trimmed down some." He pinched his nose. "Gonna upgrade. Maybe I'll finally make supervisor."

"Good for you." An ad popped up on my device—for a butcher shop in the Myrtles mall—but I couldn't really focus—because the guy—wouldn't stop—talking—I vaguely noticed a scrolling promotion for that ridiculous Tony Award–winning musical, *A Comical Furrier Funs*. I also came across a plug for the Nzinga Clinic that I'd seen around town before. A dark woman's face under a wash of sunshine: YOU CAN BE BEAUTIFUL, EVEN MORE BEAUTIFUL THAN BEFORE.

One of the nurses opened a door and called out a name. Unfortunately, the streetcar driver remained seated. He gabbed on about all the procedures he wanted to have done. Suddenly it dawned on me that he was just a lowly City employee. How the hell would he bankroll any of his dreams?

"Pilot program for municipal workers," he said. "City covers up to seventy percent. Can't say that's not fair. I'm working as much overtime as I can pinch."

A woman entered the waiting room from the examination room area. She wore a scarf like one I'd seen at work and large sunglasses that I'd once tried on and found too tight. Overall this woman looked an awful lot like Dinah. I called out to her. The woman looked at me with surprise and stepped into the hall. I opened the door and yelled her name, but the woman kept walking.

Ads kept pinging on my device. Very irksome that the ad bots tracked your movements and offered up their masters' wares. I rarely clicked on ads—why reward them?—but I needed a distraction from Chipper Charlie the Chatty Conductor.

A bookseller, offering a suite of books, to wit:

Mommy, Why Is My Skin So Dark?
Why Are All the Black Kids Sitting Together in the Cafeteria?
Lakeisha's First Perm (with new foreword by V. Sirin-Johnson!)
Dilution Anxiety and the Black Phallus
Black Past, White Future
Keep Your Child Out of the Sun!

I was about to purchase the last one when I recalled that I'd read it ages ago, even quoted choice passages to Penny.

My name was said. I glanced at the driver. He smiled at me and said good luck. A girl—I couldn't remember her name—from Nigel's school walked in with her parents. I had been struck by her round face and diaphanously pale skin in the past, even as I noticed that her parents were black. I stepped into the medical suite.

I should probably pause to say another word about Crooked

Crown, the pop star I bumped into the day Eckstein kicked Octavia and me to the curb. Other than making really annoying songs—if I never hear "Love the Real You" again, I will be very pleased—she had set in motion several fads. She was the reason, for example, that purple fur coats were all the rage among common black folk. She was also the instigator of the demel fad. It seemed ridiculous to me that one person could completely alter an entire society's image of the physical ideal. But stranger things have happened. After all, it was Coco Chanel who got white people to tan for a whole century before tanning salons were outlawed. And Hitler permanently removed the toothbrush mustache from the dapper man's fashion vocabulary.

In Crown's case, it was clear that demelanization had changed her life. She went from being a background singer in a moderately successful R&B group—Faith Colombo or Kate Sambo, I could never recall their proper name—to one of the biggest stars in pop history. Which brings me to Nzinga, who not only perfected and performed the first successful full-body scrub but was also Crown's Merlin.

The nurse in the consultation room checked my vitals. She had clearly been black . . . once. And I suppose she still was on the inside. But she must have undergone the full panoply just like Crown. The brochures called it the Spotless Special. Must be nice to get the employee discount.

Still, the work wasn't perfect. There was something not-quite-right about the curves of her lips and the way the skin tone around her knuckles was oddly dark. Even Crown suffered from these hiccups, pointed out by some of her haters on social media. That was the problem with being an early adopter of such wondrous technology. They hadn't worked out all the kinks. Fortunately, there had been improvements to the technique.

Another nurse entered, this one with dark skin and Africa-Face. What was it about people who were late of the Motherland? There was something about the cant of their cheeks and noses that made them instantly recognizable in relief to run-of-the-mill African Americans like myself. I guessed that people like this nurse's ancestors were history's victors, the lucky souls who had avoided the Middle Passage and miscegenation. Coffee never diluted by creamer.

This second nurse measured my forehead with a set of calipers. She pinched my nose. She yanked my lower lip.

"Good elasticity," she said rhapsodically, in her rhythmic accent. Still holding my lip, she jotted something on a chart.

"Whabt?"

"It means you are a good match for the program." She let go. "Still, you are going to require some effort."

"When will the doctor see me? I'm kind of in a rush."

"Excuse me, Mr. 'Kind of in a Rush,' but the doctor sees you now." She shone a penlight in my eye. I squinted.

"I'm sorry. I didn't realize—" In all the literature I read about the clinic, I'd never seen a picture of Dr. Nzinga. I'd assumed she was a man. Penny would say this was another of my blind spots.

"Do not dwell on it. After all, the place you dwell is the place you live. Shame is no proper residence." Dr. Nzinga groped my face, kneading my forehead as if I were a lump of clay. "Now. You will tell me of your dreams."

"Actually, doctor." I had a frog in my throat. This was a moment I'd anticipated for years. I was frozen. My heart whirled in my chest. I was in danger of coming across as a lunatic. "I—uh. I'm here for my son."

I pulled up a picture of Nigel on my device and told Dr. Nzinga everything. I was probably too sincere. But once I started, I couldn't slow down. I told her about my fears and the sleepless nights. About the skin creams. About how I wasn't sure if I was doing the right thing in general.

"What father is certain he's doing the right thing?" Dr. Nzinga put a hand on my knee. "Why do you think I moved my program here from Abuja? We can help your— What is his name?"

"Nigel," I said.

"We developed these protocols precisely for people like Nigel. I anticipate that his birthmark sinks to the subcutaneous layer, but his condition is relatively minor and can be revised."

I couldn't help myself. I hugged the woman.

"Now, now, good father," she said. "We are only doing our jobs."

"Does it hurt?"

"No more than removing a tattoo. Although it is much more involved than that."

"How much does it cost?"

Dr. Nzinga directed me to speak with one of the clerks. She said there were financial programs to help, if necessary.

"Once you work all that out, be sure to bring this—"

"Nigel."

"—Nigel in so that we can do a full assessment."

I floated out of the consultation room but quickly ran aground as the clerk and I reviewed an estimate sheet. The cost of the procedure had gone up since my recon visit. The success rate was over 90 percent now, but the improvements to the procedure had not made things cheaper. Short of finding a pot of gold, the bonus was my only shot.

20

It was a roaring, late spring day in the City. Bright but unseasonably cool. A sparkling patch of green, green grass. A blue jay mobbing a hawk. The happy sound of nearby hammers bringing something into being. *Pung. Kapung. Pung. Pung. Kapung.* Me and my boy. I left work early to grab Nigel per a plan I couldn't quite recall. Nigel and I walked across the grass of the Great Lawn at the School Without Walls. He wore a brown scarf and, for a change, a baseball cap, the neon-green one, without my prompting. His curly brownish hair poked out from the edges. He was due for a haircut, although I liked the way his hair partially obscured the mark. I removed his backpack and hefted it onto my shoulder. *Oof.* When did knowledge become so heavy?

"Thanks," he said with his fingers. His class was learning American Sign Language so that students who heard the magic of words would be able to communicate with those who heard the magic of silence. This meant I was learning ASL, too. The boy hadn't even peeped that morning when I kissed him on the forehead.

Suddenly Nigel hurried in front of me. He held out his hands, so I would stop. I stopped. Seeing my inability to comprehend his signs, he tried charades. We were master charadists, the pair of us.

A girl cut across the lawn. It was that dark-as-dung brat who'd ratted me out to Penny about the skin-toning cream, that time Nigel trapped himself in the closet. Like a gnat, she often buzzed around when I came to pick Nigel up.

There was no uniform requirement at the School Without Walls—they were against such orthodoxies. But just like the other times I'd seen her, the girl wore a traditional school uniform with a twist: a plaid skirt, a white top, and a purple faux-fur jacket. I took this as a sign that she was a program student, one of the kids the City gave handouts of tuition, lunch, and uniforms. I didn't like that she sometimes visited Nigel at the house. She was flippant and crude. And the dozens of twisted kinks and ribbons on her head made her look like something that belonged on the cover of a nineteenth-century minstrel ad. But Penny didn't mind her, so the girl—she had a name: Araminta Ahosi—sometimes visited Nigel at the house, where they played handheld video games or hide-and-seek, which apparently she was skilled at. At least she had some veneer of decorum. She always called me mister.

"Hey, mister," she said. "Hey, Nige." What was this "Nige" business anyway? My son didn't like people freestyling his name. Whenever I called him Nigerious or by his verbalized initials, he pursed his lips.

"You're interrupting a very important discussion," I said to the pest.

"Oh. You must have forgot about— Mmph!" Nigel clamped a hand over her mouth.

He held up two fingers. Two words. He circled his thumb and forefinger around the opposite ring finger.

"Ring," I said. He gave me a weak thumbs-up. Right track. Wrong word. "Wedding." He kept pointing up. "Wife? Penny?" Nigel hopped and did a little leprechaun dance.

"Dweeb," Araminta said.

Nigel poked out his tongue. Second word. He motioned like his stomach was covered by a balloon.

"Whale." Araminta threw her arms wide.

Nigel held a finger over his own mouth.

"Fine, boo." She put a hand on her narrow hip. "I ain't got to say nothing. I can just stand here and be quiet." She switched hips. "See? Won't say a word. I'm shutting my trap. Right now. Just like that. Zippit." She imaginatively zipped her lips shut and flung the key over the iron fence.

Nigel forced down a laugh, but my guts betrayed me, and I guffawed despite myself.

I straightened my face but chuckled again.

"Fat?" I said. "Pregnant?"

Nigel wagged his finger. He pulled his shirt collar over his head so that he was hidden like a frightened turtle. The crown of his skull emerged from the neck hole. He mock-screamed as he emerged. I was second-guessing our decision to teach that kid about the facts of life before he was big enough to hold a sippy cup.

"Mom's birthday!" I clapped my hands. How could I have forgotten? Nigel's eyes brightened, and he offered a fist bump. I shook my head. He knew better. We shook hands.

"Can I ride with y'all?" Araminta asked me.

"I don't think that would be a good idea," I said. "Tonight is a very special—"

"My dad has to work late," she said, "and I don't want to be there alone. The people upstairs make weird noises every Thursday at nine-seventeen P.M."

I sighed. Nigel had told me that her father presently held a number of menial part-time jobs, including a horrible gig for the City Department of Sanitation, removing dead rodents from drainpipes or something similarly repulsive. Her mother had tapped out of life at some earlier point.

"Fine," I signed.

Nigel signed that we had to hurry. He was right. We had much to do and precious little time. We had a cake to buy, and Penny would be home soon. Araminta took off toward the Bug. Nigel sprinted to catch up. His hat fell in his wake. I recovered it. Cake time.

Thank the fates for my considerate son, who prompted me with reminders of Penny's birthday. Or as Nigel and I rebranded it some time ago: One Cent Day. Once we cleared the whirlpool of car-bound parents and children that were in the area around the school, crosstown traffic was quite tolerable. We were skimming along like a hippo on an ice floe.

I checked the rearview mirror. They were having a conversation in sign. Nigel wasn't the type of kid to have a ton of friends. He once had a few who were especially close, but most of those he left behind at his prior schools.

Nigel and Araminta laughed audibly, breaking the fiction of deafness. What was so funny? Araminta flipped the device around. An animated ape getting blown up by an exploding cigar. Silly major-key music playing in support. They watched the sequence again and guffawed, one of them stomping the wheel well in delight.

Was there anything better than watching my shy, taciturn, neurotic boy laugh uncontrollably? My misadventures, in the final analysis, were all about pulling Nigel into a land where such giggles and happy grimaces were frequent.

The Mall of the Seven Myrtles parking lot was crowded as usual. But this didn't bother me. I didn't advertise the fact, but I was a lover of the Myrtles. It was riverfront property on the former footprint of a church and earlier tourist area that had fallen in a storm.

I got warm fuzzies each time I crossed the reclaimed cobblestone pavilion, which presently faced the water, and passed the historical statuary—our state's first governor, Jean-Jacques LePieu, clad in a fetching tricorne hat. His knee was raised high like that pirate in those cheeky rum ads. I couldn't help checking that both of his arms had hands. Some squirrel in my subconscious had been trying for decades to convince me that he had a hook. But no. One mitt held a stalk of maize, and the other a newborn babe. He had graciously just accepted both from kneeling, naked Native Americans.

The steamboat calliope tooted "I Wish I Was in Dixie," as if we weren't already.

The Myrtles combined my love of several fields of inquiry— architecture, people watching, snazzy duds—into a ginormous mise-en-scène I could stroll through without pissing off the director or the audience. The design team that built the Sky Tower also constructed the mall, so that the structures were as alike as they were different. They were a pair of elegant sisters, one tall and thin, the other wide-hipped and round-bosomed. The seemingly countless levels of undulating terraces that formed the atrium of the Sky Tower were limited to merely three floors in the Myrtles. But those gorgeous, gold-trimmed, curvilinear decks stretched onward to the edge of sight. Video panels displayed happenings in other sections of the mall such as the food court or the terrarium. A jumbo panel above showed a children's kazoo band performing at the main entrance fountain. A crew of actors in superhero costumes worked the food court.

The mall's long ceiling was a pearlescent canopy that changed colors depending on the viewer's perspective. "How does the ceiling change like that?" Araminta asked.

"It doesn't change," I said. "Your eyes are crooked."

She smacked her lips.

Nigel and Araminta played with the electronic mall directory. I didn't think I'd ever seen anyone as black as her. Did she lose herself in the dark? When she reentered the lighted world, did she have to make sure that she didn't leave any of herself behind in the shadows? A spinning compass faded away. A map dotted by hundreds of icons, each for a different business, materialized.

The mall was shaped like a stylized, seven-branched tree. The trunk sprouted from the river, and our cakery was perched near the tip of one of the upper branches. We stepped onto a conveyor belt. We passed the food court. The ersatz comic book heroes must have been prerecorded because I didn't see them. However, we passed a duo in cowboy hats playing banjos—the Myrtles hired performers to roam around and entertain in much the same way Disneyland did.

We passed stores Nigel and I had experienced before with Penny, Mama, Nigel's other friends, or any combination thereof. Here was the handmade toy emporium where a red, yellow, and blue biplane on a tether ceaselessly circled the checkout counter. We'd bought Nigel's first wagon in that place. There was the sundry shop that used to give away free photo negatives. We did that as a family when Nigel was about four. I never liked the picture. It was tucked into a closet at home.

A red-faced girl in a pinafore yelled that she didn't want to. Her mother, a woman in her twenties who seemed prematurely aged, yanked the girl by the wrist. The girl yelped. I wanted to reach out and say something. But even though I had stopped walking, I ludicrously continued to float away thanks to the conveyor belt. The mother looked right at me, as if to say, *What do you think you're looking at?*

We got off the belt at a four-way intersection. I smelled sugar, butter. Hope transmitted on an air current. Cakery Royale was close.

Just as we arrived, someone called my name. A woman with light brown skin and sleepy eyes. Zora Suhla Smits. I'd only seen her a couple of times since the first meeting I crashed at the Musée. She wore a skirt suit. I introduced her to Nigel and Araminta. "Nice to meet you," she said. Nigel said that the pleasure was all his without moving his lips. I explained the sign thing to Zora. She signed something back.

"You have lovely children," she said out loud.

"This one isn't mine," I said. "She's on loan from the pound."

Araminta growled.

"Lovely." Zora grimaced. "Can we talk for a few moments?"

"Sure," I said.

Nigel signed that they were going to the arcade in the third branch. I was about to tell him we didn't have time, but Araminta poked out her tongue. Then she grabbed the back of her own collar and led herself away. Nigel grabbed his collar and did the same.

Zora lobbed small talk at me. "Aren't we having fine weather?"

"More or less," I bunted. I was still trying to decide where Zora fit on the leadership scale. Was she an indomitable firebrand like her grandmother or the kind of malleable black figurehead that history preferred? She was tallish but young and somewhat ill at ease, as if she'd only just grown into her shell. I realized then that she was probably only in her early thirties, but an old soul. Yet I knew enough about history to recognize that the descendants of great people are rarely great themselves. Despite having some of the visual and verbal tics of their forebears, many people in Zora's position simply swam in their ancestors' wake, often for profit or D-list notoriety.

We walked into the bakery. A lanky man in a baker's coat offered free samples of bread pudding in disposable cups. I wished Penny were with me. She loved free nosh in disposable cups. The sweet shop had made my and Penny's wedding cake. We'd been hooked ever since.

"Riley tells me you're soaking up the philosophy well." I had been working out of the satellite office several evenings a week, after my firm hours, distributing pamphlets or writing drafts of manifestos for Jan, Marie, and Riley to pick apart. My job was simple: Draft position papers that argued for a nation without divisions. Instead of "out of many, one," BEG thought of America as a big bowl of milk into which tiny drops of chocolate, caramel, dulce de leche, coconut, or tamarind could be diluted out of existence. "Out of many, only one." Try as I might, I wasn't good at adhering to their fiction as I would have liked. I kept inadvertently mentioning multiculturalism, diversity, facts, history, reality.

Once I mistakenly inserted the phrase "white supremacy" into a pamphlet. I thought Riley would rap me on the knuckles with a ruler.

"Funny," I said. "I thought Riley might tell you to lock me out."

She forced a smile. "Do you know how movements change the world? Through coalitions and a belief that we can make progress, if we use all the tools at our disposal. My grandmother was an agent of change through her persistence and eloquence. When she spoke, everyone heard her. She made a difference through sheer force of will."

"Those were different times," I said. "Seems like you're doing well under the circumstances."

"That's kind of you," she said, "but not true. I've run BEG for years, and I have to admit we're in park. Maybe it's because I was educated up north. Or maybe it's because I'm too light-skinned." She seemed to be staring at my cheek when she said this. "The point is I don't care about your personal motivations. We need you."

"Me?" I asked.

"You're a talented speaker, and people in the right places are aware of you, comfortable with you. We haven't had an official spokesman in years. However, I would understand if you can't do it, with all your obligations. You have a job, and this is only a volunteer position. Plus, the glare of the spotlight can be taxing. I'm sure also you'd have to clear channels with your—"

"I'll do it." I hadn't imagined that my plan would work so well. But here I was. My path to winning over Eckstein was opening before me.

"Really?" Zora asked.

"I'm happy to help."

"What a pleasure to hear. Show up for this on Thursday morning." She handed me a glossy push card. For all of BEG's shortcomings, they could print the piss out of propaganda. The card featured the organization's pastel color scheme as well as their emblem, a stylized, palm-up hand. Ribbon cutting at the Trueblood School. Eleven-thirty A.M. Truce Garden dedication. What on earth was a Truce Garden?

A tremendous thud rocked the building, and I grabbed a post for balance. Several of the megavideo panels flashed pure white light, which died down after a moment. The people on the panels—the people by the main entrance—seemed to be attacking each other.

No. They were running for their lives.

Far down the hall, shoppers stormed through the entrance doors. They ran toward me. I began to turn tail, but—Nigel and Araminta. Where had they gone?

Someone shouted my name. "Sir, your cake." The tall baker held a black cake box by its pink ribbons. I grabbed it and ran.

I didn't use the conveyor. I probably passed Zora along the way. But I didn't notice her. I didn't notice much of anything other than intermittent groups of shoppers pointing up at the video panels along the way and, occasionally, at me. I was a good runner. I could jog a couple miles on a cool day without killing myself. But I didn't normally create the spectacle that I did now: a black man, balancing an oversize cake box on one hand, running against the tide. I was really asking for it. Security would be on me any moment.

I cleared a stand of kiosks and paused at the glass exit doors, which were veined with cracks and hard to see through. Wedging my foot into the gap, fingers reached in. Together, with the unseen people on the other side of the door, I opened it. A mass of smoke and desperate shoppers pushed in on me. A baby wailed. I was trapped, suspended in a crush of bodies. It was bad outside.

Smoke. Dust. Sirens in the distance. A thud nearby. A pile of something on fire—the LePieu statue, rendered to slag. I felt the heat of it even fifty yards away. Shopping bags and purses everywhere. A plastic Crooked Crown tiara broken in half. A dark pool of liquid. I stumbled away from the scrum and into the clear.

Children scampered like in a panicky game of hide-and-seek. A boy held his arm at a strange angle. That kazoo band! A man lay on the ground, clutching his side. Strangest of all, scraps, like plus-size confetti, green, red, and black, were everywhere.

"Go inside!" a woman in a gray one-piece, mall security, said from just beyond the molten statue. "Terror!"

A thin figure in a hard, brown mask, like something from an African arts and crafts show, shoved the guard to the ground. The figure pointed a revolver at the guard. A black van screeched, hopped the curb, and stopped. The side door slid open. A brown hand beckoned from the van's interior. The figure leaped inside. The van pulled away.

A news helicopter hovered somewhere overhead. I suddenly became aware of high-pitched voices behind me.

"Dad!" Nigel and Araminta were standing inside the mall doors. I hustled over and drew them into my arms. They both seemed rattled but otherwise okay.

"Are you crazy?" Araminta said. "Why'd you go out there?"

I gathered the children in my arms and squeezed them. "Thank god you're safe," I said.

Nigel patted my arm and pointed at misshapen letters that were spray-painted on the wall. A massive graffiti tag: ADZE.

21

We agreed not to tell Penny. What I mean to say is that when we got back to the Bug, I made Nigel and Araminta raise their hands and swear to keep their mouths shut. There were a billion police cars at the mall by the time we rolled out. Several more helicopters had arrived. Even the police department dirigible. This would be a thing. It would be on TV and the Internet. People at work would bring it up at the water cooler.

I didn't want to get into all that. We were fine. But if Penny knew we had been so close to danger, she'd be terrified. This was no way to celebrate One Cent Day.

In the driveway at home, I went over our cover story.

"But—" Nigel said.

I raised my palm to stop him. "No 'but,'" I said. "Now, tell me."

"We left the mall before it happened," Nigel said. The sun was setting. A streetlight popped on.

"And?" I asked.

"We heard about it on the radio driving home," Araminta said.

Penny opened the side door of the house, the one that overlooked the driveway. She held herself. Mama and her childhood friend, Aunt Shirls (no relation) in her horn-rimmed glasses, looked on from behind.

"Break," I said. We got out of the car. I collected the cake box from the hood trunk.

"Happy One Cent—" I said. Penny motioned for us to hurry.

"They're back." Nigel pointed.

Termites, like tiny, possessed snowflakes, swarmed around the streetlight.

"Quick," I said. "Don't let those bugs in the house."

The kids ran up the steps to the door. Penny clutched them to her body. She said she was happy we were safe.

I opened the cake box. "We were long gone," I said. Without letting go of Nigel and Araminta, she popped the back of my head. I hardly felt it. But the concept hurt. She knew.

"Don't protect me." She pressed the children close to her body, covering their ears with her hands. Nigel was so tall now that this technique wasn't as effective as it used to be. His body-side ear was almost over Penny's shoulder.

"Look," I whispered. My head buzzed. My teeth—all of them—were on fire. "They're not that fragile. Everything is fine. Nobody got hurt."

"Three died," Mama said.

"Kids," Aunt Shirls grabbed Nigel's arm. "Little ones." Aunt Shirls had a way of making the most awful facts sound mundane, so it was no surprise that she made awful facts sound like personal condemnations. Or maybe I was just being paranoid. I'd just taken my second Blue Geisha of the day, inadvisably, probably.

"Oh," I said. "How?"

The women eyed me. They knew. I felt as if my feet had sunk a quarter inch into the hardwood. Like I might continue sinking until I suffocated in clay.

"Don't tell tales," Penny said. "You were there when it happened. I saw you on national TV for a moment—"

I leaned against the doorjamb, suddenly too exhausted to argue. "You're right."

"You were standing on a message written in—" Penny whispered.

I raised my shoe, the bottom of which was covered in someone's blood. I removed the shoe and threw it across the neighbor's fence. "I'm sorry," I said. I limped to the kitchen table and put down the cake box.

Penny looked afraid. "I was worried about all of you. They say a group called ADZE was behind it."

"It can't be them," I said. "That doesn't make any sense."

"Why not?" Penny asked.

"They used to give out fruits and veggies to all the kids in the Tiko," Mama said. "They didn't attack folk."

"They all got locked up anyway," Aunt Shirls said. "Or blown up." She was right, of course.

Depending on who you asked, ADZE were community heroes or bigoted terrorists. They were a big deal until they organized a protest and tried to tear down the LePieu statue with a stolen backhoe. It was a federal crime to damage monuments that had been erected before the turn of the millennium, and the FBI arrived on the scene to arrest the whole crew.

But things got out of hand when armed statue supporters threw a grenade at the protesters. ADZE believed in armed self-defense. There was a shootout. People, including a federal agent, died. The feds chased the surviving ADZE members back to an inner-city house and dropped a gas bomb on the neighborhood not long after. The fire from the explosion spread to nearby houses recently bought by young white professionals. Over 170 people died in the incidents, including a white family fresh from Idaho. The City, state, and feds did investigations. Congress held hearings. Ultimately, ADZE was blamed for the whole mess, and the City put fences and checkpoints all around the Tiko, even though only a couple of the ADZE protesters lived there.

Police harassment made other black neighborhoods practically unlivable. With the national media pushing the story that sleeper cells of black revolutionaries were lying in wait all across the country, it was only a matter of time before other towns enacted similar measures. None of the original statue supporters were charged with any crimes.

"We tried to let you know what was going on," Araminta said. I made a face that must have registered my confusion. She held up her device. The news channel, 444, played a loop of a masked, dreaded man in a white suit firing a weapon over the crowd. The news item must have appeared before we were even out of the parking lot.

"How about some cake, Dad?" Nigel said.

"I'm not feeling well," I said. "I think I'll lie down."

"What's that buzzing?" Aunt Shirls asked.

"They coming inside the house," Mama said. We'd had the doorframes and windows weatherproofed to keep out the termites. But a line of them were streaming in from a gap in the doorjamb.

"Quick. Turn off the lights," Penny said. Termites loved lights, craved them. Making the house dark was one way to make them change their minds, to convince them that life was better somewhere else. Araminta hit the switch, and suddenly only the planes of my loved one's faces were visible, odd facets like Mama's eye whites, Aunt Shirls's glass lenses, Penny's chin, and the clean side of Nigel's face. A termite flew past my nose.

The candles on Penny's white cake hadn't been lit, but it was still the brightest thing in the room.

"We've got to cover it up!" I yelled.

But it was too late. The swarm descended.

22

Displays of affection do not necessarily come easy to me. Yes, when Nigel was still in his crib, perhaps it was easy to press his soft feet to my mouth and kiss them. Or lift him up by the underarms and nuzzle my nose against his belly as he giggled. But as he grew and began to look more like me in cant of body and cadence of walk, I found myself withdrawing. One day when Nigel was about seven, I picked him up from school—St. Moritz, a truly wonderful school—on Brighton Lane.

Nigel climbed into the passenger seat, his eyes reddened.

"Well, spit it out." I leaned across to clip his seatbelt on.

"This kid said I was a cow." It was farm day in class. The students had taken a virtual tour of a farm. At one point, the class came upon a field of amber-colored grain. A spotted cow grazed. Some genius child made a connection between Bessie and the mark on Nigel's face. I didn't want to scar Nigel with an overreaction on my part or act as if the teasing would hurt any less in the future. He would need a tougher skin to survive.

"That's silly." I started the car. "Ignore that kid, okay?"

"Yes," Nigel said.

"We're having cheese ravioli tonight."

He smiled weakly. We drove off. Having settled the issue, I placed it in a box at the back of my mind, closed the lid, and removed the skeleton key. I had a federal court brief to write, and if it didn't go over well, I'd take the blame. We'd lose the account.

We were nearly home, stopped at a red light. Vehicles flowed through the intersection. A scooter. A sedan. A tour bus. Maybe if I applied third circuit state court precedent, I could create a procedural pathway that would—

Nigel hiccupped. Not a hiccup. His head was ducked between his shoulders. He had been crying the whole time, silently. He covered his face when he noticed me watching him. Such grace. Suddenly, Nigel seemed so small, as if the Bug's bucket seat might snap shut on him like a Venus flytrap.

I swerved the car into a gas station at the last major intersection, just three or so turns from the house. I reached out but found I couldn't touch him. How had I become one of those fathers who were deathly afraid of showing any sign of tenderness? What was I doing to us?

I had been ignoring my son's predicament. Instead of engaging with his pain, I did everything to minimize it. The kid who called Nigel a cow wasn't unusual. Other kids cast similar aspersions, bullied him like it was their jobs. More would in the days to come. But I'd heard of a way to help people like Nigel. I knew what I had to do.

I put the car in drive and took us home to Penny.

Several nights after One Cent Day, Zora sent a message reminding me that I was to represent at City Hall. This was the first thing she said about the event since our brief encounter at the Myrtles, so of course I forgot all about it. We were eating dinner.

Penny looked up from her creamed spinach. "Something important?"

"BEG wants me at the press conference for the emergency ordinance signing."

"With the mayor?" Nigel asked.

"That's right, son."

"Oh no," Penny said. "You can't act all chummy with that fascist."

"She's not a fascist. She's just trying to look tough before election season."

"Human rights don't have a season."

"Don't be so dramatic," I said. "As the BEG spokesperson, I have to be there. It's just politics."

I got the impression that Zora and the mayor were frenemies at best. But since Chamberlain had always supported BEG, someone from the group had to be there. I saw it as a plum assignment, a sign of trust in my abilities and in accordance with my desire to ingratiate myself quickly into the upper echelon of BEG. Eckstein would see my face on TV. It would be proof of my involvement—of the firm's involvement—in the lives of the black community.

Zora instructed that I be ready to declaim BEG's platform, its mission statement, its accomplishments both recent and distant in time, and most important, its support for the government's action. BEG was about the safety and security of all peoples. It was BEG that lobbied for the safety patrols that watched over the Tiko and our house. It was BEG that filled in the void left by the collapse of the original ADZE with new youth work programs and the like. It was BEG that kept radical elements from passing truly discriminatory laws like the one in the next state over that required all blacks to accept tracking implants. After helping Penny and Nigel with the dinner dishes—she washed, he dried, I put away—I locked myself in the guest room and stood up reading policy and jotting speaking points on a legal pad. I scratched out lines, tore out whole pages and tossed them into the wastebasket.

As sunlight crept through the lace curtains—a design to my imagination of disembodied moth wings—it struck me that in all my years as an agent of the law, Nigel never saw me in action. Early in my career and before Nigel was born, Penny often visited court to watch me plead. Mama was present for my first argument before the state supreme court. Even Jo Jo, through some awesome trick of fate, wandered into a cross-examination I performed at a suburban law center. But Nigel, of all the people who mattered, was outside this circle of experience. The thought of my son getting to watch the old man do his thing, even if it wasn't an actual legal proceeding, filled me with a kind of manic joy. I rose from my desk and stretched, smiling like a tomcat. I patted my stomach. I could've stood to lose a couple. I pulled one of the short curls on the top of my head. It was turning kinky again. There wasn't enough time to freshen it up.

I crossed the parking lot of the Reinhardt Upliftment Center, leading Nigel and Araminta by the hands. Araminta, despite being a pest to the very core, was compliant, even pleasant. But Nigel's face was reddened by my display of parental affection. I squeezed his hand harder.

Reinhardt was in the Tiko, on the site of an old commercial sector. Long, long ago, in the very same place that we walked, Jewish, black, Irish, and Italian immigrants sold jewelry, hand-cobbled shoes, and small-batch candies from storefronts. The buildings that made up Reinhardt were once a paint factory—Pure American Paints—if memory served. Eventually, they outsourced most of production to Bangladesh. But that was only after much of the original plant was destroyed in a boiler explosion.

Colorful placards banged against light poles in the breeze. The placards were printed with slogans: STRIVE TO ACHIEVE! WORK WITH US NOT AGAINST YOURSELF! IF YOU BREAK THE LAW, THE LAW BREAKS YOU. Arrows pointed down at the pavement. There was nothing of note on the pavement.

"It's smaller than I remember." Nigel pulled his hand from mine and held the glass door open for us. I couldn't tell if he was being ironic. Reinhardt was one of the biggest complexes in the black part of town. It had once actually been outside the Tiko, but at some point, the barbed-wire fence that surrounded the Tiko reached out like an amoeba and swallowed Reinhardt.

Reinhardt contained a restaurant, a physical-book library, a police substation—Douglas's hive—an after-school work-study program, and even a Reform AME church. People went to the center to pay utilities, register themselves, and process government assistance requests. A body could spend an entire day at Reinhardt and never fail to come across something of interest.

"That's because the last time you were here," I said, "you were a lot smaller."

"My daddy ain't never let me come in here," Araminta said. "He say it's a joke."

"That's a small-minded attitude." I myself was a beneficiary of Reinhardt's programming. When I was a freshman in high school, I was selected with only ten other black kids from across the City to serve in their ambassador program. It was a huge boost for my self-confidence. A few times a month, I was transported from the rather pedantic concerns of Ms. Leni's Southern American history course (we learned mostly about the battle for states' rights) and Mr. Himmle's calculus class (my least favorite hour) to events like the press conference. We were talked about using cliché-ridden metaphors, told we were the flowers of our community—the brightest petals, who through diligence and deference would sprout into future leaders. They even gave us blazers, each embroidered with a tulip crest. I patted my crest for good luck before events. We greeted people, opened doors, and carried trays of bacon-wrapped kale. I looked pretty sharp in my navy blazer and khakis, let me tell you. Sometimes, even as an adult, I found myself absentmindedly stroking a phantom tulip on my chest.

Nigel broke away and turned to us. He held an imaginary microphone and a real index card. Some of my notes were on the card. In typical Nigel fashion, he had already run me through a few hypothetical questions in the car. He got that from his mother, his desire to see me succeed. I didn't deserve him. I didn't deserve either of them.

Araminta ripped the card in half and stuffed it in Nigel's shirt pocket.

"What's the big idea?" I asked. Nigel laughed.

"Mr. Nigel's dad," Araminta said, walking backward through Reinhardt's lobby. She motioned for the imaginary mic, which Nigel handed over. She thrust the mic at me while Nigel took imaginary pictures. "Would you rather be the Ugly Duckling or Rudolph the Red-Nosed Reindeer?"

"The swan," I said. "Although there is a certain utility to that nose."

Nigel tweaked Araminta's nose. She playfully slapped him away.

"Mr. Nigel's dad," Araminta said, "how come dogs and fruit flies have been to space but no girls?"

"Girls are already in space."

"I mean girls my age," she said.

The dark scent of red beans burbling in a pot. The salty tickle of seafood gumbo. The effervescent pinch of black pepper against catfish batter. We came to the pride and joy of Reinhardt, the Re-spectibility Cafe—yes, the name was misspelled from the start, but that was another story. All the employees were disadvantaged youth, like I had once been, though I never worked there. The youth participants were not necessarily poor or illiterate, mind you, just born of black parents.

Here, in a program administered by BEG, young people received the training they needed for careers in the food service industry, which certainly beat their other prospects: jail time or the welfare rolls. Look at that girl scribble an order. See that boy wipe down a food tray. My chest swelled at the thought of all the young people the little eatery had ushered into lives of quiet dignity.

I held up my imaginary microphone. "Dear Mr. and Miss Children, what has perfectly white fur, a cat's head, a dog's floppy ears, and—"

Someone stared at me from the other side of the glass separating the hall from the cafe. Someone very familiar but absolutely foreign at once, like a twin I'd never met. Where had he come from? He hadn't been there a moment ago. The coldness in his eyes froze me in place.

"Cousin Supercargo!" Nigel said.

"Supercargo?" I mouthed. I forgot this was one of the facilities where he worked. I pointed at my head in recognition of his head, which was as bald as a freshly shorn sheep's belly. The sliding doors opened.

"What y'all doing up in here?" He wiped his hands on his apron. Nigel hugged Supercargo as exuberantly as always.

"What happened to your dreads?" Araminta asked.

"That's a long story, missy," he said.

"Wait. How do you know him?" I asked Araminta. But they ignored me, and for a moment, as they chatted, I felt completely invisible.

"I learned some more music by heart for my school musical," Nigel said.

"Oh yeah?" Supercargo said. "So you're good to go for next week."

"He's only the bench warmer," Araminta said.

"Understudy." Nigel shoved Araminta. "Mr. Riley says I'm the backbone of the band."

"That's nice." I didn't like the fact that Riley, as a teacher at the School Without Walls, saw my son more than I did. Maybe I could somehow get Riley transferred. Nigel didn't need additional father figures. I was the first, last, and only. "No shoving," I said. But no one heard me. I was starting to panic. What if I remained invisible forever?

"I thought you were the star," Supercargo said.

"This kid named Monte is. His father donated money to refurbish the teachers' lounge. That's okay. I like Monte. I get to be a member of the band. The second keyboardist. I play the hard parts."

I took several deep breaths. I realized that in my transparent state, I could finally leave the struggle behind. I could let go. Float through the acoustic ceiling tile. Up through the gray cumulonimbus clouds. Into the ionosphere. Set a course for the dark side of the moon. If I flew overnight, I could land on that quiet little orb by morning. Set up a chaise lounge and a tray of white chocolate bonbons. Nigel would be fine. Supercargo would see to it that he got home safe. Penny would ensure that he survived the vicissitudes of being born alive into a world covered in poisonous barbs. Wait—no.

"Can we talk for a sec?" I said. Supercargo and I stepped away from the kids. "Seriously, what happened?"

"They cut it."

"But who?"

"Who else?" He rubbed the smooth brown crown of his head. "The police popped me the night of that terror at the mall."

"What did you do?"

Supercargo shot me a look of anger. "You sound like them." The police had suspected that he was involved and interrogated him for almost twenty-four hours. He didn't have to explain the rest. Under the Dreadlock Ordinance, the cops could give any arrestee a haircut if they deemed the person unsanitary. It seemed like a sound policy. With so many thousands of men locked up in close confines, the authorities did what was necessary to prevent infestations of lice and fleas. I saw it with my own eyes during a Scare 'Em Straight field trip in middle school. Even the largest prison in the City was bursting at the seams. Nobody wanted an epidemic.

Still, I couldn't remember a time when Supercargo hadn't sported a stereotypically Afrocentric hairstyle. When we were boys, he had cornrows. Later he grew a truly magnificent Afro.

Although I believed that dreads were a way to draw unwelcome attention from the authorities—clearly what happened here—I knew Supercargo took great pride in his locks. Presumably those locks had been tossed into the incinerator at the City jail, along with part of my cousin's identity.

I grabbed his shoulder and gave him a half-body hug. "I'm sorry."

"It's all right." He rocked from foot to foot, an edge to his voice. "Maybe when it grows back, I'll get a permadoo like you. Nobody mess with me then." He glanced into the cafe. "Say. Your boy old enough. You should let him volunteer sometime."

"I've got bigger plans for him than working somebody's grill." The words spun out of my mouth faster than I could catch them. "No offense."

Supercargo smacked his lips. "You've always thought you were better than me."

"Can we not talk about this now?" I checked the time on my watch.

"That's right." He undid his apron. "You're Zora's patsy."

"Excuse me?" I asked.

"She asked me first. I refused. I want nothing to do with it. I resigned from BEG the other day."

"What? Why?"

"'Cause they playing us. You see what they trying to do with them laws. They going lock down the Tiko even more than it is now. They going profile us harder and scoop up anybody for anything. And BEG going to go hand in hand with them? Want me to be a part of that? No, sir. Cannot be me."

"Aren't you being a bit hyperbolic?" I asked. "And aren't you the guy who signed me up with BEG?"

"That was a mistake. I thought I could get them to take on some real challenges. To fight what's happening. Like the way ADZE used to. This City trying to eat us alive, and all Zora want to do is grovel for government grant money to cover her salary. What's the point if we doing the man work for him?" Supercargo closed his eyes and inhaled, his chest expanding for several long moments. He turned without saying bye and disappeared into the stock-room.

Shortly thereafter I was up on a platform surrounded by digni-taries. The press corps waited below shoulder to shoulder. There were three walls and a series of panel windows that looked out on Reinhardt's garden, where some young volunteers toiled over a watermelon patch. Mayor Chamberlain stepped up to the micro-phone, raising it slightly. I liked her because, against the odds, she'd beat out the corrupt father-son dynasty that preceded her. Her signature bouffant hair never looked higher.

"Much has been said about the present state of unrest in our fair city since the occurrence in our beloved Myrtles commercial dis-trict," Mayor Chamberlain said. "I have been monitoring the streets. Particularly around the area of the Tikoloshe Housing De-velopment. We've seen an uptick in violent-crime arrests, and it is clear to me that this part of our community is on the verge of complete and total social unrest. Most important, we will bring the black supremacist group known as ADZE to justice. They will be punished for their reign of terror and for corrupting citizens of all ages to their hateful cause." She gripped the podium with one hand and raised a sheet of paper with the other. "This is a list of actions designed to address the problem. You can be assured that this administration is doing everything in its power . . ."

The police chief had already spoken, as had the emergency ser-vices administrator, two members of the council, an FBI agent, a woman from the power utility, and a guy who dealt with the City's parking meters. How could people talk so much without running out of words? My coat sleeves felt awkward against my forearms. I felt oppressed by the formality of it all, like a butterfly under glass. My armpits were moist. I hoped the woman from the power utility, now standing next to me, didn't notice. Because of our height difference, her nose was right there.

The mayor continued. "My plan will curb violence by extending the curfew at the Tikoloshe Housing Development from weekends to seven days a week."

The non-press audience members clapped. What did she mean by extending the curfew? She couldn't just lock people in the projects. Could she?

"I've already secured a contractor to raise the Tikoloshe fence and extend its parameters to encompass eight nearby blocks." The applause continued. "This is, of course, in response to the grenade that was thrown over the existing fence that destroyed a culturally significant statue of Ida B. Wells. If ill-intentioned persons can't get close to the development, then they can't harm it or our people." Mayor Chamberlain leaned forward. "There are many other initiatives, but I'm proudest of our new collaboration with federal authorities, which allows our stalwart City Police Department to hand violators of certain laws over to those authorities for deportation to the African nation of Zamunda, pursuant to an existing treaty entered under the administration of former president Palmer."

My face was hot. Supercargo was right, and I had dismissed him! The mayor's plans would strip rights from me, Mama, Supercargo, and everyone who looked like us. I couldn't be a party to it. I had to find a way out. But then I spotted Nigel at the back of the room. He and Araminta were playing some kind of game with their hands. Even here he was so oblivious to what our society wanted to do to him, as he should be. I couldn't walk away from the plan. I was standing five feet from the mayor on live television in front of hundreds of thousands of people. Octavia was almost certainly watching, as she kept up with everything political. Eckstein was probably watching, too. I couldn't lose my resolve.

"We believe that these laws"—Mayor Chamberlain pulled the mic closer—"which I will soon sign into effect, are reasonable improvements to certain ordinances already in force. And these laws are only for the health, safety, and general welfare of our citizens.

Our only aim is to create peace in our time." Chamberlain spread her arms out. "As you can see, we have a consensus among our city's leadership, including the City's historic and award-winning civil rights organization, the Blind Equality Group."

Cameras trained on me. Nigel and Araminta looked up. I gave a tiny wave.

23

Penny and I were at a picnic thrown by Octavia for clients and potential clients. I was sure Octavia had invited me to say how pleased she was with my appearance at the press conference. She might give me the promotion on the spot and end my troubles.

The only other time I had been to the mansion was Elevation Night. I didn't realize then how truly impressive the estate was. The house itself was built in the neoclassical style, all sandstone pillars and arches. I saw whimsical details that I'd missed earlier, in the darkness. Pouting angels high up, a pair of stone rabbits guarding the entrance steps, and dicelike blocks that were part of the banisters on the front porch. They spun if you pushed them.

A platter of finger food sat on each flat service while some guests relaxed in the great room smoking and watching girls play chess on the big screen.

The field behind the house sloped downward to a garden maze on the right and a gazebo on the left. How did Octavia get such a large chunk of the City all to herself?

The slope ended at the bayou where wooden canoes bobbed. Kids were everywhere.

"Is this thing over yet?" Penny asked. Her hairdresser had given her partial holiday hair, Bali braids along the left side of her head. She adopted this style occasionally, and I found it adorable.

"Almost. Just four or five more hours."

"Kill me now." Holding hands, we walked down to the bayou, but away from the hubbub. We wound up in a quiet spot. A couple in a giant plastic duck floated across the water.

"Thanks for hanging in," I said. She wiggled her fingers at me, emphasizing her wedding ring. This was part of the marital agreement, wasn't it? Every married couple has certain terms that they work out between them, some in advance. Kids or no kids? How many? Other terms they negotiate down the line, ad hoc. Who gets the side of the bed close to the TV? Who controls the thermostat? It really comes down to how much shit one is willing to take.

For example, neither of us liked the other's friends. Penny's pals were a grungy lot. They were covered in tattoos of ancient gods or Sanskrit or odd birds. They didn't bathe often enough. They hit a little too close to home when they called me Geoffrey the Butler or Remus. I just smiled in their presence. My friends were largely people I went to law school with or my fellow firm fiends, such as Paul Pavor. I had ingratiated myself with peers from fine families, people I only saw at functions like this. I remember one guy, my moot court partner. After a long night of drinking with a large group that included Penny, he'd asked what it was like to be born trash. I'd never coldcocked anyone before that night. My hand still aches in cold weather.

"We should move," Penny said. "Seriously, what about that job out west?" It was a recurring topic that she only broached occasionally. I never knew what inspired these imaginative flights.

Nigel walked down the hill. He seemed a bit deflated since the incident at the Myrtles. One of Penny's crisis counselor contacts had been talking to him.

"Dad, you're on TV." We followed Nigel to the house. In the living room, a dozen people watched Mayor Chamberlain walk across the screen to a desk and sit. Someone handed her a golden pen. I stood in the background, staring into the camera. The woman next to me on screen wrinkled her nose.

A couple of people in the living room noticed me at the door and smiled, making the connection between the two-dimensional me on TV and the real me. Eckstein, whom I hadn't seen since the Personal Hill Hospital meeting, leaned against the side of a couch. He threw a pissy look my way. Where had he come from? And why was he there? He'd made it clear at PHH that he hated Octavia and me. And why was it that people you didn't want to see were always underfoot, but beloved relatives and dead lovers went away for good?

Penny grimaced, but not because of Eckstein. The mayor rose to her feet on the screen. The audience at Reinhardt clapped. The people in the room clapped. Except for Eckstein and Penny.

The scene with the mayor shrank to an inset to make room for the national show host and a couple of talking heads.

". . . some critics call these reactions an overreaction. What say you, Mr. Pavor?"

"It's a start, but they don't go far enough. If the City doesn't have security, then what do we have? Four centuries of savage black imbeciles are enough! When I'm mayor . . ."

Dinah would later surprise me—what stake did she have in whether I thought our colleague was a bigot?—by vehemently defending Pavor. The comment was taken out of context, she would say. He was only talking about the bad blacks. In the little video box, I furtively waved at the camera.

Penny squeezed my hand. Her eyes were closed. "I can't. I just can't."

"What?" I asked. I didn't really want to know what she had to say. I mean, I wanted to know, but in the same way one might want to know how much a fender bender would raise one's insurance premium. We were outside.

"They're going to turn us into a police state," Penny said. Of course, I agreed with her. But I couldn't let her know that. If she knew I agreed with her, that would be the end of everything. No more BEG. No more plan. No more saving Nigel. Besides, it's not like a racist police state would ever affect her. And once I helped Nigel, he would be safe, too.

"Give me some credit! Do you think I'd be involved if I didn't think it would be better for all of us? Jesus. Just trust me for a change. Chamberlain isn't that bad. She's reasonable. And I've known Pavor for years. He's just playing the game, too. If he wins next month, he's not going to start shipping people back to the Motherland."

"Maybe your mother is right. It's bad enough you agree with what they're doing. But do you really have to be the fucking mascot?"

"I'm doing what I need to do to provide for my family."

"Are you really? What does that"—pointing at the house— "have to do with providing for your family?"

"Everything. It has everything to do with it. You! You told me not to give up. This is what not giving up looks like in the real world. Lord knows if I don't, you can't pay the mortgage."

"What did you say?"

"Everything isn't so easy. You don't know what it's like to be me. You act like you have an idea what it's like to walk around in my skin. You don't know what it means to be the breadwinner, and you don't know what it means to be black, Ms. Cornrows."

"That's your final answer?" She stepped back.

"I can't win with you. You want both sides of the coin every time."

"That's not even a real saying." She smiled a little through her frown. I was still always taken aback when Penny found me amusing or lovable. But I knew this fight wasn't over. Her eyes had taken on the "not cry" look, creeping moisture along the borders, a kind of red tension. In other words, she was so mad or hurt that she would not under any circumstances cry.

I suddenly became aware that several houseguests were watching us.

Penny glared. "I'm going to the face-painting booth."

"Nigel's too old for face painting."

"Who said anything about Nigel?" Her face was impassive. Completely devoid of emotion. I was in enormous trouble.

I popped a Plum dry and walked down the slope. Along the way, I swiped a pig in a blanket off a serving tray. A heavily processed version of that dreary Fats Waller song played, and the breeze slapped me with the peppery notes of a quick-seared steak. Eventually I was on the far side of the house. Penny and Nigel entered the hedge maze hand in hand. A sister stood by the opening wearing tuxedo finery.

"Hold on, baby," she said. She held a hand to her ear. "Okay. Go on."

Inside the maze, I heard the voices of people ahead of me. Every few feet there was a garden gnome or a wrought-iron chair. The hedges were about eight feet tall, so I couldn't see beyond my lane when I jumped. I wandered toward the center, stroking the sweet-scented box leaves. I plucked a tulip—it smelled of pork. I did a shuffle off to Buffalo.

"I'll have my man send you a bill for that." It was Octavia. "I have those imported from Timbuktu." She wore culottes. "Each is worth about a grand." And a sweater draped over her shoulders. She took quick steps toward me and abruptly stopped.

"You did well at that press conference." Octavia smiled bigger than I'd ever seen her smile before. It unnerved me.

"But I didn't get to say anything."

"Doesn't matter." She flourished a hand. "The optics work, sugar."

"But what about"—I looked around to make sure he was out of earshot—"Eckstein?"

"I'm not too worried about him." She grabbed my upper arms. "You getting into that equal rights group was a strong move. Very strong. I have it on good authority already that some of the other heads at PHH like it. Just keep doing what you're doing. We'll win Eckstein over in time."

If there was one thing I knew about Octavia, it was that she was a genuinely optimistic person. Now she was brimming with good vibes. That was probably why I couldn't help but ask, "So this means you're promoting me?"

She chuckled. "Finish the job. Then we'll talk." Octavia squared the sweater wrapped around her shoulders. "And watch out for the Goblin sisters." She left.

I wandered for a bit. Somewhere around what must have been the center of the maze, I started to worry that I'd never escape. It wasn't even that large or ingenious a design, but the hedgerows were thick. I couldn't just push my way through them. My device buzzed, but I didn't check it. I'd stuck my fist into a hedge just a few moments before, and something seemed to nibble at my fingers. At my feet was a brick with "Jan. '77" carved into it.

I smelled really good weed. "What are you doing in here?" I asked.

Dinah drew from a joint. I hadn't seen her in ages.

A girl in a purple bikini painted Dinah's cheek with tools from the activities tent. "I'm avoiding my father," she said. The girl drew her fingers through her long black hair. "And getting away from those creepy guards in the trees. Worse than paparazzi." She didn't look away from the design she was adding to Dinah's cheek. The girl took the joint while Dinah checked her handiwork in a compact. "You really don't recognize me, do you?"

I tried to place her high cheeks, her supple black hair, the electronic collar around her neck. My mind was in no shape for solving equations. It kept spitting out error messages. A black helicopter swung overhead. We all watched it streak by. A giant man waved at us.

The girl motioned to me to sit. She dabbed a wet brush on my cheek.

"Jesus Christ"—Dinah passed the joint to me, but I demurred—
"it's freaking Crown. Catch up." Dinah looked different. I couldn't
quite place it though. Crown had painted a frog onto her cheek.

"What happened to your British accent?" I asked Crown. She
said the accent had been part of her act.

"She's off duty now," Dinah said.

"You trying out different eye makeup?" I asked Dinah. She
shrugged.

Crown laughed. "Same thing your boyfriend said," she said to
Dinah.

"What's it feel like?" I ask. Crown tilted her head. "Your demelanization. Did it hurt?"

"Probably not that different from weight loss surgery." Crown
took a drag on the joint. "You know they have to cut all the flabby
skin away after you lose the pounds. That's how I feel. Lighter. I
walk around and feel like I'm floating. My old look was just flab
for people to, like, be judgmental about. Now I get to judge."

"Are you judging me now?" I asked.

They laughed.

"Help us figure out something," Dinah said. Her other cheek
was emblazoned with a pink orchid.

"How to deal with an overbearing parent?" Crown asked.

"You stand up to them," I said. "Be honest and direct. Make
your position known."

"I don't think that will work here. Daddy's been insufferable
since I came back to the City."

"Who's your daddy?"

"You met him. He's the hospital's CEO." Eckstein. She was
talking about Eckstein.

Suddenly I felt exposed. Did I look high? If I looked high,
would Crown rat me out to Eckstein? But I was being silly. A man
under the stress of Eckstein's position probably dropped a few
purr-pills himself. I stooped to sit with the women and awkwardly
fell onto my rump.

My own dad wasn't exactly an easygoing person. But the older Nigel got, the more I saw why Sir seemed on edge around me. Imagine being given a soft-shelled egg and having to shepherd it through a funhouse.

"Maybe you should cut your pop some slack," I said, sitting upright.

"Why should I? He doesn't cut me any." Crown crossed her legs.

"I doubt he wants anything less than the best for you. Even if he's not great at expressing it."

"He's fun to be around when he isn't trying to ruin my life."

"He can't let you ruin it all on your own."

24

A Turkish bazaar in the middle of a snowstorm couldn't have been crazier than the backstage area of the auditorium in the School Without Walls. Parents like Penny and me had crowded in with their kids, making for a space so cramped that I found myself wishing for the relative roominess of a utility closet. Backstage smelled of young sweat and candy. Ms. Kavanaugh, who normally taught English, squeezed by, sewing the back of a girl's ripped costume. Another teacher, a black man in thick glasses, darted by carrying a box of programs on his shoulder. One of the vice principals kept peeking in from the doorway and scanning the crowd. I didn't know how many students were in the show, but there in the space between the curtain and the back wall, it seemed as if every student in the school—and all their siblings—had been enlisted to the cause.

"How do you feel?" Penny asked Nigel. The family of the lead actor had abruptly left town a few days ago, changing Nigel from second banana to big apple. "Are you up to it? You don't have to go on if you don't feel like it." He wore a plaid shirt and corduroy pants, both oversize.

"Of course he's all right, Penelope," I said. Nigel shrugged.

Penny licked her thumb and scrubbed something from his cheek.

"Don't freak the boy out."

Penny cut her eyes at me.

"Nigel!" one of the parent-helpers called from the door. "Make-up!"

Penny gave him a wet kiss and a long hug. Nigel was through the door in a flash.

"Let's go get our seats before we wind up in the opening number," Penny said. It was the first full sentence she had spoken to me since the hedgerow maze several days ago. Penny and her self-righteousness! No matter how much I explained my view to her, she would never fully accept what needed to be done.

I grunted and glanced back over my shoulder as we departed. Nigel hadn't smiled the entire ride over, hadn't even spoken when spoken to by his mother. He was an electrified wire, waiting to be plucked, ready to bring down the house in a squall of electromagnetic energy.

"What is this madness?" I asked. We were walking down a side stairwell, as small girls in white robes ascended the same steps.

"Oh well, it's madness," Mr. Gonzales said. He held a wicker basket of clocks. "The teacher who runs the drama club didn't show up today, and no one can find him. But the assistant, Mr. Riley, stepped in. He's a real find. A real find, I tell you."

"Pardon me." A teenage girl hauled a bass drum onto the stage.

We got seats three rows back and off to the left. They were good parental seats because it was close enough for us to see the action and hop onto the stage in the event of some catastrophe involving our child. But we were out of the main sight line. Nigel, being left-handed, would most likely look to his left, away from us. And perhaps most important: We were so far to the front that the lowest number of observers would see me cry.

I'd learned my lesson. Through every program and project my boy had been involved in, I always told myself the same thing: *Do not cry*. It didn't matter if Nigel only played a culm (as he did to sad perfection in *The Lorax*) or was a featured performer, like when he played a donkey in that forest fantasy. I started tearing up at his first appearance. Occasionally, I made it through most of a production without the waterworks, but never through an entire one.

Suddenly and without warning, the stage lights blazed. Some faced out into the audience, and behind me many parents, cursing and stumbling, struggled to find their seats. A short blond girl stood onstage draped in white. She shook slightly, nerves. She was the only child on an otherwise completely bare stage.

"Once a boy was born into a quiet, lonely darkness, but soon he would bring musical light to the world." She walked backward, slightly tripping at one point but recovering nicely. I hoped no one else noticed. You root for these kids. You really do.

A second set of curtains lifted. Waiting there like an army of mercenaries were dozens of boys and girls dressed in white robes oddly cut to show off their white rubber boots. They sang a song about the magnificent man who touched the sun with his voice and piano. It was a little ostentatious, and the chorus was rougher than sandpaper, but so far so good. Two boys somersaulted across the planks. A shadowy figure in all black crossed the stage. I was happy when he went away.

Everything went dark. A spotlight tracked someone being pushed in a wheelchair by another kid dressed as an old-timey nurse complete with the cute little hat and red cross emblazoned across the front of her dress.

The kid in the wheelchair's face was covered in what looked like one of those "drama" masks repurposed with some brown paint. Big black shades over the mask. I didn't need to see his face though. His arms, legs, and posture screamed Nigel. Penny knew as well. She patted my arm. We grinned at each other in spite of ourselves. A temporary truce was in order.

The nurse positioned him center stage, slightly facing Penny and me. Could he see us? I couldn't tell.

"When I was a boy," Nigel said, in a creaky, mock-old-man voice that sounded a little muffled by the mask, but they had mic'd him, "I heard music from heaven." Nigel placed a hand by his ear to imitate listening. "I learned how to play the piano." He panto-mimed working a keyboard. "Then I was the one making the music." As he spoke, adults dressed all in black crept onto the stage maneuvering instruments into place: a trap kit, a bass, a guitar, and two keyboards. Kids took their places at each one except for Nigel, who limped to one of the keyboards. Each kid delivered one of the following lines with Nigel going last. "It was the 1970s." "Paisley was the most popular pattern" (tugging at her paisley shirt, polite laughter from the audience). "President Nixon resigned." "Gas was so expensive you couldn't even drive." "Not that I was driving anywhere." (Nigel, still in the mask, slumped his shoulders, un-comfortable laughter from the audience.)

Nigel grabbed the back of his mask, and my stomach tightened. The mask had been fastened with sticky strips, and the ripping was audible. Underneath, his face was all white from stage paint. The band removed their masks—the same. I was quite pleased by the face paint as it reflected the purity of the artist's intention, the tri-umph of knowledge over ignorance. Kudos to the director.

Nigel: "Me and my band pushed against the darkness!"

They jumped into a song about how hard city life could be at times. And at the end of the song, many of us parents jumped to our feet, ferociously applauding. The next hour would alternate between songs and quiet vignettes from the musician's life: avant-garde dance interpretations of the first time he tasted pizza and first girl he loved. Nigel threw himself into the role.

Several teachers and students stood in the wings enjoying the show and clapping along. When the final note played, the entire house was on its feet. Nigel bowed. Penny cried.

On the drive home, I was giddy. We all were. I stopped short of our house, near the front porch. But before anyone could get out, I accidentally let my foot off the brake, and we rolled forward a good four feet before Penny grabbed the emergency brake between the seats and wrenched it back. Our momentum carried us all forward, within the Bug's cab, three bunnies bowing. I threw the transmission into park, and we settled back, in unison, into our seats.

A long moment of silence. We glanced at each other. Brows furrowed. Mouths quivering. Eyebrows twitching. These were my faces, the only faces that mattered, the only faces that could matter. I opened my mouth to speak but accidently brushed the horn, which honked. We jumped in place at the shock of it and burst into laughter. Hard, snorting belly laughs. At the car. At the early night. At the silliness of us beneath an invisible moon on a clear night.

I doubled over in full guffaw. My hand, having migrated on its own, caressed Penny's thigh. Something about the way she sat reminded me of the morning Nigel was born. One leg curled against the dashboard, as was her habit. It had been winter, and the sun seemed reluctant to do its work. Penny's ob-gyn had warned us from the jump about the dangers of her maternity. She risked toxic shock syndrome, gestational diabetes, and a dozen other family curses, including and beyond death. She could wind up in a coma and then die. The baby could die, too. And the baby, if a girl, could inherit some of her burdens. One day during a checkup very early in the pregnancy, Penny took Dr. Sapirstein's hand and squeezed it, perhaps a little too hard: *I'm having this baby.* Dr. Sapirstein pried his fingers loose: *Yes, of course you are.*

But on the morning in question, the sky outside PHH's Labor and Delivery Suite was dark. It rained in the early morning hours, a torrent of rain that left little lakes all over the hospital lawn and dripping stalactites of water along the eaves. I had stepped in a puddle. My socks were soaked. My feet freezing.

But Penny's hair was sweat-drenched. She sat upright. Her shoulders shuddered. Her red ringlets drooped against the pale of her collarbone. And her face was pale, too pale. She exhaled and glanced out the window.

The sun rose. The hospital room blazed like the inside of a stoked oven. Penny uncrossed her legs and curled one against the railing. She placed a hand on the side of her belly. She gritted her teeth.

By my elbow, Nigel leaned against the side of Penny's seat, himself suffocating in our laugh-bubble, his upper cheeks wet, his eyes pressed shut. Penny still laughed, too. I tried to ask Penny and Nigel to stop laughing, but all I could do was hiccup with yuks myself. It would be a terrible and heavenly thing to die from amusement. But I wasn't ready to go.

I barreled out of the Bug. I stood with hands on hips. I stood on tiptoes. I counted, slowly, to five. Then to six. They got out.

"You goofuses," I said, trying on an angry face. They both watched me. "That's enough." A moment of silence—and we all started laughing again. A crow perched on the electrical line above, tilting its head in that mechanical way avians do.

"We should order pizza from Fratelli's," I said.

Nigel's face turned serious, as I hoped it would. Odd boy that he was, Nigel despised pizza. Penny and I only ate it when he was away on school trips or sleepovers.

He took the house keys from Penny. "No pizza," he said. "I have a better idea." Nigel ran for the back door. A moth, really a bullet with wings, beat against the night.

"Is he going to cook?" I asked. It had been weeks since Nigel made anything, even breakfast. Smiling, Penny placed her fingertips over her mouth and nodded. Then she kissed me.

"I thought we were fighting?" I said.

"You're fighting," she said. "I've already won. Besides, I have a honey-do list for you."

She was right. I couldn't win our argument—at least not out in the open. Besides, the key to a happy marriage wasn't to avoid going to bed angry. It was to take every chance for reconciliation. We would fight tomorrow over my work, over BEG, over Nigel. But tonight—

"This list. Does it involve bed?" I pinched her stomach.

"Why, you scandalize me, sir." She mock-blushed away from my gaze. Then she smacked her lips. "Boy, I'm getting the Polaroid. We should capture the night."

"Not the Polaroid," I said. The Polaroid was an antique made around the turn of the millennium. Penny only pulled it out on special occasions. She had used it to take that picture of Nigel on the beach. "It'll take you all night to find that thing."

"It's in the bedroom closet." She trotted toward the back steps. "I know exactly where. I just have to find the spare film cartridge."

"Oh, brother."

Penny glanced over her shoulder. "The bed idea isn't a horrible proposition. I'll take it under advisement."

In the kitchen, Nigel furiously mixed batter in a big plastic bowl. He wasn't standing on a step stool like he used to. I smelled vanilla. Flour particles suspended in the air. I didn't have to ask. He was making our undisputed family favorite, crêpes suzette. At the end of the dish preparation, we would turn down the lights. He would drizzle liqueur onto our plates and light it. For a few moments, our faces would glow in the presence of the miracle that was us. I kissed his forehead. He didn't even flinch.

I found the Grand Marnier in the cupboard and the kitchen torch on the lazy Susan. I activated the flame and admired the white-blue plume.

"Don't," he said. "You'll burn yourself."

"But—"

"Like last time," he said. Who knew that ties were so quick to ignite? Embarrassed, I put the torch and bottle on the table.

"Um. What's our fruit?" I asked.

"Raspberry." He nodded at a dish of ripe berries.

"Most excellent." I played courier, shuttling eggs, butter, lemons, whatever my bright boy asked for. How strange to watch this little person hard at work combining ingredients that would have been disgusting taken individually into something of gustatory brilliance. He poured the batter into a container—his thin arms straining against the shifting weight of the mixing bowl—and put the container into the freezer so he could poof up the whipped cream. It wasn't until he fried the last crêpe that I began to wonder what was keeping Penny. Nigel was preparing the first plate—Penny's plate—when she entered the kitchen pinching a red spiral tablet, my Big Chief Bigboote tablet, by the rings.

My god.

If she had read any portion of that journal—even just the last few weeks of entries—she knew it all: my plans for Nigel, how I intended to do it, how I prodded the boy, how much I hid from her.

"Nigel, baby." She blinked. I'd never seen her eyes like that. Focused and hard. Taking me in. Dismantling her image of me. I was afraid. "Change of plans, and this is important. I need you to pack your overnight bag for a weekend stay at Grandma's."

"But the crêpes are hot and ready."

"Now!" She stepped to Nigel as if to grab him, but he backed away from the stove.

"Wait a second," I said. "There's no need to—"

Nigel went to his room.

"Two minutes," Penny screamed. She brandished the tablet. "It fell on my head while I was searching for the camera." She pulled out the clinic pamphlet that I had tucked into the cover fold.

"Penelope," I said.

"No." Rolling her eyes, she held her index finger up as if putting me on notice that one wrong move would end me. " 'Penny hasn't suspected anything of my plans. I admit my surprise at this fact. But the lovely old girl is too deep in her own confusions to sense what I'm working on. . . .' "

"That's an old notebook."

"That part was dated last month!"

Cool. Be cool as an underground well. "I was just playing around," I said. "You know I always wanted to try writing some fiction."

Penny fumed and went into Nigel's room. A few moments later she led him out of the house.

I ran to the front windows and peeked through the blinds. The minivan was parked against the curb on the opposite side of the street. Nigel was in the passenger seat. He was talking to Penny, but she ignored him. The van lights flickered on, then off. The engine wouldn't turn over. That ratty old van was good for something after all. I could fix this. I just needed to get them back inside. If we made it through the night, we might be us again.

Penny went over to the neighbors' and banged on the door. After several moments, skinny, beak-nosed Mrs. Kravits opened the door, followed by big, panda-bear-like Mr. Kravits in gray pajamas. They talked for a moment, and Nigel entered their house. Mr. Kravits tousled Nigel's hair in a grandfatherly way.

Penny stalked back toward our house. She slowed as an electric utility truck careened past, its unsecured boom bobbing. I almost opened the door and cursed that driver out. *Idiot.* But Penny ran to the back door. I bolted to intercept her.

"You don't understand," I said.

"You're damn right I don't. Our son. That's our son! You never had the right!"

"Please sit." I grabbed her shoulder.

She threw my hand off. "Don't tell me what to do." She went to the table. I didn't see her knock the Grand Marnier bottle over, but it rolled to the edge of the table and stopped.

"Would you just calm down." I knew my mistake when I said it. Calm down? What kind of leaky faucet asks a furious woman to calm down? To my credit, she did seem a little calmer. Like Mount Vesuvius in the final moments. She walked to me in short steps. And slapped me. It hurt. I didn't move.

"What is your problem?"

"I'm trying to help."

"By poisoning our son?" She slapped at my shoulders and neck. I grabbed both of her wrists. She put one of her feet in my gut and pushed me back. I let go. We stumbled apart. "That shit corrodes steel. Don't you understand that?"

"I didn't poison him—"

"And now you want our son to go to the hospital so that they can shoot him up with things they don't even fully understand yet. All for what? So he can look more like my cousin Shane? You're that afraid of a birthmark?" Trying to strike me again. But I held on. "You coward! Afraid the cops will come after him just because they might think he's black?

"That's what they do."

"Jesus Christ, things are bad. But not that bad. Nobody's going to kill our child if he looks like you. We don't live in the Tiko. Nigel doesn't roam the streets in the middle of the night. He doesn't carjack people. Sometimes the police do awful things, but you can't build his whole life around that. The chances of something like that happening to our son are very low!"

It was then that I realized the distance between us. The talk that all black parents give their children was such an integral part of my upbringing. One night when I wanted to play after dark, Sir and Mama sat me down and basically said, *The chances of something like that happening to you are virtually assured.* Penny was aware of this phenomenon. Many white people were. But her parents never gave her the talk because it wasn't necessary, so the whole thing was just a theoretical exercise. Like trying to choose between ten doors, all but one of which led to immediate death. It's not a problem if you never have to choose.

How could two people know each other so well but not recognize so fundamental a rift? She really didn't know. She really hadn't felt what I'd felt. This was the woman of resistance. The literacy program volunteer. The fearless protester. She understood the dangers of structural inequality. She knew the value of dismantling systematic injustice.

But when it came to the basics of walking through life as prey, she had no idea. It wasn't just that Nigel would make an appetizing target for some zombie with a badge and a gun. It was all the little things that were so obvious to me. The woman switching from one side of the street to the other. The store owner following him around. The increased scrutiny from anyone with power over his freedom or happiness. All the things that would eat away at his soul and make him wonder why we ever brought him into this world. All the things that would make him me.

"Not all of us in this family are beneficiaries of white privilege," I said.

She pointed at me. "Don't you dare."

I pointed at myself. "I dare."

"Every time you want to hurt me, you pull the race card."

"My life is a race card!"

"I'll tell you something you should remember. Our son is brave. He won't crumble just because he's a little different. Unlike his father."

"Take that back." I cornered her by the sink, placing a hand on the countertop.

"No." She pushed past me.

"You think that just because you did a few marches and called out a few people over the years that you're some kind of racial saint? That's not how it works. And it won't protect Nigel. You must believe I'm trying to do the right thing. All these years together. You have to give me some credit."

"I don't have to give you shit." Penny closed her eyes. I touched her arm, and she shuddered away. She was at the door. She opened it. She closed it.

"I'm not afraid of you. But I'm an adult. That boy believed in you. Thought the world of you." I flinched at her use of the past tense.

She went to the table and sat. She righted the bottle and drank. "This is what's going to happen. I'm going to find a lawyer."

"Wait—"

"Don't make me repeat myself. I'll get the house and full custody." She was serious. I had seen her make similar declarations. When she decided to cut her losses, she cut them through and through. "I used to feel guilty about your pill problem. I felt guilty about how full of shame you were and thought if I were a better person I could get you to straighten up. But it was never about me. It was always about your demented ideas. I was too stupid to accept that before."

Penny rose from the table and went to the door. Then she was gone. I sat there for a moment encased in amber. I would not let it end this way. I could not let it end this way.

The door jammed. I yanked it open and heard a sound like a large tennis racket hitting a large tennis ball. The noise disoriented me enough that I tripped down the steps, landing hard on my hands and knees. I pulled a shard of metal from my palm. One of Penny's lost earrings. How long had it been there? A pearl of blood erupted from my dirty palm. I heard Mrs. Kravits's voice, a yelp, but I couldn't see her, as she was obscured by the house next to our driveway.

An engine revved. I expected to find the minivan gone, but it was in the same spot, the hazard lights blinking. I jogged out into the street, feeling air on my knee. I had ripped my best cotton trousers in the fall. The Kravitses and Nigel were on the Kravitses' porch. Mrs. Kravits covered her mouth with both sets of fingertips. Mr. Kravits placed a big paw over Nigel's eyes and pushed him into the house.

"What—" I said. I was about to ask Mr. Kravits what on earth he thought he was doing to my son. But I realized the three of them had been looking past me.

A white police van had swerved off the road a few car lengths in front of the minivan, taking a mailbox with it. I realized I'd never called the City to ask them to slow the safety patrols down like Penny had asked.

Where was Penny?

The street glowed yellow, then white from the moonlight, then yellow again from the van's hazard lights. The driver of the white van, a young police officer in coveralls, stumbled out. He rubbed his face and looked me right in the eye. His forehead was bleeding.

"I was coming down this way, and she just—" Suddenly, his face shifted from confusion to fear. "Where did you come from? I need to see your ID."

I ignored him and went around the front of the van. Penny was suddenly there, on the cement, perfectly still and composed, as if sunbathing on a knoll. Her skirt splayed to one side and one leg lay at an impossible angle, like that painting of the girl lying in a grassy field. Her head lay against the sloped curve of a driveway. Her eyes opened. Some blood collected on the dirt below her neck. I got down to one knee.

"Stop right there!" The officer stood a few feet away, his gun drawn. "Step away from the woman."

Penny was blinking and turning her head as if to say no.

"What do I do?" I asked. I wanted to grab her up and run to the hospital. But I knew I couldn't touch her. I couldn't straighten her ruined leg. I couldn't cradle her head against me. What could I do for her?

"Baby, I—" she said. She clenched her eyes.

Part Three

25

The toaster dings. Good. Two wedges of waffle, hot and ready. Yes, they're processed. Yes, they were probably in cold storage for a decade before purchase. But I didn't burn them this time, at least, and create a new catastrophe. Don't want a replay of when I tried to make Nigel French toast. Sticky raw egg and bubbling burned butter everywhere. Scalded my skin. But that was weeks and months and weeks ago.

Now is different. I've snipped away the deckled edges of breakfast preparation for a more modest process. Compartmentalized the routine into something I can handle efficiently, in few movements. Undercounter to sink to microwave in five easy steps. Squat, lift, shift, shake, and drop. An interpretive dance for the morning munch.

Organic syrup. Pulsing in the microwave. Half minute to the correct temperature. Cantaloupe, sliced anonymously before purchase and hermetically sealed in cellophane. No muss or fuss. One less thing to trouble the heart. Fissure the package with the tine of a fork. Voilà. Easiest thing in the world. I would do better if I could. French toast. Soy bacon. Hand-juiced juice. More than just a slice of cantaloupe but blueberries, too, strawberries, raspberries, and snozzberries. I'd have farmers come to us, riding atop their tractors. They would schlep the produce into our kitchen, trailing mud from the fields. This I would do for Nigel.

Fold a paper napkin just so. Paper, because a spreading, berry-colored stain on a cloth napkin is too much to bear on mornings like these. Set out saucers, forks, and knives for two. Just for two. Only two. Do not set a third placement. Do not dwell.

Light cuts in through the slit window as if it were the end of the day. A guillotine for dust and shadow. But it's barely seven A.M. Soon all the shadows will perish—blown away—like Hiroshima, Nagasaki, Oslo, and Perth. Don't be ridiculous. Don't bloviate. The Japanese cities, at least, are fine today.

Grab glass mugs from the freezer. Two ice cubes per mug. Just two. Only two. Forget that recurrent dream where you kiss your son's forehead and your lips stick, so you push away with your hands, but they, too, stick. Soon you are suffocating. And then a faceless, fingerless corpse.

People argue on the radio. Last month's attacks by ADZE by a dreaded man wearing a creepy wooden mask and white linen suit. Killing the killers is the only way to peace. It's what Jesus would do. Shoot them in the nads. Deport the rest, children included. But first sterilize the lot—from babies to grandparents—and implant tracking devices in their bellies that detonate if they set foot on American soil again. Pike the heads. Pike the—

Boop. Radio to classical station playing Barber's adagio. *Boop.* To station bumping Tchaikovsky. Boy, that cat sure can swing. It's all arithmetic. Exhale unhappy thoughts. Out with the minuses. In with the pluses. Kittens, puppies, and whiskers on both. Bright copper kettle. Use oven mitt to pick it up. Pour steaming water over instant coffee crystals and appreciate all the good things I've been doing for myself. Exercising at the Sky Tower gym on the treadmill overlooking downtown. Three days a week, or four if I can manage. Looking both ways before crossing the street. Greeting strangers in the elevators. Under no circumstances screaming at rude drivers or pale short people in rain slickers gawking at me from great distances. Pragmatism before teenage wasteland emotions.

I take my place at the table and stare into my coffee water, a foot-brown pond. I lower Nigel's waffle onto his plate. And the fruit.

There's an absence of noise from Nigel's room. No squeaks from his bed. No puff of cool air from his ceiling fan. Finding his door closed, I call his name. The door to my bedroom shifts, but Nigel's not in my bedroom. No one is in my bedroom when I'm not in it, even though that familiar red-haired scent still drifts on the house currents like a melody. My bedroom is empty. My life—

This is logic. The present. The here and now. Don't. Think. A. Bout. The. Past. Pull your ring finger back too far, and let the pain stake you to the ground as though you were a witch.

Nigel appears in the kitchen and says hey. I say hello and good morning. We sit at the table, faking consumption. I pour syrup onto my squares. I cut my squares into cubes. I dissect my cubes into abstract shapes. What is food even for? And whose idea was it anyway? I pour syrup over the mess until my plate is a sluice of yellow and brown, like a spring-thaw mudslide. Nigel has sipped his juice two or three times. But his glass is still nearly overflowing.

He let his hair grow out, to my surprise, for which I'm thankful. One less thing to fight over. But he still resists spot countermeasures. So I've established a market-based system to overcome his reticence. He's almost a teenager and wants things. New shoes. New shirts. Things that go beep. Things that light up. I provide a small amount of money when he uses the toning cream. A larger amount of money when he takes the antimelanin tincture. The stuff finally came in from Eritrea. It arrived one day in a box lined with white down. Tincture's active ingredient: albino turtle shell. It was said the fishermen used to throw the albinos back. They wanted fish, after all. But now they go searching for the white turtles. They have to net a couple hundred dark ones to make the harvest economically feasible. But one white hit makes a day, apparently.

Nigel doesn't wear hats anymore. I can't pay him enough to.

The tincture came in a bottle like the kind that holds cough syrup. I pour a shivering tablespoon's worth. Open the hangar, there goes the plane. He rolls his eyes when I check under his tongue with a depressor. Have to make sure he isn't holding the stuff in a pocket of his mouth. Trust but verify. I lay a small amount of cash on the table.

This is to say nothing of the puckered wound on the inside of his elbow. Once a week there is injected for a startling sum a supposedly highly effective compound of things I cannot pronounce that disperse into Nigel's young body and collect melanin in much the same way garbage men collect trash. I've noticed some change in Nigel's complexion, but I no longer trust my perception.

"It's what your mother wanted."

Nigel doesn't react for a moment. He lifts an eyebrow. "That's right, Dad. She said so herself." He grabs the cash. He grabs his bag and goes outside. He's sitting in the car, waiting for me. I'm sitting in here, waiting. I take my hat from the chair next to me.

We drive the route to the School Without Walls. No music. Too many cars drifting like angry manatees. An airless commute.

The Centurial Compilation plays through the stereo, a playlist of my favorite music from long ago, given by Sir. Nigel has earbuds in his ears, a portable game—a new purchase—in his hands, and an egg-shaped wrist device that pulses green at random intervals. Where is he? How do I find my son?

We pass a billboard atop a restaurant down one of the cross streets. It had been an ad for PHH. Then it was tagged by ADZE. Then it was painted blank. Now there's half of an *A* on the canvas, like the graffiti is redrawing itself.

I park across the street from the entrance to the School Without Walls because dozens of other cars clog the reverse lane. Nigel gets out. I shout for him to look both ways, but he doesn't. He pulls up his hoodie.

A few other students fall in behind him. The other students are a dark conclave. It's as if Nigel has collected into his sphere of influence all the kids who are anything but white. Although there is one blond girl. I get out of the car, not exactly sure why I'm following. I fail to note a city bus railroading from my left. The driver leans on the horn, which is curiously high-pitched. My hat flies off, but I catch it and press backward into the side of the car. Nigel and the others, at the top of the steps, watch me before entering the school together. I fall into the Bug and hold my hat against my chest.

26

In the Sky Tower mezzanine, people I don't know flank me on the elevator. Their bland faces I never really see. My golden reflection grimaces from the polished doors. My felt fedora is evenly pitched. My gray suit is creased to military specifications. Even the little divot in the knot of my tie is perfect. But I'm thin as a drying rack.

The receptionist greets me with hangdog eyes. It's the same every morning. What is she looking for in me? She won't get it, whatever it is. I hate a snoop. Once she tried to strike up a conversation, in friendly tones, about a father or cousin left trapped on the distant shore of eternity. I straightened my back and stepped determinedly past her. Just like now. Same as tomorrow.

I stop at Octavia's office, and she's not in. But my abacus row is nearly complete. Just a couple of more beads. Praise Theophilus. It's the one thing I have going my way. I'll make goal. I'll get that promotion. I'll help Nigel. Something good will come of all this, of my life, it will.

I keep having flashes of the first time we met, my wife and me. I was leaving the law school library after leading a class as a teaching assistant. A cold front had overtaken the City, but that didn't stop a group of activists from camping out on the portico. They were protesting a policy that kept the children of felons out of school. I picked my way through the throng. I was down the steps. I was almost to my car when Penny slammed into me. Knocked me over. My satchel full of index cards and multicolored highlighters spilled into a puddle. The same puddle I had been knocked into. My bottom was soaked with freezing water. I was ready to curse my assailant. But her bright face in relief against the gray clouds stopped me. She helped me up.

My phone chimes in my pocket. Jo Jo wants me to call him. He's been sending me messages for weeks, but I've ignored them all. I slip the phone back into my pocket. He was nice enough to give me something for my nerves and a few refills. How many months ago? He's just checking up on me. Making sure my doses are okay. I'm fine. No need for chitchat.

In my office, I hang up my hat and coat. I tell myself that I'll sit at my desk and work. I tell myself that this is a simple thing, something that I've done for about a decade. But I open the flat drawer above my lap and spend a quarter hour creating objets d'art out of paper clips: a flower, a winged thing, a very large paper clip.

Strummer, my newish secretary, enters and hands me my to-do list. There are briefing deadlines to meet, video conferences to attend, correspondence to compose. Correspondence that will be— once completed—as terse and brittle as a two-line poem.

Strummer keeps staring at me. He knows the drill. I don't much work in my office anymore. Instead, I occupy one of the smaller interior conference rooms near the kitchen. I say conference room, but it's really more of a large storage closet. No windows except for the glazed panels that open onto the hallway. He follows me in. I find his suspenders an annoying affectation. Belts work just as good.

My work—file folders and milk crates full of more file folders— is neatly arranged along the wall and table. All the technology we have these days, but we lawyers are conservative creatures. Fly me a sheet of paper over an electrical current. Watch me convert it to paper.

A legal pad sits on the table a few inches from the lip. A single blue pen waits next to the pad perpendicularly. I begin sketching notes to myself: an argument I'll need to make in section seven subsection G to overcome an opponent's prescription counterargument. Strummer fiddles with a stack of documents, fiddles with his cuff links, fiddles with his wire frame glasses, but there's nothing for him to do here. He's already made sure that my workspace is immaculate, as always. He wants me to talk. And maybe I should, but this is a professional environment, and I've important work to do.

I go to the door with the intention of telling Strummer to beat it. He must have other tasks to complete. He's answerable to other attorneys, after all, not just me. But Armbruster walks by. He pauses to put a hand on my shoulder. For a change, he seems completely tuned in to the moment. His face is unmuddled, clear, hawkish. He doesn't talk. He just stares into my eyes with a look I can't place. He could be thinking *you poor bastard* or just *you bastard*. But who knows? Who can read the minds of other people in this world?

Armbruster squeezes my shoulder and continues down the hallway. I tell Strummer to beat it.

After lunch, I'm on the floor of the Labyrinth Room flipping through client files in a bucket folder. Footsteps approach from the next aisle. Dinah's feet enter my field of vision. Still can't get used to the flats she's been wearing lately.

"Don't get up," Dinah says.

"Well, have a seat then."

"Don't be silly." Dinah places a hand on her hip. "I'm not ten years old, and I'm not at my grandma's eating a bowl of pho. Who do you think I am?" At least some things are the same.

I stand and squint. Something's changed about her. Has she had another procedure? It's possible, as I haven't seen her around much lately. Not since she revealed she and Paul Pavor had fallen for each other a while back. What else could she have done? Her eyes are one thing. What else is there? I lean in for a better look.

Dinah smiles and takes off her glasses. "What do you think?"

"What did you—"

"You can't tell?"

I can. Her jaw and her nose. She's done something to both. She looks like a different person. Still Vietnamese but whiter. As if someone hopped in a time machine and swapped out one of her parents for a Swedish person. I tap the bridge of her nose. I pinch her jaw. What a miraculous era where you can fall into a vat of sleep as a caterpillar and emerge a butterfly.

She swats my hand away, gentler than I would figure. "Does it look natural?"

I nod. I'm not sure what I should say. I can't quite lock onto the emotions bubbling up from my gut. They're just glimmers of emotions. Shadows on the wall of my psyche. I can't feel them directly.

"Paul thinks I look like that British actress," she says. "The one from those stupid end-of-the-world movies with the talking puppies. I think that's his way of saying he doesn't like it, that I should get more done." Her eyebrows furrow. "You think I look stupid, too."

I tell her not at all.

"Why does it matter what Paul—" I stop myself.

"When you put it that way, you make me sound like an airheaded schoolgirl. But yeah. I guess it did matter."

"How does it feel?"

Dinah touches her own cheek. "Like falling down an elevator shaft, but I'm not afraid of hitting bottom anymore. Well, what is it?" she asks. "Spit it out. We've known each other most of our lives. I expected more of a reaction from you, of all people. Not just a weak smile like everyone else around this joint. Except for Armbruster. Armbruster says I look like one of his nieces."

Truth to tell, I'm surprised I'm not happier for her. Trapped in my esophagus, there's a swirly colored marble of joy, disappointment, and something else. If I can't feel it all, then maybe I can interpret the swirls like reading Braille after the notches have been rubbed off. What remains?

Am I happy for her? Yes, I'm happy because Dinah is my friend. And my friend seems happier these days. Happiness is too rare a commodity not to count for something. Still, my happy is the caustic yellow of a safety vest.

"I know you think I did this for Pavor," she says. "But I didn't. Everyone always thinks I do everything to please other people. Like I make all these sacrifices to be a good Asian girl. Don't you get it even now? That's not me. It never was. That's a stereotype. And that's the only thing I've ever been afraid of—being pulled into some shitty stereotype. I don't need people to assume I'm some kind of math genius or willing to go along with whatever everyone else wants. I just want to walk to my apartment without random guys catcalling that they want to tie me up. I bet that never happened to Penny." She sighs. "I didn't mean to bring her up."

"It's okay," I say. "I'm sure P—" I can't get her name out of my mouth. "She always liked you."

"Listen up, dum-dum." She points at her face. "My face, my career, my life, has always been about what I want." She glances down at her shoulder. "And then Pavor showed up and made all this easier. My ex-boyfriends would have broken up with me for ruining their fantasies." Dinah leans back onto a file shelf. "It's still my world. But I don't mind sharing. We don't believe all the same things, but we're together where it counts. We're engaged now." She holds up her hand. The ring is ornate and loopy. More metal than jewel. "The stones are synthetic. I couldn't talk him into getting one with real diamonds. Something about not supporting savages." She wipes her eye with the side of a finger.

I ask her when will they marry.

"In the new year." She hugs me. It's the first human contact I've had in a long time that wasn't entirely about someone feeling sorry for me. Makes me feel like an empty bag in a breeze. She pauses. "I want to thank you for being my friend."

"You don't need to."

"Hush," she says. "You know it's not easy for me to say that. So don't cut me off, okay? I did some things. I made a mess that's going to get messier. But remember I'm your girl."

A gong rings inside me, a thousand miles down. Something isn't right. This is more than about her face or her new soulmate Paul Pavor.

"Things are about to change," she says.

I ask how.

"She means she sold out." Octavia is at the door. "Sold me out. Sold you out. Meet Little Lady Judas."

Fear flashes across Dinah's face, as if she thinks Octavia might haul off and punch her.

"I don't have to talk to you." Dinah turns to walk away.

"Ah-ah, sugar." Octavia grabs Dinah's arm and spins her around. Dinah tries to break away but can't. "Not so fast. You've got something of mine."

Law offices are not worlds of physicality. People rarely move, and you can go an entire year without seeing two humans touch. Violence is as rare as vibranium. Octavia's action might seem like a minor flare-up between two women if you saw it on a busy street. But up here, on the sixty-second floor of the Sky Tower, among dusty files and beige walls, they might as well be going at each other with flaming whips and broadswords.

"You were like a daughter to me," Octavia says.

"I already have a mother," Dinah says. "And I didn't do anything you wouldn't have."

"Don't sweat it, peach. I understand. Business is as business does." Octavia snatches something from Dinah's jacket. Dinah pulls away, clutching her upper chest.

I ask what in the world is going on. They've had verbal altercations before, but nothing like this.

Octavia opens her hand. Dinah's sun pendant. Octavia took it from Dinah's lapel. Dinah's not in the group anymore.

"That bitch Armbruster stole her away."

"He didn't steal anything," Dinah says. "I chose."

"Whitmore, I'm wounded." Armbruster strolls into the room. "Is that the language you use to describe your old mentor when you think he's out of earshot? Thought I house-trained you better."

"When he did everything he could to hold me back," Octavia said, pointing, "you're goddamn right that's how I describe him."

"Now, heel." Armbruster whips out a handkerchief and wipes the corner of his mouth. "Did you really think you're qualified to run this place?" he asks. "I'm not going anywhere. This is my ship. Will be till I say otherwise." He snorts and pauses in his tracks. "Octavia didn't tell you, did she? I guess she was hoping to turn things around before the deal was done."

I turn to Octavia, but it's Dinah who speaks. "Darkblum Group signed up with Armbruster. They're his client now."

"Our client." Armbruster lays an arm over Dinah's shoulder. She smiles stiffly. The significance of this strikes me all at once. Octavia and Armbruster shared the preliminary Darkblum work all year, but only one shareholder can take credit. With the company signing up with Armbruster, all the money and billables from that work will go to him and his team. Including all the billable hours from the past year. Any hours I worked on the file will go to Armbruster instead of Octavia. She won't get the credit. Neither will I. My abacus bleeds.

"My firm." Armbruster adjusts his tie.

He takes a sheet of paper out of his pocket and unfolds it. I don't have to see the words to know that it's a Racing Form containing everyone's stats.

"You'll be needing to revise this." He crumples the paper and throws it at Octavia. But the ball lands at my feet.

27

Life doesn't care about your protest. You can rage all you want, curse it, abstain from it in every way possible. But necessity rears her heavily made-up face and says, *Frown all you want, sweetheart, but somebody got to handle up on this and this and this.* In the middle of our archipelago of sadness, Nigel and I still had basic needs. Toothpaste. Tissue. Tea.

"Can I stay in the car?" Nigel asked.

"Come on," I said. He got out, and we walked into ¡Organix!, the macromarket with heart.

The problem with going to a grocery store when you're the noncooking partner is you feel like a phony. You're out of your element and assuming an area of responsibility that you aren't built for. You haven't kept track of how many cans of corn belonged in the pantry. You didn't stock those shelves. You consumed. Greedily, you lapped up every breadcrumb lovingly placed before your muzzle, always sniffing for the next bit and keening whenever you wanted more, which was frequently.

Even the layout of the building challenged me. Should I work counterclockwise through the fruits and veggies or start with the bread and sweets? What a farce. As if either choice could give me even a single moment more with—

"This is dumb." Nigel picked over a selection of grapefruit. He was wearing his hoodie up, which I hated. In profile, his shaggy hair sprang from under the hood like the legs of a hermit crab. "We're not going to eat any of this."

He was right, of course. I didn't want any of the food in the entire place. A fetid scent, of charred pig meat, rooted in the air. My stomach pulsed. *Run away,* my gut squealed.

But there was a fatherly ticker tape tangled in the rat's nest of my brain. I was depressed, and I knew it. But I had certain duties. And even if I didn't believe in the goodness of the world or have any hope whatsoever for the future, I had a job to do. All I had to do was speak the words.

"We don't get to give up," I said.

"When was the last time you were hungry?" he asked. "I can't even—"

"Listen to me—"

He gestured toward the center aisles. "I mean, we just keep buying all this stuff, and then it gets all moldy, and I have to throw it away."

"Nigel, I'm trying to tell you something, son."

I placed a hand on his shoulder. "Horrible things happen. I don't like anything now. I don't like waking up. I don't like leaving the house. I sure as hell don't like being here."

"Why are we here then?"

"I don't even like you. I certainly don't like myself. In fact, I like me less than you. So in a battle between us, you win. But this won't last forever. One day I'm going to wake up and feel like a person again. We both will."

"You're talking weird again."

"Maybe. You should try it sometime. It feels awesome. Now, I was saying that things can't suck this hard forever. And one day

I'm going to wake up and my stomach will growl, and I'm going to be pretty mad if I go to the fridge and we don't have any frozen waffles. She always made sure we had frozen waffles, just in case."

"You're trying to sound so tough. You can't even say her name."

"And you can?"

"I talk about her all the time." Nigel glanced at me, then away. "Just not with you."

I rubbed my forearm and blanched at who he might have felt more comfortable confiding in. Araminta? Riley? It didn't matter. "Well, then," I said, "you're a better man than me."

A tall figure in black crossed between the onions and the potatoes. It was Eckstein from PHH. The scowl he wore every time he saw me seemed to soften when he realized who I was with.

"This must be your boy," he said. He seemed a little frazzled. Five o'clock shadow. Ashy feet in slippers. His straightened hair uncombed.

I introduced them.

"I saw you at Ms. Whitmore's mansion," Eckstein said to Nigel, "and your mother, too, but didn't have the pleasure of meeting either of you then."

"My mom's dead. She was run over by a police officer."

"Oh."

"But don't worry." A strange smirk spread across Nigel's face. "She's in a better place now. She would have wanted us to be happy. And at least we have memories of our time together."

Eckstein's eyebrows shot up.

Nice job, Nigel. Way to sock it to him for the old man. Eckstein's shock was the perfunctory reaction I was used to seeing from the powerful trying to relate on some surface level. But then his whole body deflated.

"Don't mind him," I said. "He's just talking weird again." Nigel rolled his eyes. For a brief second, he seemed like my son again, and I felt like his father.

Eckstein leaned forward and gathered us in his arms. He smelled like coconut oil and aftershave. I looked at Nigel, who looked at me as if to ask what was happening.

"I'm so sorry." Eckstein let us go. "It's just I lost Beverley when Tyresha was small."

"Tyresha?" Nigel asked.

"Crown," I said.

"I'm sorry—I'm not very comforting, I know." He swatted away a tear.

I was jealous of him. I hadn't cried. I was so tranqed at the funeral that I felt nothing on my skin or in my soul. I recognized its presence that day, a purple-brown whirlpool gurgling inside me. It needed to get out. Nigel gushed like a busted hydrant though.

"Enough about us," I said. "How are things at the hospital?"

"Terrible, to be honest. All this business with those protesters and terrorists has the shareholders feeling quite nervous." He blew his nose into a napkin. I had seen the reports on the news. The mother corporation's stock was plummeting. They were considering selling the hospital or even mothballing it if they couldn't find a buyer. "You know my feelings about the special procedures we offer now. And I get why some in the community are upset. But it's a slap in the face to have those charlatans leading the charge. They're not even the real ADZE."

"They're real." Nigel said. "I've seen them."

"Young man, the original ADZE was a community-minded group that tried to build people up. Not kill them. They provided job training to the underemployed, healthy breakfasts to kids who couldn't get them even at school. They even put on an annual pride festival called Visions of Blackness. It was beautiful to see. My parents were heavily involved in all of it. Until the government started sending in infiltrators."

Sir would have disagreed. He thought old ADZE was a bunch of self-centered radicals. It was one thing to organize and protest, but grandstanding was almost always counterproductive, in his view. ADZE's tactics led to a whitelash, which led to the world Nigel and I lived in.

"Infiltrators?" Nigel asked.

"Sure," Eckstein said. "The FBI made a task force that—"

Something in my head clicked. A slip of paper popped out of my mouth. "That's what you should do."

"What?"

"Correction." I bopped Eckstein's shoulder. "That's what *we* should do. What if PHH threw a festival in the Tiko like back in the old days? Nothing too crazy. Just a day-long thing. Your daughter could headline it."

"But they hate her."

That's when I laid it out to him in jargon he could understand. The firm would lead the charge leveraging its connections to various community groups, including BEG, to shore up support. PHH would provide the real money, including donations to those same organizations and free swag for the festival. As for Crown—

"She just needs to say to the public what she told me when I first met her. In fact, if she works for free, it might clear out her community service."

"Gracious," he said. "I don't—"

"Go ahead," I said. "Tell me it's the best idea you've ever heard."

"The corporation has been itching to greatly expand its community medical services program." Eckstein rubbed his chin. "Demel discounts and that sort of thing, which I'm not particularly supportive of. Yet I've a fiduciary duty to present ideas that could increase our stock value. I can't believe I'm saying this, but I think we should work together on this project. I'll need approval from the board, of course."

"Of course."

"But I think we have a deal."

We shook hands, and Eckstein walked away, steering his basket with one hand and calling someone on his device.

It took everything in me to keep from dropping to the floor and break-dancing right there.

"What was that?" Nigel asked.

"That was the beginning of the next chapter of our life, son."

The Sky Tower gym floated some twenty stories above the street. It was fronted by a band of opaque silver windows that circled the superstructure. From a mile away, the gym floor looked like a metallic belt that had been cinched a little too tight. The crystal elevator that ran right of center down the southeast side of the building formed the dangly part of the belt.

"Why are we here on a Sunday?" Nigel asked, as we stepped out of the elevator.

"Because I'll explode if I have to wait until tomorrow. Wait out here."

Octavia was on one of the antigravity treadmills, chatting with someone presumably through an earbud.

"Keep up with what you're doing, Luna. Catch you later." Octavia seemed startled when she noticed us standing just a few feet away. "What the dickens?"

"Eckstein is ready to close the deal."

"Well, don't just stand there looking pretty, sugar. Spill it."

I told her.

Octavia tapped her earbud. "That's great news. You should hear Dinah shouting in my ear. She likes it too."

"Dinah?" I asked. "But she's with Armbruster now."

"That was just a ruse. Dinah is reporting back every move they make. No way Armbruster closes that deal with Darkblum with our girl throwing monkey wrenches into the works." Octavia stopped the machine, waited for the lower chamber to decompress, and stepped off the platform. "Everyone has a role to play." She wiped her face with a towel. "Pavor's going to win mayor, and he's already set to get federal funding for that demel clinic. Did you know Pavor has family in D.C.? Between that and your smooth-talking Eckstein, I'll own that hospital four or five different ways. They'll have to sign up as my client. Now, don't you feel useful?" Octavia went into the ladies' locker room.

I felt more than useful. I was rapidly approaching the fulfillment of my life's work.

Nigel stood outside the glass doors. I made a show of pointing at him, then walloping a nearby punching bag with the only combination I recalled from a long-ago summer camp. Hook. Uppercut. Cross.

28

Nigel sat on the examination table in Dr. Nzinga's office, wearing a gray hospital gown. The nurse had already drawn blood and taken his vitals. Nigel and I were like those two theatrical masks, him all frowns, me all smiles.

"Someone has a case of the pouts," said the nurse, pumping the blood pressure cuff.

"Girl trouble," I said.

I was on cloud nine thousand, of course. When I explained the plan to Octavia, she had immediately shifted into gear, throwing out the names of production companies and other contacts I needed to get in touch with. We met with Eckstein's people just two days later and signed contracts. "You'll be a shareholder within twenty-four hours after the festival is over, sugar," she said. In the meantime, I was to get Nigel signed up for demelanization. She would cover the consultation fees. She said I was a good father for working so hard to improve my son's life.

The nurse placed a hand over her heart. "Aw. It'll get better," she said. "You just have to move on, sweetie."

"I already have a new girlfriend," Nigel said. His mark seemed darker and more clearly defined under the fluorescents.

"That's the spirit." The nurse gathered her equipment and pinched his arm. I smiled at her. She winked and left the room.

Nigel asked me how long would this take. Not very long, I said. Dr. Nzinga had already explained the process to me. It was a six-month procedure, similar in some ways to the cancer treatments they used to give. The plan would play out in stages. A few weeks of primer treatments, various markers and agents added to the body to prepare it for complete demelanization. Then active reagents introduced. That was where the real work began. Epigenetic restructuring that I only understood in the broadest strokes. That was where the actual retoning of the skin occurred, among other changes to the hair and visible membranes like the gums, etc. Of course, Nigel's procedure would leave his nose, lips, and other features untouched. The changes would focus on getting out that damned spot.

But the process was also preventive and would keep him, or his once and future children, from ever being black like me. Dr. Nzinga described it as sending out millions of little demolition teams, each crashing a wrecking ball through a ghetto facade. The final stage was the bum's rush, when the tiny crews attached bombs to the melanocytic pillars and brought down the house. The procedure had been much improved with time. Crown's process had taken nearly two years.

"Let's play a game," Nigel said. I was startled when he spoke. He had been on his device, flipping from screen to screen. But now he held a pair of dice. "Double or nothing. If I win, we leave. If you win, I'll do it and never complain again."

"That's not necessary. You already promised."

"But I didn't promise to like it."

We had left before daybreak. But not before Nigel threw a fit, wrapping his arms around the porch pillars and refusing to move. He wanted that nettlesome girl to come along. She was there by our door waiting, doing her best impression of a darkened corner, when we exited. I wouldn't have it, of course. This was a private experience to be shared between father and son—a cornerstone of our future relationship. It was only by convincing him that he was making a small child of himself in front of Araminta that I was able to pry his koala fingers from the wood. He exchanged words with her. She seemed genuinely wounded.

"How do we play?" I asked. Nigel tossed the dice into the air and caught one—and then the other.

I always found the game uncouth; the men who gathered in semicircles on the streets of the Tiko were invariably society's dregs: unemployed or chronically underemployed, lacking imagination or premium insurance, empty message bottles headed for the great recycling facility in the sky.

But the few times someone convinced me to roll, I had a lucky hand. In fact, I often found favor in games of chance. Lady Fortuna knew the score and sought to help dedicated, pure-hearted men like me carry out our appointed rounds.

Nigel climbed off the examination table. I refastened the tie on the back of his hospital gown. He tossed the dice, and a good number rolled up. I tossed and a bad number rolled up. We agreed to best five out of seven, but he won the first three. Then five out of six.

"Let me see those," I said. He gave the dice to me. I eyed them and shifted them in my palm. I actually had no idea what rigged dice looked or felt like, but I had the feeling that maybe I could learn. I held one to the light.

Nigel took them from me. "They're fake, Dad."

"What?" I asked.

"Loaded."

I was astonished. My son was brilliant and wily, of course, but only a child. I never imagined him using his intelligence against me, even if only for a second. It was an inversion of our relationship. It was I who was supposed to clobber him at chess or embarrass him with feats of manly strength. It was my job to show him how cruel and uncaring the world could be, so that he would toughen up. Not vice versa.

"Why did you tell me?" I asked.

Nigel turned the dice over in his hand and threw them into the wastebasket. He shrugged.

"I don't know," he said.

Dr. Nzinga entered. "Ah," she said. "Very well to see the happy family. Are we ready to start?"

Nigel glanced at me. "Yes, ma'am."

29

One Blue Geisha Backrub will take you to seventh heaven. Two Blue Geisha Backrubs will reunite you with your maker. Three Blue Geisha Backrubs will cause your maker to throw you out of heaven for degeneracy.

My wet knees vibrated against the bathroom tile. Many hands held me by the shoulders and arms over a toilet full of expelled material. One would think that finally getting Nigel the help he needed would have calmed my nerves. Not so. If anything, since Nigel started his preliminary treatments with Dr. Nzinga, I'd been more on edge, gulping pills like penny candies. I couldn't slow down no matter how hard I tried.

Someone slapped me. "Hey, guy," the female voice said, "say something."

I glanced at the palm of my hand, which was empty. "God only knows."

"Good," a male voice said. "He's still in one piece, I guess." I experienced the sensation of being lifted.

When I came to, it was the afternoon, although I couldn't have bet on the day. I slumped out of the bed and lay face-to-carpet for a few minutes. I crawled to my feet and checked myself in the mirror. My hair was a mess, and my pajamas smelled like actual shit, but otherwise I would survive. Something crinkled in my hand. I unfurled an old to-do list with my wife's handwriting on it: call City about speeding van. Disgusted. I crumpled the paper and tossed it to the floor.

"Hey, old guy." It was the male from earlier, a youngish man, a ruddy, thin boy, one of the tribe that had been camped out back in Jo Jo's yard. "He asked me to give you this." The boy handed me a note. It was from Jo Jo. Jo Jo's yard was outside the window. I was in Jo Jo's house. This was Jo Jo's bed.

> Dear Buddy,
> This is not me. I've got to get my life back on track. Making designer whim whams and short videos was fun to do back in my college days, but I've been stalling and hoping that Casey would walk back in with the boys. But that's not going to happen, as you yourself have pointed out on more than one occasion. I get that now. Plus, I think maybe the DEA is after me. So I'm skating with Polaire. She's good for me. She believes in things. And I'm starting to believe, too. (Imagine that!) So as nuts as it sounds we're off to Oman to stand with the revolution. I hope I don't get myself killed.
> Best regards,
> Your Faithful Jo Jo
>
> P.S. I didn't leave any more geishas because we had to get an ER doctor (the kid with the red cheeks, he's a prodigy) to bring you back to life. You probably don't remember. Lay off the Plums. Seriously.
>
> Love and Rockets JJB

What of loyalty? What of brotherhood? What was friendship if a person could check out on a whim? In every instance, I had been there for Jo Jo. Held him up when his resolve turned to jelly. Acted as cheerleader, counselor, and concierge. And that Polaire— I blamed her. In a selfish, feminine display worthy of Yoko Ono, she was taking my man away just when I needed him. How would I ever get my Plums now?

I sat up in bed.

"You shouldn't sit up in bed," the kid physician said.

"No, thanks. I gave at the office. I appreciate you saving me, though."

"Don't mention it."

"Do you have anything for a splitting headache?"

30

I awoke to a synesthetic scenario: I somehow felt that I was being licked by a dog, a whimpering old beagle. But when I opened my eyes, I found no dog and no licking. Mama sat on a chair across the room from me, her occipitals moist from a fresh watering. My bedroom. What was she even doing in my bedroom?

"What are you even doing in my bedroom?" I asked, her banana bushel earrings clattering as she stood. I realized the sun's shadow was older than I would have expected. "Where's Nigel?"

"I brought him to school," she said.

"You?"

She explained that he had called her for a ride.

I climbed out of bed, belatedly realizing I was naked. I clutched the sheet around my body and grabbed my device. The date meant that it had been days—no, weeks—since I woke up in Jo Jo's bed, but that couldn't be right.

"It's a good thing I brought him. There was a government man here."

"Why aren't you at the Coop?" I stepped into the restroom suite to collect myself. It was late. I would have to forgo a shower and shave, but at least I could brush my grinners. I brushed vigorously.

Where had I been last night? I vaguely recalled taking a Chill Pill or Plum. Or a couple of both. The last of a stash I had squirreled away in the pocket of an old suitcase we never used. I would have to find a new supplier.

Mama wedged her way into the restroom. I gathered the sheet around my body to ensure that I remained properly ensconced. My head really hurt.

"The City pulled the restaurant's licenses. Too many violations, they said. We're closed."

"Are you serious?"

"I been telling you they had it in for us for months."

I recalled no such discussions. "Well, this won't stand. I'll make some inquiries. Perhaps—"

"Don't bother on that. You know how it is when they come after us. Even if we fix this one thing, they'll just find some other thing. They made that fence, that Tiko fence, bigger, so now the Coop is inside the Tiko."

"Inside the Tiko?"

"Least I still have my license for the Visions Festival. For now." She sat on the lip of the claw-footed tub. It had been a favorite relaxation of—I never got into it anymore. I preferred the shower down the hall. I worried that if I soaked in the tub waters, all my grease and grime would swirl down the drain, leaving behind nothing of me other than a few kinky hairs.

"Oh. Don't give up so easily," I said.

Mama glared at me. I hadn't seen her so angry since that time I left the Coop freezer open, spoiling a month's worth of food. "You know what you shouldn't give up on so easily? Your family."

"My family is dead."

Mama gripped her forearm and rotated her fingers around it in a wrenching motion, a habit of hers ever since she was injured that one time. I didn't want to think about how she hurt it all those years ago because that meant I'd have to think about what had happened to Sir.

"Still hurts from time to time?" I twisted the hot water handle to the max. Steam escaped.

"It never stopped."

Sir had enjoyed an early morning walk. Nothing too extravagant. Down the front steps of our building. Circle the building. Back. I wasn't an early riser, and he, despite my requests, never called on me at the time he awoke, before our neighbor's rooster crowed. But occasionally, through great force of will, I managed to rise from the depths of sleep, covered in clinging seaweed, and throw my shoes on to join him.

That particular morning I was woken up by Ms. Wendy Woods's adopted son, Dee Soyinka, much later to be known as Supercargo, who moved in with us following the killing of his mother. Specifically, Dee, younger and smaller than my seven-year-old self, once again rotated in the bed we shared until his feet were kicking me in the face. I shoved him off the bed.

What a strange morning it was. It was cold outside, but my internal furnaces were lit by the Visions of Blackness Festival, a Tiko tradition filled with arts, crafts, and music. It was a big deal during my parents' childhood but had been canceled in recent years due to permitting issues, which Sir called newspeak for the City didn't want thousands of us gathering in one place.

There was a crackle in the air that abraded my skin and the smell of lemon house cleaner from Sir's early morning efforts. The tub had cracked some time before, so I was responsible for washing off my face and armpits and doing the same to Dee.

"Ow, quit it." Dee pounded my arm, but his little fist didn't hurt. He was protesting the amount of force I used around the corners of his eyes. But you had to get in there good, or he would spend the day looking crusty. Mama would not be happy about that.

"Shut it, you clod," I said.

Mama was in the kitchen doing something to our grits, the smell of butter and salt overtaking the other house smells, the thoroughbreds of nourishment outgalloping the quarterhorses of soaking pans and stale potpourri. I forgot to brush my teeth, so my mouth tasted of sweat and cotton from biting my pillow through the night.

"This food ain't done, y'all," she said. It sometimes seemed that everything Mama made was in a state of coming but never arriving.

"Come on, Dee. We'll just starve for now."

"That's right." Mama stirred a small pot. Her face was fuller then. Chipmunk cheeks that I didn't inherit. "Y'all starve for ten more minutes."

"What's all this whining that's happening?" Sir asked. "Tell me, Lil Dee." Dee was five—old enough to talk—but he didn't. Not anymore. Sir was always trying to get him to speak up.

"It's a travesty," I said. "An aberration."

My recollection of what really happened—what I actually *saw*, that is—is, and always has been, unreliable. Maybe it's a defense mechanism, or perhaps it's just how my software operates. You could tell me that when we stepped outside, my family left standard reality. You could say that Sir became an animated boy, Mama a bird, Dee a cat, and me a dull duck, following along a wooded path. You could say that we were followed, hunted from the threshold of our door, by a creature made entirely of yellowed eyeballs, tusks, and filthy fabric fragments. That would all be perfectly fine and metaphorically true.

But I must think in terms of what I recall from this reality: that ripping cold breeze; the vibration of big commercial trucks skirting the outer limits of the Tiko for downtown; and the hand-drawn Tiko pride banners strung up in trees, on light poles, and on fences. They weren't allowed to build stands and counters, so the festival was a rickety, bedraggled affair. Not the products but the presentation. Women in head wraps sold earrings lovingly laid on a hand-quilted blanket, which lay on the ground. Men in wide-shouldered suits offered vials of perfume from the insides of their jackets. A girl pulled a cooler full of foil-wrapped pies.

"Oh. What kind is this one, baby?" Mama asked. The pie looked like a tiny moon pinched between her fingernails.

"Punkin," the girl said.

"That's different," Mama said.

The girl smacked her lips. "My daddy say they ain't have no sweet potatoes at the food salvage."

"Should we get any, Lil Dee?" Sir asked.

Dee smiled.

"Don't just smile, kid," I said. "Use your words."

"You'll hurt his feelings," Sir said.

"Get two," Dee said.

Mama gasped. Sir handed me a twenty-dollar bill. I told the girl to give me change.

"Give me a second." The girl unfurled a small roll of ones. Then she ran, pulling her busted cooler.

"Hey!" I said.

"Let her go," Sir said. "That's Magic Mose's daughter. I owe them." Dee pointed and began to cry. It was the City Police. Sir scooped up Dee, and we got out of there. We were safe. Or so I thought.

"Hold it right there," Douglas said. An electric current along my soft, hairless forearms.

"I live here," Sir said. "You know that."

"Leave us alone, you big ape," I said. Most of the people near us cleared out.

"Quiet, boy," Sir said. "Remember what I told you. Respect."

What had he told me? I would have been lost in that moment to condense it to a cohesive theory of the case. But it went something like this: You are an angel. Fate, in the guise of ordinary people, conspires to pull the wings from your body. To break your grasshopper limbs. To leave you crippled in loam. To maniacally adjust the shape of your skull. To bleed your life's blood onto concrete. To destroy you, destroy your future, to destroy your children's future. Other peoples could rely on our nation's fundamental fairness as a starting point for any hopes or dreams they might have. But you, Black Boy, were born weak but breathing and tossed into an open grave. Three quarters of Fate's work was done in our reaction to the world. In attempting to back away from hissing fauna, a rattler, or a jaguar, we find ourselves stepping off a mountaintop and falling to the jagged rocks below. Never bow to anyone, Sir would say, but don't let fools bring you down. Respecting yourself means respecting even those who don't deserve it.

"Officer Douglas," Sir said. "How can I help you, my man?"

"I got a report of a stolen beach bike, and you're the focus of our investigation."

"A beach bike," I said. "My dad didn't steal some stupid beach bike."

"Shut him up, or I'll shut him up."

"Hush." Sir squeezed my hand, hard.

The buildings of the Tiko emitted a special kind of energy. I couldn't see whether we were being watched by our fellow Tikosians up in their apartments. But we were. A screen door slammed somewhere. The voices of others far away, perhaps as far as three or four buildings over, hummed. I squeezed Sir's hand back. As soon as I did, he let go.

"Obviously, there's a misunderstanding. You see. I don't ride bikes. I have this old track and field injury that absolutely—"

"Nigga. Shut your stinking trap." Douglas's baton slapped against his palm, producing the sound of flesh on flesh, like a big happy kiss. "I know you with your murse bags and funny shoes. You think this is a conversation, but this a soliloquy."

"You mean a monologue," I said. "If it was a soliloquy, you'd be talking to yourself, Mr. Douglas."

Douglas shoved the tip of his club against my throat. Mama yelled. I went to swat Douglas's club out of my face, but I didn't need to. Mama had already pushed her way in.

There is a point of order that I'm sure you're aware of regardless of whether you are brown as mud or white as milk, that you've encountered regardless of whether you're male or female. In physical confrontations, a woman can get away with a lot more than a man. A guy who flinches while literally under the gun better be wearing a steel chest plate because he's going to take one to the heart. But in all but the most extreme circumstances, a woman has some freedom of body. She can shout, dance, and even attack without fear of reprisal.

This was what I believed. Of course, I was wrong.

In the scrum, Douglas pushed Mama to the ground. She fell awkwardly on her arm and screeched. Sir shoved Douglas. But Douglas didn't fall—he was like a reed in the water. Douglas stretched the baton to its maximum reach and pressed the tip tenderly against Sir's chin, like he was reenacting that painting where God touched naked Man. The baton flicked Sir's fedora from his head. Sir's hat grazed my shoulder like a stricken sparrow on the way down. I, like Sir, was frozen in time waiting for some music to tell me I could move again.

"What?" Douglas said to Sir. "You going to cry now? Well, go ahead and cry for me."

Sir kept his chin up. I held Dee's hand. He had the calmest head in the bunch.

"What's wrong with you?" Mama grimaced, clutched her arm. "This is how you act. Terrorizing your own people?"

"You ain't none of mine," Douglas said. "And I'm just checking out suspicious activity. Y'all the ones can't fly right."

A couple of other cops, one tall and white, the other tall and black, made their way over. Their name tags were the opposite of what one would expect.

"What's this all about, Dougs?" White, the black cop, asked.

Sir knelt by Mama.

"He didn't say you could move." Black—the Caucasian one—pulled out his gun.

"Don't," Mama said. I thought she was talking to the cop with the gun. But it was my father she was talking to.

But Sir wasn't listening. All the coolness and restraint he had exercised throughout our lives was gone. His forehead was bright with sweat. All I saw in his eyes was a lust. He stood up and went for Douglas, and it was a dance. Someone knocked me down. I skinned the back of my hand. The other two stepped in and grabbed Sir's arms. Douglas brought his baton down on Sir's forehead. I was amazed. I didn't know that beneath that skin I knew so well was a river of blood, a river that had been freed to flow down his forehead and onto his light brown blazer. Douglas cursed, but he struck again. The other cops let go, and Sir slumped, a chunk of pink face flesh exposed. A dollop of red collected at his chin, where it dangled.

"Tell me you're sorry," Douglas said. "'Less you want some more."

"Say it," Black said.

"I'm sorry," Sir said.

Mama's arm was broken. We spent the afternoon at St. Moritz Hospital. The waiting room was crowded, and hours passed before she was seen by anyone. It took Aunt Shirls coming over from her job at the Carnation Room to threaten the intake nurse and cause some movement.

We wouldn't find out for days whether Sir was alive. His apology echoed in the empty cell of my brain, and I had a reminder of the event, my brown hand scraped white before the blood came.

My father had been careless, an idiot! All his talk of respect and restraint. When it counted, he became an animal just like a common street thug. If he had contained himself, Douglas wouldn't have gone at him. But he allowed himself to be removed from our lives just when we needed him most.

I promised myself to be better, stronger, a more resilient man than he ever was. I was almost to the promised land. I would never abandon my son.

Mama nudged one of Penny's shoes out of the way and stepped over to me. "Your wife dead. That's true. But you alive. Your boy alive. Your father alive. I'm talking about the men in your life, your son and father. I see the way Nigel mopes around these days. He was such a happy child, but he slipping away. The same way you're slipping away on that junk."

"Everyone needs something to rebalance sometimes."

"I know it's been hard here since Penelope passed. I should move in here, huh? Keep an eye on my two babies. That's what I'll do."

"We're fine. We're working through some things. What can I do to prove that to you?"

"Visit your father."

"Anything but that."

"Go see him today, or I'll bring my bag in from the car."

31

Liberia. The state's oldest continuously operating prison lurked at the parish line like a hitchhiker trying to thumb a ride out of town. Liberia had been built during colonial times, during that brief period when Spaniards ruled the City. The Spaniards were appalled at some of the rules in the American Sector. Example: Under the American rules of racial categorization, anybody thought to be less than white lacked legal process to sue based on an injury to their land property rights. So while any of my lighter-skinned ancestors could buy a small plot of land or even a townhouse, if they could afford it, they couldn't do anything against the whims of white men.

It was during my research for a high school genealogy project, about an ancestor, in the bowels of the City Library's historical collection, that I came across certain documents (a deed and some arrest records) that suggested that the man, listed as an octoroon (how fortunate for him!), was the possessor of clear title to a 110 x 30 quadrant near the City's St. Denis Cemetery. That was in 1794. By 1795 he was a resident of Liberia (then called the state reformatory) for some type of public assault. By 1796 another document, not a deed, listed a man with the curiously anonymous name of John Michael Smith as the new property owner.

The great frustration with such historical documents was that they lacked a narrative. There were no paragraphs or footnotes. No sensational news clippings. Riley and the rest of the BEG would have said this was for the best. Such unpleasant events during the many nadirs of race relations in the history of our country were best forgotten. But I could never do that. I could only use my imagination and certain societal tendencies to divine what had become of this man, who was not my direct ancestor but who hung from a long branch of the family tree the way a body might.

In other words, I had to do what a hack historian might do: make things up. So I did. John Michael Smith worked for the City in some financial capacity, perhaps as an assessor. Smith, who was apparently British by birth, saw some value in the property. Maybe he discovered it and thought, *This place will change my life. I came to America searching for something to fill the hole in me. And this is that something!* Maybe he made an offer that my ancestor should not have refused. Maybe he levied a heavy tax, and when no payment was made, he called out the constable. Maybe my ancestor, bearing some resemblance to Pushkin or Alessandro de' Medici, appeared at the door and challenged Smith to a duel. But by then duels were illegal or going out of fashion. Maybe Smith had my man arrested and purchased the house at a tax sale.

These types of incidents were common in the American Sector. The Spaniards, having seen enough, shut down the American Sector jail, a converted pharmacy off the avenue. So the Americans, in a classic game of whack-a-mole, simply built a larger, nastier prison on the edge of town, in an area where even the Spanish governor's lieutenants felt unsafe. The big nasty prison? Liberia née the state reformatory.

The strangest thing about Liberia didn't occur to me until I was already an adult and had traveled a bit. Its seat at the parish line meant that it was the first thing tourists saw when they entered town from the suburban airport. In my experience, while transiting from terminal to accommodations, one might come across an ugly but productive industrial area—perhaps a shipping container facility—or a placid body of water. Not the place where that community warehoused its untouchables. But that's exactly what the City did. Upon entering the City from Schenectady or Moose Factory, one came to know the bulky, sprawly prison complex before the more benign landmarks of the various sporting stadia or even the downtown skyscrapers. I knew the stats by heart. One out of ten citizens had spent some time there. More than half of all City blacks had, and eight out of ten black men. Liberia was a vacuum sucking up all the dark crumbs.

I drove to the initial guardhouse, where a round-faced brother in black and gray fatigues operated a machine that scanned the Bug. As the wand passed over the roof of the car in much the same way that the arm of an automatic car wash does, I noted him shooting me the queerest looks, as if to ask, in both confusion and derision, what the hell was I doing there. Many lawyers visited the company. If not for the Liberian inmates, thousands of industrious criminal attorneys would be out of work. The local economy would crater.

But I admitted to being there on personal business. There had been situations where black visitors got embroiled in incidents that led to their arrest onsite. It was an extremely convenient transaction for all parties involved, like having a heart attack while in an ER.

"I know," I said to the guard as he gave me back my ID.

"What?" he asked.

"Nothing."

There were three other checkpoints. And when I parked the Bug, a spidery, youngish Latina swept the vehicle with a mirror on a stick. *Can't be too careful*. There'd been another terror attack just yesterday at the zoo. A pack of hyenas got loose.

Children watched from a barbed-wire-enclosed playground as I clicked through the stations for decent music. The guards walked me through a metal detector at the entrance to the visiting center, a tin-roofed building. The waiting area reminded me of both a hospital waiting room and the waiting area at the DMV. A crush of people. An uncomfortable mix of anticipation, dread, and hopelessness.

He would say things to me. I hadn't heard Sir's voice in decades, but I would hear it soon. That syrupy, mellifluous, accusatory voice of his. He would rant. A rant that would start with questions about why I'd never come back to see him again, why I had waited so long, why today. What right did I even have to be there? I'd thrown him away. I'd deleted him from my personal history and banished his presence from my life. Penny and I were almost married before I told her about him and even then in muted, reticent tones. She probably learned most of what she knew about him from Mama. Nigel too. But I was in the house. And I wasn't deserving of any calling out. It wasn't my fault he blew his stack. He knew the rules. He'd stepped out of bounds. Mama, me, and even Dee—Supercargo—paid the price. We lost a man because he couldn't gulp down his pride. Our whole life suffered.

After an hour, I was let into the next pen, which felt like a fish tank with its large windows and aquatic background music. Through the windows I saw a gorgeous green, not unlike a golf course. The warden seemed to have tended the lawn with meticulous detail, placing a single grain of fertilizer with a single drop of water on each blade of grass. A group of men in striped overalls straggled into view hauling shovels, picks, and wheelbarrows. Behind them, a trio of guards in white shirts and slacks followed on golf carts, short-muzzled shotguns bumping against their sides.

I went to the guard window, which was mirrored glass. I couldn't see the person behind it, but the person could see me. I was only certain that someone was there because of the fidgety shadow emanating from the steel pass-through beneath the window.

"Help?" the voice said.

"I was hoping you could tell me how much longer before my visit begins."

"Have a seat."

I sat. After a few minutes, my name appeared on a hanging monitor. An iron door opened, which I entered. The room was an antechamber. Animation on another monitor told me to use the security drawer that jutted from the wall. A pair of wafer-thin plastic sandals were in it. The screen told me to swap them for my shoes.

A tall, white-haired man greeted me in the hallway. "My how you've grown," he said.

"Excuse me?" I asked.

"From last I saw you."

"I've never been here before."

"Of course you have. I had to check the records to be sure—my memory isn't what it was—but you visited with your mother, such a nice woman. You wore a three-piece suit and bow tie. We don't get much of that around here."

I studied the man's face for a moment. His face was pale and pocked with the scars of long-resolved pimples. His skin had wrinkled, and his teeth were crooked at mildly bizarre angles. But what if I peeled back time? Flushed some life back into those cheeks. Filled in the dry canals and craters along the sides of his eyes and mouth.

"You used to have red hair," I said. "You're in charge now?"

"Assistant warden. Once upon a time I was a carrottop, but I haven't seen a scrap of red in about, oh, two decade, I reckon."

This man had been a junior administrator at the time I visited as a child. He had greeted me and Mama. The world must have been a cheerier place when fresh-out-of-school wardinistas were sent out to coddle the families of inmates. But here he was again, I reckoned. So maybe things had not changed so much, if at all. And maybe I hadn't changed as much since then as I thought.

Mama and I had met Sir beneath the central tower of the prison panopticon. The high ceiling was gray-tinted glass that made everything seem overcast, even though I knew it was sunny outside. Dozens of other prisoners walked beside us, circling the tower with their loved ones, as if we were all on a giant lazy Susan. The door guard told us that we could talk as much as we wanted, as long as we kept moving around the tower. In the tower, thirty feet up, another guard swept the grounds with his rail gun, which was mounted on a tripod. A red dot appeared wherever he pointed the weapon.

I hung a few steps back from my parents, walking stiffly in my robin's-egg-blue suit that was already short around the ankles. I had refused to get out of bed that morning. I didn't move when Mama threatened to take away my Internet privileges. But when she said the same thing about my books and notebooks, I had no choice but to get dressed and come along.

I was in a foul mood because I didn't want to see Sir. His trial came quickly, and within months of his altercation with Douglas, he was convicted of attempted murder of a peace officer. He would never get out. Never help me with another book report or shoebox carnival float. He had taught me how to brush my teeth and hold back the tears of a skinned knee. What would I never learn from him because he was incarcerated? And I kept thinking that if he'd been level-headed, we'd all be back at the apartment eating fried chicken thigh sandwiches.

They made the inmates wear embarrassing skintight white uniforms so they couldn't hide contraband. The men on either side of us were worn, deflated, pathetic. Their loved ones shuffled alongside. The high windows squeaked from the wind. I smelled the rust from the windows' hinges. With his gaunt cheeks and thin limbs, Sir looked like he was doing Día de los Muertos cosplay.

"The lawyer say you got a good chance on appeal," Mama said, her voice climbing. She wore a brown and gold pantsuit, the good luck outfit she favored on important days. "A real good chance."

"It's his job to say that sort of thing," Sir said. Mama absentmindedly rubbed her forearm. She was out of the cast but wore a wrist brace. Sir's eyes got small.

"It's better than it was," Mama said, letting go of her arm.

"I'm glad." Sir glanced back at me. "What's his problem?"

I shrugged.

"Answer your father," Mama said.

"Me?" I adjusted my bow tie, then jammed my fists into my pockets. "I don't have any problem at all. I've never been happier than right this second, schlepping around this crummy rat hole."

Sir seemed shocked.

I hadn't really talked to anyone about him. I'd shut Mama out. I'd attacked classmates who brought it up. Now my throat was hot, and I couldn't stop talking. The words spilled out of my mouth like spiders in a horror movie. "Thanks a lot, Daddy. Now, I'm just another son of a convict like most of the other kids in town. Maybe you should let me come back for 'take your child to work' day. I can help you dig ditches or make license plates. I've always wanted to work on a chain gang. They say it builds character. We'll have a real great time."

A woman with another family chuckled.

"Boy, how you going to say that to your own father who was trying to protect us?" Mama asked. "What is wrong with you?"

Sir stopped walking and grabbed both my arms. "You think this is what I wanted?" he said. "You believe I planned this?"

An intercom squawked overhead. A mechanical voice escaped it. "Resident Poopy Pants. Keep it moving. Or else." I had heard that they assigned inmates humiliating names based on their initial inspection upon arrival. But I didn't think they could be so . . . cruel.

Sir continued walking. His face was covered in sweat. No, that wasn't sweat. "Do you even know what I'd give for a second chance?" he asked.

Mama got close to him like she wanted to put a hand on his back. But we'd been instructed that physical contact was off limits.

"You could've kept your mouth closed. You told me to swallow my feelings."

Sir stopped walking again. "I was wrong. I shouldn't have ever told you that."

"Keep walking, baby," Mama said. She sent me a look of anger that turned to alarm. A red number 10 appeared on Sir's chest. It was the rail gun's laser sight. The number changed to a 9. "Come on."

"Hey, brother," an older prisoner with a beard shout-whispered. "Don't want to get caught out, my man."

"Tell your father you're sorry." Mama said.

"We're warning you, Poopy Pants," the mechanical voice said. "Noncompliance means there will be consequences and repercussions."

"No," Sir said, and hissed, "This is my fault." The number on his chest was down to 6. "You've got to own yourself."

Some other inmates screamed for him to get moving as they walked by. 5.

"I ain't trying to get zapped over here!" a man yelled, waving his arms.

"Great," I said. "Just what I need. More advice from you. Well, fuck you, Pop!" 4.

"Boy!" Mama said.

"Whatever happens, you can't give in to them, because then you'll have nothing left," Sir said. 3. His face was slick. It occurred to me that I'd never seen my father cry. I'd never seen any man cry.

The seriousness of the situation finally struck me. 2. My face tingled. The corners of my eyes moistened. I bit my tongue. I would not cry. I couldn't give him that. He didn't deserve it.

Mama grabbed Sir's arm and pulled him. Sir went along with her.

"You can't tell me what to do from inside this place," I said to myself. "You're just a ghost now."

"What was that?" The assistant warden ran his hand through his white hair in kind of an aw-shucks way. "Never mind. When I saw you pop up, I had to come down and see how you turned out."

"Well, that was kind of you."

"Not kindness, I'm afraid. He hasn't been well, your father. He's fine in body, but due to outbursts, he was transferred to psychological confinement."

"Oh." My father in chains? The thought sent a crawl up my neck. "Well, what did he do?"

"We don't talk about inmates' actions prior to adjudication as it's a violation of their rights under the Constitution to do so."

"When did it happen?"

"Again. Specifics." He held his palms up. "But sometime back. Almost a year."

"Let me see him then."

"That's what I'm trying to tell you. He can't entertain visitors."

"Entertain? Entertain! I'm not here to have tea."

The man gave a sympathetic shrug of the shoulders.

"Do you realize how long it's been since I've seen him? I have a right as a tax-paying citizen." Something clicked down the hallway. I glanced over my shoulder to see several guards moving in our direction. The guards nodded at the man. He nodded back.

"Don't cause a scene. I was only saying that it would be best for his recovery and your peace of mind not to see him. But if that's what you want."

"That's what I want."

We took a corridor that hooked sharply down and to the left, passing through several doors along the way. We'd entered another building, a building where the workers wore soft-soled shoes instead of boots and carried stun guns instead of rifles.

"Here, this is him." The warden stopped at a door. Center door: a sign of nonsense letters, a code of some kind. He shook his head as he punched a keypad. As soon as I entered, he closed the door behind me. The door clamped shut in a permanent-sounding way, causing my heart to jump. But I had to focus.

My father sat on a stiff-backed chair facing away from the door. He seemed impossibly small compared to the man of memory, small-shouldered, small-bodied, small-boned, vulnerable, infinitely vulnerable, like a child on a tricycle during an earthquake. The room was clean, the bed made, and he watched a flat screen that was flush with the wall and encased in clear plastic. That television played cartoons that had been old when Grandpa was a boy. Animated creatures attacked each other with balls of light, staffs composed of light, branches of light, and light twisted into the form of a tornado. The sound was very low. My breath was louder than the show.

"Sir?"

I walked around to him. But he didn't seem to notice me. His hands were on his knees, and his chest expanded, then contracted. His hair was carbuncles of gray, his face full of parentheses, commas, and semicolons. My father was a wizened old man now, prematurely so.

I sat on the low cot next to him. "I know it's been a while," I said. "My fault for not coming sooner. But I'm here."

The spikey-haired character on the screen flopped to the ground and grunted. His clothes smoldering, he ripped off his shirt to reveal a scarred torso.

I grabbed Sir's leg. He did not look away from the television.

"Don't be that way," I said. "We have a lot to cover. Like why didn't Othello ever realize how much danger he was in?"

Something in me assumed my father was playing some kind of game by ignoring me. Perhaps he wanted to get my full attention before speaking. Maybe he was too pissed to form words. I didn't need him to be eloquent. My heart was quickening. I just wanted him to speak.

I put a hand on his cheek. The coarseness of the poorly shaved skin surprised me. I realized with some discomfort that I hadn't touched Sir's face since I was a child. His eyes swiveled toward me. They were wide open but empty of the kindness I remembered even when he was upset with me. There was no sign of recognition at all.

I stood and gestured wildly. "Sir!" I slapped the back of my hand against my palm. "I need you to talk to me!" I paced from one side of the room to the other. But he watched me with only mild interest, as if I were a random pedestrian in a crowd. "Why didn't you warn me how hard it was to be a father? You could have told me what to expect. That was your one job. To get me ready for the world."

No reaction.

A small red light blinked above. A surveillance camera. I wondered if whoever was on the other end of it was laughing at us.

I sat again. Sir's chest moved slightly with his breath. "It's not fair for me to blame you, is it?" I grabbed his shoulder.

Sir blinked without recognition. I could have been a guard, a half-consumed glass of water, the wall.

He wasn't in there. The man who had earned a Ph.D. at age twenty-one, who could recite Gwendolyn Brooks without a pause, who had given me my words, was gone. I felt as though I were at his tombstone.

• • •

I exited the prison waiting area, with my hat in my hands, trying to wrap my mind around the fact that my father had suffered a type of identity death while off stage. No. He was on stage, but I had left the auditorium. Logic told me that he had been this way for some time. That I could have grieved for him yesterday, last week, months ago. But I was stunned by the realization that I'd managed to lose the same man twice.

I removed a Plum from a nook in my jacket and crossed a grassy field toward the visitor parking lot. I was acutely aware that the field was a shooting gallery for prison snipers. If anyone tried to escape, they'd get taken out real quick if they came this way. I wondered what it would feel like, the impact of a hollow tip through my heart.

Mama never lost him. Not completely. Not like I did. Electronic communication wasn't allowed, but they wrote each other several times a month. Over the years, she'd reported on his small victories, like becoming a trustee in the prison learning center, and his state of mind, which rose and fell on hopes of getting free. In fact, Mama must have known something was going on with him, but you would think she would have told—

I stopped dead. The Plum rolled from my fingers and bounced onto the parking lot pavement. Wearing a flowy floral blouse, my mother leaned against the Bug. She opened her arms. I didn't have to say anything. But I did.

"Mama. I'm sorry."

32

Shortly after I dropped Mama at Aunt Shirls's, I sped along General J. S. Beauregard Boulevard. The streetlights popped on in groups of three, as if to say, *Wake up you fool wake up you fool wake up*. I needed to see my son immediately. We had been drifting apart lately. But I was struck by the notion that I needed to make a few things plain. Some things could not go unsaid. He needed to hear that I loved him. He needed to know that I had his best interests at heart. He needed to know I would never leave him to fend for himself.

But where was Nigel? I sent him a message. It was time for his evening salmagundi of pills. And the hour of his nightly denatured demelanizing shot (auroxsorormab; Big Pharma name Erazamal—the stuff would settle into the nooks and crannies of Nigel's body so that Dr. Nzinga could activate it when the final phase of treatment began) would follow shortly thereafter.

I consulted Nigel's schedule: a soccer practice due to end momentarily.

I descended upon the soccer field, where girls and boys in knee socks swept across the green with the balletic grace of those who hadn't yet had their hearts broken. One of the volunteer coaches approached me.

"Nigel isn't here. I wish he was. He's a good player, even if he plays like he's afraid of his own shadow. We'll pound that right out of him. Unlike Karen." The coach took a few steps into the field— and leaped straight up into the air. "Kill it, Karen! You've got to beat it like a piñata!"

"Where did he go?" I asked.

He turned back to me but kept his eyes on Karen. "Oh, come on!" He slapped his palm against his face, then rested his hands on his hips. "You mean you don't know?"

"Know what?"

The coach threw his arm over my shoulder and shook his head. "There's always one. Every season!"

"What are you saying?" I asked.

"We haven't seen him in weeks. He said you didn't want him playing because you thought he'd get hurt. You need to have a talk with your boy. Straighten him out."

I tried calling Nigel's device. He didn't answer, but as fate would have it, I was near the Pest's neighborhood. Those two had become virtually inseparable of late. It was all I could do to set limitations on when and where they could see each other outside school. Chaperoned visits on the weekends and occasionally during the week, if there was a class project. But never at night, and certainly not without my permission. Araminta seemed quite protective of Nigel. What did she, a short pitch-black wood nymph, know about my son anyway? Yet Penny had always liked Araminta. It was the main reason I didn't forbid Nigel from seeing her.

A three-minute drive, and the duplex came into view. The house where she lived was on the last residential block before the Tiko. Up the street, the barbed Tiko gate flashed and rolled open. Security stanchions dropped into the ground. The warning arm swung up and out of the way. A family of five carried grocery bags stuffed with their belongings into the compound.

I parked the Bug in front of the duplex where Araminta lived. An old brown dog, the worst kind of dog really, lifeless as a throw rug, sprawled across the porch. A diapered brown boy, the worst kind of boy really, all snails and tails, threw a ball at the dog. I passed a lopsided oak tree, climbed the front steps, and stepped over the dog-rug. The porch was a calamity. Empty alcohol bottles and discarded toys lay about. I stepped on what could have been a shell casing.

The interior glowed with warmth, and an adult-size shadow lurked on the other side of the semi-opaque curtain. When I picked Nigel up from here long ago, the shadow had been in the same place. I rapped my knuckles against the door. I noticed that one of my knuckles was bleeding. It didn't hurt. Araminta opened the door but left the chain on the rickety latch. I asked about Nigel.

"Oh, hey, mister," Araminta said. Only her big white eye was visible. "Nigel's not here. Did you check where they play that soccer?"

"Was he here earlier?" I asked.

She said something that I couldn't hear because a trumpet in my brain was going off. I could smell Nigel. Yes, my son, like everyone I loved, had a signature scent. But it wasn't so acute that I typically made note of it. I mean, when he was an infant I used to kiss his baby-powder-scented feet and nuzzle the spring-field-smelling crown of his skull. But the present trace was linked to the way his room at home smelled lately. A sweet musk.

I lowered my shoulder. And the next thing I knew, I was inside the warm embrace of the house, tasting the odd air.

"Why'd you do that?" Araminta yelled. "You broke the door, you big crazy!" This was not true. I only terminated the functionality of the chain.

The shadow I had seen by the window wasn't a person at all. It was a cutout of the basketball player I'd seen with Nigel that night at the arena. Several other cutouts were arranged around the room: a silhouette of a woman, a full-color of the chocolate milk spokesman who dressed like a crotchety old lady in those commercials, *You bet not steal my good milks!* A medical dummy sat in a chair at the dinner table.

Another odd thing was the cleanliness of the den. The ping of pine oil, freshly applied. Dewy flowers on an end table. Not a single nit on the carpet. Not a single volume out of place on the bookshelf, where titles by Du Bois and Nikki Giovanni reminded me that the intense study of these problems did not mean a better future was on the way—

Nigel's C-Troos, the fad transparent tennis shoes of the moment, sat, like a pair of stone lions, on the floor at the far end of the couch. Araminta grabbed the shoes and hid them behind her back.

I smacked my lips and handed her my hat. "Where is he?"

She lowered her head and pointed toward the back of the house. Just then I noticed a hickey on the side of her neck.

Still following the ribbon of Nigel-scent, I passed an unoccupied room and then looped back across my own path and entered the room where Nigel had just slipped out of the closet and was trying to open the window, which appeared to be painted shut.

"Nigel," Araminta said.

He turned around with a hopeful expression that faded when he saw me. "Oh, hey, Dad." He did a little wave.

"Hello, Sonny Jim. I got you."

"I guess I'm in trouble."

"No trouble at all, other than being grounded for the rest of your ever-loving natural life. What did you think you were doing? What am I supposed to do with you?"

"I can explain."

"We'll talk when you get home. Just take your medicine." I pulled a very small water bottle and a plastic pouch from my blazer.

"I'm not going home, and I'm not swallowing more of that junk."

"Don't play. I don't have time for foolishness." I sprinkled Nigel's pills into my palm.

"He doesn't want to take them," Araminta said.

"Excuse me?" I said. "Who are you?"

"He doesn't have to either." She stepped in between us.

"This is family business, and it doesn't concern you in the least." I pushed past her with my hand open, in offering to Nigel, but he swatted it away, and the pills scattered through the air like fireworks. Araminta stepped on one of the pills, the white one that encouraged the emolliation of melanin within skin tissue. It had been worth several hundred dollars. Only powder remained.

"Stop!" I grabbed Araminta's arm.

"Leave her alone!" Nigel rammed my stomach—a soccer header, ironically enough, so he had learned something after all—and I fell onto the bed. I lay a moment. I wasn't hurt, but I was shocked. My son was in love. Dumb young puppy love. I stood up and held my palm at him. "Your own father," I said, not being sure what I meant or why I said it.

"What kind of father?" he said, his chest heaving.

"I didn't mean to shove you," I said to Araminta. I got up. "You live here alone."

"No." She looked self-consciously to Nigel. "I don't."

"I could make a lot of trouble for you. I could call my law school classmate who works for child services and have him ship you upstate. But I wouldn't do that. I have a better suggestion. You should come live with us. You shouldn't be here by yourself."

Nigel's eyebrows had shot up. At least two of us liked the idea.

"No way. I ain't closing my eyes in any house you was in."

"Mr. Moses next door looks out for her," Nigel said.

I gathered my hat from the floor, but not before dabbing my wet pinky in the powder and licking my finger. Bitter, bitter stuff. "Come on, Nigel."

"No," he said.

I told him I would call the services as soon as I stepped outside if he didn't fall in line. Nigel frowned, and Araminta nudged him.

In the Bug, I opened the glove compartment and removed a bottle with the rest of Nigel's medicine in it. I counted out the proper pills and added one. A sedative that Penny had sometimes used for insomnia.

33

By the time we finally arrived home, Nigel was limp as a soiled dishrag. I slung one of his arms over my shoulder and guided him up the back steps, as if he and I were college roomies returning to our dorm after too much fun down in the *ville ancienne*. I would have made a decent wingman for my boy, swatting away the nappy-headed beasts and subtly singing his praises to the angels among us.

We mumbled across the landing to the door. It's not every day a father sees his son high as a dirigible. Rarer still the father supplies the hydrogen. What unimaginable Chutes and Ladders we encounter. What eddies and whirlpools. What burned-out metal frames. I watched Nigel for a moment. His dull eyes. The spittle collecting at the corner of his mouth. Those reedlike arms. A helpless lamb in this world, but morally strong. Could he muster the backbone to be the kind of father I was? I hoped not.

"Hnh," I said.

"Wuh," Nigel said. "Wub," he said. "Ch—"

I pinched his cheek. "Articulation, son. You have to enunciate fiercely."

"Can we . . . chocolate cake?"

"I'll make one," I said, leading him through the kitchen and into the hallway. When he was small, Nigel would wander down into the valley of the shadow of sleep in this way, and I would point out the sights, the sweetmeat cabins and hairy-knuckled, ravenous accountants, until he made the lowest point of the valley and slipped into faultless, dreamless sleep. "We have everything we need to make a very good cake. We have the eggs and the cocoa and the flour and the sprinkle berries."

"No," he said. "Pa, no sprinkle berries. I ain't six." And then he promptly leaned forward and evacuated his stomach onto my shoes.

"I suppose you're not, huh?" I asked. What his exchange lacked in volume, it made up for in colorfulness. I wasn't as repulsed as I would have been if he were some stranger. I remember another habit of his, this one from infancy. If he was in a particularly rotten mood, Nigel would wait until just after you changed his diaper to deliver a fresh package.

I led Nigel to his bedroom, again bracing him against my body. When I removed my arm, he fell face-first onto his bed, his arms awkwardly bent beneath him. I straightened them out and prepped his shot. He had vomited the pills I gave him not even thirty minutes ago. I couldn't do anything about that. But I could fill the syringe to nearly double the usual dose. A bead of nacreous liquid pearled at the needle tip. "And I'll churn some vanilla ice cream."

"No. No. No," he said, drooling on the bedspread. "Can't be vanilla. Gotta be. Chocolate. Chocolate every day. Chocolate every nigh—" I couldn't be sure, but that last bit sounded like Crown lyrics.

In truth, I had always been a little squeamish. The sight of a firm needle against soft skin raked an ice pick down my brittle spine. And the first time I did it—that is, plunged a shiny two-inch needle into his left butt cheek—I inhaled. I sucked my teeth as if his rampant, squealing pain were my own. But when I thought of it logically, of the fact that I was doing something of profound importance for Nigel's future, all terror receded, and I was as calm and confident as a coroner over a cadaver.

Nigel sat up on his elbow. "What are you doing with that needle, Dadzel Azazel?"

"Just go to sleep, son," I said, guiding his head back to his pillow. "You have school in the morning."

"Lots to learn." His body relaxed again. I swabbed part of his skinny rump with an alcoholic cotton and let it dry. I steadied the syringe. I aimed. He popped up again. It took everything I had not to drop the syringe. "Heard about a town that's been burning underground for a hundred years. But the people call it home."

I should have anticipated that the effects of a powerful sedative on the virgin cardiovascular system of a teenager would be unpredictable. His system was on a roller-coaster ride between wakefulness and sleepfulness.

I went to the kitchen and rummaged for a drink and located a half-consumed bottle of Grand Marnier that I uncorked. I sat on the wicker chair that Penny had made during her wicker-chair-making phase and sipped my drink. Penny was a maker. She was always making things. Wicker chairs, ceramic bowls, our son. Did that make me a destroyer? The brandy tasted like nail filings.

I heard the loveliest harp music. Like something you might encounter in a fancy tea room. Or maybe in the garden of a Russian oligarch. The air felt chilly.

"I understand now why you're doing it." Penny poured me more Marnier. Her hair was shortened to a pixie cut, a style she'd given up after we married. In the burgeoning light, she seemed to wear a red halo.

"You do?"

"Oh, I was a fool to stand in your way." She tilted her head to the side and batted her lashes. "It's such a dangerous world for the great-great-great-great-grandchildren of slaves. How could I ever hope to understand?"

"There's no reason to be sarcastic," I said.

She sauntered into the hallway.

"Wait, I'm sorry. Can we just talk?"

She continued into the dining room, sat on the table, and folded her legs in front of her. She grabbed one of her old paintbrushes. Neither Nigel nor myself ever touched that little shrine of arts and crafts materials, a shrine to Penny.

She flicked the brush at me. "You didn't want to become your father. Hollowed out. Forgotten." She twirled the brush like a baton. "What happened to Sir changed him. But it changed you, too. Sent you right down this water slide." She motioned with her free hand. "You don't really think you'll win, do you?"

"I'm winning!" I said. "We're winning. All of us are this close—"

Penny grabbed my chin. "You can level with me, babe. I know you feel it in here." She patted my chest. "No matter how hard you fight to protect our son, you keep going down down down and taking him with you."

"I'm doing the best I can."

"But the best isn't good enough, is it? You're making him worse."

"I—"

"What's that?" she asked.

"I know."

Penny laughed, halfway between a giggle and snort. "Don't cry, kiddo." She climbed off the table and padded toward Nigel's room. The heel of her bare foot receded into the darkness of the hallway. She peeked into Nigel's room. She tsked. Then she smiled at me in a way I can only describe as malevolent.

"You're not my Penny," I said, suddenly fearful.

"Then what am I?" she asked, and entered Nigel's darkened room.

I reached out. My throat was so tight, I could hardly talk. "Don't go in there."

"Shut it. You wouldn't want to scare our baby." I dashed into the room and turned on the light. The spirit was gone. Nigel slept quietly, his comforter and pillows all on the floor. I went to the hall window that looked out onto the driveway. Up above the roof of the house next door, a green scarf spiraled on a current.

I woke up with a start and rubbed my face, which was clammy with sweat. My device said it was around three A.M. Nigel was still asleep. The syringe was on the dresser next to me. I grabbed it.

34

Nigel kept disappearing, and I didn't know how to stop him from going to wherever it was he went. The house had taken on a new aura. A quietude. A somberosity. I swept the floors often to gather up the brittle leaves I sometimes imagined clustered by the base-boards. I could sweep for half an hour and come back with nothing more than a blouse button.

This dead hollowness was present even when both Nigel and I were present. It was a kind of cold damp, like the feeling I had one time at summer camp when I stepped into a stream while wearing socks and shoes. Even after changing into dry replacements, phantom water crept between my toes.

But as bad as home felt on any given day with Nigel in his room, talking on the phone or jotting in his journal, it was a trillion per-cent worse when he wasn't home. In those off moments when I stopped home for lunch or when Nigel stayed late at school to participate in one club or another (I eventually requested a track-ing protocol from the phone company, which was expensive, but at least I knew exactly where he was), I had to force myself to slow down and turn in to the driveway to keep from driving through to the next part of town. A matching herculean effort was needed to climb the short run of steps to the back door. I struggled up the path as though ingots were strapped to my calves. Perversely I had to cling to my mattress to keep from floating away through the kitchen transom in the middle of the night.

These were necessary pains. If I had one duty on those days when I didn't drive Nigel home, it was to already be present when he showed up. Someone had to warm the sarcophagus for him.

I'd walk the halls turning on as many lights as I could, trying my best to eliminate the shadows and odd shapes at the edge of my vision that were neither truly shadow nor object. It never worked.

Pictures of the three of us loomed over every room. Our past smiles sneered at our present misfortune. Perhaps that was why Nigel began to fade away.

Somewhere along the way, I lost my ability to read. When I sat on the front room sofa, flipping through the pages of some recent bestseller on the American Dream, my eyes darted to and fro. They locked on the light fixture over the dining room table. The fixture was missing one of its three bulbs. Although I stockpiled fresh ones in the utility closet, I couldn't bring myself to change it. My eyes locked on the low branches of the trees outside the picture window. The branch ends were like fine hands brushing against velvet, only to reject the diamonds on display. My eyes locked on the faux-antique grandfather clock Penny had bought from a thrift store and somehow carried in on her own.

I went to the door and scanned our block for any sign of Nigel. He was over two hours late. That was his recent pattern, to show up five minutes, ten minutes, thirty minutes after the promised time. The tracking app said the service was temporarily unavailable, which happened too often for my liking.

I shrugged on a jacket and trotted to the end of the block. Nigel was approaching from a distance. A City bus rambled up the street, its headlights throwing his body into relief, an afterimage burned into the air following a nuclear catastrophe. He was still skinny as a pen refill, but taller, ever taller. When he got to me, he gave a sheepish smile. I almost grabbed his collar, but I was acutely aware of being watched by various neighborly eyes through window shades and security cameras. Even though everyone on our block knew me, had shaken my hand, quizzed me on the elections ("You're with Pavor, right?"), etc., there was always a chance one or more of them would call the police because of two big strange black guys up to no good on the street corner. Plotting evil. Threatening the security of babe and grandmother alike. That same desk sergeant would get the call. That same man would become enraged at the audacity. He'd call the Special Ward Unit down and maybe strap on a bulletproof vest for his first ride-along in twenty years.

These were trying times. Last month they'd arrested an entire family, in one of the houses just outside the Tiko, for being a threat to the general safety. A bulldozer flattened the house.

That's why I hustled Nigel into the house and locked the dead-bolt and turned out the exterior lights before I grabbed the back of his bubble coat collar.

"What do you think you're doing?" I asked.

"Hey! Let go."

"Do you know what time it is?"

"You know where I was and what I was doing."

"I've been dying waiting here for you," I said—or something similar.

"I wish," he said. He looked tired. He always looked tired lately. The bags under his eyes made him seem a little older, like the old soul he was.

"What's that?"

"Nothing," he mumbled. I tugged his collar. Nigel made a strange face, a mixture of worry, defiance, and anger that was somehow adorable. It was the same face he'd made the first time I fed him strained peas. Aircraft control denied the second plane requesting permission to land. "You act like it's a big deal. I'm sure you had plenty to occupy yourself."

"What's that supposed to mean?"

"Just leave me alone." He spun loose from my grip, leaving me with a simian paw full of coat. He went into his room and slammed the door. "I hate you." Then the sound of that awful new Crown album he had taken to. It sounded like cats yodeling into an oscillating fan. I could have simply walked in—I had disabled the lock on his door a few days earlier. But I had a different idea.

Hours later, after we both went to bed without dinner, I was startled awake by the sound of a heavy book being knocked on its face. Just as I planned. I had set the book upright outside his door. It fell when he walked by.

Fully clothed, I climbed out of bed and opened my bedroom door. Just as I did, I heard the front door shutting. I jogged to the den, past the overturned volume one of that Proust book he was reading for school, and watched from a window as he climbed into the back of a delivery van. It took everything in me to keep from flinging the door open and running into the street like a Viking warrior. But I stuck to the script. I hurriedly exited the back of the house, started the Bug, and tailed the van. I would have answers. Intrepid me.

35

I recognized the building as soon as I saw it. I'd passed it and ignored it a thousand times: my old school, the school of my father, and the school of his father.

If Booker T. Elementary was a dilapidated, second-rate public school when I was enrolled, now it was a virtual no-go zone. All manner of goblins stalked its vast grounds: the drug-addled homeless, the restless youth looking for a bad time, the desperate fugitives running to the only place in town law enforcement wouldn't follow. And that was the state of play just during school hours. Most of the students had been transferred from other schools for misbehavior or for being black, depending on who you asked. Some parents pulled their kids out to avoid the risk of getting the whole kinship locked up for failure to comply. Others gave their kids bribe money to ward off baddies or even pocket knives and mini-Tasers, if no deal could be brokered. Schools like Booker T. were the reason Penny and I never considered submitting Nigel to the public system.

It was after dark; the streetlights were on. My son was inside.

Some of the windows had been shot out and boarded over. Bullet holes pocked the bricks. A chunk of the cornerstone was missing, as if some sea monster had risen from the depths and taken a bite out of it. The naked flagpoles on the roof gave it the profile of a three-masted whaler listing toward the Antarctic.

During Sir's youth, the campus had been both an educational center and a hive of activity for so-called community activists. From that loading dock, they had distributed pallets of food and leaflets on healthy eating. In that dusty yard, children had gathered, Sir among them, for calisthenics. It was the anti-Reinhardt, run by Grandpa's cohort.

By the time I was enrolled at Booker T., the community activists had all been shooed away, locked up, or killed. The fresh fruits and vegetables had been replaced with bags of processed, genetically modified corn chips and artificially colored candy, and the overeducated staff replaced with recruits new to the profession of teaching. No one was crazy enough to drink the light brown water that slurred from the water fountains. During recess, we had to sit in the auditorium and watch films about physical fitness because the gym was off limits—an inspector found the paint was full of lead.

I crossed through an area of the yard where bike frames and overturned fifty-five-gallon drums had been discarded.

That's why I wasn't surprised when a voice called out to me as I peered into what might have been the principal's office, or a storage area for mangled textbooks: "Yo, Dice."

"Are you referring to me?" I expected to be robbed.

The voice came from a teenager. Older than Nigel, he wore a hoodie and slouchy jeans. The old "get your attention and chat" setup was a time-honored, traditional method of jacking someone. Score one for the old ways.

"Sorry, sir. I thought you were my friend." The boy took off toward a nearby fence. He wiggled through a cutaway section and kept going.

The front entrance of the school was barred closed for the night, but eventually I found a way in through one of the side windows.

I used my device for light but kept it pointed toward the floor, so as not to warn anyone of my presence. I was vaguely aware of people lurking in the shadowy classrooms. The stench of chemicals, familiar from Jo Jo's house—drugs being processed—assailed me. I focused on the unwashed floors and followed the grid of tiles. I turned off the device and let my eyes adjust to the gloom. The only sound was that of my shoes crunching on discarded things: beakers, plastic rulers, pencil cases.

I opened a pair of double doors, and a cool, earthy breeze issued from within. I couldn't see very far into the space, which seemed to expand infinitely into the darkness. It was the gym.

Like a fool, I entered.

Once, when I was small, Sir and Mama took me on a trip to Appalachia. It was Sir's idea, I think, to have me experience the kind of expansive and beautiful nature that had been paved over in the City. We rented a cabin on a hill and took short forays into the woods, Sir with a short knife concealed in his sleeve. On the third day of the trip, we visited a historic cave, where holdout rebels had barracked until only a few years earlier.

I was afraid of the cave and, as the story goes, clung to Sir's pant leg. In a surprise move, he carried me. I buried my face in his chest and entered an almost hypnotic state as my body rocked to the sway of his gait. For quite some time, I didn't look up. But I smelled him: the wash detergent Mama used on our clothes, his tangy aftershave, and that jumble of musky, manly scents that all fathers carry.

Someone tugged the hem of my knee pants. "It's sure beautiful, isn't it?" Mama asked.

I glanced up, my eyes blurry from having been squeezed shut for such a long time. As they adjusted, shimmering lights, like falling spirits, appeared.

• • •

In the vast room at the center of Booker T., a current flushed over my head as though huge fans were churning a mile away. I dropped to one knee behind a crate and peered toward what seemed like a platform around which dozens of people gathered.

A man in an abstract African mask sat on the edge of the platform, dangling his legs. He wore a white linen suit, which I had seen before. I had seen him before. I had feared him before. He'd appeared in streamed news items and as a featured player riding astride my middaymares. But I'd also encountered him in real life without realizing it at the time.

He was the terrorist leader from the Myrtles attacks and the many other incidents of past months. Of the fifty or so people in the room, a third were children. Everyone wore those spooky, elaborate, coin-slot-eyed masks.

I shivered. This was ADZE.

They were loading small packages into the back of a moving van. A tall masked woman videotaped the scene. Somehow the energy in the room was like that of people preparing for a party. There was horsing around and laughter. The movement of their limbs was loose, arbitrary. These people liked each other. One of the children, a dark-skinned girl in a long pointed mask, carried a tray of food to the platform where the leader sat. He looked over it and nodded.

"Y'all try some of this first," he said. The others gathered around and began to remove their masks.

The leader was about to take his off when something happened behind me. Two people entered, a masked man and a woman. "What are you doing?" the man said to me, his voice muffled by his mask.

"Nothing," I said. I stood up.

"Who is that?" the ADZE leader yelled. "Hold on to him!"

I ran past my potential jailers and back into the hallway. Soon at least ten people crashed through the door after me. I ran full out. I

WE CAST A SHADOW 269

ducked into the room with the purple smell. Three white kids were cooking a brew. They could have been the same kids from Jo Jo's house.

"Hey, how are you?" I asked.

"It's you," one of the girls said with a smile.

"Do you have any, you know . . ."

"For one of Jo Jo's boys?" one of the boys said. Movement in the hall.

"Never mind," I said. "Help me through."

They shoved me out the tight window. I landed awkwardly on my shoulder. It occurred to me that my pursuers were people from all over town. Cooks, hotel maids, sanitation workers. Some were kids who ran track. My point is that I wasn't going to get very far. Even if I escaped, they would know me before I knew them. I was at the far end of the school's parking lot when I saw that same boy in the hoodie from earlier. He was sitting on the trunk of an idling car.

"Give me a ride?"

"Ain't my car." My pursuers were only about twenty yards away and not very happy that I was leading them on a wild me chase.

"Help me," I said.

"Just step on that." He pointed at a blanket lying behind the car.

"What? I'm not crazy. I—"

"You want to get killed, man?"

I stepped on the blanket and fell through a hole in the ground. I landed in wet, stinky muck that splattered all around me. I climbed to my feet. I'd pulled something in my leg, but in my purplized state, I didn't feel much.

I whipped out a handkerchief, wiped off my device, and lit up the tunnel. It was the sewer system. I had heard that the City's criminal element used it for transportation and communication purposes. Cables and pipes stretched into the invisible distance. A cardboard sign even told me what street I was under.

"Why did you let him go?" a voice overhead said.

"I don't work for you, and I don't work for him. I'm just minding my own." A gunshot.

There was a light at one end of the tunnel. Hobbling, I went the other way.

36

It was Dr. King Day, and the Tiko never looked so good as it did that morning. The main promenade had been cleared of cars and vagrants, all trash swept away and concealed, every brick or siding—and the streets themselves!—pressure-washed of grimy smudges, the bushes and shrubs trimmed and pruned, fresh winter flowers planted, petunias and baby's breath, each streetlight bulb replaced, fire hydrants replugged and securely fastened, overhead power cables reinstalled, broken windows fixed, trim work touched up, eaves and gutters straightened, potholes filled, fences mended, grass resodded, gutters unclogged, swarming and hive-minded insects obliterated, lemon trees planted.

Banners as well as huge tethered balloons hung all around the quad grounds, each one emblazoned with the Visions of Blackness Festival icon, a black eye with the PHH and BEG symbols in the silver and bronze positions.

Of course, the Tiko was close enough to home that I walked over in full finery: my best brogues, a heavy velveteen coat that I'd only worn once, and an ascot. My job would be easy. Just blend in but be seen. The professionals had handled the main preparations. I was an ambassador or, as Mama called me, a figurehead.

People, my people, walked toward the grounds and were in their finest too: a sister in a slinky purple dress with her matching hat and matching man, a brother in head-to-toe zebra skin, his woman likewise, pregnant women carrying the unborn in their zeppelin-bellies, old women in boxy floral dresses and old men in Kangols and gold rings, both groups swaying to an old beat only they heard, a group of brothers in bejeweled football jerseys and flat-billed caps, a flock of small children dressed in rainbow-colored jumpers, a trio of teenage girls in feathers, a family re-union in all white wearing shirts that prayed for a loved one to rest in peace, a woman with hair styled to look like a fruit basket, an-other with braids that fell to her ankles, a basketball team in black sweats cutting across the grounds and towering over the rest of us, as if they were the only adults in an endless rumpus room, politi-cians with primped hair and party pendants on their lapels, a gag-gle of cosplayers appearing as Japanese warriors with humongous swords, fairies, human-animal hybrids, steampunks, comic book super-types, and imaginary creatures I'd never imagined, sorors and fraternities sporting windbreakers glowing with Greek letters, bodybuilders, virtually naked in tank tops and short shorts despite the cold, and a woman absolutely naked except for her piercings and body paint. And yes, even a few white people.

I felt as one for a change. Not different. Not set off to one side. It was as if a brother from another planet asked for samples of every kind of black person the City could offer up before the world exploded, and the Tiko was the site of our disembarka-tion.

I used the staff entrance to avoid the line, flashed my badge, and slipped into the central quad. I passed a 444 field news truck. To my delight, I noted representation from the national media all around. I wasn't entirely comfortable with their presence, as the media tended to focus on the community's negatives. But what could they detect here in the belly of positivity? In the distance, the group Fate's Rainbow performed. They were too far away to see clearly, but I knew from the preparations that they were the singing group Crown originally sang backup for. They swayed back and forth in their skintight gray outfits belting a vaguely familiar song from my college years. The lineup was posted on stakes here and there. First Rainbow, then the rap duo the Chucks. Then Crown herself, appearing for the first time in ages without her monitoring collar.

The open area near the stage was already crowded with those who wanted a prime spot to see Crown. Nearer to me, tents were arranged in lines that ran on for blocks. Every manner of art, craft, and penetralia was being sold in these tents: ancient grains from the Motherland, perfumes and gimcrack potions, colorful textiles, handcrafted comics, rings, necklaces, and bracelets. One man offered to sell me a handful of "soul beans." I declined.

I followed the smells. There were as many food stands as craft tents. Nigel had stayed with Mama overnight—I wondered whether the Booker T. incident was my imagination running away because I found Nigel in his bed asleep and snoring when I returned—and I knew that I could find them somewhere around here. There they were. The booth matched the other stands, white boards with blue lettering, but I couldn't help but grin like a monkey. In a coup, I'd pulled some strings with Octavia to get Mama a prime position near a major pedestrian intersection. I couldn't reopen the Chicken Coop, but I could do this. It was a small thing but necessary. The City had expanded the Tiko boundary lines to include the Chicken Coop, Mama's home. Since technically the City owned all property in the Tiko, this put Mama at risk for being evicted. My string pulling was the opening salvo in Operation Mama Protection.

They didn't see me, so I hung back for a moment as festivalgoers flowed around me. You can't go back. I understood that. But for a moment, I felt lucky enough to have been tossed back on a wave of time to when lowercase Nigel worked Mama's kitchen for the first time, smudged across his small face with batter, but handling his end of the bargain.

Now they worked efficiently. That much hadn't changed. But he was taller than her, taller than Penny had been, streaking up like a bottle rocket to meet me. Still scrawny of limb and awkwardly small around the shoulders, but no one's baby by any means. He prepped bundles of chicken, and Mama dunked a basket into the fryer. Aunt Shirls and Araminta handled the money. They all wore matching long-sleeved shirts with CHICKEN COOP emblazoned across the front.

My mind had been playing the usual tricks on me. I knew what day of the week it was (Saturday) and what the festival was all about (encouraging pride in a community not allowed much). But as hard as I tried, I couldn't remember basic details, such as where I worked or who my son really was. No, I wasn't panicked, because I knew these were temporary effects. I would regain my senses when I needed them. But there was something about Araminta that I couldn't place. The Pest seemed happy and smiley, but I noticed an edge to her, like she was waiting for bad news.

"O, Lord, it's gone rain." Aunt Shirls lifted her glasses and squinted at me. She took money from a customer and gave it to Araminta. "Look who done showed up."

I stepped behind the counter and hugged Aunt Shirls.

"You're early for tomorrow," Mama said.

"Early for next year," Nigel said.

"Oh," I said. "You two have yolks. Yuk." I turned to Araminta. "Minty, back me up here. I'm outnumbered."

"Uh-huh," she said.

"You look tired, son," Mama said. "Did you sleep?"

The question was whether I ever woke up, but I wasn't going to raise that query with her. "What do you need me to do?" I asked. "Prep all this?" I gestured to the folding table, which held various foodstuffs. "I came to get down and fry some chicken." I grabbed the pepper mill.

"Uh-uh," she said. "Nigel and me got a good system going. You're on stocking."

"You do appreciate that I'm not dressed for stocking."

"I appreciate you better get to work, boy. Make sure we're good to go on serving plates and napkins. Then fetch me some ice for the cooler. Plus, get those . . ."

Like that, I was in the fold of Mama's restaurant again, displaced and only built to last for a few hours on a not-too-chilly-to-enjoy February day. Working with my hands. Carrying boxes. Sweating and loving every moment of it.

I was some distance away from the booth, disposing of cardboard boxes, when Nigel and Araminta ran by me wearing knapsacks. What were they up to? I followed them through the crowded fairground, which had suddenly become an obstacle course. I dodged festivalgoers, produce carts, and garbage cans. They ran into an area behind the stage, near the fences.

I should have simply called my son's name. Made my presence known. But I couldn't. I was fascinated.

They placed their knapsacks on the ground and removed sculptures. No—masks. Wooden abstract masks like the ones I'd seen in Booker T. They were ADZE masks. My son was a terrorist.

Nigel looked right at me as he raised the mask. He stopped, the mask just above him. There was no flash of recognition, no sign of surprise. He lowered the mask onto his head.

His mask was mostly white with dark indentations to represent features, eyes, ears, hair. Araminta was already wearing her mask. Hers was oblong and pointed with something like a smile carved into it. She tugged Nigel's arm.

"Wait," I said. But the children ignored me.

They jimmied open the locked fence. ADZE came in through the opened gate. Dozens of them, all in wooden masks. They rushed past me toward the front of the stage. Crown ran off stage, even as her band and dancers continued to perform.

One of the ADZE men threw a smoke grenade at the stage. The crowd near the stage screamed.

I couldn't find Nigel and Araminta, but I spotted a familiar figure standing on the ground to the side of the stage. A man dressed in an all-white suit wearing an all-black mask with magnificent dreads coming off the back. There was an athleticism to the way he shifted from leg to leg and flipped his cudgel from one hand to the other, like a tennis player might. His muscularity. That hair. The police had shorn my cousin's hair as if he were a sheep. But that didn't mean I wasn't missing something.

He glanced at me, then followed the others into the open spaces. What I saw next was hard to fathom. Hordes of terrified people running in different directions. Closest to me, a scrum. Festivalgoers and ADZE fighting with fists, flag posts, and clubs. The security personnel were mostly average people in neon T-shirts hired to keep fans from the stage. They were as terrified as everyone else. A couple of hundred yards away, a news helicopter listed down sideways and slammed into the ground, unleashing a plume of dirt and smoke. The helicopter didn't explode, but there was a squealing noise as the tail broke free and bounced across the ground.

My family, Araminta and Nigel, were in the middle of this hell. And Supercargo was responsible for it all. I found him by the stage, beating the face of a security staffer with his cudgel.

I came at him from an angle, shouting. He didn't acknowledge me. I would rip off that mask and shove it down his—

"Supercargo!" I said.

I grabbed a handful of dreads. He whirled toward me. But the mask, with attached dreads, stayed in my hand. He wore a ski mask underneath. If I pulled off the ski mask, would he have another mask beneath?

He watched me with what could have been bemusement. I

didn't need to get the mask off to know that he wasn't Supercargo. The eyes were all wrong.

"Who are you?" I asked.

He drew back his cudgel.

"Dad," Nigel yelled. I turned.

"Son?"

The Plums kept me conscious after the first blow. But others came.

37

The Punu mask on Octavia's hope chest was turned facedown and filled with candy corn. She was on her phone finalizing plans for some deal that I wasn't involved in. I waited on the orange couch, my knees together. The lump on the back of my head throbbed. I watched the City through her high window. The river was low that day, exposing muddy banks and detritus for miles upstream.

My Nigel was somewhere down there, he and Araminta. Perhaps holed up in a safe house. Perhaps wandering the streets and begging for change to buy clean drinking water. I had dedicated my life to protecting him from the myriad dangers of black boyhood, only to watch him succumb to the worst dangers of black boyhood. Now my son was a suspect, a label that would haunt him as long as he breathed. It was perfectly kosher to charge a thirteen-year-old as an adult, and any adult who was accused of doing what Nigel would be accused of would face death.

Octavia said a frustrated goodbye to the person on the phone and flopped down into her chair. She pointed to the door, which I got up and closed before returning to my seat.

"Sometimes I feel I'm talking to a rock with that one." Octavia went to the mini wet bar, poured two fingers' worth of whiskey, and gave me a glass. I could tell from the color and smell of the stuff that a bottle of it could purchase a wedding dress or cover a semester of tuition at one of the better City universities. She toasted, but I didn't drink. "Listen, I'm sorry your boy is missing. I'm sorry he was mixed up in all that crazy, too. But know two things. One, he's a smart kid and he'll turn up. It's just a matter of time. He'll realize he can't survive underground, and he'll give you a call because he wants the new Crown album or a good slice of pizza.

"Two, you have my word that the firm will support your family with any legal issues that may arise. We have an arrangement with the Bienville Firm, who'll do any criminal defense gratis. At that age, who knows what's right or wrong anyway?" She eyed my glass. "Not thirsty?" She tossed back the rest of her drink. "Suit yourself," she said. "Let's make this official."

She placed my glass on the edge of her desk and gestured to the abacus.

"This is a difficult time. I get it. But I can't let the moment pass without acknowledging the good work you've done for me, for this firm, and for the whole town, really." Reaching across, with thumb and forefinger, she slid the final bead into position. "Everyone came through. Dinah, Pavor, even you. The best team won!"

Octavia crossed to me and handed over a stack of stapled papers.

"What's this?" I asked.

"PHH is delighted."

I knew they were. Despite the debacle, PHH had gotten great press for volunteering to treat the casualties at no cost, including the victims' busted noses and lips, which they would slim down if asked.

"This is the representation agreement between Seasons and PHH." She flipped a couple of pages into it. "Look at these rates! This is hands down the biggest deal I've ever been lead on. Armbruster's contingent—what's left of them—is eating crow."

Armbruster's right-hand man had been arrested by the feds for embezzlement. I had the vague notion that somehow he had been set up, but greedy lawyers weren't unheard of. Either way, Armbruster's entire team was under federal investigation and an internal administrative review.

"The committee is going to bump me up to shareholder in charge next quarter. But I'm interim SIC effective immediately. And you know this means you're with me. Everyone on my team gets a bump. Bumps for all of us. An outbreak of bumps. But—" Octavia stared at the door and laughed. "Jack, what are you doing here?"

Armbruster stepped into the room. His suit was wrinkled, and he looked like he hadn't slept in days.

"No games, Whitmore," Armbruster said. "You called me."

"Sugar, what possible use could I have for you?"

Armbruster tried to close the space between them, but I blocked him. He was lighter—frailer—than he looked.

"My, my, Jack. Do calm down. A man your age has to be careful of his blood pressure." Octavia strolled back to her desk. "I remember why I had them send you up." She pulled her purse from one of the big lower drawers and produced one of her sun pendants, which she placed on the desk. "Since your group was dissolved, that means you're one of mine now."

Armbruster huffed and stomped out.

"I'll have Strummer send it down to you!" Octavia called out.

She opened a checkbook and wrote. "As for you, I don't want you to have to wait another second for what you earned." She pinched the check out of the book and pressed it into my hand. "That's your full bonus and then some, right out of my personal business account. When the official firm money comes down, you can just write that one over to me."

My palm was numb. I glanced at the check, more to make sure I hadn't dropped it than to read it. But I did read it, and it was more than I could have dreamed. Was this the value of my soul? I wouldn't even have to use the meager savings I'd set aside. I recognized that Octavia could have always done this. She could have done it months ago, even on Elevation Night. I'd fought so hard—for what? Nigel was gone. I would never see him again. There would be no procedure. No conciliation to a better future. I didn't deserve the money. I never deserved it.

"Why are you doing this now?"

"You're a good man," she said. "Don't ever think otherwise."

"I quit," I said.

Without missing a beat, she laughed. "You can check out, but you can't leave."

I repeated myself. "I need to do something—anything. I can't do this anymore."

She said my name and chuckled. "Sugar, I understand you've had a tough time. But if you think I'm letting you do something stupid, you're stupid. And you and me both know you're not stupid, genius." She pointed at me. "Go find your boy. Take some time off, as much as you can stand. Recharge. You're benched."

38

Time passed. Every now and then I got a message through my device that literally stopped me in my tracks. Was it every twenty-third message or every thirty-second? It could have been every other. I'd get a text or email, and something in the sender or subject line would trick my eye into thinking it was a communiqué from Nigel. The message might say "Greetings, Dad," to my initial glance. But on closer inspection the letters would perform a fire drill in which they rearranged themselves into an advertisement for the City Metropolitan Museum of Art, where I was invited to "Come Say Goodbye to the Dadaists." Or maybe I'd get a social media note from "Your Son" that resolved into an unsolicited holiday hello from a forgotten someone named "Burson" I sat next to in third-grade typing.

Nigel disappeared years ago. I sold the house three years ago. The house was too big for me alone, and suddenly, the market got red hot. I would have been a fool to sleep on the opportunity, so I bought an overpriced but tiny condo a three-minute walk from my office.

I hired a personal trainer and nutritionist to help me get healthier. I purchased cookbooks but usually ordered out. I even dated occasionally, but none of the women I met made an impression. It was nice to have someone go with me to firm functions, but they weren't Penny.

Work was fine. I was a shareholder, after all. I still worked most closely with Octavia but also teamed up with Dinah and Riley, who actually came back to the firm after leaving the School Without Walls and doing a brief stint as executive counsel for Mayor Pavor. He seemed happier since he returned. I'd even taken on a few small business clients of my own. Pavor was in his second term, and some of the Black Safety Laws, as they came to be called, had tightened statewide, such as the right to use public facilities after dark. And the City condemned the Tiko. The whole neighborhood. Eventually PHH bought the land and was nearly done building its sprawling, state-of-the-art replacement for the ramshackle original.

But some of the old Tiko structures, including the Chicken Coop, were spared the wrecking ball and converted to condos. The whole nastiness disheartened Mama, who moved to Canada with Aunt Shirls. I visited them twice a year, at summer solstice and Canadian Thanksgiving. None of us could find Supercargo, who simply vanished without so much as a goodbye.

And then one day as I was pecking out a brief in my condo—it turned out that condo living suited me—an email pinged through from Jo Jo, whom I hadn't heard from since he left town.

Such a strange aspect of our friends that we consider them constant. The childhood pal we last see in grade school is still fundamentally the same goofball we meet in middle age. Our college buddy who leads the ragers and keggers remains the same insecure animal at his core. Our first love is always our first love, even if she is in the arms of some barrel-chested child oncologist.

But Jo Jo's email was not from the same laconic brother I'd loved all my adult life. His voice was unwrapped, loose, joyous. After their stint in the war, he and Polaire moved to the Netherlands. They had triplets, age four. They skied with the children in tow and lived in a cabin a short hike from a mountain. They all, kids included, took pictures of the mountain, which the family sold to collectors around the world. Polaire volunteered in a nearby school. Jo Jo injured himself in a skiing accident—a tree ran right into him!—but was almost completely recovered, except for recurring migraines. A picture was attached to the email: his new family standing on a mountaintop, Jo Jo and the others all in matching red sunglasses and gear—one of the clone children noticeably smaller than her siblings—the colors of the snow and tree leaves digitally enhanced to a level of ebullience unattainable in nature.

He had been trying to contact me for months. But his calls to the firm were fruitless, his emails bounced back. Of course, I should have known. I had changed my name within the past eighteen months to break with the past. To renew my life. When he called, the receptionist, a new girl from Minnesota, had no idea who he was asking for. Only select persons had my new email. The complications of being a transracial person.

In any event, he appended a note messaged to him. It was from Nigel.

> Hi Dad,
> I wanted to tell you not to worry. Don't search for me. I'm doing fine. I'm sure you are, too. Leave me be.
>
>
> N

And in the second attachment, which was initially incomprehensible to my eyes and, therefore, ignored: Nigel's location, typed in by Jo Jo and laid out by longitude and latitude as determined via the IP address Nigel had used to send the original message.

Part Four

39

The hills and mountains around my Appalachian destination, Carrier Falls, made for a scenic journey. As I drove, my mind wandered to the ancient Confederate battalions. The ones who a couple hundred years earlier marched northward in defense of the Beneficent Institution. How many of the very best young men were taken by conscription? How many sacred Southern sons gave blood and spirit back to the earth for the Lost Cause of the landowners?

Which reminded me. I checked the revolver in the glove compartment and was comforted to see it there in all its snub-nosed glory. It had belonged to my grandfather and was given to me on my eighteenth birthday by Mama, who was a believer in armed self-defense. I'd never used it. I brought it because there was no telling what I might come across in my search for Nigel. One-handed, I removed the gun and tried to spin the cylinder as I'd seen in films. It didn't work.

I might encounter any variety of woodland creatures, hillbillies, or for that matter, Nigel. There was no telling what level of brainwashing he had experienced, or who held him captive. Force might be a necessity. I had no intention of losing him again. Not after all that had happened. Not after all the time that had passed.

One of the pleasurable aspects of driving the hidden highways and byways—along State Route 342 at that point—was coming across raw Americana. Advertisements painted on the sides of barns. Abandoned wells. General stores cum military recruitment centers. The drive itself was mostly unremarkable except for my mind's tendency to conjure up unpleasant daydreams. At a rest stop, I saw a kind of fata morgana—a flickering image of Penny, Nigel, and me seated on a knoll, as if picnicking. I continued through that stop without resting.

Later, after traveling through a particularly winding stretch of road, I came across a delightful old-fashioned filling station—it only had one pump. A handwritten sign promoted homemade blackberry winter pie. As I stood at the pump feeling the current pulse through my fingers, I noticed people inside staring at me, taking my measure. The observation wasn't violent, and I figured they were suitably impressed. Trusting that I was very close to Nigel's location, I had dressed that morning at a local motel, the Magic Hound, and put on my very best seersucker—a darker tone to suit my skin—and brogues. A pocket watch chain dangled from my vest pocket. I had a new paper fedora from Paris. I wanted Nigel to see me at my smartest.

A young couple came out of the station. A black woman and a ginger man. They mistook me for a doctor who had given them free care at some point in the past, a Dr. Holm. I insisted that I wasn't who they thought I was, but they seemed so happy in the assumption that I almost felt bad in having to assert my real identity. The whole thing was very odd, and I couldn't help but feel that I was somehow in danger. They absolutely would not accept payment from me. After getting assurances that I was heading in the direction of my destination, I sped away.

When was the last time the gun had been fired? I had no idea.

Had it ever been cleaned? How did you even clean a gun? With dish soap? Formaldehyde somehow seemed appropriate. But I couldn't worry about that. I put it back and slammed the glove compartment door shut. Immediately, I heard a *whapp,* and the Bluebird, my new car, shook violently. Flat. Damn. Tire. No spare.

A single mountaintop looked down on me from the near distance. I asked my device to tell me where I was. But the search screen drooled in response. We could send astronauts to Pluto, but we couldn't make an electronic device that got reliable reception in a gulch. A trio of eagles flew by. No, two eagles and a military drone.

I waited for some time, leaning against the Bluebird's trunk, but no vehicles passed. Luckily, I had come prepared. My outrigger pack, which I had ordered from a women's home and garden company, included dried meats, a coffee pot, a compass, a sexton, an altimeter, a duck-billed sun visor—pink, so I kept it stowed—and most important, a custom topographical map of the area. After some frustrating attempts to use the materials to fix my location, I was fairly certain that I was less than three miles from Nigel. It seemed like an easy trek except for a purported natural gas field to the east. I could avoid it by simply walking straight thataway.

I wished I had just one Plum. Then I scolded myself for the thought, using the litany my addiction counselor had taught me: *You're a good man riding a bad road. Walk if you must.*

I hadn't taken one in three years.

At dusk, I lit off into the hills with my pack jauntily clanking in time to my steps. To distract myself, I sang, although I stopped due to a splitting headache. The smell of unseen furry animals reminded me that life went on around me all the time without any difficulty whatsoever, so just relax. This was nothing more than a leisurely hike through spindly trees and kudzu. But about thirty minutes into the action, I was gasping for breath. A raindrop hit my shoulder like the sky was saying, *Hey, buddy, up here, don't you forget about me.* Shortly thereafter the drizzle intensified to an even shower, to a steady spew, to darting spikes that rebounded from every direction.

The rain let up as I crossed a small summit. It was there that I heard voices nearby. I couldn't quite place it. Was it a radio? Was I near a church? I trotted in the direction of the voices, which sounded like the chant of Native American people on a long, hard trail.

After a few minutes traveling in the direction of the sound, I found nothing. I recalled what an expert psychiatrist once explained: *If you start to hear voices, stick your fingers in your ears; if the voices go away, you're sane.*

I held my fingers in front of me as if that would help. Slowly, I brought them to the sides of my head and plugged my ears. My heart beat. My breath sounded distant, but clear enough to follow each draw and exhale. No voices. I sighed and unstuffed my ears. The chanting came back, but closer than before and greatly changed. I saw movement beyond the foliage. It wasn't chanting but vaguely gospel-style singing. Curious, I moved closer still. The music shifted again—banjos. Radio! Had to be a radio. Who the hell had a radio in the middle of a mountain wood? Suddenly the voices sounded angry, drawling, questioning. The movement in the brush picked up, and dogs barked. It wasn't a radio, and I wasn't tracking them. They were tracking me. I ran.

My pack made too much noise. Whoever was out there could go anywhere I went and maintain their distance just by listening. I might as well have been under a spotlight. But I needed my provisions. What chance did I have if I just dropped my stuff and ran for it?

They, whoever they were, closed in on me from the east. At one point, I could have sworn that they were right on top of me. The foliage to my right parted. In a lightning moment, I told myself to stay calm and see whether it was friend or foe. But my body—in that same split second—made other arrangements. I hopped, as if goosed, and slipped in the mud, careening down a hill butt first, prickly branches stabbing me, berries bouncing off my skin, my pack serving as a toboggan.

I came to rest maybe a hundred yards away, in a muddy ravine. Then the gun tumbled away from me and went off. The muzzle flash was small, but the blast was louder than I would have thought possible. Fearing that I'd shot myself, I climbed to my feet slowly, checking the workings of my arms and legs as if I were a marionette. But other than being wet down to my underwear and covered in muck, I was fine. I also felt lighter. I reached around and discovered that my pack had disintegrated during my fall to earth. All that remained was the base and the straps. I rummaged through the underbrush for my things, locating the compass and the gun, which I tucked into my belt holster. It was impossible to find the other items in the descending gloom.

Oh. And something was in the trees right above me.

At first, I thought it was nothing. Shadowy leaves and branches danced on the breeze. A bird—a warbler, probably—chattered in the high dark green. Its agitated, twittering melody brought Duke Ellington—conked hair and all—to mind. Something crunched, and the song stopped abruptly.

Something moved in the upper branches, and my stomach shrank to the size of a walnut. The thing in the trees was white-furred and about as big as a large cat or small ape. I didn't move, hoping it wouldn't see me. Or at least I tried not to move, but my body wouldn't stop shaking. And the animal was getting closer. I sprinted—forget the remains of my pack—scanning the trees as I ran.

I stopped to catch my breath in a clearing. A branch fell, bruising my shoulder. The creature climbed down toward me, its forelimbs scissoring, its bill-like jaws mimicking the sound of the bird I'd just heard.

It followed me as I ran, jumping along the tree limbs as easily as I would stroll down a street. I tripped on some kudzu and scrambled to my feet, cursing. Then the animal flew, like a flying squirrel. I'd never be able to outrun it. But I remembered: *The gun, you idiot!* The animal groaned above me. My hands failed. I couldn't make them stop vibrating long enough to unholster the gun. Just then I noticed a shimmering surface beyond the edge of the woods. The shimmering area was a small pond, black as a mirror. I leaped in without even slowing down.

The water was cold! But once I was submerged, the bottom emerged into view. Rock formations lurked. At the shore, that thing splashed into the water. No way. Was it really swimming? Its head was submerged, and great splashes of water shot out as it moved. My leg cramped from the coldness. I struggled to the center of the pond and dove.

I found an opening, a smallish, phosphorescently glowing portal. I swam along the tight, underwater corridor for a while. It was very narrow, and it didn't seem to lead anywhere. Worse yet, there wasn't enough space to turn around. I couldn't go back if my life depended on it. In a panic, I exhaled, and bubbles ran up my forehead, like a clutter of hairy spiders. I was running out of air, and everything inside me said to turn back, fight, return to the surface, *you fool.* But I kept going. Suddenly the rock ceiling above me cleared away, and I was in a dim cavern. Gasping, I climbed onto a muddy shelf and shivered with my back pressed against the rocks. I shook out the gun from its holster and aimed it at the surface of the black water.

Eventually my eyes adjusted to the dark. The cavern was bounded by high, smooth walls. My body was a phantom. My hands and feet came into focus, reluctantly. One by one white specks appeared above me as if answering a silent roll call. I couldn't tell if I was watching the night sky away from the lights of the City or minerals in a rock ceiling. Scar-chasm.

Funny how it made no difference. Vast cosmos or submerged tomb, the space gave me, for the first time, a sense of how endless the big dark really was. The stars were just punctuations within a blackness that went on in all directions for eternity.

I stood with the gun pointed at the glimmering water for half the night. I was freezing, wet, and I had no idea how to get out of my cocoon.

40

The next morning I woke up alive. I was stunned to find myself still in something like a dark, airless tomb. Still lying, I yawned and rubbed my eyes, taking note of the fact that I could only see the faintest outlines on my fingers in the gloom. My lips tasted like dirt.

Not remembering where I was, I rolled my legs over the side of the rock outcropping, as if to get out of bed, and slipped. Back in the chilly water, I found myself fully awake in an instant. Splashing around and yelling, my voice reverberated in the chamber. At least I wouldn't need a bath.

I was in an optimistic mood. There was no creature. There were no chanting ghosts. My dread had been purely manufactured by an overactive pyloric valve or a cluster of long-fried synapses. I'd panicked in the dark and conjured up the whole dumb nightmare. Typical. Now that I was back in my right mental mind, I just needed to find a way out so that I could reclaim my Nigel.

I got out of the water and leaned against the rock face—I really didn't want to jump back in—and felt something jab my shoulder blade. I turned around. The wall was irregular. Some sections of the formation were big enough to put my entire bare foot on. The gun lay on the ground where I'd left it the previous night. I grabbed the gun and let water dribble out of it. I didn't know if it would ever fire again, but I stuffed it back into the holster. Then I climbed. Near the cavern's ceiling was a shelf, now clearly visible. A stream of fresh air hit my face. Freedom.

I unfolded into a sun-dappled morning. I stretched my arms and admired the freshness of the breeze. Green leaves goldened. Dew twinkled grass. Floral scents. Dripping wet, I started in what I hoped was the right direction. Rabbits and squirrels darted around the landscape. I came across a log fence, which I clambered over, and entered a field of grazing cows. I was never a big fan of the farming life, but had a measure of respect for the people who brought forth the flora and fauna that conglomerates processed into sluice and pulp for our consumption. But there were no megatractors here, no skyscraper silos. What would my life have been like working to bring forth goodness from the soil, coerced by a whip? I wasn't hardy. I would have died from cholera or consumption. Or been whipped to shreds for the master's amusement.

Quonset huts appeared at irregular intervals. Occasionally, I saw someone hacking at the hard earth with a pickax or pulling chopped wood on a rickety cart. The farther I walked, the more activity I came upon. I arrived at an expanse where a group of folks of seemingly every race plucked green beans. People in plain cotton clothes carried buckets of water from a well. Was that a cotton field? Many of the women and girls wore flowers in their hair or bell-sleeved dresses. Some of the men and boys, too. Commune.

In the heart of the commune, it was an active morning. Newly planted evergreens swayed in the breeze. Hens clucked across the dirt road. Who could say why? People stood outside the huts talking about crop rotations and an upcoming pageant. Children chased dogs. Dogs chased cats. How big was the commune? The central road stretched beyond my sight. My son was here, or he was nowhere.

I approached a Latina girl and asked after Nigel. She had a sable-tipped paintbrush tucked in her hair, and feathery earrings dangled from her lobes.

"I don't know anybody with that name," she said. "Maybe try Claremontville, thirty miles north." She eyed me warily before walking off with the easel and canvas she carried.

I noticed more and more of the locals dropping their conversations to watch me. I had a feeling I was attracting too much attention. I kept my head down and avoided eye contact.

"What happened to this guy?" A man in a faded yellow baseball cap checked me out from head to toe. He was medium-brown and very tall, with a reddish beard. Suddenly I felt severely outclassed. I hadn't paused to take stock of my condition, but it dawned on me that I had the psychotic drifter look down pat. I wiggled my dirty toes, which had ripped through my remaining ruined sock. Earth and grass stained my seersucker pants. My shirtsleeve was ripped at the shoulder.

A crowd had gathered around me. I ran a hand through my hair. "What kind of farm is this? Cotton? Peanut?"

"This is New Rosewood," Artsy Latina reappeared sans canvas and easel. But she gripped a pitchfork. "You should go back to where you came from, mister."

Yellow Baseball Cap carried a shovel, which he pointed at me.

"Who sent you?" a wild-eyed blond girl in overalls said. She had a hoe.

I held my hands up. "Listen. I just ran out of gas and—"

"Answer me," the blonde said. "Where did you come from?"

"The City."

"That's almost six hundred miles from here," Artsy Latina said. "Come on. We'll show you the road back."

The blonde grabbed my arm. "Or we can bury you in the corn. Your call."

I twisted away. "Hold on. I'm just trying to find someone very important to me."

Then she raised her hoe.

"Easy, Dopey," Yellow Baseball Cap said.

"Why?" Dopey asked. "First the government sends drones. Now they're sending snoopers. Next thing it'll be troops, and then developers. Ain't that right, Doc?" Dopey nodded at Doctor Artsy Latina. They were using code names.

Doc nodded back. "The last thing we need is fresh trouble."

"You kids sure are rude," I said. "You ever hear of the concept of hospitality to strangers? I haven't eaten in a day. And there are weirdos in the wood."

Yellow Baseball Cap had put his shovel down and was standing off to the side watching me with arms tightly folded across his chest. He stepped closer to the group of us and chuckled with a sheepish look of guilt. "I almost didn't recognize you." He placed a hand on my shoulder.

"No way, Watchdog." Dopey said. "This is *that* dude?"

Nod. Under the cap, beard, and black man's skin was my boy. My Nigel.

41

Doc and the girl in the overalls, Dopey, forced me at the point of a pitchfork into a partially curtained area where I was made to climb into a steel washbasin—the kind you might use for a large, filthy, shaggy dog.

They dumped scalding-hot water on me, water that had a strong medicinal punch to it that flared my nostrils. Something about delousing for the protection of the community. I wasn't sure where Nigel had gone, but it occurred to me that he was likely not in control of his movements. He may have been barred from coming to me by one of the others. Worse, he may have been brainwashed into not wanting to see me. The thought made me shiver even as steam rose from my skin.

Nigel.

It wasn't too late. Yes, he was dark-skinned. And the mark—it had darkened and spread beneath that beard. Where did it go, and where did it stop? The overall blackening of his skin made the mark almost unnoticeable . . . almost. But then again, his whole body was basically a mark now.

I would get him back to the City for treatment. It wasn't too late. It was never too late as long as we were on this side of the void. Dr. Nzinga stood ready to help. And if not her, then one of the other clinics that had popped up across the nation. She'd licensed her techniques, and they were being used from sea to shining sea. All over the world, even. Yes, some other magician could cast their spells, and Nigel would rise. Even if he was now almost as dark as me—well, as dark as I once was.

Out of the bath, I put on sandals and a belted, caftan-type garment they called a tupa. Once I was fully dressed outside the little shack next to the baths, Dopey came to me and picked through my hair with a comb.

"Can I help you?" I asked.

"Hush, man," she said. "Can't have you spreading bad luck. And keep your hands where I can see them. I know you're some kind of sicko."

I winced. What had these people convinced my son to believe about me? What false memories and manufactured fears? No doubt there had been some sweat lodge session. Some dark guru presiding. That master would have coerced Nigel to find the so-called source of his so-called pain. No doubt they contorted my son against me, so that he would embrace them and whatever their feeble ideology directed.

A dark-skinned and very pregnant girl in an empire top ambled over. She looked like she would walk right through me if I didn't get out of the way. But she stopped just short of that and stared at my face. Her black features were unmistakable. Araminta!

Unlike Nigel, and except for the obvious, she still looked like the annoying girl who drove up my blood pressure every time she opened her mouth. Something crashed inside me. I hadn't realized how much I missed her.

"That's so weird, mister." Araminta pulled my cheek, as if to test its substance. "God damn."

"Watch your mouth, young lady," I said. "Need I remind you—"

"You really damn did it." I swatted her hand away.

Her face slid from offense to softness. Then she gave me a warm hug, pinning my arms against my body. It was the first act of kindness any of the New Rosewoodians had shown me.

"Looks like you got into a little trouble," I said.

"Looks like you got a lot white." She grabbed my hand and turned it over in hers. "What's white and white and white all over?" She poked my chest. "You are."

I had almost forgotten about my demelanization. If there was anyone crass enough to broach the issue of the work I had had done, it was Araminta. To be honest, it wasn't something I thought much about anymore. Sure, when I was undergoing the process at Personal Hill, I obsessed over my improving visage. It had taken several long months (which felt like an eternity of visits to the DMV). And each week, after a session, I would compare my retoned face in the mirror to the memory of my darker self, fading into the grasslands of the past. Each time I smiled. I smiled when I saw my reflection in storefront windows downtown or in the winking waters of the Myrtles mall fountain. I smiled at the strange absence of recognition of my otherness. When white men saw me, they shook my hand as they would the hand of a brother or old college pal. When white women saw me, there was no fake chumminess to compensate for their fear that I might snatch their purse and run. I was just a man on a mezzanine minding my matters. Uncle George. Mister Smith. Good old Norm from the tavern. I marveled at this new sense of normalcy like a fish that suddenly realized it could breathe out of water. But the novelty wore off eventually, and I took on an unexpected but comfortable invisibility.

A pickup truck tore up the dirt road, trail pluming dust. It stopped hard. The engine knocked as the driver rolled down the window.

Nigel sat in the driver's seat. "It's time to go, Dad."

42

My son killed the engine of the dented pickup and leaned out the window the way a train engineer might. This threw me. In my soul of souls, Nigel was still an adolescent, younger even.

But even wrinkles in time get sorted out. And once free of the truck, Nigel swaggered toward me and Araminta. My, he really was tall. Even taller than I realized in our quick exchange earlier. His long stride cleared the distance between us in a few steps. His green eyes—Penny's eyes—were unchanged, thankfully. Unfortunately, there was the issue of his skin, which was fair-angel-fallen-into-the-mud-pit brown.

This Nigel was much darker than the boy I'd raised. He vaguely reminded me of some of my lighter-skinned cousins on Sir's side of the family. These cousins had been older than me when I was a child, and I hadn't seen most of them since adulthood. But I had been jealous of their worldliness, their masculine beauty, the hint of final assimilation into whiteness they heralded. Still, it wasn't my cousins, whose names I could hardly remember, that I thought of when my son came to me just then. In fact, it wasn't really a thought that I experienced so much as a feeling that caught me by the collar from behind.

Where is my gun?

The weapon had been tucked into my belt holster when I made it to the commune entrance. But I must have lost it before my delousing. I glanced around. Which one of these kleptos took it? One of the cotton pickers? Doc? Dopey?

During my woodland journey and before my flight to the underwater tunnel, I had raised the gun to eye level and pointed the muzzle at a grand old evergreen. I had choked the trigger—*pop*—and relished the sight of mottled bark exploding away from pearlescent flesh. I still smelled gunpowder in my nostrils.

I worried that Nigel and Araminta saw my thoughts in a bubble over my head. But now that I was paying attention to them, it was obvious they weren't paying attention to me. They were shouting at each other. She kicked the wheel of the truck. He pounded the hood with his fist. What was the fuss?

He wanted to take me somewhere right away, and she wanted to come along. I pleaded for calm, and they told me to shut up, simultaneously. I recognized the pattern of their argument as one I once knew well. This was the exchange of two people who had been grievously in love for years. Two souls who had been divided prior to their disposition on Earth and now were angry at the effort of trying to fuse the jagged halves back together. They wore wooden bands on their ring fingers. I wished Penny could see them now.

These two new adults—so greatly changed from their larval stages when they fed on the leaves of the garden Penny and I planted—frankly astonished me. They were a family of two, soon to be three. And inside the big swell of Araminta's belly was a precious baby—my grandchild. A person who would hopefully not take after me in any significant way, who would favor my Penny, inside and out, if there were any justice in the multiverse. But then again Araminta was still black as a meteorite—

"Look, Minty," Nigel said. "I"—he shot a look my way—"have to do this."

"This ain't what we talked about," Araminta said.

Nigel placed his hands on her shoulders.

"Fine," she said. He kissed her forehead. With that, Araminta tugged his beard.

When I got into the truck, my door wouldn't close. Nigel instructed me to pull the handle when I shut it. We were already in motion before I fully latched the thing. Crumpled notepaper and fallen leaves cluttered the floorboard. The truck was a beater for sure. The tailpipe banged against the bumper, adding to the noise that made the truck sound like a bundle of pots and pans tumbling downhill. A jagged crack ran down the center of the windshield. The passenger rearview mirror was missing so that the bracket seemed like an empty eye socket, silently appraising my worth.

We hung a right and curled up the mountain road. Dark valleys and wooded slopes all around us. Jackrabbits leaped along gravel, their eyes glowing like diamonds.

"This is certainly in the middle of nowhere, isn't it?" I asked.

"It sure is."

I turned to Nigel. "You like this?"

He gave a small nod. "It's quiet, and the air is clean."

"I sold the house," I said.

He nodded again. "Oh."

"It was too big for just me."

And again. "That makes sense."

"That doesn't mean you can't come home, son." Up to this point, Nigel had been focusing on the shadowy road. His voice was flat, and his eyes betrayed nothing more than vacant concentration. Whatever ideas they had fed my son seemed to have turned him into a drone. But at my last comment, something flickered across his face.

"Home?" He glanced at me.

"Yes. The condo is small, but I have a rollout, and wait till you see—"

Nigel opened his mouth to speak, then closed it. He took a half breath and placed a hand on my forearm without looking away from the path.

"We'll talk when we get up the mountain," he said.

"But I really think we can—"

"Dad." He smiled. I had been shushed by my own son, who now seemed to be laughing at something foolish about me. I stared at my hands, confused. We didn't say a word for the rest of the ride. The rattletrap cacophony of the truck was abrasive. The silence? That was worse.

43

The truck pulled onto a drive off the main road, which continued back down the other side of the mountain. We were on a smooth expanse where the curvature of the formation mimicked the Earth's. Soon we came to a small lodge with a tower attached to one side, so that the building looked like a toy soldier shouldering a rifle.

Nigel got out, slammed his door, and grabbed a full cardboard box from the back of the pickup. As he approached the building, he gestured with his hand, as if to say, *Come on, old man, don't be afraid.*

Inside, an ax and cords of wood lined the back wall as though the occupants were prepping for a long, hard winter. A window opened onto the back of the mountain, where leaves shone in the starlight. Below in the valley, the commune firelights were Lilliputian, the faint rooftops benign as mushroom caps.

I peeked into a side room. A mattress was pushed against the wall under a dreamcatcher. On the mattress lay a partially wadded-up dress. The dress was like what Araminta wore.

I stepped back into the main room. "You live here."

Nigel rummaged through a hutch. "I spend most of my days up

here on lookout while Minty does her counselor thing. Unless it's harvest time. Then it's all hands on deck. Or on field if we're being particular." He paused and grunted to himself. "No one comes up here because it's so far. I guess that's what I like about it most."

The place was simply furnished but contained a certain warmth. There was a potbellied stove, a rough-hewn table with benches, and a colorful mandala-esque hemp rug. Rumpled papers, mechanical pencils, and old textbooks—many by authors I remembered from my schooling like Nolan; Shrumley and Aloise; and Hatter, Wang, and Jonson—were everywhere.

"Still reading, I see."

"It gets pretty dead, so I go up in the tower." Nigel pointed up.

A trio of rifles were propped on a rack near the fireplace. He had placed the opened cardboard box next to the rifles. A familiar holstered weapon sat on top of some linens.

"What's with the insurrection?"

"I handle the guns and ammo because I'm in charge of security. Sometimes we get unwanted visitors." I furrowed my brow. "Anyway, most of those books are Minty's, though. She's been studying extrapolational humanism."

"Is that my revolver?"

Nigel went over to the box and picked up the holstered gun. "Yeah. They took if off you because they thought you were from the government." He unholstered it, went to the stove, and with his free hand flipped on a propane burner to warm water. "We don't keep much up here. I'm having tea if you want some." I nodded.

"Why'd you come?" Nigel placed the gun on the table.

I casually lifted the weapon and tried to spin the chamber. Again, it didn't work, but I saw it was still loaded. I gathered the holster and secured it and the revolver around my waist.

"I was very worried about you after the festival," I said. "I searched everywhere. I almost went bankrupt paying a PI to find you. I searched flophouses and under cold bridge overpasses. One freezing night, leaving a mixer at the City Rail Station, I saw a boy sleeping on a mat by an exhaust vent. I tried to wake the boy, who I quickly determined was dead. For a moment, I thought he was you. It sickened me, that boy's death, and the idea that you might be as dead as him."

"I'm sorry I didn't tell you where I went," Nigel said. "That wasn't fair. But I needed to protect myself." He placed teabags in two mason jars on the table and poured steaming water into them, one at a time.

"Protecting you was my job."

"Dad." He shook his head. "Are you sure that's what you were doing?" He handed me a jar of tea.

"How could you say that? When you ran off with those terrorists, I thought I'd never see you again."

"That's all well and good, skip, but I wasn't kidnapped. I enlisted."

"Don't play with me." I had no idea what kind of charade Nigel was playing at, but I wanted to shake some sense into him. I couldn't let him see my frustration. I was his father. I was in control.

"Who's playing?" Nigel took a sip of tea. "I joined ADZE along with some other kids. Not long after that mall attack, that was."

"You wouldn't join up with terrorists. Not willingly. They must have gaslighted you into thinking it was right."

Nigel looked me in the eye. "You were my hero. I thought you were good. Whatever you said, I sopped it up with a biscuit. 'Wear a stupid hat for your own good, Nigel.' 'I know the needle hurts, but I would never hurt you, Nigel.' 'I love you, Nigel, so grin and bear it, Nigel.'" He imitated my voice so well that I was afraid to open my mouth, afraid of what might come out. He pulled off his faded yellow cap and tousled his hair. "That's why I still keep this thing."

He turned it over in his hands and sniffed it. "It's a reminder, I guess. I don't want to forget you. I can't afford to. Everything you did to me, I really believed was for the best. Even the way you convinced me to lie to Mom about what you were doing. But then I met Minty at school. Boy, did she help me turn my head around. We had this long talk at that plantation you went to for your job. She helped me see things that were right in front of my nose. Better yet, she helped me see my nose. But I still remember what we were like before I woke up."

"Araminta wasn't even with us at the plantation."

Nigel leaned against the table and grinned in a way that made me squirm. "Oh, sure she was. Her neighbor brought her along to babysit one of his kids. You and Mom were sleeping when she threw a rock at my window and told me to meet her in the woods."

"No. That's not true. Your mother and I found you splashing around that dirty pond all by yourself."

"Dad." Nigel sighed and rubbed his hands together. "Minty was right next to me. In the water. The whole strip-down-naked-and-free-yourself thing was her idea. But that's beside the point. The point is that she was the first person who understood me. Her dad, her real dad who died before I met her, had his own demons. Did bad things to her. She was the one who told me that maybe you really meant well but couldn't help yourself. She was the one who said I couldn't depend on Mom to shut you down. Minty thought my plan to run away made all the sense in the world. But I had always been too chicken to do it. She made me feel less crazy."

"Because of her, you joined a group of killers."

"I was wrong to join them." Nigel stood up, his shoulders slumped. He inhaled. "They were saying what I wanted to hear. The leader told me that the people who died at the mall were an accident. He never even used weapons! No guns. No bombs. People got so freaked out whenever we showed up, they would stampede and hurt each other. But really, I didn't care. I thought if a few people got hurt, so what. Because I was selfish and angry. One of the men did bring a bomb to the festival. I don't think anyone knew what he was up to. But it was too late. After, the adults abandoned us outside town with nothing. A bunch of us hopped a train, but only a couple of us got off near the commune."

"Who took you from me?" I stepped toward him. "Franklin? Supercargo? Your wife's neighbor? Octavia? Just tell me."

"No one took me, Dad." Nigel folded his arms and exhaled in exasperation. "As bad as things were with them, they were better than with you. You were so afraid of everything. I mean, you wouldn't even let me call myself black."

"You're not black," I said, a bit of spittle leaping from my mouth. "You're mixed. Two-fifths Irish, one-fifth German—"

"And you?" he asked. "What are you?"

I didn't answer, and I certainly didn't tell him about my new ID, which listed me as "American White."

"Remember the day you rubbed that max-strength bleach on me? It may as well have been battery acid the way the stuff burned." Nigel leaned forward. "You left. But I didn't tell Mom about it because I couldn't. She always knew you were up to something, but she would have been too hurt if she knew about that. I mean, she might have gone after you with a frying pan. Or way worse. She might have fussed for a while, cooled off, and forgot about it like she did with everything else 'cause she felt helpless, too. I mean, in the back of my head, even I kept thinking you might change. And I knew better. Both of us did!"

"We had our disagreements, but—"

"She wanted out. She cried all the time when you weren't there. Even when she thought I couldn't hear. One night she locked the bedroom door and turned up the TV in there—that *Unsafe Wherever You Go* show was on—but I heard her. She used to say nothing was wrong with crying, but she couldn't let me see that, I guess. I made dinner—enchiladas and churros. When I called for her, she wouldn't come out. So I wrote a note and slipped it under her door. After a while, a letter popped out from her side."

I grabbed Nigel's arm. "I know you hate me, but this—this revisionist history is foolish."

He stepped around me and fumbled through piles of paper on the floor. He grabbed a notebook and tossed it aside.

"Dammit." He opened a narrow door by the fireplace that was camouflaged to look like part of the back wall. The faux logs swung toward me. There was a stairway behind the door. He entered without saying anything.

I followed. The stairs were narrow and rickety. In the dull light, a lizard crawled into a gap in the wood.

The bell tower's ceiling was high, and at the top of the vaulted ceiling, a massive yoke crossed from one side to the other, but there wasn't any bell. Nigel knelt by a chest, his arms plunged deep inside.

"I knew I had them." He stood up. "What did you say you call it when you're trying to prove you're right? You give the judge something for the truth . . ."

"Truth of the matter asserted."

"Yeah. That. I submit these for that."

There were two slips of paper. One was a long rectangular strip with pastel flowers and chickens around the border. We had a to-do list affixed to our fridge by a magnet. This was one of those pages, faded by years. The other paper was narrow and flimsy, a receipt. I glimpsed Penny's handwriting. I had wondered where all the things that had disappeared around the house went. Nigel must have planned his own disappearance for some time to make off with so many artifacts.

"No," he said, "read this one first." So I read the to-do list slip, which was dated years earlier and scribbled in Nigel's handwriting.

Dear Mom, Let's go somewhere safe where he can't find us. We can drive to the ocean and float across.

Another note. This was the receipt. I touched the sunken paper where Penny's pen had creased the page. Her fingers had held that paper. Her palm had brushed the edges. Some of the ink was blurred by the pressure of her skin. She had always hated the tyranny of grammar and capitalization rules.

> *dear my favorite chef i know that your father and i must seem pretty odd to you. there are problems in the adult world that you will face when the time comes. but for now i need you to understand that we both love you very much. food smells great. i'll have some tomorrow. p.s. i promise things won't always be this way and maybe we'll go away, me and you*

I sat on a low stool, covering my mouth with a hand. Nigel was trying to convince me that he and his mother were plotting an escape. What a ridiculous notion. Penny had been upset, for sure, but there's no way she would have ever left me. She loved me. She wouldn't have left. Not for good.

"She's right to say I didn't need to understand then. But I do now. I'll ask again, Dad. Why did you really come here?"

"You asked me that, and I told you—"

"You said it was because you were worried about me and my safety." Nigel lowered and shook his head. "But come on. If that was the case, this would be a happy occasion. You would have hugged me and said how much you missed me, and then you would leave. But look at you. Look at your beady eyes and tense shoulders. Me and my friends used to follow you around sometimes to see what you were really like. I know you. You haven't done what you came to do. You're still on duty. That's why you brought this old gun." He patted the gun at my waist.

"Don't be ludicrous. This was for my protection. It was a long trip through unfamiliar territory." I didn't make eye contact. I tried, but I couldn't.

"What's that old story about the rabbit who saves the snake and is surprised when the snake bites him, but shouldn't be because snakes gonna snake."

"You have no right to look down on me. I'm your father! I always took care of you. Did everything I could to make sure you believed in yourself even when the other kids laughed at you. I stood up for you. I protected your self-esteem, and I'd do it all again."

"You can't understand, can you? A little while ago you said that you thought I hate you. But that's not right. I forgave you a long time ago because, you're right, you'll always be my father. But that doesn't mean you're worthy of holding that kind of power over me. I never realized how much I needed to tell you that to your face, to show you that I control my life. And after tonight—"

"Enough!" I pulled my gun on him. "You're so far gone, you don't even know it."

Nigel glanced at the gun, which was a few inches from his heart.

"Dad," he said quietly. "You're my father."

Nigel stared at me with a serenity that I'd never seen. For the first time, I realized that his mind was a planet unto itself. During our years together, I'd only caught brief glimpses of that distant world with my telescope. But I suddenly understood that I couldn't make him do anything now. To the extent I'd ever had any influence over my son's orbit, that influence was gone. He was gone from me. He reached out and gently moved the gun downward and to the side. I dropped it. My legs weakened. I found myself on my knees, my arms wrapped around his legs.

"I'm not letting you stay here," I said.

"Dad?"

"Stop talking and do as I say," I whimpered. I couldn't quite catch my breath. I wasn't even sure he could understand me. "You're my boy. It's my job to take care of you. Is that so wrong? Just come with me. Please."

Nigel held me back enough to sit down on the floor next to me. He put an arm around my shoulder and lightly squeezed. For a moment, I felt the movement of his chest against my side and his breath against my ear. He made a sound something like a chuckle. Somehow this calmed me.

"Dad. You need to go home."

I glanced up. His cheek was wet. He wiped it with his wrist. Then he wiped my cheek, too.

I shook my head.

"I know you're afraid," he said. "But that's something you're going to have to figure out how to deal with. I'm not leaving with you. This is where I belong, and I love who I am."

I pulled away from Nigel and placed my back against one of the wooden table legs. "I know." I rubbed my face. I was embarrassed to cry in front of my son, but there was something else I felt, a feeling that rose up and startled me. I was envious. I couldn't say that I'd ever stood so firmly for anything I believed in. But he had. "Why are you so stubborn?"

"I get it from Mom."

"Who else?"

Outside, something backfired. An engine rumbled. Nigel went to the window. He peered down the road.

"Minty?" He looked as if he had just seen a flying saucer crashland. He hurried downstairs. I went to the window. Araminta and Doc were untangling themselves from a motorcycle and sidecar. Nigel entered the field of the headlight. By the time I got downstairs, he and Araminta were arguing again.

"Why would you come up here in your condition?" Nigel asked Araminta. Then to Doc: "And why would you bring her?"

"As if I could stop her," Doc said. "Her water broke as soon as you left."

"Neither of you gonna tell me where to go," Araminta said. "If you thought I was going to have this baby alone while you picked your teeth with your crazy old man, you a dumbass."

"You could have just called me!"

"You mean on this?" Araminta pulled a walkie-talkie from Nigel's pants pocket and waved it in his face. "You had it off, goo-fus."

"Oh. Sorry."

"I had a mind to— Ooh." Araminta grabbed the side of her stomach.

"Let's get her back to the infirmary," Doc said.

They brought Araminta to the back of the pickup and lowered the gate. But once they had her situated in the truck bed, Doc turned to Nigel, who had taken a seat next to Araminta, and said there was no way they would get down the mountain before the baby came. Doc asked for blankets, hot water, and a few other items.

"I'll get it," I said.

But Nigel raised a hand to stop me. "We don't need your help." He attempted to get up, but Araminta squeezed his hand and told him to stay.

"Let him help," Araminta said. "We're short—unh—staffed."

I went inside and collected all the things, and extras like pillows and a canteen of drinking water. I found myself going back into the lodge for more and more—towels, a flashlight, bug repellent— and circling the pickup truck like a satellite on each trip, speed-walking, jogging, sprinting, mentally cartwheeling in orbit around my son, his wife, and my arriving descendant. Eventually, more people from the commune rolled up in a busted green van. Others arrived on scooters. Suddenly, we were surrounded by a dozen or so others who sat in a semicircle around the impromptu delivery room, lighting candles and incense, playing music and singing prayers in languages I didn't know, and laughing in the breeze.

I worried for Araminta. Her screams made my fillings vibrate. What if something went wrong? She lay on a cushion of blankets in the pickup bed, and Nigel alternated between stroking her hair and wetting her forehead with rags.

I was hovering over them when Dopey tapped my arm.

"Hey," she said. "Sit with us." Which I did. Dopey handed me two small bundles of cloth tied in heavy twine.

"What are these?" I asked.

"He asked me to gift-wrap your weapon and ammo."

I sighed. The moonlight intensified as clouds gave way to the infinite vast above and stars spilled across the void like jewels across velvet.

"You ever feel as though there are questions you can't answer?" Dopey asked.

"Never," I said.

The sound of crying from the back of the pickup. I scampered to my feet. The musicians strummed and sang louder, and everyone cheered. The baby was wrapped in beige swaddling. *It's a girl,* someone said. She was a lovely little gumdrop with a doll's nose and eyes that seemed to ask what did I think I was looking at. She was very dark, nearly Araminta's color. But she might lighten with time.

Dopey got behind the wheel of the truck.

Araminta's and Nigel's faces were both dripping wet. Nigel beckoned me, and I leaned over the side of the pickup bed so he could speak into my ear.

"Tell me something, Dad." Nigel took his daughter's chubby hand.

"Anything."

"Do you honestly think you would ever be able to accept her looking the way she does?"

"I—" I stopped myself from speaking and looked down.

"At least you're really thinking about it. I appreciate that. But we don't need that in our lives. Go home. Enjoy what you've done to yourself. But don't haunt us anymore."

44

I believe there are two states of being: living and living dead. This is the division between moose and taxidermied moose, majestic oaks and the hardwood floors of a Creole cottage, the curious man I was before I found Nigel and the shadowy simulacrum I became thereafter.

The aforementioned minor events from a short period of my insignificant life compelled me to jot down these notes in my Big Chief Bigboote notebook. In retrospect, I realize that like Mary Magdalene and Dante before me, I've suffered a kind of social death. I've been thrown off the social step stool. I have a name and a country, but I'm no longer a husband or father. And I no longer possess an identity I recognize. My fumbling attempts to make sense of my absurd predicament—the iron bars persist even with my eyes closed—have been less than successful, as you have seen.

After my return to the City, I took a leave of absence from the firm and set out with nothing more than my fedora and a surplus duffel. One day I boarded a bus in Selma. The next, I disembarked from a monorail in Gujarat, India. I rode a seaplane in Sri Lanka, a jitney in Jakarta, and a pedicab in Perth. I lost my money and passport in a nightclub in Antananarivo, Madagascar, so I was forced to stow away on a cargo ship bound for the mainland.

But that vessel was attacked by pirates. The last thing I recall was men, with machine guns on their backs, scampering up the side of the hull. When I came to some days later, I opened my eyes in a hospital bed in a kingdom by the shore. I'd been shot in the back. Or the front. The physicians were unclear about that as the projectile traveled through my body, rendering the point of breach an issue of semantics. I would live, but some nerve was mutilated, making my left foot useless. I also had a deep slash wound on my cheek. Still, I fared better than the half-dozen or so crew whose bodies were never reclaimed from the Indian Ocean. After weeks in that sanatorium, I was given what belongings they had found—notebook, fedora, sun pendant—and pushed out to fend for myself.

The kingdom is an odd place. There's a battle between civilizations being fought nearby, and it's caused untold numbers of people to seek refuge here. In the shantytown where I live, we're all stacked atop each other like kindling, doing our best to survive. Pickpockets and confidence brothers outnumber doctors and schoolmarms on this prairie. A man must keep his head on a swivel if he wants to retain anything of himself. I suppose I could try to make my way to the nearest U.S. consulate, which is in the middle of that war, but I can't bring myself to do so.

The question I get most often, only slightly more than *Say, my friend, what hyena mauled you?*, is *Why are you here?* I don't look like most of my fellow displaced humans. My living space is a tiny lean-to in a cluster of a thousand similar structures. I have a pot for cooking, a cot for sleeping, and a pillow for my face in case some Othello wanders into my story and wants to put me out of my misery.

One notable development bugs me whenever I happen to glance at the hurt areas of my body. The skin over my wounds came back in my old coloration. The healing slash on my cheek looks like a slowly expanding brown crevasse. I hope Dr. Nzinga is able to correct this hiccup in her otherwise excellent and—dare I say it— godly process. Nobody wants tar babies coming out of the margaritaceous lady parts of recently demelanated ex-welfare queens. But as has been so often the case during my tales of tilting at windmills, I digress.

I mind an outdoor kiosk for a discredited expatriate reporter from Holly Springs, selling old-fashioned newspapers. There are more Americans here than I would have guessed. My boss was stripped of her citizenship and deported to this place a decade ago. I trade shifts with a centenarian moonbat who yammers on about missing his basement full of lights. My neighbors in the flea market are lovely local women who take pity on me and ply me with food and drink. One of them even devised a makeshift brace for my extremity. Another gave me a puppy, an adorable mutt called Laika. The women think I'm a shy, damaged man. I can't argue. At night, the women return to their families. I spider to my corner. Laika falls asleep in the crook of my arm.

As often as I can, Laika and I hitchhike to the savanna, where we hunt for old coins and other artifacts. Plumes of smoke billow on the horizon, and it's said that bandits roam the night searching for workers to use in their forced labor camps. We never stay out past sunset.

Still, unrest notwithstanding, this is a beautiful land of swaying grass and pristine watering holes. Giraffes frolic in the distance or nibble on tender high leaves. Some days I lie under the Adansonia, which provide heavenly shade. I jot in my notebook, which I keep on me at all times. Sometimes I sketch. I'm not very good, but something about the movement of my hand across a page tends to lessen the quivering of my fingers.

I'm resigned to the fact that I'll never see my son again and that he'll never forgive me for my transgressions. For every practical purpose, I'm dead, by his request, which fits the Oedipal scheme quite nicely. Elsewhere in these scribblings, I believe I apologized. But here at the end of my revels, where you, dear reader, must imagine my presence for me to exist at all, I take it back.

A part of me believes that I wronged Nigel by interfering with his so-called natural development. That I should have left him to his own devices, to play in the killing sun, dally with darkies, and enjoy Nubian culture in all its carcinogenic glory. I should have let my son's voice merge with the voices of his peers and listened to the harmony from a doting distance. The inference is that I snatched something from the kid. But the truth of the matter is that I was no normal father, Nigel was no normal son, and America was no normal nation.

I sought to arm my boy with magic potions and enchanted swords, or at the very least provide a sturdy wooden shield. I once believed my intent was to never harm him. But that's not true. I meant to hurt my child from the first day I met him, when I was a giant and he was a papoose. I needed to hurt Nigel the way a physician introduces a junior varsity version of a virus so that the body knows what to do when the all-star team shows up.

In these shabby pages, I've obscured and dissembled for Nigel's sake. I've changed names and places. I've fiddled with time and space like some punk demigod. Perhaps more than anything, I've tried to tell my life as I experienced it at the time, without knowledge of things to come. I couldn't have known at the beginning of the narrative that I would end up in this state. But it seems inevitable now.

As much as I hate the electronic world gaze that inspects and examines with neither understanding nor empathy, I have placed Jo Jo in possession of this text by sending it to him in the same way that he communicated Nigel's message to me. Estate lawyers use an old scheme for the distribution of property to heirs. Roughly, for it's not my specialty, if a person dies, their child inherits the baggage. If the child dies, the grandparents. If dead patriarchs and matriarchs, then distant relations. When all kin have been wiped from the Earth, the People take all. Jo Jo will forward this treatment to my son when I'm dead and gone. But if strangers are reading these words, then neither he nor I remain.

In truth, I have no illusions that these jottings will ever be seen by anyone who would be moved by my ravings, let alone my Nigel. But I can pretend for just a moment, can't I?

I need you, Nigel, to read this addendum to the foregoing narrative and take some insight. These words are what's left of my heart, and they're for your eyes only. Not to save you, because I realized long ago I could never promise such salvation, but to give you access to my fractured psyche to use the information as you will. Perhaps you will know me better than I myself.

I can't dwell on things over which I have no control. The past is a shipwreck. I can only offer you some fatherly advice from my side of the chasm. Be kind to your Minty. It took me too long to realize what a shining soul she is. Show my granddaughter— Oh! I would give my good foot to know her name, her favorite foods, the color and shape of the monsters under her bed. Show my dear grandbabe how much you love her every day. Shield her from poisonous influences, especially suspect texts. Keep her out of the sun. But above all, teach her to think for herself. Provide the tools she needs to prosper, given the limitations this conventional reality has placed on her.

And if I could ask one small thing of you, Dear One, it would be that you occasionally think of your father—even after my body has returned to stardust, and I am nothing but the ghost of an angel in mossy chains, haunting endless grasslands in search of a spear tip sharp enough to finally cut this knot.

Acknowledgments

Writing a novel is synonymous with living a life. I thank those who helped me live a good life and write a good novel.

Tanzanika Ruffin: soulmate, genius, contrarian, North Star.

Ma and Dad—rest in peace: who gave me whimsy and a love of people.

Victory Matsui: editor, whose wisdom and grace brought this book to its best form. Chris Jackson: publisher and editor in chief of One World/Random House, who greenlit my dream. PJ Mark: agent, whose competence, confidence, and optimism aligned planets.

Tad Bartlett, brother-in-arms, who has the soul of a poet, the mind of a supercomputer, and the heart of a lion. Terri Shrum—rest in peace—sister-in-arms, whose incredible kindness and talent continue to inspire me. Emilie Staat, sister-in-arms, a gifted writer who read everything and gave out gold stars.

Che Yuen, whose short stories and humane example inspired me to ignore limitations. Jamey Hatley, who pushed me to tell honest stories and who used tarot cards to predict this very moment. Mat Johnson, first reader, wonderful mentor—a nicer guy could not happen to me. James Nolan, fearless teacher and friend.

Ben Morris, early reader and expert technical editor. April Blevins Pejic, early reader and encourager.

Susan Kagan, Bryan Block, Sabrina Canfield, Amy Serrano, Emily Choate, J.Ed. Marston, L. Kasimu Harris, Amy Connor, Cassie Pruyn, Kelly Harris, Denise Moore, Janis Turk, Susan Bennett Vallee, Keri Rachal, Zach Bartlett, Andrew Kooy, Alex Johnson, Larry Wormington, and all the members of my writing group, the Peauxdunque Writers Alliance, for providing safe harbor.

My writing community: Barb Johnson, Neal Walsh, Rick Barton, Amanda Boyden, Joseph Boyden, Randy Bates, Kay Murphy, Joanna Leake, Richard Goodman, Zachary Lazar, Jami Attenberg, Wells Tower, Rodger Kamenetz, Moira Crone, Alexander Chee, Roxane Gay, Laila Lalami, Kiese Laymon, ZZ Packer, Rachel Kushner, Charles Blackstone, David Mura, Nicole Bartlett, Rosemary James, Joseph DeSalvo, Melissa Remark, Cate Root, Chris Lawson, Willemijn Lamp, Joris Lindhout, Maaike Gouwenberg, Loraine Despres, T. Geronimo Johnson, Naomi Jackson, Sarah Broom, Garnette Cadogan, Tom Piazza, Robert McKee, Jim Randels, Kurtis Clements, Danielle Pellegrin, jewel bush, Mary Jane Ryals, and Ms. Pauline of the long-defunct Bookworm Comics in New Orleans East, who encouraged all her young patrons to read as much as possible and go to college.

Thanks to Read My World, Deltaworkers, VONA, and the Middlebury Bread Loaf Writers' Conference for institutional support.

To my family, who gave me a reason to tell stories: the Ruffins; my brother, James, and the Alexanders; Ms. Claudia, Ernest M. Washington, Jr., and the Washingtons; Auntie Edie and the Brandons; and the Jourdan family.

PHOTO: © CLARE WELSH

Maurice Carlos Ruffin has been a recipient of an Iowa
Review Award in fiction and a winner of the William
Faulkner–William Wisdom Creative Writing Competi-
tion for Novel-in-Progress. His work has appeared in
*Virginia Quarterly Review, AGNI, The Kenyon Review,
The Massachusetts Review,* and *Unfathomable City: A New
Orleans Atlas.* A native of New Orleans, Ruffin is a grad-
uate of the University of New Orleans Creative Writ-
ing Workshop and a member of the Peauxdunque
Writers Alliance.

loweramericanson.com

Twitter: @MauriceRuffin

Facebook.com/mauricecarlosruffin

About the Type

This book was set in Bembo, a typeface based on an old-style Roman face that was used for Cardinal Pietro Bembo's tract *De Aetna* in 1495. Bembo was cut by Francesco Griffo (1450–1518) in the early sixteenth century for Italian Renaissance printer and publisher Aldus Manutius (1449–1515). The Lanston Monotype Company of Philadelphia brought the well-proportioned letterforms of Bembo to the United States in the 1930s.